Adventures About To Begin

Adventures About To Begin

a novel

Allen Therisa

The Book Guild Ltd

First published in Great Britain in 2023 by
The Book Guild Ltd
Unit E2 Airfield Business Park,
Harrison Road, Market Harborough,
Leicestershire. LE16 7UL
Tel: 0116 2792299
www.bookguild.co.uk
Email: info@bookguild.co.uk
Twitter: @bookguild

Typeset in 11pt Minion Pro

Printed and bound in the UK by TJ Books LTD, Padstow, Cornwall

ISBN 978 1915603 319

British Library Cataloguing in Publication Data.
A catalogue record for this book is available from the British Library.

For Clifford Palmer, my mother, father, Carol, Glyn, Michelle, Tracy, Rosa, Ms Coxall and Matteo. Thanks also to Clarence Allen and everyone else who was so encouraging when I was banging away at the keyboard.

From a Jack to a King lyrics, as written by Ned Miller, reproduced by the kind permission of Jamie Music Publishing Co (www.jamguy.com).

1

I was watching a fight when Granddad Patrick died.

Granddad Patrick was from Mum's side of the family. Granddad Ronald, who was from Dad's side, was diagnosed with lung cancer when I was four. I don't remember him much (or what I was doing when he died).

The fight is between two old fat guys who are punching each other in the middle of the pavement on Waterloo Bridge.

'It was all a bit strange,' I tell Kelly on the phone afterwards. 'And not unlike something out of *The Bill*.'

Kelly's my younger sister by a year.

She never remembers my birthday.

'Did the police have to come and break it up then?' Kelly asks after a while, not sounding particularly interested. *Coronation Street* is on in the background and I'm too tired to be annoyed that she isn't listening to me.

'No, there were just these Japanese tourists—'

'And how do you know they weren't Chinese?'

'Because they looked more Japanese than Chinese to me—'

'That's borderline racist, that is. Right on the border, in fact, and almost in Passport Control—'

'Anyway – and not that it is racist – it was only at the end that a couple of those Community Support Officers turned up—'

1

'And they never do anything because of all the Health and Safety—'

'But by then it was all over.'

'So, it wasn't anything like *The Bill* then?'

'Well, no, not really, now that I come to think about it.'

'I don't really like that programme anyway.' Kelly sniffs, any interest she may have had in my little story quickly draining from her voice. 'It's just a load of running about in car parks and arguing over overtime if you ask me.'

And she should know, being such a devotee of all things Sky Digital.

'Yes, I suppose so.'

I'm near the National Theatre as the impromptu brawlers are enthusiastically swinging at each other in the middle of the bridge, surrounded on either side by a circle of Japanese tourists following the throwing of each punch on their video cameras.

Because they are Japanese; I can tell that by what they're wearing, if nothing else (and not because I'm racist, borderline or otherwise).

By the slurred swearing, I would also say that the two fighters can very well be drunk, or possibly homeless or probably both. Nobody seems to mind the swearing and least of all the tourists, who I think are all quite excited by it all – the thrilling unpredictability of modern London life and all that.

I take my phone out of my pocket, wondering whether to stop and watch or walk on by, as if this were a perfectly normal metropolitan scene that you could see every day if you knew where to look (i.e. Peckham), and there is the voicemail from Mum.

Everything changes right there and then.

YOU HAVE ONE NEW MESSAGE

It is never a good sign for Mum to phone before the end of *EastEnders* (non-omnibus edition) and, since she's still at the care home, I know she can only really be phoning for one thing.

I listen to the message, ready for the possible inevitability.

'Hello, darling,' Mum says after a short pause, her voice all sad and relieved. 'I'm just phoning to tell you that your grandfather passed away this afternoon. The carers said he was asleep at the end and that he did not appear to be in any pain. They said it looked like he was dreaming.'

Then she stops speaking and I look up at the sky, which is bright blue and hurts my eyes.

'You can call me back if you like,' Mum continues after a while. 'Michael and Joan are coming over later to sort out the funeral arrangements and then I'm going to speak to the consultant.'

Mum used to be a nurse before she took early retirement because of problems with her heart.

'Try to get hold of me once you get this message if you can. Goodbye, my darling.'

And then she is gone and I'm left staring at the sky as the two Police Community Support Officers come plodding up the pavement, immediately prompting the two old fat guys to stop their sparring and run off laughing in the direction of the Strand.

Typical.

'Well, that was a complete waste of time,' the sweatier of the two officers complains to no one in particular, as they come to a shuffling halt in front of me. 'To be honest, I don't know why we bother sometimes.'

He tilts his head and touches the radio on his shoulder.

'Waterloo Bridge incident dispersed.'

He pauses and winks theatrically at his companion.

'Heading back to the station now. Over.'

Then they wander off in the opposite direction, as I phone Mum back (who answers almost immediately, almost as if she knew that I would be calling her at that exact moment).

Which is spooky, if not totally unexpected.

'Hello, son, and thanks for phoning back.'

'I'm sorry I missed you earlier,' I say, staring over the bridge and down on the river, 'but I was watching a fight.'

'Oh,' Mum says, a little confused (as she has every right to be). 'Well, putting that aside, darling, if we can indeed do that, did you have a chance to listen to my full message?'

'I just picked it up—'

'It's just that I couldn't get hold of Daniel, but Kelly was stoic.'

'Stoic?'

'It means she took the news with calmness—'

'I know what stoic means,' I say a little too quickly and in a way that immediately makes me feel guilty. 'Sorry, I shouldn't speak to you like that.'

'That's OK, darling,' Mum sighs without a hint of surprise to her voice. 'Kelly is going to tell your brother, I think, when she speaks to him later tonight.'

Daniel and I hadn't spoken since his wedding two and a half years ago.

'That's good.'

Kelly complained I was being stupid and that there were more important things in life to be concerned with (and about which she would know, being so constantly right about everything family-related, as she always seemed to be whenever it mattered in that strange way of hers that always made Christmas such an ordeal).

'I'm really sorry, Mum.'

'I'm sorry too, though I do think it was for the best because at least now he's not in any pain.'

'Yes, I suppose so.'

Then we both fall into silence.

'Who was the fight between?'

'I'm sorry?'

And I suddenly remember the time Granddad took me fishing in Whitstable and we got soaking wet because it rained all day long, even though the forecast said it was going to be fine.

'You said there was a fight?'

Granddad and I ended up eating chips in a bus shelter.

'Oh, it was just a silly punch-up between a couple of old drunks, but I think they were only playing silly buggers, to be honest with you.'

'Right.'

And then we fall into a dismal silence all over again.

2

Two weeks previously, Mum and I had visited the Evening Meadows Care Home, where Granddad was to receive some intermediate treatment after his scheduled transfer home from the Queen Elizabeth Hospital.

Not that he cared that much where he was being sent.

'Because why they bother with all the bloody backwards and forwards when I'm going to die anyway is beyond me.'

Kelly is immediately suspicious when I get her on the phone after the ambulance has left and Granddad has started to settle, if reluctantly, into his new room.

'What exactly is "intermediate treatment" anyway? And be quick, please, because I'm supposed to be on my lunch break.'

Kelly is also supposed to be on a new diet (which is never a good state of affairs where she is concerned).

'I think it's the care that the hospital arranges for you, to get you back on your feet—'

'Or into a wheelchair—'

'After you are first admitted and stabilised, but before they send you home again,' I say, essentially making it up as I go along. 'Or possibly to somewhere else for a different kind of treatment altogether—'

'Actually, they had a special report about this on *GMTV*,' Kelly continues, using the authoritative tone we had come to know so very well over the years. 'It's to prevent bed blocking and the associated paperwork that the blocking of such beds entails. Lots of old people

6

have been left cold and confused waiting for taxis in hospital car parks as a result over the past six months, or so Eamonn Holmes said.'

An overweight porter comes plodding up the corridor, whistling and pushing a laundry cart filled with blue plastic bags.

'Isn't that "early discharge"?'

The porter shuffles past, the wheels of his cart squeaking forlornly as he goes.

'That's right,' Kelly says quickly. 'It was early discharge. "Early discharge and an NHS too underfunded to care" – or something like that. Now, I'm sorry, but I've got to go. My tuna salad is ready and I'm frankly starving.'

*

The intermediate treatment was after Granddad's first stroke, or possibly his second, since he had suffered something of a funny turn a little over a year before, playing bingo with his brother in Blackpool (though at the time we put that down to too much sun and Guinness).

'Bloody trams and donkeys is all that bleeding town's good for anyway.'

The visit to the Evening Meadows Care Home is organised for the first weekend after Granddad's transfer from the hospital and Mum is especially keen that it should be as stress-free as possible, taking into account his potentially delicate post-stroke condition.

'And I don't want to argue when we get in there, no matter what happens.'

Though I think Granddad was more than a little stressed even before we arrive.

'They've been poisoning me, you know, spitting in my food and putting pills in my porridge. I'm sure of it.'

And this is as soon as we walk into the room.

'Nice to see you too, Granddad.'

'It's a bloody, ruddy disgrace.'

At which point he suddenly grips my hand and won't let go.

'I haven't eaten breakfast since yesterday, just to be on the safe side. Bloody muck it is anyway. Boiled eggs and cold toast. Disgusting.'

Mum sits down carefully at the bottom of the bed, rolls her eyes and takes off her coat.

'Oh, Dad,' she sighs, not quite loud enough for him to hear, and then smooths down the sides of her jumper, which she had finished knitting only the week before and which has a sort of brown and green zig-zag pattern on the front.

'The things you come out with sometimes.'

Despite having recently retired, Mum continued to take great pride in looking younger than her sixty-three years, both in her dress and in her personal appearance. Her make-up was a testament to the magical power of Boots No7 and she never left the house without a leisurely promenade before a full-length mirror, no matter how many people were waiting downstairs (or honking their car horns outside).

'They're not poisoning you, Granddad,' I say, trying to sound as reassuring as possible whilst easing his grip on my hand, 'even if the breakfast here is a little—'

'Unappetising,' Mum adds helpfully, bouncing about on the bed to make herself more comfortable. 'Or unpalatable – either will suffice in the context.'

'Basic but filling,' I continue, doing my best to ignore Mum's in no way strange interjection. 'Besides, you're being cared for by medical professionals here and they know what they're doing.'

'Huh, that's what they said about Harold Shipman,' Granddad grunts, and I suppose he has a point.

He squeezes my hand even harder and looks like he is going to say something important but then just goes quiet.

'Are you at least going to have some lunch, Dad?' Mum asks, as Granddad finally lets me go and relaxes back into his chair.

'I'm not touching that either and I'm not going to eat again until I leave,' Granddad replies, rubbing at his legs, 'just to be on the safe side.'

'Oh, Dad, honestly. I shall have to bring in sandwiches and bananas if you carry on like this.'

'You ruddy well do that, but it won't make a difference.'

Sniff.

'Bloody bananas.'

He had once been a large, heavily built man with a booming voice and a stern, rolling humour, but now here he was, smaller and more vulnerable than at any time that I could remember and, though still round, he was no longer the jolly or mischievous man we had come to love. Now he was just frightened.

'And what about you, Noah?' Mum asks, brightening her tone and turning to me. 'Are you going to have a McDonald's later?'

'No, I don't think so. It's an unethical corporation that treats its workers particularly badly. I'll probably have a Pret a Manger, instead.'

Granddad snorts and rolls one hand round the other. 'Don't talk daft. All McDonald's do is sell beef burgers and milkshakes. You used to like them when you were younger.'

'Oh, Granddad—'

I reach over, smooth down the last of his white, wispy hair and kiss him in the middle of his bald spot.

'Get out of it,' he grumbles, trying to elbow me out of the way (though not that hard, I notice). 'And find out what they're putting in my food.'

He'd had the stroke the week before, followed by much crying on the part of everyone concerned (once the ambulance had left), as we were all worried that he was being neglected and we were the ones doing the neglecting.

'He died of a broken heart,' Mad Aunt Joan would announce later, after the funeral and to anyone that would listen.

Unfortunately, I couldn't get away quickly enough to avoid her partially informed opinion.

'There can be no doubt about it and we all broke it for him, do you know that?'

'Well, I really don't think I—'

'Smashed it into tiny, little pieces.'

Though to be fair she had been on the whiskey all morning.

'As sure as if we'd used a hammer and tongs on his oh-so-vital organs.'

And anyway, it wasn't even remotely true. In fact, Granddad was very well looked after, particularly during his stay at the Evening Meadows Care Home (despite all his arguing and shouting for no good reason whenever the tea trolley came round) and he was just as cared for after they sent him home.

Though he wouldn't be at home for that long, as it turned out.

3

'All we have to do is introduce special spoons, wire in some significantly brighter lighting and put down non-slip carpeting – which I expect you can help me with – and everything will be fine.' Mum beams, doing her best to reassure anyone who may be listening, once the community nurse has finished opening and closing the kitchen cupboards in preparation for Granddad's return from the care home.

'Right, special spoons. OK, got that.'

I'm the only other person left in the room, so Mum's particular show of confidence is largely all for me.

'And they're not called adaptations – or adaptions, I can never remember which it is – for nothing, you know, and it's these very adaptations which are going to keep your grandfather in his own house, right here in Mineral Street, which is where he well and truly belongs.'

So there.

'Non-slip carpeting?'

'It has rubberised and high-grip backing.'

'Are you making all of this up?'

'I most certainly am not!'

Affronted now, in a slightly theatrical way.

'And shame on you for even thinking such a thing.'

Granddad had saved for a deposit to buy his own house for five straight years after moving to London from the Welsh coal-mining village of Mountain Ash.

'Soot, injury and debt were all that my father knew or my mother saw, year in and year out, with only hope and prayer each Sunday as a reward.'

Granddad was never interested in following his father down the mines, not for a moment.

'Bloody coal-mining is only for the broken man and the beaten donkey.'

Or, for that matter, in making a life for himself in Wales.

'A land of beauty sitting above a well of misery.'

After surveying the house at 47 Mineral Street, with its high dusty windows and long, sloping back garden, he made a generous offer that was accepted almost immediately by the owner, with the first mortgage payment scheduled to begin on 28 August 1939.

Timing was never really Granddad's forte.

The house was, however, reasonably priced and a short walk from Woolwich Arsenal, where Granddad had just started a job in an armaments factory (and which was about to become more demanding of his time, thanks to the actions of a certain Adolf Hitler).

'You know that off-colour brickwork in the wall at the back of the garden?'

Mum was always one for a good family mystery.

It was why she had an annual subscription to *Woman's Weekly*.

'Behind the gooseberry bushes?'

'Well, that was where a Luftwaffe incendiary exploded one night during the Blitz. It caused quite the local uproar, according to your grandmother.'

'I thought it was where Uncle Brian crashed his new Ford Anglia because he was drunk behind the wheel.'

Sharp intake of breath.

'And how did you find out about that?'

'Kelly told me.'

Which she had, obviously.

'After Beverley told her.'

About which I was largely guessing, though it was a pretty safe bet that that is indeed what had happened.

'Actually, it was Brian and his stupid car, now I come to think about it. And that not so little accident on his part played merry havoc with his insurance, I can tell you. Not that it bothered him that much.'

'Because of the Pools win—'

'Because of his silly bloody Pools win, yes.'

Slightly awkward pause.

'So, are you going to help me put down this non-slip carpeting, or not?'

*

It would take the Battle of Britain and the real bombing of London (as opposed to Mum's made-up blitz of the capital) for Granddad to experience his first passionate embrace with a certain Marjorie Blakestone – soon to be his future and only wife – during a particularly dramatic night-time bombing of the city's docks.

He was twenty-five and she was twenty-seven, though only one of them knew what they were doing at the time.

'She was as beautiful as Marlene Dietrich and as fiery as Bette Davis,' Granddad told me and Kelly once, as we stared at an old wedding photograph he kept hidden at the back of his wallet.

Kelly is incredulous. 'Look, she's smiling.'

I swallow hard. 'I know. Doesn't she look…'

At which point my mind goes completely blank.

'I think the word I'm looking for might be "sweet".'

'Those three years we were married were the worst of my life,' Granddad snorts, as the words dry up in my mouth. 'She was mad as a snow goose in summer – sweet, my arse.'

Kelly and I make frightened eyes at each other as the photograph quickly goes back into the wallet and Granddad wanders off whistling *Nellie the Elephant*.

'Marlene Dietrich?' Kelly asks in a whisper, as Granddad disappears into the kitchen. 'But she looked nothing like her.'

'I know,' I whisper back. 'Though the Bette Davis bit was possibly closer to the truth.'

'The hooded eyes?'

'I'm just saying.'

Through the course of the war Granddad calibrated shells during the day at the Royal Woolwich Arsenal and, on every third night, manned a gun battery down by the river, romancing the slim and spirited Marjorie in between his patriotic threading and firing.

All until 1942 when, with the war turning the Allies' way, Marjorie secured Granddad's ring on her bony finger and finally became the respectable woman she had always secretly wanted to be. Despite what the neighbours said.

Patrick and Marjorie Tribe.
Forever & ever.
Until death

(or something equally significant)

do us part.
Amen.

'This is the happiest day of my life and, if we can only make it through this terrible war, I see nothing but a bright and happy future ahead for the two of us,' Granddad drunkenly announced towards the end of his groom's speech, and just before the start of yet another air raid.

Sitting tight-lipped beside him, Marjorie picked silently at her wedding bouquet.

'So here's to Marjorie, my very own wife and true love. For, no matter where I happen to end up, fighting for my country here or even abroad – if that does indeed happen – it will always be you, my beautiful Marjorie, that will be in my heart and thoughts for all my waking days.'

Cue a quick sprint on the part of the wedding party to the nearest air-raid shelter.

Though the truth was Granddad had already been saved from any prospect of any actual fighting at the front, due to the seriousness of his previously little-known "chest condition" which, according to Uncle Michael (who knew all about Granddad's little-discussed war record), only came to light after a particularly wheezy engagement party down in Bournemouth, and just before Granddad's call-up papers were due to be sent out in the post.

Fortuitous.

'It was a miracle he made it through the Blitz at all, to be honest with you, what with his catarrh and the accompanying incessant coughing,' Uncle Michael slurs, waving a half-empty bottle of Jamaican rum in Granddad's general direction during a particularly cold and icy Christmas evening. 'Can you imagine what it must have been like down there in that shelter, what with all the damp and dust? The bronchial discomfort and wet gasping don't bear thinking about and I should know, having always been a martyr to the asthma myself.'

An episode of *Dad's Army* is on the television, drunken relatives are falling asleep in both the front and back rooms and, sitting in his favourite armchair, Granddad is drumming his fingers on his belly as Uncle Michael continues in his drunken and, by now, free-flowing recollecting of the past.

'Of course, if it hadn't had been for that chest infection your grandfather might not have been around to marry your grandmother in the first place if you come to think about it.'

At which point Granddad gets up sharpish and turns the television over to ITV.

'And just imagine how differently things might have turned out then.'

Kelly turns to me, looking genuinely startled.

15

'Can you imagine that?' she asks, in hushed, trepidatious tones.

'No, not really.'

'No, nor can I.'

In between haphazard flak-firing into the night skies of London and Marjorie conducting the 122 bus in and out of Plumstead garage, the happy couple managed to raise three children (Stephanie, Michael and the slightly troublesome Brian) and create something resembling a happy home: Granddad dutifully tending his meandering back garden while the redoubtable Marjorie stitched cushion covers when not already engaged in her own special war effort, making amorous eyes at the local ARP warden.

It was an occasionally happy marriage.

'Bloody stupid woman,' Granddad grunts, before sitting back down for the start of *The Morecambe & Wise Christmas Special*. 'Facing the Nazis every day would have been preferable to getting into bed with her each night of the week – when she wasn't off on her bloody air-raid patrols, that is – if my chest had been strong enough to get me to the Western Front in the first place.'

He suddenly winces and clutches at his heart.

'Heartburn,' he reassures us eventually, before popping a chocolate Brazil into his mouth. 'Can you check the *Radio Times* to see if there is nothing better on?'

It was not long after VE Day that Marjorie departed Plumstead unannounced and without warning one particularly blustery Sunday afternoon, apparently to visit her flu-struck sister in Chatham for just a few days, or until the poor woman was no longer suffering from what could have been a very severe fever and was well and truly back on her feet.

A short and cheerful note was left, propped up against a jar of marmalade on the kitchen table, for when Granddad returned home, rain-soaked from the Arsenal.

I imagine I will be back by Thursday at the latest, trains permitting.

There is no need to be concerned, as Deborah mostly has a strong constitution (though she has always been susceptible to a dismal draught, the poor woman) and I am sure that she will be as right as providence will allow, once she has had a chance to rest and recuperate.

I have packed enough clothes for Stephanie, Michael and Brian, and they are all looking forward to seeing the Kent countryside with me and to getting some fresh air into their lungs, so don't go looking for them in the garden.

All my love until we are all once again reunited.

Yours, forever.
Marjorie

Though as it turned out the saintly Marjorie was ensconced with a meter reader named Robert in what he liked to boast was his very own detached cottage (actually a three-storey that he rented from the Gas Light and Coke Company), a little further down the Kentish railway line, near Sittingbourne.

Just along from the cement works and up from the creek.

I imagine that I will be back by Thursday at the latest, trains permitting.

As for the children, they were eventually returned by a miraculously recuperated Deborah, just in time for tea the following Wednesday.

There is no need to be concerned.

But their mother never did make it back to Plumstead (trains permitting) and divorce proceedings began less than a year later.

Yours, forever.
Marjorie

After which, and as the years passed by, Granddad's house, with its haphazard decorating styles (within which no room had any discernible relation to any other) and assorted collection of furniture collected apparently at random, would become our playground and familial harbour, whether Granddad appreciated our partially announced arrivals, suitcases thumping on the hallway carpet, or not.

'Wouldn't it be wonderful, darlings, to go and visit your grandfather in London? Because it has been such a while and he does get so very lonely without the company of his loving family.'

Until one day, at the height of the heatwave in 1976, the suitcases thumped down onto Granddad's hallway carpet for the very last time and Mineral Street became our new home.

'Well, you could have bloody well called first. There's a reason I had the phone installed, you know.'

Which was all rather unexpected.

'I wanted to before we left, Dad, I really did. But we were late leaving for the station as it was and the rain was pelting it down, so there was just not the time, I'm afraid.'

For some of us, anyway.

2

'According to the community nurse, we should have the adaptations and mobility aids ready just in time for when your grandfather gets out of Sunny Meadows—'

Mum is becoming obsessed with adaptations and, more recently, with mobility aids as well.

I blame her subscription to *Woman's Weekly*.

'Evening Meadows—'

'Yes, Evening Meadows – that's what I said – and the changes are, I would say, on the whole mostly affordable, what with the grants and my savings. So everything is entirely for the best and as it should be.'

'"Everything is entirely for the best"?'

Mum narrows her eyes, not unlike a cat looking down upon a cornered and somewhat injured mouse, and then smiles her most radiant smile.

Be afraid.

'Yes, and without confusion or deviation in the matter.'

Release of the smile.

Which in itself is something of a relief.

'Do you not agree with me, my darling?'

I swallow hard on what is left of my doubts and reply as sincerely as I can. 'Yes, Mum, I absolutely agree—'

'And, my dearest darling?'

Clearly, a little punishment is in order. What have I missed?

'And the changes are, on the whole, mostly affordable.'

19

'Very well then.'

Subject closed.

Evening Meadows is what Granddad's GP once called "An outstanding BUPA Care Village with a sector-leading reputation".

Whatever that is supposed to mean.

He even had a brochure to show us (though not to take home, as he only had the one copy) and which did indeed show how outstanding the "Care Village" was, in glossy and very colourful photographs, featuring ducks splashing playfully about on a pond and nurses grinning in a day room.

'It really is extremely highly rated and particularly for this geographical catchment area.'

This was just after Granddad had been put on oxygen following his first (or possibly his second) stroke.

In reality, however, Evening Meadows was more of a care home than a village (unless a single-storey building with a social hall and a wheelchair-accessible garden constitutes a village), situated halfway between Plumstead train station and Thamesmead.

'It's a very nice care home – or village, if you must,' Mum opines to me and Kelly a little too breezily the following evening, after we have gathered in the front room for an impromptu family conference.

Granddad's yet-to-be-done washing-up is still in the sink.

'In fact, I was very impressed when I was shown around by one of the care managers, and particularly by the standards of food hygiene as demonstrated in the kitchen.'

Kelly frowns at this point but says nothing.

'The nurses all appear to be very nice as well – kindly women, I would call them – though I don't think you'd want to get on their wrong side, which is probably why the residents are so well behaved, I would imagine.'

'Right then.'

Kelly takes a new notepad from her handbag and flips it open.

'What was that name again? Sunny Meadows...'

'Evening Meadows Care and Respite Village...'

And now I'm the one that is confused.

'Where does the "Respite" bit come from?'

'It's all on the website,' Mum snaps, brushing off my question with a flick of her wrist. 'Actually, I'm pretty sure it's on the website – which is an org and not a com – though it is also a little slow to load, so you might want to make yourself a cup of coffee while the homepage comes up.'

'OK,' I say, no more the wiser. 'I think I've got that.'

*

Two hours later, Kelly's earlier grudging cooperation with Mum's plans has pretty much evaporated.

'I don't care what she says, because that place is a shithole.'

Oh, dear.

Kelly is shouting into her hands-free so as to be well and truly heard (though she really doesn't have to worry on that front) as she is making her way back to Faversham. 'Dean says he's going to park up by the station next time we visit and we'll have to walk the rest of the way to the care home—'

'Care village—'

'And don't you start – even if it is raining. Dean says he'll bring his umbrella if he has to.'

Dean is Kelly's "life partner", though not her fiancé, and definitely not her husband, which Kelly always made sure everybody was absolutely one hundred per cent clear about at all times, or whenever the subject came up.

Which was (and is) often.

'And it's more than a five-minute walk, I can tell you. Dean has already had the *A to Z* out.'

'Are you and Dean planning on coming with me and Mum to see Granddad this Saturday?' I ask, as carefully as I can, once a gap opens up in the could-be conversation. 'Because I'm sure he would really, really like that.'

Because he really, really would.

'Of course, though Dean's got to sort the insurance out on his new car first. But don't worry because we'll be there. I've already told Mum and she's going to meet us before we go down.'

'I thought I was picking her up—'

'What, in that ridiculous boy racer wagon of yours?'

Deep breath.

'It's a Golf GTI, Kelly, not a—'

'It's something that an eighteen-year-old should be driving, not a thirty-eight-year-old fully-grown man. You should get yourself a nice proper saloon like Dean's just bought, and I'm sure you'd be able to get yourself a decent trade-in if you tried hard enough, just like Dean did after a little prodding on my part.'

Just a little prodding?

Dean's brand-new Ford Mondeo could comfortably seat five, according to Kelly, and has a very accommodating boot for both luggage and groceries.

Though Dean had actually wanted a BMW 3 Series.

'I'm thirty-nine,' I say, as calmly as I can, once Kelly has stopped her energetic hectoring and I can get a word in.

'What? Sorry, but you're breaking up on me—'

'I said I'm thirty-nine, not thirty-eight—'

'Really? Are you absolutely sure?'

'Alright then, see you on Saturday,' I say, as cheerfully as I can, keen to get off the line before another flare-up. 'And if I park up near the station we can all walk down together, I suppose.'

'I suppose so,' Kelly sighs, 'though Dean's not coming in when we get there. He doesn't like hospitals, or care homes for that matter, after what happened with his brother. So he's going to feed the ducks with Chloe instead, even if it is raining.'

'No Adam?'

'Unfortunately not. He's got army cadets and has to go, as he's up for a commendation for rugby-tackling a teenage shoplifter outside the Rainham Tesco.'

5

During his stay at Evening Meadows, Granddad had his own little room – a grey linoleum box with a window looking out on the railway line – within which he flirted with the nurses and dozed off whenever the floors were waxed.

He was particularly keen on the flirting and the warm laugher it generated, though his views on the nursing staff were rather nuanced.

'They might all be wogs, but they are all very lovely ladies.'

This is before the black nurse who has just shown me, Mum and Kelly to Granddad's room has even reached the end of the corridor.

'You can't understand a bloody word they say, not half the time anyway, but they are all very nice.'

Mum laughs nervously (and loudly), her eyes darting towards the open door as she extracts a tub of Nivea Creme from her handbag. 'Oh, Dad, the things you say sometimes.'

Granddad suddenly grabs my arm and waves towards the doorway. 'And especially that big fat one when she comes round with the drugs trolley in the afternoon.'

'And is that when they are trying to poison you?' I ask, as Kelly smirks and opens the wardrobe. 'Or do they only do that in the morning?'

'You're bloody stupid, you are,' Granddad grumbles, pushing my arm away. 'She wouldn't poison me, not that one. She's always extra careful to get your name right before she gives out the pills.'

'This place stinks of stale urine and Dettol,' Kelly complains, icily surveying the empty shelves of the wardrobe. 'And the nurses talk about you behind your back—'

'You look nice, darling,' Mum interjects, obviously keen to change the subject as quickly as possible. 'Have you lost some more weight?'

Which Kelly might have done, not that I'm that bothered.

'Perhaps around the hips?'

In fact, since starting her water aerobics, Kelly had transformed herself from the leggings-wearing party girl that always seemed to be texting from down the pub, into a far more serious and minimally made-up young professional, who wore her severe bob and dropped dress sizes with a grim sort of pride.

'Half a stone,' Kelly sighs, before closing the wardrobe door with a slight bang. 'Not that Dean would notice, of course.'

Though on balance I think I preferred the Kelly of old.

'They do not talk about me behind my back! And this is my home, for the time being anyway,' Granddad suddenly announces, jabbing a finger at Kelly's wardrobe-nosing. 'So I would appreciate it if you'd keep such views to yourself, thank you very much.'

'Well, temporary accommodation or not, it is still not your home,' Kelly mutters, almost under her breath, 'and I do not like it, not one bit.'

'I don't care what you like, or do not like, because it is still my home, for a few more days anyway.' Granddad's eyes fix on Kelly's back like he could burn through it with just a stare. 'I've even put my cross on the wall.'

Which he has, just above his bed and hanging at a slightly wonky angle.

We all look dutifully up at the cross.

'Well, I suppose it is while you're having your intermediate care,' Kelly concedes at last, obviously a bit intimidated by the crucifix, which now seems to be pointing directly at her. 'But that doesn't mean you're never going back to your real home, because you are. Mum's even had an alarm line put in.'

'That's right, and it does work,' Mum adds a little too quickly, a hint of tepid triumphalism in her voice. 'In fact, I've tested it three times already.'

'Bloody stuff and nonsense,' Granddad grumbles. 'And who's it going to call, anyway?'

'A help centre, because they will – help, I mean.'

Granddad turns and winks at me, and I want to laugh, but instead all I do is stare up at the crucifix.

'Well, they're still putting strychnine in my tea and cyanide in the coffee.'

And here we go again.

Kelly swallows, then closes and opens her eyes. 'No, they're not, Granddad, it's just the sweetener. I was the same when I started on the Weight Watchers.'

Granddad awkwardly lifts one leg and crosses it over the other.

'It is Nescafé and poison, I'm telling you. That's why I don't drink it anymore. Bloody filthy muck.'

'And on that controversial note—'

Kelly zips up her jacket and swivels her handbag over her shoulder.

'I'd better go and check how Dean is getting on. He only has so much bread for the ducks and Chloe still hasn't decided if she wants to go to ballet at half-five or not.'

She leans over, kisses my ear and then pecks Granddad on the cheek. 'If I don't come back, until next time,' she coos, waving vaguely in our direction as she heads for the door.

'I didn't know Chloe was into ballet,' I say.

'She wasn't originally,' Kelly sighs, pausing to straighten Granddad's name card on the door. 'All she was interested in was being a vet, but then she changed her mind after watching a documentary on the Discovery Channel where they had to put a kitten down because it had something wrong with its paws.'

Granddad shakes his head.

'Bloody vets, they're worse than the bleeding doctors.'

'Anyway.' One last wave. 'Ciao for now, if this is indeed goodbye.'

And then she marches off down the corridor, leaving me, Mum

and Granddad with the crucifix, which now seems to be pointing directly at us.

Awkward silence.

'She only came because she wants my money,' Granddad mumbles eventually, almost to himself.

'Oh, that's not true, Dad,' Mum says, a little too late. 'She came with us today because she loves you.'

'All she loves is whatever she'll get from the sale of the house, just like the bloody lot of you. You're all only waiting for me to die, including you.'

Which is rather harsh, even for him.

'Granddad, now that really is a horrible thing to say,' I admonish him, drawing on as much gravitas as I can rustle up under the circumstances.

Mum looks like she is going to add something but clearly can't quite work out what that something should be, so instead just turns away.

'Besides, it's not true. Actually, nothing would make us happier than for you to live a long and happy life.'

Granddad just ignores me and looks out the window, muttering, 'Silly bugger,' under his breath.

'And shame on you for even thinking it in the first place,' I continue, maintaining my tone of slightly thin seriousness.

'Shame on you, you mean.'

I look craftily at my watch.

'And what are you looking at that ruddy thing for?' Granddad mumbles. 'They'll ring the buzzer when it's time for a nap.'

'I didn't know you got to have naps.'

'Bloody stuff and nonsense. And what does it matter, anyway? I'll be gone soon enough, no matter what any of you say, and then you can do with the house whatever you want.'

And here we go again.

'I wish I could take an afternoon nap,' I say eventually, meaning every word.

'Best part of the day if you ask me. Though they do wake you up for visitors.'

My eyes meet Mum's, but neither of us say anything.

'It's true, though. I'm nothing without that house. I'm a moving bloody body, waiting to lie down and go cold.'

Mum looks like she might cry but instead just rubs more Nivea into her fingers.

'Oh, Dad, honestly.'

I lean towards Granddad's chair and put my arm around his shoulder.

'You're too cruel for your own good, Granddad,' I whisper in his ear, 'and none of what you're saying is even remotely true.'

'It is true and it's the least you all deserve for putting me in here in the first place,' he says with renewed vigour, shrugging me off in the process, 'and for letting me live so long.'

He looks down at his hands.

'I want to die and that's all I know.'

Then he suddenly squeezes my arm. 'They're trying to kill me, you know – my own kith and kin. But I've hidden all the money that should be in the bank so they can't get their hands on it.'

He relaxes his grip and taps at his nose.

'They think I've completely gone upstairs, but I've still a few rooms they don't have the keys to.'

I place a hand over his and hold on to him.

'I don't doubt it, though everyone does, love you, I mean—'

'Eh?'

'You moany bastard.'

'I heard that,' he says quietly, gripping my arm even tighter.

6

The following evening I'm fidgeting about on the posh sofa in Granddad's front room, next to Mum and Fatty (Mum's latest half-ginger moggie), and waiting for Kelly to come back on the phone.

'I'm thinking of getting another cat, to keep Fatty company,' Mum says, as Fatty stretches out his paws on her lap. 'Or possibly a Labrador.'

The front room had always been significantly grander than the back room, though it never did have a television.

'Because cats don't really like each other that much, do they?'

What the front room did have, however, was the posh sofa, a long heavy dining table, four equally heavy matching chairs, a glass-fronted display cabinet showing off Granddad's best china and a very large Grundig radio that Dad had given Mum as a Christmas present back in 1974.

'A bit like humans in that regard, I suppose.'

The radio had taken a lot of wrapping, apparently, and remained Mum's pride and joy (she being the familial apostle for all things Radio 4).

'Hello. Sorry about that,' Kelly yelps in my ear, fighting to be heard over what sounds like *Casualty*, 'but I had to separate Chloe and Adam fighting in the kitchen.'

Fatty licks his paws and then rubs them over his ears.

'Will you please turn that down, Dean?'

'What were they fighting about?'

'Oh, nothing important, just what to listen to on the radio while I make them do the washing-up. Dean, I am talking to you—'

'Anyway, Granddad was fine when we left him. In fact, I think that underneath it all he's secretly loving all the attention he's getting,' I assure her, as next to me Mum makes a sort of snorting sound and flicks imaginary fluff from her skirt. 'The staff really can't get enough of him and he's got all these interesting new friends he can talk to now.'

Mum actually starts snorting properly at this, much louder than before, and with a "Really?" inflexion that probably could be heard all the way to Faversham (without the aid of a mobile phone signal to get it there).

'Is Mum with you?' Kelly asks suddenly. 'Dean, for the last time, will you please turn the television down!'

'No,' I lie, giving Mum my best "don't make a noise!" eyes.

Mum looks a little confused and gives me her "What have I done?" face.

It is all in the eye contact with my family.

'Anyway, that's what he needs in my opinion,' Kelly continues authoritatively, almost as if she has become Granddad's social worker. 'He must be so vulnerable in that great big house, despite Mum's efforts to take care of him, and it does get so very draughty, what with all those gaps under the windows and doors. What Granddad really needs are people his own age to be around, to have a good argument with.'

Kelly had become very keen on the healthy benefits of arguing, or "domestic conflict resolution", as she insisted on calling it after she and Dean paid over the odds for a Family Therapy Residential Weekend in Rye to stop them fighting all the time.

Not perhaps the best spend of £300 (plus VAT), as it turned out, though they did learn some helpful, if rather confusing, phrases as a result.

I don't think Kelly had ever felt so validated.

'Well, anyway, that's what he's got now and if he wasn't so paranoid

I'm sure he would realise that it was the best thing for him, in the round.'

Though I am not entirely sure I'm entirely convinced by that.

In the round.

'He's not going to stay, though,' Kelly says, clearly not over-impressed with my nuanced assessment of Granddad's current state of mind, 'and I bet you all the money tied up in that big old house of his that I'm right on that score.'

'What makes you say that?'

'Because he told me when you were talking to the black nurse.'

Which was about Granddad's (possible) dinner later that evening – an egg salad, with fruit and jelly for dessert.

And who has jelly these days, except old people (obviously)?

'He told me that if he could he'd rather die at home, instead of ending his days in that stupid bloody care home.'

I don't say a word, as Mum leans in even closer to the phone, her face tight with concern, or possibly nosiness.

'Well, it's true,' Kelly deadpans, obviously sensing potential disagreement in my silence. 'Are you still there, or have you put the phone on the table?'

'Yes, I'm still here and, yes, I can believe it,' I answer at last.

'Then why have you gone all quiet on me?'

'Because you're being a complete bitch as per bloody usual, that's why.'

Which is true, though I shouldn't have said it quite like that.

Mum moves her head away and rolls her eyes.

'No, I'm not. That's just a vicious lie!' Kelly snaps, her voice filled with satisfaction at having made me so argumentative. 'I'm just the only one in the family that doesn't pretend everything's so rosy all the time, that's all.'

Which is also partly true.

'Anyway, regardless of what you may or may not think, he is going to come home so he can die in his own bed, whether you like it or not—'

At which point the phone goes (thankfully) dead, probably because Kelly's phone credit has run out.

'What was that all about?' Mum asks before I have a chance to tell her.

'Kelly thinks that Granddad would rather die at home than stay at Sunny Meadows.'

'Evening Meadows—'

'Evening Meadows, that's right—'

'Oh, he does not want to die – neither here nor indeed anywhere else for that matter, despite what he may say when he's feeling particularly maudlin—'

'Like he is most of the time?'

'Well, yes, but as far as Kelly's concerned, that's just her being her usual depressing self, that is.'

Mum takes a breath and then reaches for a mug of brown tea sitting half-forgotten beside the radio.

'I mean, I do love her dearly – more than dearly, in fact – but the truth is that your sister can't contemplate human fragility without instinctively reaching for a shovel.'

'I don't doubt that,' I say, before the second part of what Mum has just said sinks in and I realise I don't quite understand what she is talking about. 'I'm sorry?'

'Your grandfather is not thinking about dying,' Mum sighs slightly wearily, 'or indeed is anywhere near dying.'

She pulls a ball of pink wool and a couple of knitting needles from where they have been shoved down the side of the sofa and jabs the needles in the air.

'He's convalescing, that's all. And once he's finished with his convalescing he'll be happily back here in his own home and that, my darling, is quite simply the end of the matter.'

She rubs one needle against another, loops a thread of furry wool onto it and then starts the magic needle twitching which will eventually lead to the creation of a cardigan of some kind, or possibly a jumper.

'And as for Kelly, I don't know why she says these terrible things sometimes, I really don't. She's always looking for the very worst in people or in reasonably challenging situations, no matter how beautifully the sun may or may not be shining at any given time.'

It's because she's a bitch.

'She worries, that's all,' I say.

Mum puts down her knitting needles and gives Fatty a quick stroke as he slips from the sofa and waddles off in the direction of the hallway.

'Oh, I think there's a little more to it than that, my darling.'

Without thinking I say, 'Wouldn't it be better for Granddad for him to to stay at Evening Meadows for a little bit longer?'

Mum looks at me suspiciously and re-clutches her needles.

'I told you, he wants to come home and be here with me, after he has finished the prescribed process of respite recuperation.'

'And here is where you're going to find him one day, Mum, lying dead on the front-room carpet.'

I stop talking. That had come out all wrong.

'Or, if not dead, then perhaps with some kind of sprain—'

Mum rolls her eyes and takes a breath.

'You're worse than your sister, you really are—'

'I'm sorry, it's just that—'

'No, no, and you complain when she gets started.'

I take hold of Mum's hand, which is wonderfully warm.

'I know that Kelly tends to look on the dark side, but she does have a point – in a roundabout sort of way – concerning where it's best for Granddad to live, now that he has had a confirmed stroke, and we do have to recognise that what Granddad wants is not necessarily what's best for him—'

'That is a wicked thing to say!'

'And it's not good for you, Mum, either.'

She shakes me off with a determined flick of the wrist.

'He's not going back into Evening Meadows and that is final, you insensitive animal, and once he does come home I can assure you, my darling, that he will go on to enjoy a full and fruitful life here in his own home, which he fully owns and actually wants to live in.'

'Fruitful?'

Honestly, sometimes I think that all Mum's listening to Radio 4 was doing her more harm than good, no matter how much it kept her company when she was tangled up in her knitting.

Without warning Mum suddenly stands up.

'You are doing the right thing,' I say quickly, in case it's too late and I have hurt her feelings beyond the opportunity for quick repair. 'I want you to know that and that I'm behind you, whatever you choose to do.'

'OK then.'

She sits back down again.

'Now, let's talk about something else. How are things going at work?'

'No, let's not talk about that.'

'Really?'

Dear God, no. After all, if we were to start talking about "work" it would only be a few short steps to the dreaded "relationship" discussion and what I was going to do for my fortieth birthday (which would be nothing involving the family, obviously) and then I'd be the one reaching for the shovel.

'Certainly. Now, let's get back to Granddad instead.'

'You know after your grandfather had his examination at the Queen Elizabeth—'

'After the first stroke?'

'After the first stroke, that's right, your uncles applied all of their not unsubstantial and collective pressure to have' – fingers in the air – '"Their Grandfather" admitted to' – and once again – '"A Professionally Managed Home" as quickly as possible. They were worried, you see, about what would happen with the house—'

'Though to be fair, Mum, everyone was worried about what would happen with the house—'

'And that's just a terrible thing to say!'

Mum looks like she's about to stand up again, but instead, all she does is poke a needle in my general direction.

'There's more to it than that. They were concerned for him as well, and about his wishes. It's just that those concerns also happened to coincide with their own financial sensitivities, that's all, which is understandable if you think about it.'

'It's why they're always so miserable all the time.'

'Yes,' Mum sighs. 'It's the price you pay when you feel like you have no choice but to be so appallingly selfish all the time.'

'Is it, really?'

Quick rub of the needles, clickety-click.

'Oh, I don't know. But one thing I am sure of is that my father is not going back into Evening bloody Meadows when he can stay here in his own home, regardless of what happens, and we are all going to have to do whatever is necessary to make sure he is taken care of right here, in Mineral Street.'

Fatty pokes his head around the door and yawns.

'Now, what else did your sister have to say for herself, when she wasn't worrying about the afterlife and in which high-backed chair your grandfather was most likely to drop dead in?'

7

As it turns out, less than a week later Granddad is indeed back in his own home (much to Mum's satisfaction) with some new medication, a folding walking stick and a selection of special cutlery (which Mum is particularly proud of).

'Join me in the kitchen, please, Noah, once your grandfather has made himself comfortable.'

I have driven Granddad back from the care home as no ambulance (or even a taxi) was available to do so, due to "an unexpected and unprecedented increase in localised demand".

Whatever that means.

It had been something of a struggle for Granddad to fold himself up so that he could actually get into the Golf and, possibly as a result, since returning he has refused to settle.

'As you can see,' Mum announces, holding up a dessert spoon with a plastic handle as soon as I come into the kitchen, 'all the new utensils are especially suited for the more wobbly wrist and have an easy-contour grip.'

'Is that the technical term?' I ask, carefully weighing the spoon in my hand.

Because it certainly could be.

'Well, I'm sure it is,' Mum replies loftily, snatching the spoon back and dropping it into an open cutlery drawer. 'I can look it up after *The World Tonight*, if you like, just to be on the safe side.'

In the hallway, Granddad starts waving his walking stick about to get our attention.

'Mum, I think Granddad—'

'Why do you do things behind my back all the time?' Granddad demands loudly, pointing the stick at the new and very white handrail running up the stairwell.

'Because if I didn't I wouldn't have any fun in my life,' Mum mutters with more than a hint of mischief, before shooing Fatty out the way and joining Granddad in the hall.

'And then where would I be?'

I quickly follow and cross my arms in an authoritative manner, before eyeing the offending handrail with as much sternness as I can muster. 'It's only a high-visibility handrail, Granddad,' I tell him. 'It's to help you with your eyes.'

'There's nothing wrong with my bleeding eyes,' Granddad grumbles, waving his walking stick about once again. 'Now, where are my ruddy glasses?'

Mum smiles at me and I smile back.

'Now, Dad, Noah is going to look after you this afternoon while I'm at work—'

'With all those bleeding do-gooders—'

Mum had recently started volunteering at the local Sue Ryder shop on Plumstead High Street.

'But he can't stay long after *Countdown*, I'm afraid.'

'Oh, to hell with the bloody lot of you.'

Granddad leans on his walking stick and scratches at his arthritis. 'The sooner I'm bleeding well dead, the better.'

'You do not mean that!' Mum gasps, genuinely shocked.

'Oh yes I bloody well do,' Granddad mutters, shuffling off in the direction of the kitchen. 'Every ruddy word of it.'

I nod for Mum to come and join me in the front room.

'Are you sure it wouldn't be a good idea for him to return to the care home?' I ask, as gently as I can, once we are alone. 'Perhaps for a couple more weeks at least?'

I sit down on the posh sofa and pat energetically at the free space next to me.

'What did you just say?'

I pat even more energetically.

'Oh, get out the way, stupid ruddy cat!' Granddad snaps at a squealing Fatty, who has joined us after clearly becoming bored slinking about in the kitchen.

Mum purses her lips and then sits down abruptly on the sofa.

'I'm going to pretend we are not having this conversation,' she says, looking straight ahead, 'even though we so obviously are.'

She leans over, turns on the radio and *The World at One* fills the room with a slightly hysterical report on teenage obesity and the ever-present dangers of carbonated drinks.

'And I certainly don't want to – have the conversation, I mean.'

We shuffle about on the sofa, which, like the rest of the house, is as uncomfortable to sit on as it is to look at.

'This place is not designed for comfort,' Kelly had complained once, as we shivered, waiting for the fire to get started. 'It's more of a sit-up-and-take-notice kind of house.'

Another thing that Kelly was (annoyingly) right about.

As for the posh sofa, it was usually covered in cat hairs (because of Fatty) and piles of magazines that Mum was always going to recycle, once she could get round to doing it.

You really wouldn't want to sit on the posh sofa for too long.

Not unless you absolutely had to.

'I don't mean to upset you, honestly,' I say at last after the radio report has finished, 'and I'm sorry if I have.'

A copy of *Woman's Weekly* slips to the floor.

'So you should be. Besides, I thought we had put all that nonsense to bed.'

I take hold of Mum's hard-skinned hand and tickle her palm.

'But Evening Meadows is very nice and there are other homes if you don't like that one—'

'It's BUPA and it costs a fortune,' Mum snaps, still looking ahead, her face exhausted. 'And God knows we haven't the money.'

'But there are some more affordable ones as well, probably.'

I run my index finger round in a small circle in her palm.

'I can show you the websites if you like.'

On *The World at One* a woman starts talking about roadside bombings in Baghdad.

'Do you think that all these terrorists have been driven mad by the invasion and George Bush and Tony Blair?' Mum asks suddenly.

'Well, I—'

'Because of all the airstrikes and the religious fanaticism?'

Mum had a habit of going off on tangents like this. After a while you got used to it, though the trick was not to get too distracted whenever it happened.

'Possibly, though why any of that would make anyone want to make bombs and blow up people who are only trying to help is beyond me.'

And now I am the one that is distracted.

'Because it doesn't really seem to have that much to do with anything, does it?' Mum asks quickly, looking sideways at the radio as if she thought it (or possibly even Al-Qaeda) might be listening to us right now. 'And it's certainly not a very God-fearing form of behaviour.'

'No, not really. But they say it's because they'll go to heaven and live with lots of virgins and that makes it alright – especially the virgins bit.'

'But that's a lie, though, isn't it?' Mum asks firmly.

'Yes, I believe it is, even if they want to believe all that nonsense,' I say, keen to get back to Granddad and away from confusing Middle Eastern politics, though Mum clearly is having none of it.

'I was pretty upset about Iraq the first time around, but I wouldn't kill people because of it.'

I sigh and give up the fight.

'Me neither,' I say at last.

Mum looks at me, her eyes shining with the sharp intelligence that we had come to respect and love over the years. 'Which is why I ask, do you think they have all gone mad?'

A severe weather warning comes on the radio – flooding in Yorkshire, apparently – and for some reason, I remember the time we crossed a bridge to visit Granddad's sister in Wales and got stuck in a traffic jam halfway across. Granddad made jokes about how they must be checking the passports on the other side and we all laughed, apart from Uncle Brian, who was doing the driving and was worried about the car overheating.

'Yes,' I say after a while, watching Fatty nonchalantly pad his way into the hallway. 'They probably have all gone mad – and in a very bad way.'

In the kitchen, Granddad starts banging about and grumbling.

'Put him back in the care home?'

'Put who back in the care home?'

'You said to put your grandfather back in the care home.'

'Yes, because I think that—'

'But this is his home—'

'Mum, please—'

'And it is where he belongs.'

Granddad bumps into something – the kitchen table, by the sound of it – almost as if he has been listening to our conversation and waiting for this very moment to act.

'I don't mean to sound harsh, I really don't. But you should consider it as a viable option.'

Fatty squeals as the banging in the kitchen continues, possibly because Granddad was now stepping on his tail.

'I can't just put him back into the care home, regardless of whether it is a' – fingers in the air – '"viable" or even a bad option, come to that,' Mum sighs, taking hold of my hand and rubbing my wrist with her fingers. 'Aren't your hands cold.'

She firmly squeezes my palm in an attempt to press some life back into it.

'He's not an old dog, you know, and he doesn't want to lose his independence.'

I'm tempted to recall the time a couple of months ago when

39

we found Granddad at the bottom of the stairs, with Fatty twirling around his ankles, but I keep quiet.

'Well, can't you encourage him to agree to have some regular respite then or, at least consider getting some proper help in?'

Mum abruptly stands up and then starts rummaging under the magazines for her knitting.

'It might be a good idea,' I continue, a little startled by Mum's sudden movement. 'Perhaps if only in the short term?'

'What does he need professional help for?' Mum snaps, finding the half-knitted jumper she was searching for at the back of the sofa. 'He's got me, hasn't he?'

And with that, she settles back down on the sofa with her needles and wool, one ear on the potential fall about to take place only a few short feet away. 'Anyway, he'll be fine,' she says, rubbing the needles together. 'And you can trust me on that potential fact, my darling.'

'But what about the local area?' I ask as the needles go back and forth. 'Plumstead's really run down now and it's become quite dangerous, what with the gangs and everything. There are always empty beer cans outside the Co-op.'

'That's only because the bins aren't emptied often enough and, besides, it's not that bad. It just needs a little regeneration, that's all.'

'It needs a bit more than that, Mum...'

'Well, maybe.'

'Maybe, yes?'

'Maybe, possibly, though I don't care because this is where I was born and where your grandfather wants to finish his days. This has been his home for more than sixty years and that means something.'

She holds her knitting up and squints.

'You'll understand that, one day.'

'Well, at least give some thought to what you might do, afterwards.'

'After what?'

Needles down.

'After, you know...'

'No, I don't know.'

'Yes, you do.'

Needles up.

'You shouldn't be speaking about your own grandfather like that. It's not respectful.'

Conversation over.

8

1976

I found a blue box in Granddad's attic once.

It was not long after we had left Dad for the last time.

You could get into the attic by pulling down a special ladder Granddad had added inside the hatch. If you opened the hatch and then pulled on a rope the ladder dropped down, section by section until it just about touched the landing carpet.

It was a marvel of engineering, even if the ladder itself was a little bit wobbly.

'I made it myself,' Granddad announced proudly, as he prepared to pack our suitcases away, 'and now the attic is as accessible as any other part of the house, though you have to be careful where you stand when you're up there, in case you come through the ceiling.'

Mum said not to go into the attic or to be impressed by her father's modest engineering skills either. 'It's potentially a very dangerous piece of apparatus,' Mum warned us sternly, as Granddad grinned and nodded enthusiastically at the fully descended ladder standing erect beside her, 'and it is in no way a potential source of fun or, indeed, excitement.'

Absolutely not.

Which was an open invitation, obviously, to investigate the potentially dangerous attic, once Mum was snoozing in front of the television and Granddad was down the pub.

Even Kelly is excited.

'Tell me what he has hidden up there,' she whispers, as I climb the narrow ladder into the darkness above, a torch shoved down the back of my jeans, 'and try not to fall and break a leg in the process, as I don't want to be coming up there myself to rescue you.'

'I won't need rescuing, thank you very much.'

'Oh, yes, you will.'

At the top of the ladder, I turn on the torch and look around.

'Can you see anything interesting?'

Kelly's voice is suddenly all hot and tight with expectation.

'Not really, apart from a load of old rubbish.'

'That's a shame.'

I swing the torch round onto a narrow avenue of mismatched floorboards running the length of the attic, flanked on either side by rolled-up carpets, broken vacuum cleaners, discarded floor lamps and cardboard boxes wrapped in brown tape.

'And it smells up here.'

Which it does, of warm dust and bird feathers.

'Plus there are lots of cobwebs and probably spiders to go along with them.'

I decide to take my life in my hands and advance gingerly along the floorboards.

'I'm investigating further back.'

'Well, hurry up then.'

Kelly is clearly starting to sound worried.

Or possibly bored.

'Because I think Mum has stopped snoring.'

And then the torchlight falls upon a stack of empty orange crates with a big blue cardboard box sitting almost proudly on top.

'Bingo,' I say quietly, though I'm not entirely sure why, as there is no one close enough to actually hear me and, besides, it's only a blue box (though it just seems the right thing to say, regardless of who is or is not around).

'I'm going back down for a bath,' Kelly shouts up (so much for the

43

almost whispering), obviously even more bored than she was before. 'Don't forget to close the hatch properly when you come down.'

'Will do.'

Though my brain is already plotting on how to sneak the box downstairs even before I have even opened it.

'See you later then.'

Kelly stamps off down the stairs.

'And don't worry because I won't be long, not long at all.'

I wait for Kelly's stairway-stamping to finish, then tuck the mysterious box under my arm and quickly sneak it down to my bedroom, where I place it carefully on top of my bed. Then I check on the landing for Mum's snoring (which is continuing, despite what Kelly says) and for Kelly's bath running, push the ladder back up into the loft and stand on top of the banister to close the hatch.

'Do you need the bathroom?' Kelly suddenly yells up from downstairs. 'It's just that I want to read for a bit when I'm in there.'

'No, you go ahead,' I say loudly, but calmly, using my best "I'm really cool about it, actually" voice, before jumping off the banister and running back into the bedroom before Kelly can ask any more of her stupid girl questions.

Downstairs the bathroom door bangs shut.

'Alone at last.'

I sit on the bed and carefully lift the lid off the box.

'And what exactly do we have here?'

Inside the open box is a pink, satin-covered birthday card, with a squashed, purple, plastic flower and big, silver, curly writing on the front.

With our fondest & loving thoughts
Wishing you all the best for your 21st!

'Right then.'

Not exactly what I had been expecting.

'OK.'

I open the card.

Here's wishing you
A wonderful day
With the best of good fortune
Coming your way
And lots of good luck
Good health & good cheer
To bring you real happiness
All through the year!

A bundle of letters is underneath the card, written by Mum to Dad between 1972 (much excitement about the new Asian neighbours) and 1974 (lots of complaints about queues at the petrol stations), tied together with a faded pink ribbon.

I don't think the snowing will ever end and Dad is driving me mad. Noah won't stop crying and though he won't say it, I think it's because he misses you.

Interesting.

Also, when you return, can you bring a new iron, as Dad's keeps giving me electric shocks, and a coat for Kelly, as hers is now too short in the sleeves.

Actually, not so interesting.
'Damn.'
Dad was on the Rhine back then, digging tank traps for the army, while we were staying "very temporarily" with Granddad in Mineral Street for our first "special holiday away from your father".
Dad lost the top of one of his fingers once, building a bridge in Minden when it was cut off by a girder.
'It didn't hurt when it happened,' he told me afterwards, showing

me the butterfly stitches at the end of the stump, 'though they did have to give me a little injection in case it got infected.'

That was his only injury in all his years in the Forces.

I swallowed hard.

'But weren't you worried, about bleeding to death?'

He put back on the little black leather sheaf that covered his modest amputation and wiggled the stump at me.

'No, son. At the time I just tied a shoelace round the knuckle as hard as I could, then had a quick cigarette and it was fine.'

I wanted to be sick, but I also wanted to be like him, even with his half a finger.

'And now I've almost forgotten there used to be anything else there. It's funny how things change and you adapt because you have to.'

That was just before we left for the first time for Granddad's in a rush of tearful suitcase-packing and hurried goodbyes to the neighbours.

If we could only put the past behind us, we could be a happy family again.

We were only supposed to be staying "for a couple of weeks and almost certainly for no longer this time", though we also had to bring our winter clothes, after being promised that it would be a good opportunity to "spend some highly valuable and special time with your grandfather", while Mum wept in the kitchen and we all did our best to ignore the constantly ringing telephone.

Until one day it stopped ringing.

9

'She's crying again.'

'I know. I can hear that.'

Me and Kelly are playing in the middle of the road outside the front of the house and pretending that we are not worried about what is really going on.

Which we are.

Obviously.

'Stay where I can see you,' Mum had cautioned us between her sobbing, as we ran out the front gate that second afternoon after our cases had been safely packed away. 'And make sure you listen out for any cars that may be coming down the hill,' she continued, almost as an afterthought, before blowing her nose in a damp hankie. 'Because they do come so very fast round the hidden bend in the road and you can never be sure what injuries they may cause if they do so unheeded.'

As Daniel still couldn't talk properly (and could not be let out on his own without supervision because of his habit of randomly running into the path of oncoming traffic) he had to stay inside with Mum and her crying, which left me and Kelly free to make friends with the neighbours.

'So, you run to here and hide for one minute and then you run to here and count to a hundred.'

It is just after lunch, our first proper lunch in Mineral Street (spam and pickle sandwiches with warm Dandelion & Burdock), and we are kicking the kerb with Tommy Smith from next door but one, as he tries to explain the rules of his new and slightly mysterious game.

'And it has to be a hundred, and that last bit is very, very important.'

At which point Tommy takes a quick breath as Kelly delivers a theatrical frown, befuddlement hanging heavy on her face.

'I don't get it.'

Tommy Smith wore glasses, had freckles and spiky blond hair ('Strawberry blond,' Mum called it, 'even though both his parents are dark brown or auburn where their follicles are concerned, depending on the light') and tended to get over-excited very, very quickly.

'Yes, you do,' Tommy suddenly whines, frustration at Kelly's lack of "getting it" making his voice go higher and higher. 'It's really, really simple, actually.'

At which point Kelly tucks her hair behind her ears and crosses her arms.

This could be trouble.

'No, I do not, and I know what I do and do not get, thank you very much, Tommy Smith.'

She wipes sweat from her forehead with the back of her hand and then smears it down the side of her jeans. 'And I think on that point we could not be any clearer even if we tried.'

Tommy had been attempting to explain the rules of his game, except that it was too hot and neither Kelly nor myself really understood what he was going on about.

'This is just making my head hurt,' I say, shaking my hair and pushing a finger up my nose to have a good scratch because it is starting to get hay-fever itchy. 'Tommy, are you sure you're not making it up as you go along?'

Tommy suddenly looks cornered and his eyes dart left and right, even though there is actually no one on either side of him.

Which is weird.

'Yes,' he yelps. 'I mean, no.'

We had only been at Granddad's one day and I already knew that Tommy Smith wet the bed.

That was the first real secret that Granddad told me when we were in the back bedroom and he was showing me which drawer was mine and where the extra blankets were kept.

'There's always washing on the line in the morning,' he said, drawing back the curtains and nodding in the direction of Tommy Smith's garden, 'and it's usually pyjamas and bedsheets.'

Still, as we were to discover, Tommy was good at making up games, even if it was a little confusing when he was trying to explain the rules of his new ones, and especially when he was thinking and talking at the same time which, as we were to discover, he tended to do a lot.

'It's perfectly simple,' Tommy suddenly gabbles, waving vaguely in the direction of his front door. 'Even my brother understands it and he's only three and a half.'

Kelly raises a slow and very sceptical eyebrow. 'I frankly find that difficult to believe,' she says coolly, 'as Daniel can barely understand a word we say and he is, I would like to point out, significantly older than three years and six months.'

Daniel was, in fact, five years and two months old, though he acted a lot younger than that. Kelly was convinced that he was a little bit mentally handicapped (or had "very special needs", as one of his teachers put it once when we were still living in Farnham).

'Oh, you're just being bloody stupid, you are,' Tommy says quickly, his voice straining with frustration, 'and you're only pretending you don't understand the rules of the game so you can be the centre of attention.'

'Alright, keep your T-shirt on,' Kelly snaps, biting her lip and looking like she is trying to work out if what Tommy is saying is actually true. 'And I'd appreciate it if you didn't raise your voice to me, thank you very much, as I am but a girl.'

I shield my eyes and try to see if she is joking (Kelly could be quite crafty when she wanted) or being serious (in which case things could get nasty pretty quickly), but then Kelly just shakes her hair and sneezes.

'It's just too difficult, Tommy, honestly.'

It was time to steer this potential storm safely back out to sea if that were indeed possible.

'Perhaps we should go inside and play some Cluedo or Monopoly instead?'

'No, it's not difficult at all and I think I've got it now,' Kelly announces all of a sudden (probably because she secretly fancies Tommy a bit and wants to show him that she is actually on his side, despite her earlier angry words). 'All you do is count up in your head, going one elephant, two elephant, three elephant, four elephant, like so—'

'Oh God, now this is getting complicated—'

Tommy stamps his feet and angrily crosses and then uncrosses his arms. 'No, that is not how it works!'

'Actually, I might want to play that Cluedo, after all—'

Though the truth is that both me and Tommy secretly want to go and start fires behind the garages up on the Common, which we instinctively know would be far more enjoyable and interesting than this.

'Why elephant?' I ask, speaking for both Tommy and myself at the same time.

'Because otherwise, they're not real,' Kelly replies too quickly.

Tommy blinks rapidly against the achingly bright sun. 'What's not real?'

'The seconds, stupid! If you don't say elephant it's not real time and you find everyone too easily.'

'Oh, right. Elephants, seconds, got it.'

Then Asghar comes running out of his house, grinning and carrying a football.

'Oh no, here comes Asghar,' Kelly sighs, before wiping at her forehead. 'Which means things are going to get even more confusing than they are already, though they were far too confusing to begin with.'

Asghar is a bit older and taller than me, has a big boy moustache, shiny Asian hair and lives right next door. From the minute Asghar's family had arrived, Granddad had called them "bloody Pakis" (even though they were actually Sikhs and came from the Punjab).

'Alright, you lot,' Asghar shouts out, dribbling his ball across the road towards us.

'Hello, Asghar,' I say, trying to sound as cool as possible, as he smacks the football hard down onto the tarmac.

'I heard you making a racket,' he says, kicking the ball to the kerb, 'and you've only been here two minutes.'

Which isn't strictly true.

'You alright, anyway?' he asks no one in particular, looking all excited and bored at the same time. 'You noisy, bloody bastards.'

'Yeah, we're alright,' I answer before anyone else can get a word in. 'In fact, we're better than alright, we're doing just great.'

Kelly looks at me funny. 'You idiot.'

Asghar shields his eyes with his hands and squints at us. 'What are you up to? Anything interesting?'

'Just trying to sort out the rules to a new game,' Kelly says, as I take a much-needed breath. 'Now go on, Tommy, what were you saying?'

'Granddad told us you'd come and have a chat,' I blurt out, without thinking and even though it isn't strictly true. 'We're going to be staying for a while, and Mum says probably for the rest of the summer as well.'

And that isn't true either.

'Yeah, I know all about you staying,' Asghar says without looking at me (and clearly not that interested in what I'm telling him either). 'Your granddad warned us yesterday. Your mum and dad splitting up, are they?'

'No. We are simply on a short holiday,' Kelly answers curtly, 'while Dad finishes his posting overseas and nothing more. Now, Tommy, what were you saying?'

'I've forgotten now.'

'Oh, Tommy,' Kelly sighs.

'Anyone want to play five-a-side?' Asghar asks brightly.

He runs to the kerb, picks up his ball, throws it into the air and then catches it without even looking.

'Yes!' Tommy whoops, punching the air with a happy fist.

'Result!'

'Come on then,' Asghar says, and we drift away, following him up the road towards the Common.

'Excuse me.'

All except Kelly, who crosses her arms, unmoved and watching as we leave.

'Are you coming or what?' I shout back, as it quickly becomes obvious that Kelly will not be joining us and that we have obviously insulted her in some way.

'No, I'm going to do some reading with Daniel instead,' Kelly replies tartly, and then she turns and walks back to the house before anyone can object.

'Are you sure?' I ask as she marches off up the garden path, her arms still firmly crossed in front of her.

Please say yes.

'Very much so,' Kelly sing-songs, before going back inside the house.

She was like that, Kelly – unpredictable and annoying – though why she would want to read with Daniel, who can't understand what you're saying at the best of times, when she could be watching us play football up on the Common is a total mystery to me.

'OK,' I say, as the front door slams shut. 'See you at dinner.'

Then the three of us turn into Ancona Road and Tommy Smith falls over because he hasn't done his shoelaces up properly.

10

Later that night, after Kelly has helped Granddad with the washing-up, the two of us sit at the top of the stairs with Daniel, listening to Mum arguing on the telephone in the back room.

It is very hot.

'That is not true... Because I'm telling you that is simply not true... Oh, I most certainly did not say that!'

'Oh, dear.' Kelly leans towards Daniel, puts a finger to her lips and then says in a loud whisper, 'Be very, very quiet.'

Daniel grins, giggles and then wraps his hands around the top of his head.

'Doesn't it bother you that he just laughs whenever you say anything to him?' I ask, nodding at my gurgling younger brother.

'No,' Kelly says sharply, all affronted and over-the-top offended, before hushing me so that she can hear Mum's arguing better. 'Actually, in a way, I quite like it because at least he doesn't tell me any lies.'

The arguing downstairs gets even louder (but also more muffled, which is odd), though we can still just about hear what is going on.

'And what would you know? You've never been around or interested in sorting things out...I did not say that either... And I most certainly never said that!'

'Well, sometimes it's a bit weird,' Kelly concedes finally, once the muffled arguing has died down, 'but he does still listen to what I'm saying, which is good.'

She leans back against the flock wallpaper. 'Sort of.'

'Mum's going out later and she's not coming back until tomorrow,' I say, not really paying attention to Kelly or to the fading argument downstairs, which now seems to have settled down into a sort of leisurely bickering. 'She's picking up some No7 from Mad Aunt Joan, because she forgot hers when we left, and then they're going to the bingo together.'

'Is she really?' Kelly asks, coolly raising an exaggerated eyebrow. 'And how can you be so sure that she won't be coming back?'

'Because she told Granddad. I heard them in the hallway.'

I suddenly feel both proud and guilty at the same time because of my shameless snooping, but it doesn't dampen the feeling of excitement that I have at telling Kelly what I know.

'They've closed the swimming pool,' Kelly announces suddenly, sitting forward and obviously not remotely interested in the outcome of my skilful spying, 'and I don't think they're going to be re-opening it again until the autumn either.'

'And how would you know that exactly?'

Now it was my turn to be apparently uninterested.

'Munira told me,' Kelly continues, her voice heavy with self-satisfaction, 'when you were up on the Common playing your stupid game of football.'

That bloody Munira.

Asghar's sister, younger than him by a year, was also only about a quarter as cool as her brother (though Asghar was pretty cool so that probably made her a little bit cool). Kelly and Munira were thick as thieves and three times as annoying together as when they were apart (though even apart they were very annoying).

In the back room, Mum laughs a loud, mocking laugh and then starts to cough.

'And why are they doing that?' I ask, trying to hide my annoyance at being so effectively trumped in the news-gathering department by Munira and my sister (and you had to be careful because some days you couldn't be sure what Kelly did and didn't make up, so it was always best to be laid-back and ask the right questions if you wanted to get the complete truth out of either of them).

'Because no one would leave the water and it just became too congested, apparently.'

'It's because of the heatwave,' I say with as much authority as I can muster on such a muggy night. 'They were talking about the reservoirs running out of water on the *News at Ten* and how they might have to turn off the water to everyone's taps if it gets any worse.'

'And I can believe it,' Kelly gabbles, suddenly over-excited for some reason. 'Granddad says we'll have to keep the skylight open tonight because otherwise it'll get too hot to breathe properly and we might all suffocate in our sleep. Well, he didn't say the last bit, though it does make sense – but then the flies come in and buzz around at the top of the stairs and that's even worse, in my opinion.'

Worse than what, exactly?

'That's because they're too stupid to fly out again,' I say, as two bluebottles buzz their way up the stairs, 'so they just go round and round in stupid fly circles until they bump into each other and then they die.'

Quick breath.

'God, it's hot,' Kelly sighs, turning her feet round and round. 'Too hot and too bothered.'

'It was ninety degrees today, at least.'

'Was it really?'

'Well, so they said so on The News.'

'You and The bloody News.'

Daniel reaches up and tries to pull at Kelly's hair, but she deftly steers his arms away before he can really annoy her.

'Do you want to be a newsreader or something when you grow up?'

'Not especially.'

Which is true, because I don't. What I actually want to do is to go into the army and make something of my life (and to get away from Kelly).

'Oh, get off, Daniel, you annoying sod,' Kelly snaps, as Daniel reaches up once again to grab at her hair. 'I said, stop it!'

But Daniel won't stop his hair-grabbing, so I get up, go into the bedroom and take down a wooden fort from the top of the wardrobe.

Granddad had made the fort two years ago and filled it with green plastic World War Two soldiers after Daniel had scraped his knee in the back garden and wouldn't stop crying. The fort had battlements covered with blue wallpaper left over from when Granddad decorated the front bedroom and the soldiers were mine from when I still used to play with soldiers.

'Here you go, matey,' I say, putting the fort down on the carpet in front of him.

Daniel grins and claps his hands together, his interest in pulling Kelly's hair immediately forgotten.

'Had World War Two soldiers in the medieval ages, did they?' Kelly asks tartly, as Daniel starts assembling his toy army on the carpet. 'Or was a time machine invented during the Second World War just to give the Allies something to do when they weren't busy fighting the Nazis or winning the Battle of Britain?'

Just where does she get all this stuff from?

From books, I reckon.

She's always been into reading.

'I don't know,' I say, repelling Kelly's attack as vigorously as I can (even though I don't really understand it). 'And anyway, I don't care. It's only for Daniel to play with and he doesn't know what he's playing with—'

'Yes, you do care,' Kelly snaps, waving her hands about to make the meandering flies go away. 'You care more than you make out, you do. I heard you crying last night, before you went to sleep, you big baby.'

One of the bluebottles crashes into her hair.

'That's why Mum made you apple crumble for after dinner – not that you're bothered about her feelings.'

'Yes, I am! That's just a big, bloody lie.'

'No, you're not, and, no, it isn't. You just think about yourself all the time, you do. With you, it's all Noah, Noah, Noah, and the rest of you can all go to hell.'

Downstairs Mum's coughing gets even worse.

'You're a ruddy cow, you are,' I almost shout, not caring who can hear me, 'always snooping on other people's business and being so bloody horrible all the time!'

Daniel pulls up the drawbridge.

'And I do care, about Mum and Dad, and Daniel, and even about you—'

'But you're always first in the queue, you are.'

And it's obvious now, by the speed and implicit venom in her little speech, that Kelly had worked out what she was going to say, long before we had even started arguing, and that I had just walked into a trap of her own very skilful making.

'Everyone comes after you because that's the way it's always been and the way it's going to be forever and ever, no matter what happens to anyone, because with you it's always Noah, Noah, Noah!'

Then she pushes her hair back, pulls her ears forward, waggles them at me left to right, and for the first time I notice that she has had her ears pierced.

And when did that happen?

'Listen to me,' Kelly squeals, her voice becoming even higher and sneery, 'because I'm Noah and nothing else matters except me. Everyone else could all be dead for all I care.'

Then she lets go of her ears, shakes her hair free and I feel so angry that all I want to do is smack her in the face.

'I do wish you were all dead,' I shout right in front of her, before getting up and marching to the bedroom, 'and especially you, you mad, bloody cow.'

Downstairs the door to the front room opens.

'What's going on up there?' Granddad shouts up the stairs.

'I said I wish you would all just piss off and go away because you're all bastards!'

'What did you say, young man?'

'He's swearing, Granddad,' Kelly says matter-of-factly, her voice suddenly all calm and over-amplified. 'And he's not making any sense or telling the truth. All he's doing is swearing.'

'I can hear that!'

But I don't care.

In fact, I don't care at all.

'You're all a bunch of bastards, every single one of you!'

And I slam the bedroom door shut as hard as I can (then hope that no one comes up the stairs to open it) and sit down on the floor.

'I hate being here.'

Because I do.

'Hate it, hate it, hate it.'

Then I start to cry, even though I don't want to.

'And all I want to do is to go home.'

11

Granddad's funeral was on a Wednesday.

Mum did the food with the help of her best friend, the darkly mysterious and vaguely Transylvanian, Rosella.

'Who was always very cheerful when sorting out the donated clothing at Sue Ryder,' according to Mum. 'No matter how many bags we had to get through.'

Both Mum and Rosella were roughly the same age, give or take a few years, and both had a passion for knitting.

'And please do make sure you don't annoy your sister,' Mum warns me the night before the funeral after I have phoned to see how she and Rosella are getting on cooking the sausage rolls and chicken legs. 'Because it's bound to be a stressful day, what with one thing or another—'

'You mean the actual funeral service?'

'Yes, of course I mean the actual funeral service, and don't be facetious so late in the evening. Also, bear in mind that Kelly is likely to be more stressed tomorrow than she usually is—'

'Why? Is she bringing the children?'

Things were always better when Chloe and Adam were around, regardless of how much they annoyed Kelly by being under her feet.

'Yes,' Mum sighs, leaning in even closer to her phone, 'and Dean with them, even though he's put on a little weight recently and doesn't

59

want any more attention paid to his ever-expanding waistline than he's getting already. Or Kelly doesn't want his slightly round belly to get any spare interest that might be going – it is inevitably one or the other.'

Dean's gradually widening and apparently troubling waistline had, for some reason, become the subject of much semi-heated speculation on the part of Kelly and Mum over the past year. It was a simmering matter of some concern and a bit like the war in Afghanistan (though not quite so distressing or bloody, obviously).

'And have they decided yet on whether they are getting married in the foreseeable?'

'No,' Mum snaps, 'and I've warned you before about trespassing into that particular minefield of non-conversation, have I not, Noah?'

It was never a good sign when Mum ended a sentence with your name, and especially when it was also so heavily underlined.

'But I thought they were looking at having a wedding next summer.'

'Yes, it was either going to be that or possibly in the autumn, depending on when Dean could get the time off work, though now he's facing redundancy—'

'He's being made redundant?'

Now, this was news, as Dean had been working in the Argos warehouse near Canterbury for the past year or so.

Though perhaps not for much longer.

'Well, he might be made redundant, according to your sister—'

'Is it because of his belly?'

(Pregnant) pause, followed by sudden and very stiff breathing on the line. 'What did we just agree about, concerning your facetiousness?'

'I'm sorry.'

'And so you should be. Anyway, now they don't know whether to save their money because of the threat of the potential and onerous redundancy or to spend it on a fortnight in the Caribbean Sandals because, as you know, your sister does like it hot, hot, hot. Rosella, the quiches, if you please.'

'When did the warehouse say they might be making Dean redundant?'

'Oh, they're just changing his shift pattern because of these new Polish workers that are coming in—'

'Polish workers?'

Working at a distribution warehouse in the middle of Kent?

'Well, they're either from Poland or possibly Portsmouth – it was one or the other, though you know what your sister's like—'

'A little bit pessimistic in her outlook?'

I can hear Mum's sudden energetic finger-wagging all the way from Plumstead. 'Now, you listen to me and you listen very carefully.'

Pause.

And now the voice a full octave lower.

'Because I want this to be a good day and something that we can all look back on with a certain affection, despite the unavoidable serious circumstances involved, and I do not want it to be ruined by lots of your pointless and self-serving arguments or theatrics, regardless of the pain that either may inflict on your sister or the social embarrassment it will undoubtedly cause to me – which it will because it always does.'

The pain that either may inflict on your sister?

'Do I make myself as clear as polished crystal in that regard?'

'Yes.'

'Genuinely and honestly?'

'There will be no theatrics of any kind, I promise.'

'Very well then.'

The previous and happier (if slightly stressed) tone returns to the line. 'Because I love you all, you know that, no matter how much you may annoy me in all your individual and oh-so-exhausting ways – except for Adam and Chloe, obviously.'

'I love you, too, Mum.'

'Alright then, and thank you. Now, Rosella, it is time to prepare the egg and ham pie, and do please wash your hands before you start on the pastry-rolling, my darling.'

The next morning the house is alive with relatives erratically descending from near and far, as Mum holds court beneath newly teased highlights and in a cloud of Chanel No. 5.

'Noah, my sweet darling, you've arrived,' she coos, before letting me fully into the hall and kissing me briskly on each cheek.

'I was doing my hair when the doorbell went.'

'And what were you doing with it exactly?'

'Oh, just ensuring it's worth the money that I paid for it.'

She steps daintily back and gives me her best "ta-da!" pose.

'So, what do you think?'

'It's very...'

Oh dear, this could be tricky.

'Regal.'

Hold on, no, that's not quite right.

'Stylish and...'

Think, Noah, think.

'And, my darling?'

Chic?

Could "chic" be the word that I am searching for?

'Chic?'

Mum smiles and twirls in the middle of the hallway.

Yes, that's clearly much better.

'And worth every penny, I would say. Though it did cost a pretty one or two, and I can assure you of that.'

And now, with the twirling over, there are even more kisses on each side of my face.

'Darling, thank you. You see, you can be quite charming when you make the effort. Oh dear, and now you're just one big smudge of lipstick.'

She wets a thumb and rubs at my right cheek.

'Sorry, but I do appear to have covered you in Amethyst Shimmer. And, just so you know, Joan and Michael have not long arrived from

Spain and I think Joan might well have had a drink or three on the plane coming over.'

'She's not completely drunk, though, is she?' I ask, as a vision of Mad Aunt Joan clutching a bottle of champagne and falling into her swimming pool on Mum's sixtieth swims into view. 'Or possibly asleep?'

'No, love, she's just being energetic and amusingly conversational, that's all.'

'Well, as long as she isn't slurring too much.'

Mum takes a kindly hold of my tie and slowly but firmly tightens the knot. 'And try especially not to be alarmed when you see Michael.'

'Why, is he drunk as well?'

'No, dear, but he is wearing a T-shirt. They were going to pick up a proper shirt at the airport but they couldn't find one without some kind of motif on it, apparently.'

'But Mum, it's a funeral—'

'I am fully aware of that fact, darling.'

She lets go of the tie and straightens my collar.

'However, your aunt and uncle believe they have no need for astringent formalities on the Mediterranean as, according to Joan, Spain is a far more relaxed and friendly society than Great Britain. Though I put that down to the exhausting Mediterranean sunshine.'

'I thought it was all bullfighting and riotous football supporters, myself.'

A sudden release of the collar.

'Yes, darling, but that's just the Catalans.'

Mad Aunt Joan suddenly appears at the end of the hallway, draped in black lace and clutching a chinking glass in one hand and her Mauzer air dog, Charlie, who immediately starts growling the minute he sets his twitching, watery eyes on me.

'Well, if it isn't Noah,' Mad Aunt Joan slurs, waving her glass in my direction. 'And don't you look handsome?'

Rub of the dog under its chin.

'Doesn't he look handsome, Charlie?'

Charlie growls even more loudly than before.

'That's right, he does, doesn't he?'

'Joan, darling!' Mum gushes, turning and smiling slightly manically, before nodding at the glass in Mad Aunt Joan's hand.

'So you found the whiskey after all—'

'And have you put on a little extra weight since I saw you last?' Mad Aunt Joan asks, ignoring Mum and sweeping up to throw her arms around me, despite the growling dog now clutched to her bosom. 'Because a little bird did tell me that you have been gaining a few centimetres, if not actual inches, around your troublesome waist area.'

'That's Dean, Joan,' Mum mutters under her breath.

'And you need to be careful at your age, Noah, as everything, including one's metabolism, starts to get oh so much slower as you grow older – everything apart from one's lust for life, of course.'

She lifts her veil, revealing a heavily tanned and deeply lined face dominated by thick black glasses, hanging on the tip of her nose.

'Though even that can become such a heavy burden to bear as the physical form starts to so tragically fall away.'

'Is that a fact?' Mum asks sharply, as Mad Aunt Joan gets her veil caught in her glasses. 'Scientifically proven or otherwise?'

'Oh yes,' Mad Aunt Joan says, finally untangling her veil. 'Because carbohydrates and emotional pain together can be a potentially lethal combination. Something you might want to consider, Stephanie, and especially at your age.'

'I've not that long retired, Joan—'

'Such a cruel time in any woman's life—'

'Stephanie, are you tossing this salad?' Rosella shouts up from the kitchen. 'Because I have now found the balsamic vinegar.'

Mum looks immediately relieved – though not for long.

'Is Daniel not coming, Stephanie?' Mad Aunt Joan asks, rolling the ice around in her glass. 'Not even for his own grandfather's funeral?'

'No, he's still in Sweden,' Mum says, the relief dropping from her face, 'though he said he should be back in the country within the fortnight.'

'Oh, that is such a shame,' Mad Aunt Joan says, pushing her glasses back up her nose, 'and so very long after the funeral as well.'

I step away, hoping to make it to the front room before my escaping absence is fully detected.

Mad Aunt Joan, however, has other ideas.

'I'll be with you in but a minute,' she sing-songs, slightly menacingly as I escape. 'Have no doubt on that fact.'

Then she joins Mum in the kitchen, as Kelly and Chloe come down the stairs, followed almost immediately by the distant sound of a flushing toilet.

'That woman is mentally unstable and she has a dangerously good memory,' Kelly hisses when she reaches the bottom of the banister. 'And how's that for an unhelpful combination?'

She awkwardly kisses me on the cheek and then squeezes my elbow.

'Hello, you. I'm sorry we never made it for your fortieth.'

And then before I can say anything she says, 'Do you like my new outfit?'

I look her up and down.

'Very nice,' I say without thinking.

The "new outfit" consists of very tight black trousers, an even tighter black polo neck jumper and black leather boots. All in all, it is very Kelly in its fashionable severity.

'Very smart,' I say carefully.

'Come on,' Kelly says, taking my arm. 'Everyone's here and they're already getting on my nerves.'

At which point Chloe, who is ten (or possibly eleven), giggles and slaps Kelly's arm. 'Mummy!' she squeals in the theatrical tone we have all become familiar with. 'Don't be so rude!'

Kelly narrows her eyes, but Chloe keeps smiling, clearly overjoyed at the fact that she has just become the centre of attention. 'That's so wrong, Mummy,' she continues, wagging her finger energetically in Kelly's direction, 'and so very, very naughty of you on such a sad, sad day.'

'Sorry,' Kelly says, suddenly apparently overwhelmed by guilt. 'But it is true. I could hear the angels calling when Michael was going on about the problems he keeps having with EasyJet. I mean, there are other airlines you can fly with, you know, apart from the budget ones. You can get a really good deal on British Airways to Bilbao these days if you book early enough and don't mind which airport you fly from.'

She blushes and then looks even glummer than she did before.

'And now I just feel worse.'

She nods towards the front room. 'Come on. Dean's here and he's looking forward to seeing you. Just don't ask him about his weight or his recent shingles incident.'

And now the shingles?

'Did he drive you all here?'

'Yes!' Kelly snaps. 'But I can drive as well, you know.'

Then she marches me and Chloe into the front room, where Dean and Adam are laughing and pinching each other in front of the fireplace.

'Hello, Dean,' I say, casually checking if he has indeed put on any additional weight as everyone seems to think he has – and which he hasn't.

'Noah, matey.' Dean grins, still pinching his son, who is two or three years younger than Chloe but who looks so much younger and more fragile than his sister, while she has the physical presence of an off-season junior sprinter.

'How you doing, London gay boy?'

'Dean!' Kelly yelps, immediately suffocating the potential outbreak of good humour in the room. 'I've told you before about the homopholobic jokes, haven't I?'

'Sorry,' Dean mumbles, giving me quick "stupid bloody women" eyes.

Though the truth is I had always had a soft spot for Dean, ever since he had started going out with Kelly more than a decade and a half ago, partly because of his easy, good humour and partly because of his steadfast refusal to be remade by my sister into her idea of what constitutes perfect boyfriend material.

'Have you been to a funeral before?' I ask Adam, as he ducks behind his father.

'No,' Adam squeaks from behind Dean's back.

'Really?' I ask.

'Yes,' Adam says, his voice wavering.

Then he covers his face with his hands.

'What, not even for a pet?'

Adam shakes his head again, his face still covered by his hands, and then slips fully under Dean's arm.

'You're just being silly.' He giggles.

'And there's nothing new there,' Kelly sighs, just loud enough to be heard.

'Why don't you show your Uncle Noah your new braces?' Dean asks, rubbing the top of Adam's head with his free hand. 'And stop being so stupid in the process.'

Adam drops his hands from his face and rubs his head on Dean's shirt.

'Don't do that Adam, please,' Kelly says automatically. 'It was fresh on only this morning.'

Chloe leans forward and slaps her brother's arm.

'Adam, do as Mummy tells you and show Uncle Noah your braces.'

'Chloe!' Kelly snaps, pulling at Chloe's arm.

'If we don't put them on him now, they'll cost five grand later,' Dean says, as Adam finally opens his mouth and reveals his new and highly controversial dental scaffolding for all the world to see, 'and no amount of bridgework is worth that amount of money.'

'Wow,' I say, as Adam's oral metalwork is fully revealed.

Chloe immediately looks around, clearly sensing her sudden loss of the spotlight.

'Amazing...'

I lean forward to peer at the neat metal wires lacing Adam's teeth as his father squeezes his son in a neck lock until his tongue pops out.

'How are they held in place like that?'

'With special brackets,' Kelly says, touching Dean on the arm, who immediately releases Adam from his grip.

'But still, that's two thousand pounds' worth.' Dean chuckles, before remembering where he is and why we have all been brought together. 'Though we were able to put it on the insurance,' he continues, his voice suddenly becoming sombre.

Adam rubs at his neck while his sister narrows her eyes at him.

'Have you not even buried a toy of some kind?' I ask Adam, returning to the former topic of conversation. 'In a secret garden burial or something?'

Adam looks up at his father. 'I don't bury toys,' he says, his voice trailing off as he realises the ridiculousness of what he is now saying.

'Well, you had better get used to it,' I say, looking at Kelly, 'because this will probably be the first of many more funerals to come.'

Kelly rolls her eyes and shakes her head.

'You're a miserable bastard, you are, sometimes,' she sighs, before staring out the window. 'In fact, you're all too morbid, the whole bloody lot of you.'

'It's true,' I say, winking at Adam, who giggles and covers his mouth to try to stop any more happy laughter escaping from it, 'whether you like it or not.'

Chloe starts silently laughing and looks at her father, who is grinning with one careful eye on the back of my sister's head.

'It most certainly is,' Dean deadpans, rocking gently on his heels, 'and we're none of us getting any younger, now that the top deck has gone.'

Kelly suddenly turns back from her window-gazing.

'And I'd take that stupid smile off your face if I were you,' she says coolly, 'because Dad and Isobel are getting out of a taxi and it looks like they might have already had an argument.'

12

Isobel was Dad's second wife and, taking everything into account, a woman that possessed the diplomatic skills of Henry Kissinger combined with the mental resilience of Margaret Thatcher.

'Shall I show Granddad my new braces?' Adam asks, looking up at Dean as Kelly joins them in front of the fireplace.

Each and every one suitably on parade.

'No, mate,' Dean says kindly, stroking his son's hair. 'He has more important things on his mind today.'

Kelly points her frown in my direction.

'And you should be thinking about your own grandfather – God rest his soul – and not about how to entertain everyone all the time with your stupid funny-man routine.'

Typical Kelly, always looking for an opening.

'I am thinking about Granddad,' I reply as casually as I can, 'and I am not entertaining anyone.'

'No, you're not,' Kelly says with a sly smile, 'not even slightly.'

For a moment no one speaks, then Kelly goes all guilty.

'When did you last see Granddad, anyway?'

The doorbell rings and there is a commotion in the hallway.

'About two weeks ago, when he was doing his physiotherapy.'

The front door opens and the commotion advances towards us up the hallway.

'He was doing quite well at that point, or so the community nurse said, anyway.'

'Oh,' Kelly says sadly. 'I take it all back, then.'

Dad appears in the doorway, looking at least half an inch smaller than when I saw him last, which was only a year ago.

'Well, hello, hello!'

'Hello, Dad,' I say, looking around him into the hallway.

'Where's Isobel disappeared to?'

'She's already nipped down to the kitchen to swap recipes and probably some gossip as well, I would reckon, with your mother,' Dad replies, slipping his wallet into his trouser pocket. 'Women, eh? Always a mystery.'

When I was a child my father was a tall, apparently constantly smiling soldier with jet-black hair worked up into a modest quiff which always seemed to be flattened down by his uniform beret. Now, happily settled into his retirement and more recently with the ever-diligent Isobel by his side, he was heavier, softer and increasingly grey-haired, his trademark quiff long gone.

Dad suddenly claps his hands together and surveys the room.

'And why all the long faces?' he asks cheerfully. 'Is it because of the funeral?'

Kelly wearily shakes her head and then steps forward for a kiss. 'Oh, Dad, the things you say. And you didn't drive up then?'

'No, we got the train and there was a terrible altercation on it. Some drunken hooligan without a ticket punched one of the inspectors.'

He rubs at Kelly's shoulders and then shakes Dean's hand.

'There was an ambulance and police dogs at the station. Alsatians, by the look of them, and hungry with it, though they keep them like that, don't they, so they can attack quickly enough when needed.'

Adam nips back behind his father.

'It's a sad business, though, today, isn't it?' Dad sighs, opening his arms to encourage Adam and Chloe to jointly give him a hug. 'Come here, you two – both sad and inevitable really, when you come to think about it.'

'He was eighty-nine years old,' I add, waiting for my hug.

'Or ninety,' Kelly mutters under her breath.

'Ninety and not a year too late.' Dad chuckles, before finally getting round to me with his hugging. 'And let's be honest, because there are much worse ways to go.'

Kelly frowns even more.

'So, all in all, I think you have to say that it could have been a lot worse,' Dad continues, ignoring Kelly, who is now chewing her lip furiously. 'And he was as cared for as he could be, especially at the end. Where's Daniel?'

'Still in Sweden,' Kelly answers before anyone else can get a word in. 'He's trying to give up his smoking, but it just makes him too grumpy, apparently.'

'Even more grumpy than he usually is,' I add without thinking.

Nobody laughs (though Kelly looks even more annoyed if such a thing were indeed possible).

'I think I see,' Dad says carefully, pushing his hands into his trouser pockets to rattle his loose change about. 'Your grandfather was comfortable at the end, though, according to your mother,' he continues, obviously not overly concerned by Daniel's reportedly grumpy demeanour, 'and you can't deny that fact.'

'Apart from when he was suffering from the stroke,' Kelly mutters, 'or strokes, plural.'

'Yes, that's true,' Dad says and then adds, as if he is thinking it for the very first time, 'though he was certainly a good man, was Patrick.'

Then we all fall silent and listen to Mad Aunt Joan and Isobel laughing in the kitchen, as Mum suddenly exclaims, 'Oh you can't say that, Joan, I mean, honestly!' with no great seriousness or intent.

'Why didn't you drive up, Dad? Is your car playing up again?' I ask, genuinely interested in Dad's latest motoring travails for some reason.

'Oh, I've decided to give all that up.'

'Really?'

Now, this is interesting, as Dad has owned a maroon Rover 800 since John Major was in Downing Street.

'Well, it's been nothing but a year of mysterious non-starting and escalating garage bills. Last time they said it would cost a small fortune just to replace the alternator, so I thought, what's the point?'

A ghost of a juddering saloon, complete with fake wood trim and velour trim, rattles through my mind very, very slowly.

'It's probably for the best,' I venture at last, sensitive to my father's sad loss. 'After all, they only become more trouble than they're worth when they reach that stage.'

Dad nods sagely. 'That they do,' he sighs, studying the pattern in the carpet, which Granddad told us once had been in the foyer of the Greenwich Odeon before they turned it into a bingo hall. 'Though letting go can be very difficult all the same.'

We all join him in his melancholic carpet-staring.

'I've got a Golf GTI now,' I say suddenly (though I don't know why, to be honest).

Dad perks up on hearing this news, however.

'So I heard. Punitive, though, is it? The insurance, I mean.'

'Not for the area, though I did have to tell them I was parking it in a garage and not on the street.'

'Because of all the car thieves?'

'That's right, Dad, because of all the car thieves.'

Kelly rolls her eyes.

'Afternoon, everybody!'

Simon, one of the cousins that me and Kelly never really saw enough of (even though he only lived in Hayes and was roughly our age), pokes his head around the door and immediately starts counting heads.

'Don't mind me. One, two, three—'

'Hello, Simon,' Kelly says without undue enthusiasm.

'Have you lost some weight, Kelly? Four, five, six—'

'On the Zumba,' Kelly answers brightly, standing up a bit straighter than she did before. 'Every other weeknight, with a special class on a Sunday before we go down the pub.'

'I thought that was a country in West Africa,' Dad chuckles, his eyes darting around the room searching for potential laughter. 'One of the more touristy ones, isn't it?'

Kelly takes a deep breath. 'That's a very old joke, Dad, and it wasn't that funny the first time round – which was, I might add, years ago.'

'Just so you know, the hearse is on its way,' Simon announces to everyone in the room (and out of it) before tapping the outcome of his headcount into a calculator. 'And it's a brand-new Volvo – first time it's been used, apparently.'

Kelly's previous stab at good humour evaporates immediately. 'That's nice,' she says.

Simon slips his calculator into his jacket pocket and then strides right into the middle of the room, where he holds out his hand to my father. 'Frank,' he says solemnly, as Dad shakes his hand, 'it is always a pleasure to see you, Sir.'

Then he carefully retraces his steps back into the hallway.

'Who was that?' Dad asks after Simon has left.

'That's Michael's son,' Kelly says authoritatively. 'He's planning on saying something at the church and he is very nervous at the prospect, apparently.'

'I didn't recognise him.' Dad grins, happily overstating the obvious. 'But he certainly looks like his father, doesn't he?'

Which is an odd thing to say as Simon is tall, thin and pale as milk, whereas Uncle Michael is short, overweight and as orange and wrinkled as his wife. They do both have brown curly hair, however, though Simon's is receding a little more slowly than his father's.

Kelly sighs wearily and with a certain theatrical flourish. 'He's studying to be a disability advisor, according to Mum, and is very good at wheelchair basketball as a result.'

She fixes her eyes on Adam and Chloe.

'Now, get your coats on, you two, please, and remember what I said in the car about no giggling in the church.'

'But Mum,' Chloe whines, wrapping her arm too tightly around her father's waist, 'the hearse isn't even here yet and it's not even that cold.'

From behind his father, Adam leans round and tries to shove his sister away. 'Chloe, get off.'

'No, you get off, you sod.'

'Chloe! The hearse will be here soon, young lady,' Kelly snaps, her eyes ablaze. 'And you heard what your Uncle Simon said, so get yourself ready!'

Dad takes a careful step to the side.

'Besides, the fresh air will stop all this silliness and giggling. So don't just stand there staring at me, the two of you – get your coats on now!'

13

When we arrive at the church Mad Aunt Joan and Uncle Michael are already directing mourners to their pews and mild confusion is in the air, possibly because of the sudden outbreak of rain, which had greeted the funeral party as it drove up Brookhill Road and into the church car park.

'It's best not to hover,' Uncle Michael shouts from the entrance of the vestibule, as friends and relatives dart from their cars and into the shelter of the church. 'Because the weather's only going to get worse before it gets any better. If it gets better at all, of course, which I don't think it will.'

Beside him, the vicar, who must be half Uncle Michael's age, wipes at his forehead and attempts a comforting smile for the benefit of the damp figures vigorously shaking off rainwater as they dash inside.

'Such a sad and disappointing day. Good morning.'

A short bus ride from Woolwich Arsenal Station, Saint Peter's the Apostle Roman Catholic Church, with its gloomy, red-brick majesty, which had always been slightly at odds to the grey council estate that surrounded it, was where Mum and Dad had married, back in the summer of 1965.

'And please do be careful as you make your way to the pews because of the wet floors and our associated Health and Safety obligations. Thank you.'

Despite the rain, however, inside the church everything is calm and smothered in organ music, while Granddad's coffin is surrounded

75

at the foot of the altar by white, red and green floral arrangements and draped in a Baner Cymru.

I don't want to look at the coffin and, judging by the glassy look on Mum's face as she stares grimly ahead, neither does she.

'So how is Spain?' Dad asks Mad Aunt Joan, before shaking rainwater from his jacket. 'Have you and Michael had a chance to fully settle in with the local culture?'

'I think so, though we are going to have to start learning the language if we are to stay any longer,' Mad Aunt Joan sighs, as Dean ushers Adam and Chloe into our allocated pew. 'Because the truth of the matter is that we really would be lost without Maria and that frightens me more than a little, I can tell you.'

Maria makes the beds and mops the floors at the villa in Spain.

'It's like being a hostage when we're there sometimes, and not in an exciting way either, I can tell you.'

Isobel momentarily looks a little confused. 'I don't think—'

'I do miss it, however,' Mad Aunt Joan continues, remorseful and still a little bit drunk from her earlier whiskey. 'Especially with this awful, wet British weather.'

'It's not that bad,' Dean says, grasping a struggling Adam in one hand and a giggling Chloe in the other, 'and I'm sure it'll pass over by the time we leave the church.'

'Oh, this rain won't be going anywhere for a long while yet, just you wait and see,' Mad Aunt Joan admonishes him. 'It will continue to fall remorselessly now, you can take my word on that probable fact, and then it'll be nothing but rain and misery until the day is over, I assure you.'

And now it's Dean who looks confused.

'It's only a light shower, Joan—'

'You may think that, Dean, but years of personal loss have taught me that the insinuations of apparently changeable weather can be very much otherwise.'

'Alright then,' Dean says, clearly desperate to escape this particular "conversation". 'Mystery solved, then.'

'Or started,' Dad mutters, just loud enough to be heard.

'Of course, you don't get this kind of tedious drizzle in Spain,' Mad Aunt Joan continues, more to herself than to anyone else. 'There it is either a genuine Mediterranean storm of full and marked violence or it is nothing at all.'

'Is it now?' Kelly asks wearily, quickly joining us after having a crafty fag outside next to the bins. 'Is it really?'

'Oh yes,' Mad Aunt Joan continues, now even louder than before. 'In my experience the Mediterranean weather is, like its people, more forthright, passionate and, when required, also torturously hot.'

'Well, it certainly sounds suitably sweaty, if nothing else,' Kelly mutters, slipping her coat off her shoulders. 'Apart from when the sun is not actually shining, I suppose.'

Mad Aunt Joan tugs at her veil, which falls abruptly down over her face.

'Thank you, Kelly. Now, if you will excuse me, I do need to prepare myself for the sermon. So if anyone needs further assistance of any kind I will be with my son and daughter as they gather their thoughts for the emotional turmoil that lies ahead.'

And on that note she turns in the direction of the altar, where an agitated Simon is holding a growling Charlie next to a freshly permed and almost painfully thin Rachel, together with what Mad Aunt Joan had excitedly told us earlier was Rachel's "new close and very personal friend, Sapphire, an Italian riding instructor now living in Bishop's Stortford".

'Such a difficult and testing time, though Rachel and Simon are being so very brave, and the indomitable Sapphire has proven to be such a support for my daughter, as well as to her own delightful horses, of course.'

All eyes turn to Rachel and Sapphire, who are grim-faced with grief and wearing identical fuchsia trouser suits, starched white blouses and shiny, black court shoes.

'So, if anybody needs either myself or my children or indeed Michael, we will be gathering our collective thoughts as best we can. Good day to you.'

At which point Mad Aunt Joan marches off down the aisle, swerving a little to the left as she goes.

'Careful not to trip over the coffin,' Dad mutters under his breath. 'Or into it.'

'Frank, stop that!' Isobel snaps, before swallowing her laughter. 'It's not right or funny, so stop it right now.'

'But I—'

'I don't want to warn you for the last time, Frank. Just you settle yourself down before it's too late.'

'Too late for what?'

At the front of the church the vicar appears at the pulpit.

'Shall we begin, ladies and gentlemen?' he asks, his voice booming around us as the last of Granddad's Welsh relatives shuffle in and take their seats at the back of the church. 'And thank you all for coming on this sad and very wet occasion,' he intones gravely, before pausing to adjust the height of the pulpit microphone. 'Also, can you all hear me without any unnecessary interference to the audio connection?'

At the back of the church a man shouts back, 'Yes, and bloody well get on with it!'

Which is from one of the Welsh relatives, obviously.

'Very well then…'

And my eyes are suddenly hot and heavy after the torturous journey up the A206, while the church is warm and dry, so I am more than happy for the vicar to say whatever he wants, for as long as he wants, just so long as we can stay out of the rain that is now pounding onto the roof above our heads.

'Mr Simon Tribe will begin the service.'

Kelly nervously eyes the coffin.

'I keep thinking it's going to fall over,' she whispers in my ear, 'and he's going to come tumbling out onto the floor.'

'That's if he's even in there,' I whisper back. 'I'm convinced they swap the coffins over just before they open the doors to prevent that very thing happening.'

'Really? Is that legal?'

'I wouldn't have thought so.'

Simon and Rachel awkwardly step into the pulpit.

'Oh God, here comes the speech,' Kelly mutters. 'And now I need to use the toilet.'

She shifts uncomfortably in her seat.

'Though I don't suppose I'll get a chance now.'

We had heard the rumours of what Simon was going to say for weeks.

'He's been drafting and re-drafting that eulogy and going through all your grandfather's papers,' Mum had warned me on the phone the night before, 'and Rachel's coming round first thing to help with his timing.'

'That's very like Rachel.'

'Oh, it is. With the two of them everything is in the schedule and rehearsal.'

'And has she told anyone that she's a lesbian?'

I had been curious to know how long Rachel would be able to keep up her current "could-be heterosexual" pretence, especially now that a video of her singing *I Will Always Love You* on a float at Brighton Pride was doing the rounds on computer disc.

'No, she has not, and I've told you before that is not going to happen,' Mum snaps down the line, before lowering her voice. 'And now if you'll excuse me I have some chicken legs to breadcrumb.'

The next morning both Rachel and Simon managed to remain suitably tight-lipped about who was going to say what and how long it would take the two of them to deliver their mysterious pieces at the service.

Which turned out to be all very intriguing.

'Is she still a lesbian?' Kelly whispers in my ear as Simon taps at the pulpit microphone. 'Or at least bisexual?'

'As far as I know,' I whisper back, 'though nobody wants to talk about that, or at least not in front of her, anyway.'

'I'm not going to look at him while he reads this, in case I laugh,' Kelly says, her voice already starting to wobble. 'Because I know I'm just going to – it's because of the nerves.'

I elbow her in the ribs and bite my lip.

'You're horrible, you are.'

'It's going to be funny, I can just feel it—'

'And it is not going to be even slightly amusing.'

Then, as if to spite us all, Simon starts telling a story about what happened when he stole some money from Granddad's wallet (which was more of a purse, really, though we never talked about that) and how he was tortured by guilt because of what he did, especially once he was caught, and that Granddad had him pay the money back without telling anyone.

'Well I never,' Dad says cheerfully behind me. 'You really do learn something new every day.'

Uncle Michael and Mad Aunt Joan shuffle awkwardly in their pew and look down at their bibles.

'I wonder if he charged him any interest? Because knowing your grandfather, I bet he did.'

Still in the pulpit, Simon bows his head.

'And when I had paid him all the money,' he says, before wiping at his nose, 'he gave it all back to me so that I could go skiing with my friends in Switzerland.'

Nobody says anything.

At the back of the church a mobile phone goes off.

'And that was a lovely holiday, though I did sprain my ankle on the nursery slope the first day we were there.'

Then he steps carefully out of the pulpit and I can't help but notice that beneath his trousers he's wearing Homer Simpson socks.

'Now I come to think of it, I've heard that story before,' Dad whispers in my ear, before putting his arm around Mum, who is sniffing into her sleeve. 'There, there,' he says kindly. 'I think we've all been very touched by Simon's very affecting admission of theft.'

But I'm more intrigued by the skiing holiday.

After all, when did that happen?

Though on second thoughts I couldn't recall ever seeing Simon on any of the compulsory family camping expeditions that scarred our childhood, so perhaps his off-piste adventure story has some truth in it after all.

'Your grandfather always did keep a close eye on his wallet,' Mum sniffs through her tears, 'and not just on pension day, either.'

'I'd look under the floorboards if I were you,' Dad consoles her, 'or at the bottom of the garden.'

'Frank, stop that, please!' Isobel hisses gently, as Rachel steps up to the microphone and carefully unfolds a sheet of paper.

'Now, if you would allow me, ladies and gentlemen, I would like to tell you about all the things that will always remind me of my dear grandfather.'

'Oh no,' Kelly whispers, bowing her head. 'Now I am going to laugh.'

'I'd like to start by reminiscing with you about the sweet old man I loved and what he meant to me and, I hope, to all of us.'

I brace myself.

'Dandelion & Burdock, fried eggs and three-pawed cats, burnt toast and hard, slippery gobstoppers, cold, wet Guinness…'

Beside me, Kelly makes a sort of choking sound.

'Jars of rusty screws and rubber bands in a ball, rainy summer outings, false teeth and homemade beer in a bucket…'

I look to the coffin, willing it to pop open.

'Poker games on a Sunday afternoon…'

The vicar flicks at his watch.

'Camping sites and cold, rusting showers, ration books and cabbage with fried mashed potato. Unsafe bend-in-the-middle shelving…'

I'm tempted to add old pornographic magazines at this point (and we're not talking about anything as classy as *Penthouse* or *Razzle* here) but keep quiet.

'Sweat-stained rugby shirts and cold white lard, not-quite-hot-enough baths, communal toilets on isolated French camping sites…'

Kelly now appears to be having an asthma attack.

'And warm cuddles on miserable, do-nothing Sundays.'

Rachel suddenly stops speaking and folds her notes in half.

'You were such an important part of my life, Granddad,' she says hesitantly, 'and I'm going to miss you so very much.'

'Oh dear,' Dad sighs, and I am suddenly very relieved that I didn't laugh when I could have done (though Kelly is noisily clearing her throat in a very embarrassed fashion, I notice).

'Well, now I just feel terrible,' Kelly mumbles, pulling at her handkerchief, 'and it's all your fault.'

'And how did you work that out, exactly?'

'Because you should have stopped me. You know you should.'

'You need to take more responsibility for your own actions,' I say, actually meaning it.

'I do take responsibility. It's just the shock of it, that's all. And now I need another cigarette.'

'Ladies and gentlemen,' the vicar announces with measured sensitivity as Sapphire leads Rachel out of the pulpit, 'perhaps now would be a good juncture to attempt a hymn, which will be sung in Welsh.'

'Oh dear God,' Dad mutters. 'I think I'd rather hear another of Rachel's poems.'

12

At the end of the service, six of the Welsh male relatives march to the front of the nave, touch at the Baner Cymru and then, with a certain amount of effort, lift Granddad's coffin onto their shoulders.

Behind me, Mum starts to cry.

'Come on, you,' Dad says gently, rubbing at her arm, 'you know your dad'll be frowning if he could see you now.'

Which doesn't make much sense, really, but you can see where he is coming from.

'I just wish I could have told him how much I loved him, despite all his shouting and swearing,' Mum sobs through her tears, her voice juddering gently up and down. 'It was all just too bloody difficult at the time, though, because of his dementia and everything.'

'I know,' Dad says as Granddad's coffin goes past. 'But it'll all be for the good come the end, though, Steph, you'll see.'

Which doesn't make much sense either.

Kelly looks confused, her eyes swollen with tears.

'What end?' she whispers, as we shuffle out of our pew.

'I don't know,' I whisper back, before joining the slightly haphazard line behind the coffin. 'I suppose he means when we all meet up again, you know, upstairs.'

Just in front of us, one of the Welsh relatives frowns at me.

'Sorry.'

'Apart from that bloody Marjorie,' Kelly mutters under her breath, as the coffin is carried from the church and out into the fading rain, which now seems to be blowing its way towards Abbey Wood. 'I mean, there's only so much goodwill in heaven.'

And on that, she most definitely does have a point.

*

'Well, that went better than I thought,' Dean says, as the back doors of the hearse close on the coffin and Kelly searches in her bag for a box of matches.

'I thought so,' Kelly sighs, elbow-deep in the bag. 'Even the singing was alright at the end, though I didn't understand a word of it, to be honest with you.'

She finally finds her matches and then lights a cigarette, despite the rain-speckled wind blowing against her face. 'It was both very touching and well-paced,' she coughs.

'The hymns were certainly good and I even saw Dad singing – and he hates hymns,' I say, as Kelly frowns at a giggling Adam and Chloe, who have just discovered something amusing in one of the church litter bins.

'Is it because he's an atheist?' Dean asks.

'No, it's because he's tone-deaf.'

'Watch yourselves, you two,' Kelly warns us, as Great Aunt Catherine totters over, supported by Mad Aunt Joan on one side, her veil blowing wildly in the wind, and a very stern-faced Rachel on the other.

'Oh, blimey,' Dean mutters, looking down quickly at the wet pavement. 'I knew I should have stayed with the kids.'

We rarely saw Granddad's only sister these days, and hardly ever out of her electric wheelchair (or "mobility carriage", as she insisted on calling it whenever she got the chance). A tiny, grey, trembling woman, apparently constantly on the verge of tottering over when not safely sat down, Great Aunt Catherine was as loyal to Wales as her brother had been and rarely travelled beyond its borders.

Mobility carriage or no mobility carriage.

84

Not unless she absolutely had to.

'I won't stop,' Great Aunt Catherine cackles, once she is close enough to be heard. 'I've been awake far too long as it is and the rain has only made me more tired than I was when I got up this morning.'

Then she smiles encouragingly at me and looks Dean up and down, before touching delicately at my forearm.

'And is this…'

Pause.

Shift of the dentures.

'Your other half, Noah?'

Kelly sucks ferociously on her cigarette.

'No, no,' I say as gently as I can. 'This is Dean, Kelly's husband—'

'Boyfriend!' Kelly snaps, angrily tossing her barely smoked cigarette into the kerb. 'Because we're not married, there's no prospect of getting married and I thought I had made myself clear in that regard on a whole number of occasions.'

Quick cough.

'I mean, we had made ourselves clear in that regard.'

'Sorry, that's right. Dean is Kelly's boyfriend,' I correct myself as soon as Kelly takes a breath. 'My mistake.'

'How are you doing?' Dean asks Great Aunt Catherine, apparently unconcerned either way by his non-marital status, before leaning over and extending his hand, which Great Aunt Catherine touches with the tips of her fingers.

'You're very like Noah,' she says, patting his forearm affectionately. 'Especially around the eyes and the high hairline.'

At which point she releases her two assistants with a flourish and turns to wobble slowly over to the Welsh pallbearers, who are joking and shoving each other against the side of the hearse.

'She did that on purpose,' Kelly fumes, looking quickly at Dean in case he is tempted to disagree.

Or indeed laugh.

'Congratulations on a very nice poem,' I say to Rachel, who is looking at Dean, a little confused. 'It must have taken some time to write.'

Rachel smiles modestly and gives her best impression of Princess Diana. 'Thank you, Noah. That is very giving and sensitive of you. Though to be honest, it wasn't the writing of the poem that was the challenge but knowing when to stop.'

'I can imagine,' Kelly mutters under her breath.

Mad Aunt Joan places a Rothmans in her mouth.

'Can you really?'

Kelly reaches into her bag and offers Mad Aunt Joan her matches. 'Yes, on most days, when the kids are not getting on my nerves too much, I can.'

'Though to be honest, Noah, it really was the least I could do and the composition was, I think you'll agree, a fitting tribute to such a fine and noble man,' Rachel continues, holding her perm out of her eyes as it starts to blow about in the wind. 'Now, if you will excuse me, I need to focus myself on the advancing cremation.'

And with that, she glides off with Mad Aunt Joan to join Sapphire, who is swinging her car keys next to a bright red Ford Focus.

'I know sod all about writing,' Dean says, zipping up his jacket as Chloe and Adam run up to us, their arms outstretched like aeroplane wings, 'but that poem of Rachel's was bloody awful.'

Chloe smacks at his arm.

'Bad daddy!' she yelps, before shaking her head. 'What are we to do with you, Mr Naughty?'

'Put me in a shoebox and throw away the key?'

'Well, it would be a start. Though it would have to be a bloody big box,' Kelly sighs, with a hint of a smile. 'Why don't you show the kids the flowers, Dean?'

Dean looks momentarily baffled. 'The flowers?'

'The funeral wreaths that go with the coffin—'

'Oh yes, of course,' Dean replies sharply, before leading Adam and Chloe over to where the mourners are shuffling past and pointing at the floral arrangements.

'Did you see Mum and Dad when Rachel finished that bloody poem of hers?' Kelly asks, rummaging about in her bag as Chloe re-appears with a big smile on her face.

'Go back to the beautifully arranged wreaths and stay with your brother and father,' Kelly snaps without looking up. 'I will be with you in a minute!'

Chloe dutifully turns on her heels as Kelly pops another cigarette into her mouth and strikes a match.

'Stay with me a minute while I have this,' she says, blowing smoke into the cool air, where it hangs momentarily above her head like fog. 'Mum and Dad were almost holding hands when they thought Isobel wasn't looking.'

And which of course Kelly had been.

She takes another lungful from her cigarette and then blows the smoke out of the side of her mouth. 'I think Dad started it, though I could be wrong.'

I look past her to where Mum, Dad and Isobel are laughing over a wreath that spells the word "Gramps" in white roses. 'And what do you think that was about?'

'I don't know. But it probably doesn't mean anything.'

'I suppose so,' Kelly says, suddenly losing all interest in her potential Mum, Dad and Isobel could-be scandal. 'Though I think it's nice if it shows he still cares.'

She suddenly waves her cigarette about.

'I need to give up because of the kids if nothing else. Last time I saw the doctor he gave me a DVD to help.'

'Was it any good?'

'Not a patch on *Titanic*.'

She takes another couple of quick drags and then tosses the smouldering cigarette into a puddle. 'It's not good for you, though, is it?'

'No, not really. Though there are probably more important things to worry about.'

We walk over to the flowers.

'I saw Mark the other day.'

I stop walking.

'Did you speak to him?'

'No,' Kelly says calmly. 'It was at Bluewater and there were lots of people about.'

'So you could have been wrong.'

'I wasn't wrong. Believe me, it was him.'

'But you could have been, after all this time.'

'It's not been that long.'

'It's been years—'

'But it's not like he's emigrated or anything.'

Though then again he could have done for all I know.

Kelly looks me straight in the eye.

'Believe me, it was him.'

'I do. Believe you, I mean.'

'And he saw me as well,' Kelly says coolly, and then she walks away as if nothing has happened.

15

'Never look directly at the pygmy men after midnight.'

When Granddad could still hear what you were saying he would proudly show off his front room, within which everything was at its best, presentable and right, all ornaments dusted, each surface lovingly polished to a warm glow. He even used to lock the door to the front room to prevent anyone going into it on their own, until one day he lost the key and had to take the lock off.

'After midnight is the magic hour and the magic hour is not for mortals or for children either.'

Neither Kelly nor myself had been allowed into the front room on our own before, but now, after only a few weeks in Mineral Street, here was Granddad inviting us in as if it was a very special occasion indeed.

'Though you can't stay for too long, mind.'

Kelly looks worried at the prospect but tries to hide her fears.

For myself, I could not be more thrilled if I tried.

'Should we fear the pygmy men?' Kelly asks with a slight tremble to her voice, as Granddad pushes the creaking door open for the three of us to enter the dimly lit room. 'And do they have special powers?'

'Oh yes,' Granddad whispers, waving us in. 'They have very special powers indeed, over the mind and the soul, and they know everything that is to be known about all things. So heed my warning well.'

'Like in *Look and Learn*, you mean?' Kelly asks half-expectantly, peering past the open door.

'Definitely. Though perhaps not so scientific in their ways.'

In the middle of the room, on the heavy oak dining table that is Granddad's pride and joy, a hand-carved wooden army stand keenly to attention, watching our awkward shuffling into the room with wonky eyes.

'And that power comes from this!'

A flick knife suddenly flashes in Granddad's hand and then, just as quickly, it disappears again back into his trouser pocket.

Kelly gasps.

I swallow hard.

'For it is the blade that is man's best friend, not the dog.'

He looks at me with the cold, hard eyes of a man who had survived the Blitz (and marriage to Marjorie Blakestone).

'Do you understand me?'

'Yes!' I yelp.

'Good, but don't ever let your mum see you playing with knives otherwise I'll never hear the end of it. Now, let me show you a snake I made from a chair leg.'

Granddad liked to carve and the big-headed figurines facing the front room's heavily curtained windows were the product of all his chipping and scraping over the years.

'What's that horrible smell?' Kelly asks suddenly, wrinkling her nose, obviously starting to get bored.

'It's a special mixture of shoe polish and varnish,' Granddad grunts, moving a fat horse with short legs on the tabletop. 'You'll get used to it after a while – it's like Vicks.'

We breathe in as deeply as we can.

'It's good for your lungs,' Granddad wheezes. 'Cleans them out good and—'

Cough.

'Proper.'

My eyes start to water. 'Really?'

More coughing now, even wetter than before. 'Y-ye-yes.'

And then we all stumble back into the hallway, sneezing and wheezing and grasping at the wallpaper.

'Now, go play outside,' Granddad splutters, pointing us in the direction of the front door, 'while I get the dinner on.'

'What are we having?' Kelly asks, wiping at her eyes. 'Is it lamb?'

'No, it's not lamb.'

'Or pork? Because I do like pork, especially with crackling.'

'No, it's not pork.'

'Is it turkey then?'

'At this time of year? Does it look like it's snowing outside?'

Kelly opens the front door and hot summer air wafts in as if from a baking oven.

'No, not really.'

One last cough.

'Well, it wouldn't be turkey then, would it? Summer is not for turkeys or for Christmas pudding, if you please. Now go play outside, because today's dinner,' one last splutter, 'is going to be something very special and unique.'

We finally turn and march out the door as ordered.

'Do you think it'll be beef?' Kelly asks, once we are safely outside and Granddad is back whistling in the kitchen. 'After all, beef is nice.'

We climb up onto the garden wall and stare down at the road.

'Where's Mum?' I ask, convinced we will not be eating beef for dinner.

'She's at Mad Aunt Joan's.'

Still?

'Did you hear her crying last night?'

'No,' Kelly says too quickly. 'I did not, as I was fast asleep.'

Which is just a downright lie because Kelly is never, ever fast asleep.

'You're making it up, you are. I heard you walking about, unless you were sleep-walking – which obviously you weren't because you never have done.'

'I was walking about actually, you snoopy sod, because I had to go to the toilet,' Kelly snaps, bouncing off the wall down onto the pavement. 'Sometimes I have to go to the toilet in the night, you know, or I might end up wetting myself and the bed with it.'

She wanders off along the pavement, picking at her hair.

'You liar,' I say, not quite loud enough for her to hear, and then tilt my head back to squint at the sun. 'Why are girls so bloody deceitful all the ruddy time?'

*

An hour later the dining table is fully laden and me, Kelly and Daniel are hungrily perched in front of our plates, cutlery in hand.

'What's this?'

Kelly's knife and fork hover mid-air, neither knife nor fork going anywhere.

'Is it French? Because it certainly looks foreign to me.'

Next to me Daniel sneezes.

'Or possibly Turkish?'

Quick sniff, roll of the nose.

'And it smells funny.'

Which it does, sort of.

'Can you not smell it?'

The air is hot and ripe with the aroma of slowly roasted chicken and each of our plates is filled to the brim with gravy and vegetables, but something is clearly wrong.

'What smells funny?' Granddad waves his fork in a sort of circular motion above the table. 'I don't know what you're talking about. It's only roast chicken and vegetables.'

Kelly and Daniel stare down at their plates and right there, in that empty, dead moment, I suddenly realise that Granddad has just crossed the line which divides us, the normal people, from those dirty old shufflers you tend to see sleeping on park benches with hats over their faces.

'Well, don't just wait staring at your plates – get stuck in.'

There is no going back.

'Otherwise it'll only go cold.'

Kelly tips her knife and points at something bobbing about in her gravy.

'There, right there. What are they, exactly?'

'They're called capers,' Granddad grunts, chewing on a ball of fat and thigh. 'I got them specially from the Co-op just for you.'

Then he swallows and starts making a slurpy "mmmm" sound, before licking carefully and repeatedly at the greasy corners of his mouth.

'They're spicy and cosmopolitan, and you'll learn to love them, just like you did with garlic.'

'I don't like garlic, it makes your breath smell—'

'They're maggots,' I say without thinking.

Kelly's cutlery trembles in her hands.

'Where's Mum?' she asks quietly.

'Still at Mad Aunt Joan's,' I say quickly. 'They're going over a *Freemans* and eating aubergine on her wicker three-piece.'

'On her what?'

'It's in Mad Aunt Joan's new conservatory.'

'They're not maggots, they're capers, and they're very, very tasty,' Granddad snaps, slicing decisively into a potato. 'So go ahead and try one.'

Swallowing hard, Kelly turns her head and stares at me.

'Well, what are you waiting for?'

Daniel picks up his fork.

'I think they are maggots,' Kelly says calmly. 'In fact, I think you will find that one of them might even be moving about, or swimming, to be more precise, right now in my gravy.'

That's just a lie. I can tell that without even looking down at Kelly's plate, though it might also be true if you don't look too closely enough (Granddad's eyesight had long ago started to play up and recently he had started using a magnifying glass to do the crossword, so actually what would he know?).

'I'm telling you, they're capers.'

Granddad lifts his fork and we watch, wordlessly, as a bunch of spiked maggots disappear into his mouth.

'What?' he asks at last, genuinely confused by our open-mouthedness.

A thin rope of gravy dribbles down his chin.

'Well, don't just sit there. Your dinner's waiting to be eaten.'

Kelly gets up from the table, her eyes on the door.

'Oh no, no…'

'Kelly, are you alright?'

'No, no, no…'

'Come back, you stupid girl!'

Then Kelly starts making this high wailing noise and runs into the hall, before darting up the stairs without looking back.

'Get back here, you silly child. There's Arctic roll for afters—'

Daniel spikes a maggot and lifts it to his mouth.

'Or you can have a fruit salad.'

I reach out, take hold of Daniel's wrist and the maggot wriggles off the fork before splashing back into the gravy.

'Oh, for Christ's sake.'

Granddad slaps down his knife and fork, marches round the table and picks up our plates, spilling gravy and maggots everywhere.

'You kids drive me crazy sometimes, I swear to God.'

Upstairs Kelly runs howling up and down the landing, apparently unable to take a breath.

'Bloody maggots, my arse. You kids are just ignorant of good Gallic cooking, that's all.'

Beside me, Daniel looks crestfallen as Granddad stomps off into the hall.

'And you can cut out that racket as well!'

I turn to Daniel and rustle his hair because he looks so hungry and doleful.

'Cheese on toast tonight, I think, matey, and that's if we're lucky.'

For a second Daniel looks like he's going to say something.

'Yes, that's it...'

I take hold of his hand.

'Go on, you can do it...'

But then all he does is look down at the table and starts pushing spilled gravy about with his finger on the tablecloth.

16

'Mum, wake up.'

The next morning the maggots are history and I am in Mum's bedroom not making a nuisance of myself (regardless of what Kelly might have to say on the matter).

'Mmmmmmmm… leave me alone.'

Lying on her side, with only her head visible over the top of the blankets, and with a bedspread clutched up tightly around her neck, Mum seems to be almost on the verge of snoring (even though it is mid-morning).

I shake her shoulder extra hard to help her wake up.

'Mum, can we go next door to play?'

'Ne, nah, nahh, gahhh…'

'Noah, you had better not be disturbing your mother,' Granddad shouts up the stairs. 'She needs to be back in the workshop in a couple of hours, no matter how much sleep she has had.'

That mysterious workshop.

We didn't know what they made there (apart from that it had something to do with central heating) or how Mum was suddenly an employee of the workshop (almost as if her new job had been arranged even before we had left Dad) or why she was working such strange hours, but lately, it was all we heard about.

'I'm not disturbing anyone!'

'Yes, you are. I can hear you.'

'No, I'm not.'

I turn and make for the door and, as I do, Mum starts snoring properly.

'I'm just looking for something.'

'My flaming arse you are.'

I run down the stairs.

'Anyway, Mum's fast asleep. In fact, I think you might find that she may even be dead.'

At the bottom of the stairs, Granddad eyes me suspiciously.

'And where do you think you're going?'

'To see Asghar and Munira.'

'Well, don't go eating any of their food. It'll only put you on the pot.'

'You shouldn't speak about them like that. They're not aliens, you know.'

I bounce into the kitchen.

'In fact, I think you'll find that they're Asians.'

Granddad heads for the stairs.

'Bloody Pakis is what they are, and they're taking all our bloody jobs.'

Out in the back yard, Kelly is waiting for me, holding Daniel's hand as he chews on a dandelion.

'She said yes,' I sing-song as casually as possible.

'You liar,' Kelly snorts, not even bothering to consider the evidence in support of my potentially spurious claim. 'I bet you didn't even get to speak to her.'

'Yes, I did, and she said it was OK, just so long as we are back in time for The News.'

Long seeds with fluffy white heads begin to drift from Daniel's mouth.

'Alright, you lot!'

Leaning over the wall dividing our back garden from next door, the dreaded Munira, thin, Asian and of Kelly's age, grins down at us, her long black hair rising and falling on the morning breeze.

'Well, are you coming or not? We're just about to make chapatis.'

Asghar pops up next to his sister. 'Did your mum say it's alright?'

'She's still asleep,' Kelly says flatly, 'and she should not be disturbed under any circumstances, real or otherwise, when she is so sleeping.'

A slightly hysterical woman starts shouting from the other side of the wall.

'It's alright, my mum's in,' Munira squeals for some reason, nodding over her shoulder, 'and you're all welcome to come and help in the kitchen.'

She drops out of sight and then smacks down hard onto the concrete on the other side of the wall.

'See you in a minute then,' Asghar yells, before also disappearing off the wall. 'And don't worry because Mum's really good with little kids.'

Daniel starts pulling himself up the wall by a stray washing line that's snapped in the middle.

'Daniel, wait here, please,' Kelly sighs, before looking at me and shrugging.

I shrug back.

'Come on then,' Kelly says, half-bored and half-intrigued all at the same time. 'Because I suppose we don't have a choice, do we, strictly speaking?'

She takes hold of Daniel by the neck of his T-shirt and pulls him down the garden to where the fence has a hole in it.

'Though we won't have to eat any of their food, will we?' I ask, not knowing if I'm asking the question or thinking it out loud.

Or possibly both.

'No,' Kelly says, shoving Daniel through the hole. 'Besides, I've already told Mrs Bukhari you don't like anything spicy. You won't even have mustard on your beef burgers, you won't.'

'That's not true.'

'Yes, it is.'

I follow Kelly and swing a leg over the fence because the hole in the fence isn't big enough for me to squeeze through.

'I put mustard on hot dogs. And tomato sauce.'

On the other side of the fence, Kelly couldn't be less impressed if she tried with my culinary assertion.

'Well, that's hardly exotic, is it?'

Then she frowns in a slightly concerned matter (though that could be because the sun is in her eyes).

'And it's not exactly what they're used to either.'

'Granddad calls them Pakis,' I say, lowering my voice in case anyone might hear.

'That's due to him being ignorant of foreign customs,' Kelly says sharply, one careful eye on the fence. 'And fearful of strangers. It's because he's old, in my opinion.'

Which is sort of true. When he got flu last year and slipped in the kitchen because the lino was loose, Mrs Bukhari brought him minestrone soup and did the washing-up and Granddad still complained about the strange interlopers next door and the care and consideration they insisted on bringing him.

'I'm sure she's been thieving from me,' he complained when he was back on his feet and able to search for all the things that Mrs Bukhari was supposed to have stolen while she had been in the house. 'And I'm not talking just about my money, either.'

'You don't know what you're talking about,' Mum scolded him, as he poked behind picture frames and under cushions. 'Mrs Bukhari wouldn't steal from you. In fact, she wouldn't steal from anyone. It's against her culture, probably.'

Granddad rolled his eyes on hearing this and reached down the back of the sofa, his tongue jammed between his teeth. 'You'll learn,' he admonished Mum, before coming up with a lost fifty-pence piece. 'Just because they smile to your face doesn't mean they're not stabbing you in the back.'

He flips the coin to where I am hiding and spying behind the partially closed door.

'Here boy, go buy yourself a Coke,' he says, winking at me.

Which I did.

Kelly, on the other hand, could not have been more excited by the shouting and door-slamming from next door, or the young girl that always seemed to be at the centre of all the neighbourly commotion and who would quickly become her new best friend, despite what Granddad might have had to say on the matter.

'And don't embarrass me in front of Munira,' Kelly warns me when we reach the Bukharis' back door. 'And whatever you do, do not, under any circumstances, be sick on the floor.'

The door opens and Munira sticks her head out.

'The whole family is here,' she whispers, rolling her eyes, 'and they all want to meet you, so you'd better come in right now.'

She opens the door and a roomful of grinning, sari-wrapped women beckons us in.

'Crikey.'

I gulp and push Daniel in first.

'Yes, yes, welcome, welcome—'

Mrs Bukhari grins and scoops a wooden spoon from a huge pot on the cooker as we are suddenly surrounded by the women.

'Come, come—'

She pushes the spoon at Kelly, who blushes and then tries to smile before carefully sucking the smallest amount of soft brown lentils as possible from the spoon that hovers in front of her mouth.

'Is it nice?' I ask, as Kelly opens her mouth, goes, 'Ohhhh,' and waves her hand in front of her face. 'Oh, blimey O'Reilly.'

'Well, is it?'

At the back of the kitchen, Munira sighs and then hops onto the top of a dented chest freezer. 'I can get you some water if you like,' she says, swinging her legs over the side. 'Or some cold Fresca.'

But then Kelly's face brightens. 'It tastes of coconut and raisins,' she says approvingly, wiping at the corners of her mouth, 'and it's not bad, either.'

She turns and smiles at Mrs Bukhari.

'Can I have some more, please?'

Then, before Mrs Bukhari can answer, Kelly snatches the spoon from her hand and shoves it back into the curry.

'You don't mind, do you?'

She scoops up more lentils from the steaming pot, quickly blows on them and then steers the spoon in Daniel's direction.

'Here, taste this.'

She shoves the spoon into Daniel's automatically opening mouth.

'Try some, but remember to breathe through your mouth.'

Daniel splutters, chews a bit and then opens his mouth again for more, as applause ripples around the room.

'There, he likes it!'

Munira stands up on the freezer to get a better look.

'Do you want some?' Kelly asks, nodding enthusiastically in my direction.

'I don't know,' I bluster, not at all keen to try the strange lentil mixture. 'In fact, I'm not sure I'm really that hungry.'

Suddenly everyone is staring right at me.

'I mean, I don't usually like spicy food.'

Munira starts flapping her arms about like a chicken.

'Because it just makes me feel a bit sick, to be honest.'

'Cluck, cluck, cluck—'

'And I do have an unusually delicate stomach.'

Asghar totters into the kitchen, arms outstretched and bouncing a football on his right knee.

'Go on, try some,' Kelly pleads, jabbing the spoon at my face. 'After all, it's curry, not maggots.'

'No, I'm alright,' I say, as casually as possible. 'I might try it later, though,' which isn't strictly true because it's supposed to be fish and chips tonight and I am saving myself.

'You big baby,' Kelly snorts dismissively.

'You're the baby!'

'No, I'm not, you are!'

Asghar kicks the football towards the open back door.

'Goal!'

Except he kicks the ball too wide, so instead of disappearing out the door and over the wall into Granddad's back yard (probably), it ricochets off the doorframe and bounces back into the kitchen.

'Here, try it, man,' Asghar says, snatching the spoon out my sister's hand. 'You're just being a big bloody idiot, you are.'

Kelly looks around for another spoon. 'Amen to that,' she mutters, just loud enough for everyone to hear. 'A big, fat baby, in fact.'

Asghar scoops up a spoonful of curry from the saucepan and lifts it towards my mouth. 'Go on, give it a go,' he says, grinning at me. 'You've nothing to lose.'

'Really?'

'Yes.'

And without taking my eyes from his I open my mouth and the spoon slips onto my tongue.

'See. Not so bad, is it?'

I swallow hard and Asghar grins at me, even wider than before.

'You're totally right,' I say, keeping my mouth open because the curry is so hot. 'It really is lovely.'

'Told you, didn't I?'

Asghar hands the spoon back to Kelly.

'He just needed to taste it, that's all,' he says, before dribbling his ball back towards the door.

'Result!'

I stare at his arse and inside my head, this voice is going, 'Do not look at his arse, absolutely do not look at his arse,' as Asghar's football goes SMACK, SMACK, SMACK, against the kitchen wall.

'Asghar,' Mrs Bukhari snaps. 'No, no, no!'

And then he turns, looks over his shoulder and winks at me.

'Do you want to come, Noah?'

Asghar's head is all hazy and framed by the sunshine outside the kitchen door.

'Do I?'

'Well, do you?' Kelly asks, a hint of malice in her voice.

I hand the spoon to her.

'Yes, please.'

And I follow Asghar out onto the hot garden concrete of the Bukharis' back yard (that used to be grass before Asghar's mother got the builders in) and we kick his football about until it goes over the fence at the bottom of the garden and gets squashed by a bus.

17

'Oh boy, it's hot.'

The next day me, Daniel and Asghar are lying on the burning concrete in the Bukharis' back yard and we are all blinking up at the sun.

'They said on The News that it's only going to get hotter and hotter, and I think they're right.'

Asghar tries his best not to sneeze and wiggles his nose.

'Hay fever,' he says eventually. 'I always get like this in the summer.'

'I know what you mean,' I reply, not understanding what he's going on about but fascinated by the up and down movement of his nose anyway. 'It's to do with the pollen and the bees and the wind, I reckon.'

Daniel giggles and points at a cloud.

'What is it, Daniel?'

I sit up and wipe sweat off my arm.

'Yes?'

Daniel smiles, opens his mouth and takes a quick breath.

'Go on...'

But then Munira appears in the kitchen doorway.

'Here it is!'

Asghar sits up, immediately bored.

'What's she going on about?'

'I don't know, but she seems to be quite excited about something.'

Munira totters across the concrete in a pair of her mother's wedges, holding up a large cardboard box as she bears down on us.

'I've found it, I've found it!' she babbles, slipping as she wobbles on the concrete. 'I didn't think I would, but I did!'

Kelly emerges from the kitchen, swinging her hair and trying to look cool, but I can tell that she's excited.

'Yeah,' she says, for some reason.

I try not to look at Asghar and move my shorts down as casually as I can.

'I told you they hadn't got rid of it!' Munira squeals.

She clatters to a halt in front of where we're sitting, tips the box upside down and a shower of what looks suspiciously like make-up spills out and onto the concrete.

'Ooh,' Kelly murmurs, looking over Munira's shoulder. 'L'Oreal, very nice.' Then she kneels down and yelps, 'Ouch!' because the concrete is so hot.

I catch Asghar's eye.

'Girls,' he snorts, smiling slyly at me across the dishevelled eyeshadows.

'There's always stuff they can't sell in the Cash & Carry because it gets damaged before they can put it on the shelves,' Munira babbles, before excitedly retrieving a tube of mascara from the cosmetics pile. 'Usually, they throw it away, but not anymore!'

She immediately starts applying the mascara to Kelly, who kneels and leans forward, blank-eyed and blinking. 'This is called Tantalising Night,' Munira whispers, as the mascara brush sweeps over Kelly's eyelashes, 'and it is very, very ladylike.'

Asghar touches the bottom of his big-boy moustache with the tip of his tongue.

'Oh yes,' Kelly moans as the oppressive eyelash-blackening continues. 'I can feel it, and it does indeed feel truly feminine.'

I swallow hard and try to look away from Asghar but can't.

'Daniel,' I say, gesturing for him to come sit next to me. 'Why don't you come over here?'

But he just ignores me and rolls over into the make-up, waving his arms about.

'This is very smouldering and has the ability to make you look like a true seductress,' Munira coos. 'Because that is what you are deep down – a smouldering and evocative woman of the seventies.'

Asghar sniggers and shakes his head. 'Bloody stupid is what you are.'

Munira narrows her eyes and swivels in his direction. 'And what would you know?' she demands, eyes blazing. 'All you're interested in is stupid bloody football and wanking.'

She jabs Kelly with the tip of the mascara brush.

'Munira!'

'Your bedroom smells like a swimming pool half the time.'

I cover the front of my shorts with my hand.

'Bloody stupid, mate,' Asghar sniggers, before lying back on the hot concrete and giggling up at the sky. 'Girls are just stupid and boring.'

I cannot stop looking at him and I don't want to either.

'Yeah, I know, mate,' I say as Munira returns to painting my sister's eyelashes and I can see Asghar's stomach from where his T-shirt is riding up.

'And now the right one...'

Asghar has hairy forearms, which he strokes with the top of his fingers when he thinks no one is looking, and right now he is so close that I can smell the washing powder on his clothes (which is Daz).

'No man will find you irresistible wearing these summer shades.'

My heart goes BUMP, BUMP, BUMP like it wants to jump right out of my chest, and it gets louder and louder with each beat as Asghar's foot starts rubbing lazily left and right against my knee. He doesn't even know what he's doing (though I certainly do) because he's still giggling at the clouds and not paying any attention to me at all.

'Now let me do you,' Kelly says to Munira.

'Yes...'

And my cock gets warmer and warmer in my shorts.

'Oh, Munira...'

So I swallow and look away but then turn back again because I just can't stop and it feels so good.

'Do it, do it…'

All I want to do is stare at Asghar.

'I can feel it and it is so beautiful…'

Kelly takes Munira's mascara brush and re-twirls it as Munira, shoulders twitching, gets ready for the application of the mascara on her eyelashes.

'I'm going to make you look really rather lovely,' Kelly moans. 'Just like a princess.'

'Yes,' Munira pouts, her lips wet, her mouth open. 'Do so, please.' Then she closes her eyes and Kelly touches her face before retracing the mascara over her eyelashes. 'It just feels so nice and sensual…'

'Doesn't it…'

Munira opens her eyes.

'Really, really lovely, in fact.'

Kelly holds up a small mirror.

'Oh…'

And Munira blinks and turns her head, taking in the smudged reflection in front of her. 'Cool,' she moans, almost to herself, 'so graceful and womanly.'

'You look a bit like an Asian Suzi Quatro,' I say without thinking, and it is only once the words have left my mouth that I realise they are true because, what with her hair and the way she is pushing her lips forward, Munira does right now.

'That's right,' Kelly sighs without taking her eyes from Munira, 'but without all the leather.'

'Now let's do you again,' Munira announces suddenly, turning the mirror on my sister, who blinks and twitches as one of her eyes jams shut.

'Oh, Munira…'

Munira reaches for her face.

'Don't move, do not move,' she says, placing a thumb on Kelly's eyelid. 'Not one little inch, or it could be fatal.'

She begins to pull Kelly's eyelashes apart.

'Now, take a deep breath…'

Kelly's eyelashes snap open.

'There you are. They're now back in the right working order,' Munira reassures her, wiping her hand on the front of her jeans.

'And close…'

Kelly closes her eyes.

'And open…'

Kelly opens her eyes.

And this time Kelly's eyelashes mesh and unmesh without any further difficulty.

'You need to let them dry first,' Munira says, using a tone just like the one they use in big department stores when the assistants stand in your way and talk to your mum when all you want to do is go to the café.

'That way you will have dramatic and provocative lashes without any unnecessary gluing.'

Asghar sniggers under his breath, props himself up on his elbows, and I shake my head in a manner designed to reassure him that I am very firmly on his side.

'What a load of rubbish.'

After all, we are immune to this kind of silliness is what our laconic slouching is communicating and, by the way that Asghar is leaning back, I can tell that he's getting the message that I am subtly sending him.

'I don't know why you bother, mate.' He chuckles, though I think he's talking more to Munira than to me. 'You look exactly the same to me, only with make-up on.'

'Yeah, mate,' I say, suddenly revelling in the liberating use of the word "mate". 'It's not like you need it or anything.'

Kelly looks at me like I've just been sick and then Munira leans over and shoves Asghar, who falls back laughing and curling his legs up to his chest.

'You bloody idiot.'

Without thinking I look up at Asghar's bedroom.

'Because that's all you are…'

If I can only get him up to his bedroom, my brain is going, then I can lie down next to him (because we are both so tired, what with all the sunshine and the cosmetics and everything) and perhaps even touch his moustache and fall asleep on his shoulder.

'You're just being stupid, Munira. You don't need mascara and face-painting and all this make-up.'

And my cock is starting to hurt a bit because it's trapped by the elastic of my pants, so I laugh, quickly pull at my shorts and turn back to Asghar. 'I could do with a bit of a lie-down,' I say, as casually as possible. 'I think I might even have a bit of sunstroke…'

Kelly looks at me funny.

'Or something.'

For a second Asghar looks like he's going to get up (and maybe offer me his hand, so I can fall against him as I stand and then have to hold on to him to steady myself because one of my legs might have gone to sleep due to all the sitting down), but before he can, Daniel unscrews a lipstick and starts drawing on the concrete.

'Oh no, my dad's going to kill me!' Munira squeals as Daniel traces a big pink line around a ladybird.

'Daniel, you little monster!'

Kelly snatches the lipstick from his hand and snaps its lid back on in one quick motion.

'I've told you before about playing with other people's things when you know you're not allowed.'

She takes one of his hands and gives it a little slap.

'It's not like you haven't been warned or anything.'

Daniel immediately starts to whine, like a miniature air-raid siren, as he always does just before the real tears start to fall.

'Because I did, I warned him,' Kelly proclaims, a little nervously. 'I've told him plenty of times.'

The whining gets wetter and louder.

'Shut up,' Kelly hisses, nervously eyeing the wall dividing us from next door. 'Please, Daniel, stop it.'

Mrs Bukhari appears at her lounge window, peering around the curtains.

'No, no, he's fine,' I say, raising my voice and stifling my erection. 'He just needs some paper to draw on, that's all.'

I nod encouragingly in Daniel's direction, but he just ignores me and keeps on howling.

'He needs to learn to respect other people's property,' Kelly says, using her best For Public Consumption voice, 'because sometimes he can be so very unnecessarily anarchic.'

She pulls Daniel to his feet as Mrs Bukhari comes running out of the house, arms outstretched, ready to take Daniel away.

'Are we going upstairs now?' I ask Asghar, my thoughts falling out my mouth before I can organise them properly. 'Perhaps to have that lie-down or something?'

Munira grabs Kelly's arm.

'Let's go listen to some music away from this lot,' she says, nodding dismissively in the direction of me and Asghar.

'Yeah, you boys are just losers,' Kelly sneers, before following Munira, her mother and a now-giggling Daniel back into the house.

'I'd better go as well, mate,' Asghar says, standing up and dusting down his T-shirt. 'I've got some maths homework to do and it's bloody hard.'

Do not look at his cock.

Absolutely do not look at his cock.

'OK,' I say, standing up and putting my hand in my pocket.

'Cool, mate.'

'Catch you later then,' Asghar says, slouching off towards the house. 'Or maybe tomorrow.'

Suddenly Mum appears over the top of the garden wall.

'Can you kids please keep the noise down?' she pleads, bobbing up and down (probably because she is standing on tiptoe on the other side). 'I've got to be back at the workshop in precisely one hour and thirty-five minutes and it is simply impossible to sleep with all this racket going on.'

'I'm sorry,' I say quickly, taking my hand out of my pocket.

'And so you should be, what with your brother crying – and is he alright, by the way?'

'Yes,' I say as reassuringly as possible under the circumstances.

'And with you lot chattering on about "mate" and "football" and God knows what else, it's near impossible to establish a sensible shift routine round here.'

'Sorry,' I say again, trying to sound like I mean it this time.

'Alright then. And now I'm going for a bath. If your grandfather has remembered to put the hot water on, that is.'

And then she disappears as quickly as she first appeared and I look up at Asghar's bedroom, where he is jumping up and down on his bed and grinning down at me.

'Asghar!'

18

'Follow me, Munira.'

Outside my open bedroom doorway, Kelly has her arms outstretched and is balancing an *Encyclopaedia Britannica* on her head.

'Make sure you do everything I do without any hesitation or distraction—'

And she is being especially annoying.

'Keep your head up at all times, just like Miss World. And now walk—'

Munira follows my sister in her hesitant footsteps across the landing, Granddad's telephone directory (*London South East Edition*) wobbling on her head as she goes.

'Imagine the audience clapping because they really do love you, Munira, and not just the men, and turn, and bend...'

The floorboards creak and groan under Kelly and Munira's laboured attempts at being ladylike.

'Place your hands on your hips and smile for the judges before turning back again—'

'Oh, for God's sake!'

I have been trying all morning to put some Scalextric together with Daniel and frankly could do without all this girlish distraction from our complicated track-laying.

'Kelly, would you please give it a rest?'

Daniel licks the bottom of a police car.

'Feel like a lady, Munira, act like a lady, be a lady—'

'Kelly, shut up!'

'No, I will not shut up!'

The *Encyclopaedia Britannica* hits the carpet.

Smack!

Followed almost immediately by the telephone directory.

Bang!

'And anyway, you're just being bloody jealous!'

Followed by clumping across the landing, quicker than before, as Kelly marches determinedly towards the banister.

'Just because I've got interesting and intellectually stimulating things to do and you haven't.'

Behind her, Munira sniggers and then follows as the two of them escape downstairs.

'You loser!'

I angrily snap two pieces of track together.

'Oh, piss off, the pair of you.'

Downstairs the front door opens, someone blows a raspberry (which could only be Kelly) and the door slams shut.

'She's a complete bitch, isn't she?' I say, drawing Daniel into my secret boy-conspiracy. 'Her and her stupid bloody friend.'

Daniel sticks a finger up his nose.

'Useless, bloody females of the species.'

I take the now-wet police car from his hand.

'Do you want to play *Space: 1999*?'

Daniel sneezes.

'OK then, let's go.'

I pull my brother to his feet before poking my head around the bedroom door.

'All clear. The building is now girl-free, apparently.'

On the landing all is quiet, so I nip across to the banister to confirm that Kelly and Munira have indeed left the building (and are not lying in wait for me, which they have done before) and I usher Daniel downstairs.

'Follow me,' I whisper, leading my brother quickly out through the kitchen, into the back garden and towards Granddad's shed, 'as I introduce you to the future of interplanetary space travel!'

After quickly checking that Granddad is nowhere to be seen, I throw open the door of the shed, take a last look back at the house (to make sure that the coast is clear) and then shove Daniel inside.

'Don't touch anything, or at least not until I tell you to,' I whisper, carefully closing the door behind us. 'That's right, wait for your orders.'

Daniel looks momentarily confused, so I steer him over to the side of a workbench, which is covered with a collection of old light switches, car parts and discarded pipes that I had rescued from the loft when everyone was at Tesco.

'What you see before you...'

I flick a switch and the control panel crackles into life.

'Is the Command Centre of Moonbase Alpha!'

A light bulb pops.

'Pretty cool, don't you think?'

Daniel leans over, prods at a fuse box (or a computer memory bank, to be more precise), yawns and rubs his face.

'You can be the co-pilot if you like,' I say, nodding and lifting Daniel onto an old dining chair.

'And what do you think of that?'

Before he can answer I quickly secure my brother into the chair with an old seatbelt and then hop onto a bar stool that Granddad had brought back from the tip.

'Let the deep-space adventure begin!'

We lean over the console.

'Commander Koenig to Moonbase Alpha. Do you read me, over?'

Daniel giggles, claps his hands together and wiggles excitedly in his seat.

'Helena, this is an emergency. Put the Medical Centre on standby...'

A meteor hurtles over our heads.

'Twenty parsecs to landing...'

I point in the direction of the window.

'Blackhole at twelve o'clock.'

Daniel starts bouncing up and down.

'Commander Koenig, aliens on the launch pad,' I shout over the mounting turbulence. 'Can you hear me, Koenig?'

'*Brrrrrrrrrrrrrrbooooooooom!*'

I take hold of Daniel's hand.

'Pull up, pull up—'

Daniel throws his head back, laughing.

'*Keeeaaaaaahhhhhhhhhooooooooo!*'

'I don't think I can hold it, Alpha. We're losing control…'

I shake the back of Daniel's chair and his head jiggles about.

'Too fast, Koenig. You're breaking up…'

Then I reach down and flick the switch on an old Hoover connected by an extension lead to a socket in the kitchen.

'Helena, we have serious radiation burns, Helena—'

Warm air blasts at our ankles.

'Alpha, we're breaking up, we're—'

'What the bloody hell are you doing?'

Granddad stands in the doorway, hands on hips and with a tea towel over his shoulder.

'Because, unless you have a good excuse, you are in big trouble, young man!'

He looks down at the extension lead and then turns to follow its taunt journey back into the house.

'So that's why the meter's been going round like topsy.'

I swallow hard and try to control my breathing.

'And why is he tied to the chair?'

Using my foot I turn off the Hoover, which whines and sighs before going back to sleep, and carefully unclick my brother's seatbelt.

'You're going to burn out the motor if you bugger around with it like that,' Granddad complains, as Daniel slides off the chair and slips past Granddad into the back yard.

'I'm sorry.' I rub my foot along the still-hot Hoover. 'I would never want to damage your vacuum cleaner.'

Granddad shakes his head and whips the tea towel off his shoulder as Kelly appears at his elbow.

'And just look at the mess you've made.'

Kelly shrugs her shoulders up and down.

'Not *Space: 1999* again. Boring.'

Then she turns and tramples away after Daniel.

'It's egg salad for your tea tonight,' Granddad grunts, before turning to leave. 'Freshly made and special, with a vinaigrette dressing.'

He stops and points a threatening finger in my direction.

'And I want all that rubbish put back where you found it before you sit down to eat.'

'Yes, Granddad.'

'Bloody *Space: 1999*. You need to be playing outside in the fresh air.'

'But it's too hot!'

I kick at the Hoover (accidentally).

'I went red all over my back yesterday and I felt sick afterwards.'

Granddad rolls his eyes.

'Don't you worry about that,' he says unreassuringly, 'because once your top layer peels off you'll be as good as gold and, besides, it's not that hot, it's merely warm and possibly a little close.'

'There's nothing to do outside,' I complain, rubbing at my neck, 'and the roads are melting. It said so on TV last night.'

Which is true, sort of; there was a story about the paint melting on a slip road in Ipswich on the *News at Ten*.

'No, they're not. It's just a sunny break from the norm and nothing to be concerned about. That bloody Reginald Bosanquet doesn't know what he's talking about half the time, even when he is half-sober holding court between the ruddy commercials.'

'But I had to sleep with the window open again last night.'

'Well, just so long as you keep a cricket bat next to your bed like I told you to so that if you hear anyone moving about you can hit them over the head with it as hard as you can, then everything will be fine.'

My stomach starts to hurt.

'Now, do you want that egg salad or not?'

'No, I don't.'

Not that I'm that worried about the heatwave (not really).

'I don't even like egg salad.'

Because, after only a couple of weeks of cloudless skies and newspaper headlines ending in big exclamation marks, I was even starting to enjoy what was fast becoming "A RIGHT REAL SCORCHER!" regardless of what they were saying on The News.

'Are you sure? Because I can put some pieces of ham in it if you like.'

'Alright then,' I say quietly, starting to feel hungry all of a sudden. 'But only if we can have salad cream as well.'

19

The next day after work, and because the sun is shining, Mum joins me in the garden to listen to the radio (which is turned up too loud in the kitchen).

Mum is sunbathing.

But I am dreaming of Asghar.

'Let this sultry weather continue forever,' Mum sighs, slipping her sunglasses on and offering herself up to the cloudless sky. 'It would certainly make everyone stop worrying and start enjoying themselves for once.'

'Can I try on your sunglasses, please?'

I am on my stomach with my arms by my side, staring up at Asghar's bedroom window.

'No, you cannot. You'll only bend the frames.'

'No, I won't.'

'Yes, you will.'

Granddad marches up the garden path towards us, a knotted handkerchief on his head.

'Here it comes,' Mum mutters without turning her head. '*Dad's* bloody *Army* without the jokes.' She pulls at her bikini bottom. 'And it wouldn't hurt your grandfather to be a little bit sunnier in his outlook.'

I had never seen Mum in a bikini before.

Usually, she wore a black swimming costume and lots of Ambre Solaire if the sun came out, but her new bikini was bright green and tied with thin straps at the back.

'Look at you,' Granddad says pointedly, as he starts wiping down a sun lounger. 'Parading yourself like that in the middle of the lawn, and it's hardly as if you're a Hollywood starlet or anything.'

'Thanks for that,' Mum sighs, getting up and wiping grass from her back. 'This is, I would like to point out, my free time, the sun is still shining and what do I have to put up with – the moral bloody custodian of Mineral Street!'

She takes off her sunglasses and hands them to me before flip-flopping away up the path.

'And I'm still only thirty-four, you know!'

'Just about,' Granddad grunts, as the offensive green bikini disappears from view. 'And with three innocent children to bring up as well.'

I giggle and turn over in the grass.

'And don't you stay out too long either,' Granddad warns me as he folds up the sun lounger. 'It'll only put you off your dinner – which tonight is homemade pizza.'

I turn back in the direction of Asghar's bedroom and slowly rub my cock into the grass.

'Just another couple of minutes and then I'll come in.'

Sweat runs down my forehead.

'Where the bloody hell are you, Asghar?'

Mum pokes her head out the open back door.

'Actually, I will have those sunglasses back, please. I'm going to the shops.'

I stop rubbing.

'And they had better not be smudgy.'

*

'There's going to be water rationing!'

With no warning whatsoever Kelly takes a deep breath and launches into her full-on opinion mode as we finish our homemade pizza (which is really just cheese on toast sprinkled with chopped cucumber and tomatoes, but we don't say anything).

119

'And we're going to have to use jerrycans and communal showers and there's going to be "share a bath days", whatever they are.'

When Kelly is in this sort of mood there is not much point in talking back or contradicting her.

'It said so in *The Guardian*.'

'Huh, that ruddy *Guardian*,' Granddad grunts, as he clears away the last of the plates from the table. 'Bloody stuff and left-wing nonsense, that is.'

He takes a cold boiled egg from his shirt pocket and taps it on the tabletop.

'And it's dangerous, probably – not that your mother would notice.'

It was because Mum had started reading *The Guardian* that Granddad had got so worried.

'As well as being bloody expensive with it.'

Mum said she liked reading the controversial newspaper "for the woman's page", though none of us knew what she meant by that, to be honest, and we were all a bit intimidated from probing any further in case she suddenly went all feminist on us and started making speeches over the washing-up.

'We need to be careful,' Granddad continues, as Kelly rolls her eyes as theatrically as possible. 'This could turn into a sit-in or a walk-out, like the one they had at Ford. So best pretend nothing is happening and it'll all just go away of its own accord.'

'But nothing is happening,' Kelly sighs, folding a slice of bread, ready to pop it into her mouth. 'She's just reading a newspaper, that's all.'

Granddad tussles her hair and wipes his hand on the front of his trousers.

'That's right, that's all she's doing. And we're going to keep it that way, aren't we?'

Nobody says anything.

'Can we go up the Common and read books with Munira, please?' Kelly asks after a while.

'Yes, but make sure you stay away from any Jackie Collins or the buses, because you know I don't trust the drivers.'

Kelly frowns as Granddad crushes a hollowed-out egg in the palm of his hand. 'I can kill with these hands,' he says, shaking eggshell from his fingers. 'Or deliver babies, whichever is required.'

20

Up on the Common, the crickets are chirruping with lazy abandon as we find a place to sit and read.

'Granddad's going mad, you know,' Kelly announces casually over the top of her *Cider with Rosie*. 'Munira says it's because he's getting demented and it's only going to get worse as he gets older.'

On a park bench by the bus stand, a bare-chested skinhead in England football shorts and dusty work boots strokes the face of a girl with long, blonde hair who's wearing a red boob tube and white culottes.

'Why do they do that?' I ask, not particularly interested in Granddad's (supposed) dementedness one way or another.

Kelly looks up and eyes the couple on the bench with icy disdain.

'It's like a disease,' she says carefully. 'Once they get the virus inside them they're done for and it's all sex and snogging, your brains go flying out the window and you never come down for tea. Just look at what happened to Cheryl Travers.'

Cheryl Travers, who lived on the other side of Mineral Street, had taken up with Gavin Henderson from the church bike club and now they never left Cheryl's bedroom, no matter how hot or sunny it was outside.

'She's turned into a zombie and it's all his fault,' Kelly sighs. 'She'll be pregnant and living in a bed-sit before she's eighteen, just you wait and see.'

Getting pregnant and living in a bed-sit was the worst thing in the world (if you were a girl) and, despite the apparent escape route it appeared to offer from exams and over-emotional door-slamming, having a baby was no joke.

Even I knew that.

'It's a slippery and sticky slope, every inch touched with peril.'

The skinhead moves his thumb in a slow circular motion on the girl's chin.

'Anyway, Cheryl's only after one thing and it's not Gavin's Chopper.'

Then the girl smiles, opens her mouth, and the skinhead pops his thumb in.

'Cheryl told me Gavin pulls the curtains the minute he comes over and that he watches her in the mirror when she takes her bra off, even when he's supposed to be looking the other way.'

The skinhead slowly moves his thumb in and out of the girl's mouth.

'Well, I think it's disgusting,' I say, swallowing hard. 'She should be thinking about her exams and not about how long they can snog for every time her mum's at Sainsbury's.'

Kelly studies the blatant thumb-sucking going on by the bus stand.

'And I bet she's thinking about going on the pill,' she adds dismissively.

Munira appears in a cloud of dry earth, dripping lolly juice everywhere.

'They didn't have any Cornish, so I got you these,' she says, thrusting a couple of Zooms at us.

Kelly pushes her hair from her face and takes one of the lollies.

'Much appreciated, thanks.'

Juice runs down her hand, but she licks it off before it can reach her wrist.

'How much?'

I shift so I can get a better view of the skinhead, who is now smiling, as the blonde girl runs her hand up and down his thigh.

'Don't worry about it. The lollies are on me,' Munira says, licking hungrily at her 99.

'Great!' Kelly grins. 'Though I could pay if you wanted me to.'

Munira sits down right in front of me, so I have to lean to the right to see past her. 'Well, do you want it?' she asks, holding out the last of the Zooms before biting into a Flake. 'Because it's dripping into my palm.'

'I thought they didn't have any ice cream?' I ask as casually as I can under the circumstances.

'Cornish. I said they didn't have any Cornish.'

Munira waves her free hand in front of her mouth because her ice cream is so cold.

'Blimey, blimey, blimey.'

Vanilla drips onto her knee.

'Oh, it tastes like paint, this.'

Kelly licks her Zoom.

'What colour?'

'Magenta, no... oatmeal.'

'Oatmeal? What colour's that, then?'

'It's like porridge but not so salty.'

Munira waves the spare Zoom at me.

'Well, do you want it or not?'

The skinhead and the blonde girl suddenly stand up, then she turns away from him, shaking something from her hair – flying ants, I reckon – at which point the skinhead tugs at the front of his shorts.

'Yeah, thanks,' I say, taking the Zoom and shoving it into my mouth as quickly as possible before the top falls off.

'You're in a world of your own, you are,' Munira says.

The skinhead and the blonde girl bump their hips into each other and walk off in the direction of Ancona Road.

'Yeah, it's the sun – it makes me go, you know,' I say, gulping down the scrunchy frozen sugar as quickly as I can, 'a bit crazy.'

'Yeah. And we know what you're crazy about,' Kelly mutters under her breath, 'you dirty bloody bastard.'

Then she stands up and dusts off the grass from her legs.

'Come on, you sordid little lurker, let's go back and see if Cheryl is about.'

'I am not a lurker.'

'Yes, you are. You're all eyes and ears, you are.'

'Oh, get lost.'

But I get up anyway.

'You don't know what you're talking about,' I say, and we walk down Griffin Road doing the lean-back thing you have to do because the road is so long and steep, then have to speed up again just before we reach the turn for Conway Road.

'Dad says we're going to France this year,' Munira announces for no good reason as we get near the bottom of the road. 'He says he's renting a country chateau – which is a bit like a bungalow, but with its own swimming pool – and you ride everywhere on bicycles and go swimming in the afternoon because it's so hot, and there are mosquitoes everywhere.'

Pause.

'Where are you going for your holiday?' she asks lazily.

Kelly and I long knew this was coming and we had already worked out what we were going to say and how we were going to handle it if the dreaded "holiday" question came up.

'For our holiday, you mean?'

'Yes, for your holiday.'

Kelly said the important thing was to be super casual if it happened like it didn't matter and that everything was OK and who cares anyway?

'Oh, you know...'

We come closer to Granddad's house and for a second I think that we will be able to make it and that Munira will have to go in before we have to answer, but then I see a shiny brown Morris Marina parked outside.

Munira suddenly looks confused.

'I thought we were going to see Cheryl.'

'Change of plan,' Kelly says quickly. 'And now, if you'll excuse us, we do have to go in.'

But then the gate is suddenly further away than it should be and we can't walk fast enough because Munira has her bloody sandals on.

'You are going away, though, aren't you?' Munira asks, clip-clopping along as quickly as she can to try to keep up with Kelly, whose speed is now approaching that of a trot.

'I mean, you're not staying here all summer, are you?'

Kelly opens her mouth as if to say something, but before she can get any words out Mad Aunt Joan and Uncle Michael come striding out of the house wearing matching shorts, T-shirts and backpacks.

We all stop walking.

'Hiya,' Mad Aunt Joan coos, breezily waving at us as she reaches the gate. 'We've got a little surprise for you out back, though nothing to worry your little heads about.'

'Your grandfather's in the garden,' Uncle Michael says, opening the boot of the Marina, 'and he's got the big one up.'

He tilts and drops his backpack into the boot of the car as Mad Aunt Joan twists around so that he can then take hers.

'You alright there, Asian love?' Mad Aunt Joan asks, grinning and nodding at Munira.

Kelly takes a breath.

'I think we might be going camping,' she sighs finally, at last answering Munira's earlier question, 'and I doubt if we'll be going abroad or indeed outside of England come to that.'

For a moment Munira doesn't say a word.

'Oh… right.'

Then Uncle Michael slams the boot of the Marina shut, before chasing Mad Aunt Joan back up the garden path, his hands outstretched so he can tickle his wife around the waist.

'I've never been camping,' Munira says, as they disappear back into the house. 'Does it mean you have to wee in a bucket?'

'Yes,' Kelly answers grimly. 'Unfortunately, sometimes it does.'

Munira opens her front gate without looking at us.

'I've got to go in for my dinner now,' she says, before darting back into her house as quickly as possible. 'But I promise I'll send you a postcard from France.'

'Bugger,' Kelly sighs, as Munira's front door slams shut with an almighty bang. 'Bloody, bastard, bugger.'

21

'This has got nothing to do with me!'

In the back garden, Mum has her arms out, attempting to block our path as we come racing out of the kitchen.

'Honestly, it's completely out of my hands,' she says, wiggling her fingers about. 'I'm just being swept along despite my protestations because, as you know, I was only more than happy to return to Butlin's, even if it does bring back painful memories of arguments with your father.'

She takes a quick breath.

'But your grandfather was having none of it.'

Kelly tries to dart beneath one of Mum's surprisingly long arms but Mum is just too quick for her. 'Barry Island has always been one of my most favourite destinations,' she continues, 'be it Welsh or not.'

Kelly, however, has seen and heard enough.

'No! No! No! Not now, please, not with the new term coming up and what with the heatwave and everything!'

With a frown Mum steps aside to reveal Granddad, Uncle Michael and Mad Aunt Joan pulling and yanking at Big Blue as it wobbles about on the lawn.

'Ta-da!'

'But we can't, we just can't!' Kelly wails, running across the lawn and nearly colliding with a camping table before running back again.

'Please, not Big Blue! I'll do literally anything.'

Big Blue was the tent Granddad had bought off a French woman on the Walworth Road three years before. '*Très magnifique*, and it can sleep six!' he had announced proudly, the first time he put it up in the garden. 'It even has its own kitchen.'

Which it did, even if the kitchen in question was just a couple of old folding tables with a bowl for the washing-up. Inside, the tent smelt of melted plastic and paraffin, and when the wind blew, the poles bent in the middle.

'Oh God,' Kelly groans, leaning against Mum for support. 'This is even worse than I imagined and I have, I would like to point out, a very vivid imagination.'

Mum gives her a cuddle and then squeezes her shoulder.

'There, there, my darling. It's only a canvas erection. There's no need to be so aghast.'

Kelly shudders, shaking off Mum's comforting hand.

'It's a living, flapping nightmare, and there is no way I am staying in that,' she shrieks, pointing in the direction of the bright blue monstrosity in the middle of the lawn. 'I would rather sleep in the car.'

'Now, now,' Mum comforts her, as I try as hard as I can not to laugh, 'there is no need for all this high emotion. Besides, you won't have to sleep in the car.'

Kelly immediately relaxes. 'Because I won't be going?'

'No, my darling, because you'll be in the two-man with your brother here and there's plenty of room inside the two-man if you lay head to toe. So you don't need to worry on the comfort front.'

Granddad peers out of Big Blue looking sweaty and clutching a handful of tent pegs.

'Afternoon campers, all corners secure,' he huffs, wiping his brow, 'though do please ensure that the lines are appropriately tightened there, Joan.'

Mad Aunt Joan smacks at the grass with a mallet.

'Thank you, Patrick. I have been doing this for eighteen years now, I'll have you know, both here and on the continent.'

She thumps a fresh hole into the lawn.

'And in that time I have found that practice does indeed make perfect.'

'I'm just saying because otherwise it'll only be lopsided and catch the wind if not properly tethered,' Granddad says, before dropping his voice, 'and then you'll only complain when you can't get any sleep done.'

'This is the worst summer of my life,' Kelly complains, before reaching out and grabbing at Mum's blouse.

'Darling, please, my bra—'

'Mum, I'm begging you. Is there nothing you can do?'

'Kelly, the cups—'

'Nothing at all?'

'Now, this is what makes us the family that we are,' Granddad chuckles, marching up and tapping my sister on the head with the mallet, 'the doing and the sharing, the fun and the adventure.'

'Is it really?' Kelly sniffs. 'Is it, honestly?'

'Oh yes, there is quite simply nothing better than this sense of familial adventure. You'll learn that as you grow older and slip into stupefying maturity like the rest of us.'

He taps me on the head with the mallet, which only makes me laugh and doesn't hurt at all.

'The thrill of a roaring fire, the curious noises of the night, living without the modern accompaniments of life; these are some of the important skills for a man to learn and for women to learn as well – in case the men are incapacitated.'

Mum frowns. '"Incapacitated"?'

'Yes, by nuclear apocalypse or natural disaster – flooding.'

'And when was the last time you saw any flooding?' Mum asks dryly.

'1965.'

Kelly jabs me in the hip.

'That was the year you were born, wasn't it, idiot boy?'

She turns to Mum. 'Did you go camping that year, Mum?'

'No, love. Your father and I spent a charming weekend in West Berlin because of his extended posting on the Rhine. It was quintessentially Bond-like, I can assure you.'

'See, told you, German love-child-boy.'

'Anyway,' Granddad continues, waving his mallet about, 'this year's expedition is going to be the best yet, with three cars, the same number of families and six tents. It'll be like the war but without the urgent evacuations or bomb damage.'

He walks back to where Mad Aunt Joan and Uncle Michael are struggling to flatten a groundsheet. 'Trust me, children, because this particular adventure will be truly the best yet, and all taking place under a great big open-top sky. Who could honestly ask for more?'

Kelly slaps at her sides.

'Oh, God! You lot are absolutely bloody ridiculous, the whole ruddy lot of you!'

'Language, please, Kelly,' Mum sighs, not sounding that bothered.

Kelly looks up pleadingly into Mum's eyes. 'I mean, can't you see? It's just not right for a girl. Camping's more of a boy's activity, it's just so dirty, smelly and cold.'

'That it is, my darling,' Mum coos, stroking Kelly's hair.

Then she winks at me.

'But unfortunately, it's also something we have to grit our teeth over and deal with and that's just the way it is. You'll understand, one day.'

She steals a kiss from Kelly's cheek, before disappearing up the garden path back to the kitchen.

'I'll be doing the potatoes, if anybody needs me,' she sing-songs over her shoulder as she goes, 'and, they will be all roasters tonight, my darlings.'

Kelly crosses her arms.

'"Understand one day"? We'll see about that,' she mutters, 'because I am not doing anything I don't want to. It's my human right or rights, plural.'

'Oh yeah?'

I cross my arms as well.

'And what are you going to do about it?'

'You'll see,' Kelly purrs. 'And if you watch closely enough, you might even learn something, camping boy.'

'You're bluffing.'

'Oh, am I now?'

'Yes, you are.'

'Well, let's find out, shall we? Because you're going to be the only one sleeping under canvas this summer and I'm telling you that for nothing, camping boy.'

And with that, she flicks hair from her face as Uncle Michael trips over a tent peg.

22

The next morning we pack the camping gear into Uncle Michael's Marina and then wait patiently outside the house for Uncle Brian and Uncle Terry to arrive so that our camping adventure can begin.

'You do know the best way to reach the M2, and then how to navigate us en-route to Faversham, don't you, my love?' Uncle Michael asks Mad Aunt Joan as she leans on the bonnet of the car and has a crafty cigarette before we leave. 'After all, we don't want another Barcelona misadventure, do we now?'

Mad Aunt Joan gives her handbag a reassuring pat.

'Don't you worry, sweet husband of mine, because the map is right here, all present and correct and ready for inspection whenever we finally do get a chance to get a move on.'

'Which will hopefully be by the end of today,' Mum mutters, as she straightens Daniel's T-shirt. 'Or perhaps by the weekend, if we're lucky.'

From up at her bedroom window Munira looks forlornly down (though there has been no sign of Asghar all morning, I notice) and even gives Kelly a little wave, just as Uncle Terry's black Ford Granada comes roaring up the road, horn honking and lights flashing, followed immediately by Uncle Brian's bright blue Austin Maxi.

'Oh God,' Kelly sighs, as Uncle Michael gets into the Marina and Mad Aunt Joan tosses her cigarette down a drain. 'I'd do anything not to have to go, I really would.'

'You don't need to worry your pretty little head like that,' Granddad reassures her, putting his arm around her shoulder and giving her a big squeeze. 'Because this is going to be fun and not something to get all unnecessary about, just you wait and see.'

Kelly gives him one of her looks, but Granddad remains in high spirits regardless.

'Right then, happy campers. Are we all ready to depart?'

*

An hour later we are on the A2 heading for Dartford and Kelly is sulking even more than when we were still in Mineral Street.

'Hey, listen to this—'

I'm not sulking, though, unlike Kelly.

'Must we?'

I'm just excited.

'I mean, is it the law to do so or something?'

On the radio David Cassidy is singing something about love and Uncle Michael is doing his best to hum along whilst maintaining a steady fifty-five miles an hour, as he is wont to do whenever driving on a potentially dangerous motorway (or an A road, come to that).

'Yes, I'm afraid you must, Sulky Sarah.'

It is very, very hot.

'No, we don't, and that is not even my name, you idiot.'

All of the Marina's windows are open (if not all the way down, because of the noise and flies), whilst in the back of the car, jammed in next to me and Kelly, Mum is half-heartedly fanning a sleepy Daniel on her lap with a well-thumbed *Woman's Own*.

'He knows that's not your name, darling,' she says without sounding particularly concerned either way on the matter. 'He's simply being something akin to amusing.'

Me and Kelly wiggle about next to her trying not to sweat too much, despite Mum's languid magazine-waving.

'Speak up, Mr Noah,' Mad Aunt Joan shouts from the front passenger seat, 'and share your knowledge with all of us.'

133

Kelly makes an urgent sort of grunting sound as Mum chuckles at a giggling Daniel as he buries his face in her blouse.

'Must you?' Kelly snaps.

A Sherpa van shoots past, a roll of carpet flapping on its roof.

'Apparently, the campsite has got a games room with a ping-pong table, communal showers, freshly painted kitchens and a barbecue area with genuine log seating.'

Mad Aunt Joan turns down the radio and puts on a pair of sunglasses.

'Sounds lovely,' Kelly mutters through gritted teeth, 'really quite becoming.'

A red Beetle convertible full of whooping students draws up in the lane next to ours.

'Oh, that's nice,' Mum coos as the students wave at her. 'They seem to be happy young people, don't you think?'

In the Beetle, one of the girls suddenly lifts her T-shirt and jiggles her breasts at us.

'Good Lord!' Uncle Michael splutters, momentarily putting his foot down on the accelerator. 'I mean, honestly!'

The Beetle takes a turning for the M25 without indicating.

'Ignore them, Michael,' Mad Aunt Joan orders her husband, furiously winding up her window as the Beetle disappears from view. 'They are clearly under the influence of something that could very possibly be illegal.'

'I should say so,' Uncle Michael stammers, sucking furiously on his pipe. 'Quite disgusting and totally unnecessary, my dear.'

'Oh, please,' Kelly drawls, shaking her sweat-matted hair from her face. 'You would think no one had seen a pair of breasts before. They're perfectly natural, you know. Even I've got them.'

Mum frowns at her. 'Thank you for that, Kelly.'

'What? I'm just saying.'

She slumps back into her seat.

'I mean, God!'

'Cheer up, love,' Mad Aunt Joan shouts over her shoulder. 'Because we'll be at the campsite soon enough, don't you worry.'

I put down the leaflet I've been reading and wiggle about on the seat to find a cool spot.

'Would you please sit still?' Kelly hisses furiously. 'You're getting dirty-boy sweat all over my legs.'

On the radio, Kenny takes over from David Cassidy.

'Oohh, turn it up, Michael,' Mad Aunt Joan coos all of a sudden. 'I like this one.'

She puts down the map she has been folding and re-folding for the past half an hour and peers over the top of my head.

'The next turning on the right,' she mouths with a theatrical flourish, gesturing with the map at the back window. 'Past the petrol station.'

'They won't be able to understand you, Joan,' Mum sighs, just before kissing Daniel's hair. 'So, you are wasting your time and breath, I'm afraid.'

"They" are Granddad, Uncle Terry, Nice Aunt Emily and their two timid children, Charlotte and Peter, who are in Terry's Granada just behind us.

'Two more miles. Let the others know.'

"The others" are Uncle Brian, Moany Aunt Barbara and their three sons, Martin, Michael and Thomas, who right now would be slapping each other on the legs in the back of Brian's Maxi as Barbara dutifully repeated the word 'Boys!' from the front of the car, as she flicked her way through a *Daily Express*, looking for the crossword page.

It was what they did as a family whenever they were all together for a day out like today.

'On the right and not the left.'

The Granada flashes its headlights at us.

'Wasting my time, am I?'

'Yes, I believe you are,' Mum sighs with calculated nonchalance, as she does her best to ignore the headlight flashing behind us.

'And it's a sharp turn,' Mad Aunt Joan shouts, jabbing furiously at the passenger window. 'So be careful, otherwise, you'll only miss it.'

Kelly rolls her eyes, clearly less than impressed by Mad Aunt Joan's convoy synchronisation.

'Would you please shut up!'

Behind us, the Granada indicates, accelerates and then pulls up alongside, as Emily furiously winds down her passenger window.

We all involuntarily lean to the left.

'What was that, Joan? I couldn't hear properly because Terry was saying something in my ear.'

Mum snorts under her breath.

'Next right,' Uncle Michael yells, pointing his pipe in Mad Aunt Joan's direction. 'And it tends to come on without due warning, so please be aware.'

'Confirmed. I'll let Terry know,' Emily shouts back, just before the Granada drops back behind us once again.

I twist in my seat and watch, fascinated, as Brian's Maxi attempts to overtake the Granada without much success.

'They get a lot in for such a small car,' I say, marvelling at Barbara's packing skills. 'And it doesn't look too heavy up top either, despite all their bags and cases.'

'And to think he wanted to buy a Renault 5.' Uncle Michael chuckles. 'But I told him the trouble he'd have with the parts and the servicing, and in the end, he saw the virtues in British Leyland.'

'Oh, for God's sake,' Kelly splutters, tetchily crossing her arms as only she can. 'Do you think we could talk about something else, please, apart from cars and directions and female breasts?'

Mum tuts and puts down her magazine.

'Kelly, could you not, please?'

'I'm just saying!'

'Well, don't, thank you.'

'Though by the looks of things,' Mad Aunt Joan says, studying the rest of the convoy over the top of our heads, 'they appear to have understood us perfectly, Stephanie.'

She lifts her sunglasses.

'Tried and tested methods always succeed in the end, young

Noah,' she says, winking at me. 'As you'll discover in time, I'm sure.'

'I just want to die,' Kelly mutters, before resting her head on Mum's shoulder. 'And as painfully as I can, if such a thing is possible and not against the law.'

'No, you don't,' I say as Daniel bursts into a fit of hand-clapping. 'You're just saying that to be a cow.'

'And will you please shut that window?' Kelly snaps, furiously eyeing the rear-view mirror. 'It's like a ruddy wind tunnel back here.'

'Nearly there, young travellers.' Uncle Michael chuckles, turning up the radio. 'And adventures about to begin, I'm sure.'

23

Two hours later we are huddled around a picnic table in a lay-by, just outside Teynham.

'Oh dear, oh dear—'

As Daniel runs around making choo-choo noises, Mad Aunt Joan unfolds her map and then traces the line of a B road on it with one of Mum's knitting needles.

'You see, I believe we went wrong here, at the junction when we were rudely overtaken by the oil tanker.'

Beyond the trees surrounding the lay-by, a dog starts barking.

Mum zips up her jacket.

'And it's Esso's fault, at the end of the day, because by the time we reached the roundabout we were already well off course.'

The knitting needle meets a crease in the map.

'Then after the church, we were just too far behind the others to be able to keep up with them properly,' Mad Aunt Joan continues, her voice taking on the tone of a military officer. 'Or, indeed, to see them at all or know which direction they had eventually chosen to take.'

She raises the needle and taps it in the palm of her hand.

'Either way and, taking all circumstances into account, we are very much detached, I'm afraid.'

Kelly looks up at the darkening sky, sensing danger as only a teenage girl can.

'Why don't we just put the tent up here, then?' she asks, fear nibbling at her voice. 'After all, it is starting to get quite late.'

'I'm afraid we cannot do that,' Uncle Michael sighs, rubbing the back of his neck. 'For this area is for picnicking and resting purposes only.'

'Well, we're resting, aren't we?'

'No, we are not. What we are is lost,' Mad Aunt Joan answers sharply, searching in her jacket for a packet of Bensons. 'Plus, there is also an additional problem which we really must take into consideration at this potentially traumatic time.'

'Which is what?' Mum asks wearily.

'Well, my dear, the situation is demonstrably clear in its severity,' Uncle Michael continues, handing his wife a box of matches. 'You see, we have the tent canvas for Big Blue but, unfortunately, we do not have its poles.'

Mad Aunt Joan extracts a match from the box.

'Or the ropes,' she adds quickly.

All eyes turn to the tightly packed bundle lashed to the roof rack on top of the Marina.

'I do not believe this!' Kelly squeals, running back towards the car.

'Well, can't we radio the others?' Mum asks, one eye on Kelly as she starts circling the lay-by. 'Perhaps using your CB radio or something?'

'There is little value in such an endeavour, my dear,' Uncle Michael advises her calmly. 'For neither Brian nor Terry have working citizen band radios with which we would be able to do so.'

'But I thought Terry had one, for the boys?'

'Oh, he does, and in fact, I fitted the aerial for him, up in his loft. The boys use it when they have finished their homework in the evening, to converse with passing lorry drivers.'

Uncle Michael takes hold of Mad Aunt Joan's hand.

'So you see, we are, I am afraid, very much on our own in this contemporary dilemma, until we can come up with a suitable plan of action to thus get out of it.'

'In that case, what are we going to do?' Kelly demands, back amongst us, only this time even more agitated than she was before.

'Because we have to do something, otherwise we could all end up dying here.'

She slaps her sides and advances on the picnic table.

'Well, hello!'

'Hello, Kelly,' Mum sighs, not looking up from where she is nibbling at Daniel's ear.

'I mean, can't someone go up to the road and make a telephone call to the emergency services or the mountain rescue or something?' Kelly demands, wiggling her hands about. 'There's bound to be a telephone box within a few miles. It's the law.'

Kelly is not so much talking to us right now as making a speech to the whole lay-by (not that there is anyone else to hear it, apart from us, unfortunately).

'Oh dear, oh dear.'

Mad Aunt Joan rolls her eyes and takes a deep breath.

'Oh my, oh my, oh my, oh my.'

I carefully take Daniel's hand and step back from the picnic table just in case.

'There is simply no point in calling the police,' Mad Aunt Joan continues, resting her head on Uncle Michael's shoulder. 'We've just become dislocated from the others, that is all, and there is quite simply nothing that anyone can do about that situation.'

'Plus, there is little that the mountain rescue can do either,' Uncle Michael adds, more to himself than to anyone else, 'this not being a mountain or a coastal location.'

Suddenly a vision of one of those great big yellow helicopters with an RAF officer swinging on a rope drops into my mind and I am in the RAF officer's arms being winched up and everyone is shouting, "No, Noah, please don't go."

'Well, we can't stay here all night, can we?' Kelly snaps, clapping her hands together and pulling me instantly back down to reality. 'That's just a fact of the current situation, isn't it!'

At which point the RAF officer winches himself up into the helicopter and I am left on the ground, with everyone going, "So you're back then?"

'I mean, why are we even still here?'

Kelly waves her arms about.

'Just look what's happening around us!'

Mum's eyes dart around the lay-by.

'Because they're not going to come back tonight, are they?'

Mad Aunt Joan peers over Uncle Michael's shoulder.

'And now it's getting dark and it's just not safe to stay here.'

Kelly's voice begins to dissolve into tears of panic.

'I mean, it's just too dangerous, isn't it?'

Mum gets up from the table.

'Kelly, dear—'

'Oh no, you do not, Mother,' Kelly snaps, stepping sharply back. 'Because this is all your fault.'

Mum looks aghast.

'And how do you work that out?'

'"Come camping," you said, "for the last time," you said, "because then we'll be going back to your dad and we won't have to do this ever again."'

'Did you say that, Stephanie?' Mad Aunt Joan asks delicately.

'I may have done,' Mum gabbles, attempting a smile, 'though I can't remember my exact words, to be honest. There was just so much packing to do.'

'But it's not true, is it?'

The tears in Kelly's voice creep even closer to the surface.

'Because we're not going back to Dad, and I know we're not because you said on the phone last night that we're going to Sittingbourne instead.'

Which is news to me.

'Mum?'

'I was just talking to your grandmother about having a little stay, that's all,' Mum splutters. 'Now, come here, darling, and let me put a cardigan around you.'

'Oh no, you do not!'

Kelly takes another step backwards.

'No cardigans, no cuddles and no Sittingbourne either. I want us all to get back into the car, for Uncle Michael to turn that car around and for the six of us to drive back to London so that I can have a hot bath and sleep in my own bed.'

Her tears finally break the surface.

'And then we won't have to do any more bloody—'

A black Ford Granada shoots past the lay-by.

'Kelly!' Mum squeals.

'—camping.'

Mad Aunt Joan and Uncle Michael run past Kelly, back towards the car, followed almost immediately by Mum.

'After you, Michael!'

'On my way, Joan!'

I take hold of Daniel's hand and follow the others as a bright blue Maxi pootles after the Granada.

'Really?' Kelly asks, wiping the tears from her face. 'Really and honestly?'

She turns and stares as Uncle Michael scrambles to start the Marina, using too much clutch.

'Are we going back to Plumstead after all, because everyone has finally come to their senses?'

The Marina lurches forward, as Mum throws open the rear passenger door and urgently reaches out.

'Oh, get in, you teenage hysteric,' she shouts, gesturing at my sister. 'Can't you see there's a chase on?'

I scramble round to the other side of the car and throw Daniel onto the back seat.

'And chases like these don't wait for anyone's convenience, you know.'

And with that Mum pulls Kelly into the car, Uncle Michael put his foot down and we splutter out of the lay-by in third gear.

24

Just after 9pm all the cars in our mini-convoy are finally reunited, lined up and cooling their engines in front of the locked gates of the Happy Families Camping Village.

'This has been the worst day of my life,' Kelly sighs, wetting a finger and drawing a heart in the condensation on the passenger window, as Uncle Michael honks his horn for the third time. 'And I'm counting that birthday when I got food poisoning and couldn't get out of bed to go to the toilet when I say that.'

'Oh, it's not that bad,' I console her, as a bone-thin, narrow-eyed man eventually approaches the padlocked gate barring us from the campsite.

'Double diarrhoea, that was,' Kelly sniffs, 'which is something I would gladly have again, rather than have to go through with this so-called "holiday".'

And by the sad tone of her voice, it's clear that she means every single word.

'It's exciting, though, isn't it?' I say, in a final attempt to make her feel better. 'Adventures have indeed begun and we haven't even got inside the campsite yet.'

'Well, I'm sorry, but none of you can come in,' the bone-thin man announces from the other side of the gate.

Uncle Michael rubs his eyes and leans out of the driver's window. 'And why would that be, may I ask?'

The bone-thin man strokes at his chin for a moment.

'Because it is too late,' he says, barely stifling a half-smile. 'There are rules, which we are required to abide by, and it is my job to ensure that such law-abiding does indeed take place.'

'What's he saying, Michael?' Mum pipes up from the back of the car, agitated because she has been wanting to use the toilet for the last ten miles or so. 'Is there an insurmountable problem of some kind, my darling?'

'No, Stephanie, just a little local difficulty that I am seeking to iron out.'

'Well, iron quicker, Michael, would you please, my darling.'

'I'm afraid the rules are paramount,' the bone-thin man continues, ignoring Mum's protestations of urgency. 'They are what made this country great, what once maintained our glorious Empire when there was indeed an Empire to maintain, and they are all that remain today against the power of the unions and in rejection of the work-shy anarchists and Trotskyist students who are doing everything they can to ruin this honourable nation and turn it into a satellite of the Soviet Union.'

He takes a deep breath and straightens his tie.

'I was stationed in Malta, you know, with the Royal Air Force.'

'Such a beautiful country,' Uncle Michael sighs, almost under his breath.

'Indeed it was and I believe it still is,' the bone-thin man says with nearly as much affection.

Behind us, Uncle Terry honks his horn then Uncle Brian winds down the driver's window of the Maxi and shoves his head out.

'Will you please hurry up? We're suffering a starving back here.'

He quickly winds the window back up again.

'Hear, hear!' Terry shouts. 'We have been on the road for several very hot hours, you know.'

'The rules are clear and fair,' the bone-thin man intones gravely, before raising his voice, 'and no one gets in after eight in the evening.'

Uncle Michael opens his mouth.

'And strictly speaking, as this is a Friday, it is also the case that we close the gate at seven to prevent the obvious and inherent dangers of late-night drinking, this being a family site. And since it is now five minutes past nine, which is some time after seven, as I am sure you will agree, I am afraid that you and your friends—'

'Loved ones,' Moany Aunt Barbara hollers from behind us.

'And I don't even want to be here!' Kelly shouts, just to keep her oar in.

'In which case you and your loved ones will have to turn around and find somewhere else that is more suitable for your camping needs because this barrier gate will not, I am afraid, be lifted any time this evening.'

'Right, that does it!'

Mad Aunt Joan is out of the car and slamming the door behind her before anyone can intervene.

'Oh dear.'

The bone-thin man takes a quick step back on the other side of the gate.

'Avert your eyes, please, children,' Uncle Michael mutters, winding up his window. 'And your ears, if possible, as this could get very unnecessary indeed.'

'Does this mean we will have to go home, after all?' Kelly asks, her voice rising with hope and expectation. 'Perhaps even tonight?'

'No,' Mum sighs wearily, 'it does not. Though we may have to put the tents up next to the motorway.'

She taps her foot up and down.

'Please do come on, Joan… my darling.'

'Because we could,' Kelly continues. 'In fact, all we would have to do is take the—'

'Oh, will you please shut up, Kelly!'

At the gate, Mad Aunt Joan gesticulates, points and then opens her handbag while the bone-thin man on the other side of the gate shakes his head gravely.

'Come on, old girl,' Uncle Michael mutters, rubbing his fingers up and down the steering wheel. 'Don't let us down now.'

At which point Mad Aunt Joan says something, the bone-thin man steps forward to look even more closely in her handbag and then he quickly unlocks and opens the gate, before delivering a stiff salute at the side of the road.

'Bingo,' Uncle Michael mutters, turning the ignition.

*

Come midnight, me and Kelly are crammed into the two-man tent at the bottom of the campsite, together with Charlotte and Peter.

'Well, I'm glad that's over,' Peter gushes the minute the tent is zipped up. 'If Joan hadn't opened her purse and flashed her money like that I don't know what we would have done.'

'You can say that again.'

I'm trying to get comfortable in my sleeping bag, but it's not easy with everyone else jammed into the tent.

'I thought Mum was going to wet herself back there.'

'Dad was the same.' Charlotte giggles, taking up all the room as she fidgets about on the groundsheet next to me. 'He said he might even have to use the bottle.'

Kelly looks at me, confused.

'Use the what?'

Charlotte and Peter were roughly our age but were very, very Kentish in their outlook; she a deep blusher with a habit of stroking her knee whenever her nerves kicked in, while Peter was all itches and mournful stares (a state of affairs which, as we could not help but notice, tended to manifest itself whenever he got caught staring at a girl's breasts or touching himself when he shouldn't – which was often).

'I nearly fell asleep in the back of the car,' Charlotte yawns, ignoring my sister, 'and Peter had to wake me when we got here. I was snoring. Or so he said.'

'She was,' Peter gabbles, eager to get back in on the conversation, 'and she was talking in her sleep. She kept going, "Neah, Nah, Neah,

Nah," so I elbowed her till she woke up and then she had dribble all down her chin.'

Charlotte rolls her eyes knowingly in Kelly's direction.

'Peter Tribe, you are such a terrible liar.'

Peter scratches his forehead and does his best not to look down Kelly's top.

'I most certainly am not.'

'Oh yes, you are,' Charlotte continues, 'and you're a very poor one at that.'

She turns to me.

'Sometimes I swear he says all these things just because they dropped him when he was a baby and had to put him in an oxygen tent until he got better.'

'No, they didn't. I rolled off the bed was all that happened,' Peter snaps.

'Oh, they just said that to stop the Social Services taking you away,' Charlotte says, shaking her head. 'And anyway, whatever happened, there's still a bump on your head where your double crown is.'

Peter tilts his head forward (which means his eyes are now almost totally down Kelly's top). 'Do you want to feel it?' he asks excitedly. 'Because you can, if you want to.'

I reach over and trace my fingers over the top of his skull.

'Oh yes, it's all silky,' I say, genuinely intrigued.

'You'll go bald there when you get older,' Kelly adds quickly, resisting the urge to lay her fingers on his scalp. 'Just like a monk, probably.'

Peter tilts his head back.

'When there's lightning it twitches.'

Charlotte shakes her head.

'Which is just another shameless tissue—'

'It does! It's like electricity in my brain.'

'You are such a complete fabricator,' Charlotte sighs. 'You just say these things to make yourself look more important and don't think we don't realise that fact in every instance.'

'What's going on with Moany Aunt Barbara and Uncle Brian?' Kelly asks suddenly, clearly bored with Charlotte's berating of her brother.

'They're having a meeting,' Charlotte says, moving her hand to the leg of her jeans, 'to talk about the mortgage or something.'

Kelly raises a theatrical eyebrow.

'Are they really?'

I turn and look at my sister more closely.

'What do you mean?' Charlotte asks, scratching at her jeans.

'Well, I heard Granddad talking to Uncle Terry when they got back from playing crib the other night,' Kelly says quickly, obviously to get the words out before any of us can stop her. 'And Terry was saying that Brian would have to stay with Granddad for a couple of months while he sorts himself out and that's why we're going to Nan's.'

Which is news to me.

'Kelly?'

'What?' she snaps, obviously not appreciating my distracting her from her malicious fun. 'Can't you see I'm trying to help here?'

Peter lifts his gaze from Kelly's breasts, his left eye going ten a minute.

'While he sorts what out?'

'The separation.'

Not far away a cow moos.

'Well, he can't just walk out, can he, because of the house and the new schools in September. He's got to find a place of his own and, when he does, Moany Aunt Barbara will need to stay with you lot and then she's bound to be upset and crying, and everything.'

'Who said that?' Charlotte demands. 'Because it's the first I've heard and Mum tells me everything.'

'I told you. Uncle Terry said so, the other night.'

For a second no one says anything.

'A separation,' Charlotte repeats bleakly.

'For how long?' Peter asks.

No one wants to say the dreaded "D" word.

'Who knows? But they'll be telling Uncle Michael and Mad Aunt Joan right now, I reckon.'

Kelly seems to be enjoying herself now, and the more Charlotte and Peter get more and more intimidated by her words, the quicker Kelly seems to be shovelling them into their laps. 'It's so they can get it all organised once they get back – what with the packing and everything – because there's bound to be a lot to do, especially straight after the holiday.'

I don't know about Charlotte or Peter, but I have heard enough.

'Give it a rest, will you?' I say, pulling at the zip of my sleeping bag. 'Your voice is like an alarm clock on a Monday morning sometimes.'

'What do you mean? I'm just saying.'

'Just being stupid, more like. That sort of thing is not something to laugh about, you know.'

'Who's laughing? I'm just reporting what I heard so that we can all be more sensitive in the morning when they're all bound to be upset.'

She turns back to Charlotte and Peter, who are staring down at the groundsheet. 'Because they are – there's obviously going to be tears and trembling lips over the boiled eggs.'

Charlotte looks like she is going to cry any minute.

'I'd better get back,' she says quietly. 'I've got to put my cream on as it is.'

Then she stands up, yanks the tent flaps open and nods at her brother.

'Come on, Peter.'

Catching one last twitchy look at Kelly's heaving chest, Peter gets up and reluctantly follows his sister out of the tent.

'I was only doing what was right,' Kelly pleads, not entirely convincingly, 'because it's wrong to keep a secret inside. It's a well-known medical fact.'

'I believe you,' Charlotte says, in a cold, flat voice.

'Goodnight, Noah.'

'See you at breakfast, then,' Peter adds mournfully, obviously reluctant to leave, despite all the dramarama. 'I think they've got Sugar Puffs here.'

And then the two of them slip out of the tent.

I turn to Kelly the minute they are gone.

'Why do you have to be such a bloody mare all the time?'

'Don't say that to me, you queer bastard.'

Queer?

Why did she call me that?

'All I was doing was telling the truth and Mum's always telling us to do that.'

'Oh...'

I am suddenly so angry that I can't even think.

'Why don't you just piss off!'

And I crawl out of my sleeping bag and push my way out of the tent, not even bothering to find my jacket first.

'Noah, what are you doing? Come back,' Kelly shouts as I march off across the grass, not knowing exactly where I was going. 'Please don't leave me alone.'

But I ignore her and instead go and sit on the wall at the end of the campsite and try to control my breathing.

'Noah!'

Charlotte and Peter I just know would have gone back to their tent so that Charlotte could cry and Peter could comfort her, and all I want to do right now is murder Kelly, partly because she hadn't told me about Uncle Brian and Moany Aunt Barbara before she told Charlotte and Peter, but also because for the first time I'm starting to wonder what else she knows that she isn't telling me.

'Come back, Noah, please!'

From the wall you can see the lights of the village we passed on our way in, and one of them isn't working properly and keeps blinking on and off.

'Noah, I'm sorry.'

And all I can think about is the number of bedrooms at Granddad's and which one Uncle Brian will be staying in with all his stuff before we have time to leave, and about Charlotte and Peter, who are bound to be visiting all the time (and what will that be like, what with all the crying and the coming and going and the queues for the bathroom?).

Footsteps swish towards me through the grass but I don't turn round.

'Mum says you're to come back and go to bed,' Kelly says carefully, before climbing up onto the wall beside me. 'Because soon they'll be turning all the lights out.'

Which is a blatant lie.

'Because they do that, you know, to save on the electricity.'

I don't say anything (though I am tempted to point out that tonight I will be sleeping in a sleeping bag and not a bed and that they couldn't turn off the lights, even if they wanted, because that would be illegal and not very sensible).

'Which can be very expensive for a campsite like this.'

But all I do instead is stare at the village and wish I was on my own and away from my stupid bloody sister.

'It's not that bad here, is it?' Kelly says after a while. 'And at least there aren't that many cows.'

Pause.

'Which is good.'

'I thought you liked cows.'

'I'm more into horses now,' Kelly adds quickly, before scooting along the wall towards me. 'And ponies.'

'Did you really hear Mum talking on the phone to Nan?' I ask, not able to keep the question inside any longer.

'Yes,' Kelly answers carefully. 'After Uncle Brian had gone home, Mum came into the sitting room and telephoned Nan from there. She kept her voice down, but I could still make out what she was saying.'

'Did she say anything about Dad?'

'Not much. Just about his posting being extended and something about a petrol station.'

'Why would she be talking about a petrol station?'

'I don't know. Anyway, it was a bit difficult. I could only hear one side and that was a bit whispery.'

'And did she say when?'

My mind suddenly fills up with the tennis tournament I'd planned with Tommy Smith (obviously not now going to take place) and about Asghar.

'No,' Kelly says, even more quietly than before. 'So it might not happen at all if we're lucky.'

In the village a dog starts barking and then a man comes out of a house and starts shouting at the dog, but the man sounds a bit drunk so doesn't make much sense.

'We need to get back,' Kelly says at last.

'Yes, I know.'

There doesn't seem any point in talking anymore, not really, so we just sit on the wall and listen to the dog barking and the drunken man shouting until Mum calls us to come back because it is getting late.

'Come on,' Kelly says, slipping off the wall. 'Let's just see what happens.'

'OK.'

And I follow her back to the tent.

25

'You listen too much to other people's private conversations, you do.'

'No, I do not,' Kelly snorts, affronted and aghast at my frank accusation (as well as being a bit excited by it as well).

We are in the front room watching *The Basil Brush Show* with Munira, who is clearly bored by the laughing fox on the television.

'I'm simply vigilant, that's all, and Granddad's always telling us to be vigilant – because of the IRA and the threat of bombs and such and such.'

Munira and Kelly are balanced on pouffes whilst I am in an armchair, swinging my legs over an arm and scuffing the carpet with my feet.

'Anyway, that is a horrible thing to come out with like that,' Munira says, turning to give me the evil eye. 'Kelly's just keeping on top of all the relevant local affairs and sharing what she knows, that's all.'

'Well, she's always wrong. Like that time she said Granddad was having a heart attack when all that happened was he had a bit of wind because of a dodgy steak and kidney pie.'

Kelly looks momentarily confused.

'But you don't complain when I hear things you want to know about, do you? Then you're all trunky and lapping it up and tell me more, more, more.'

'Oh, that's just a lie.' I yawn, slightly affronted, but determined not to show it. 'I'm just curious about what's going on in the world, that's

153

all, and not in other people's lives the way you are. I respect people's proper privacy and so should you.'

'You're the liar,' Kelly says, her voice suddenly louder than it was before. 'And besides, it's not like I hide on the stairs listening for the phone to ring or anything. It's just that when something happens, if I am near, then I'll listen if I'm not doing anything of equal importance at the time.'

Which is just another lie. Kelly was fast becoming the biggest snooper in the world, with better hearing than Jaime Sommers.

'Well, you were wrong about Uncle Brian and Moany Aunt Barbara splitting up and us having to go to live in Sittingbourne, weren't you?'

Which is completely and totally true.

It had been weeks since we had got back from the campsite and Uncle Brian was still with Moany Aunt Barbara. There had been no arguments at all during that time or opening of train timetables, or suitcase packing and, as a result, I was beginning to wonder if Kelly had got the separation thing wrong or, worse, had made the whole thing up.

'Do you think so?'

Kelly sits up and twitches her nose.

'We'll see,' she says calmly, before giving Munira one of her mysterious looks. 'Though I'm sure everything will be revealed in due course to your full and total satisfaction.'

'Really?'

'Yes, really,' Munira pipes up, sounding just like my sister. 'I have a feeling that the full truth will shortly be revealed, just like Kelly says, and that feeling is strong, I can tell you.'

Kelly climbs off her pouffe and marches across the room in a purposeful fashion.

'And, if I were you, I wouldn't bank on everything turning out all hunky and dory,' she says, once she reaches the safety of the door and has waited long enough for a sniggering Munira to join her. 'In fact, I wouldn't bank on it at all. Not unless you want to lose a lot of valuable money in the process, and that is all I have to say on the matter.'

And then the two of them slip into the hallway before darting, giggling, up the stairs.

'Ah-ha!'

I jump onto the pouffe newly vacated by Munira and roll it around under my feet like a surfboard.

'The pouffe is mine!'

On the television, Basil Brush nods his head up and down like he is going completely mad.

'Don't panic, Mr Mainwaring,' I say, for no reason whatsoever, and then jump down onto the floor.

'Crisis over.'

Boom! Boom!

*

'Now, watch very closely.'

We have only just finished eating beans on toast for dinner and now me and Kelly are upstairs, pressed against the front bedroom window with Kelly trying not to breathe on the glass.

'That just goes to show what you know,' I scold my sister as, down below, Uncle Brian and Moany Aunt Barbara emerge onto the garden path holding hands. 'That's true love, that is.'

Uncle Brian and Moany Aunt Barbara had just spent the last of the afternoon drinking brandy and playing Monopoly with Mum and Granddad in the front room and now, here they were, touching each other in public all over again.

'You were completely wrong,' I say quietly, leaning onto Mum's dressing table to get a better look at the renewed love revealing itself outside. 'In fact, I think you might even be losing your evil powers.'

'It's because of her,' Kelly says carefully, not taking her eyes from the curious affection going on below. 'Women make men civilised. That's why there's so many wars and murders. Men are just plain evil without the female touch.'

'That's not true.'

I pull at the sleeve of my T-shirt and try to work out if it is.

'Anyway, one thing's for certain: Uncle Brian's definitely not moving in, which means we're not going to Nan's or anywhere else for that matter.'

'We'll see,' Kelly says in that tight, hard voice she uses when she is absolutely and completely right about something. 'And then, if we do, perhaps you'll also learn a thing or two in the bargain.'

I really could slap her sometimes.

'Something important and perhaps even life-changing.'

She touches the window and takes hold of the curtain.

'He doesn't love her,' she says, precisely and calmly. 'He's just doing all of this for show.'

And sure enough, when the front door is closed and Granddad has marched back up the hall, Uncle Brian lets go of his wife's hand and they walk away up the road without talking.

'Told you,' Kelly says triumphantly, releasing the curtain. 'All men are bastards.'

I want to say something.

'I don't know what to say.'

But just then something goes bump next door.

I instinctively grab hold of Kelly's arm.

'Do you think that's Mrs Douglas?'

Kelly looks genuinely startled.

'Please don't start up with all that nonsense,' she splutters, unable to fully hide her nervousness. 'She's just an old woman and not the monster you want to make her out to be.'

I let go of Kelly's arm and we both rush over to the wall.

'In fact…'

Ears to the wallpaper, just in time for another bump.

'Sometimes I think that you're the monster – the juvenile monster of Mineral Street.'

Without warning the bedroom door opens and we both stand back, ready with excuses.

'Oh, it's you!'

But then we see it's only Granddad and return immediately to the wall.

'Now, don't you trouble Mrs Douglas,' Granddad chastises us, waving at the wallpaper. 'She's a private woman who likes her own company. And the one thing she does not want is to be spied upon by you two.'

'Honestly, Grandfather,' Kelly sighs, covering her free ear with her hand, 'the things you say sometimes.'

'She's a very kind old lady as well, I would very much imagine, and you should respect her wishes.'

'But there's obviously something going on,' I say, praying for another bump (or perhaps the sound of a body hitting the carpet). 'You can just tell.'

'You're going to stain the bloody wallpaper if you carry on like that, young man—'

'Shhh,' Kelly hisses. 'I think I heard something.'

Granddad steps forward and takes hold of our free ears in each of his big, fat hands.

'You'll learn one day,' he says, leading us to the door without any concern for our potential aural injury, 'that being left on your own is the one thing that you come to value in this God-forsaken life.'

He releases us onto the landing.

'Now go outside before the sun goes in.'

'But it's boring,' I complain, holding back on the top step as Kelly bounces down to the hallway below. 'And there are ants everywhere.'

'Not in the back garden, there aren't,' Granddad snaps, closing the bedroom door. 'Besides, we'll be starting another game of Monopoly soon, if you're interested in joining us.'

'That's even more boring,' I moan, and bounce down the stairs after my sister.

'Did you hear anything else?' Kelly asks once I re-join her by the coat stand. 'Cries for help, perhaps, or possibly the wailing of someone in pain?'

'I heard something that could have been crying,' I say, playing with an umbrella that has a handle shaped like a duck's head. 'Or it might have been sobbing.'

'What's the difference, exactly?'

'Well, one's more wet and sad and the others like a hysterical hiccupping. What I heard was crying, I'm sure of it.'

'No, you didn't,' Kelly snorts, before opening the front door. 'You are such a complete and total liar.'

'Yes, I did! Well, it was either crying or possibly a rat going up and down the skirting board.'

Munira is waiting on the doorstep, blowing Hubba Bubba and half-heartedly bouncing a yo-yo up and down in her hand.

'He says he heard Mrs Douglas crying,' Kelly says, not taking her eyes from me. 'But I think he's making it up to appear more interesting than he actually is.'

'She's dead, she is,' Munira sneers, catching the spinning yo-yo as it rises towards her. 'So he couldn't have.'

'I think you might be right, though,' Kelly says, suddenly going all serious and mournful. 'There's certainly a funny smell coming from under the floorboards and it's not fluff or discarded breadcrumbs.'

We all go into the front garden to frown at the late-afternoon sunshine.

'Perhaps it's a pigeon,' I say, catching a sneaky look next door, 'that flew in through an open window, couldn't get out and is now a maggot bag.'

On the other side of the gate, Mr and Mrs Bukhari are arguing and pointing at their withered roses.

'It's Mrs Douglas that's rotting on the carpet, if you ask me,' Kelly says, shielding her eyes from the sun, 'and she's being eaten by stray cats or perhaps by spiders.'

Mrs Bukhari smiles and waves at Munira.

'You're sick, you are,' I say (though I'm secretly loving what I am hearing). 'And anyway, I did hear something and it wasn't cats or spiders.'

'What was it then?'

'I don't know. It was a sort of like a tap, tap, tapping sound.'

'You idiot,' Kelly snorts, suddenly losing all interest in my potentially interesting recollection. 'That's not Mrs Douglas—'

'Tied up by burglars and banging her foot on the floorboards, desperate to get our attention?'

'No, that's just Andrew Harper practising his jiu-jitsu.'

'Practising his what?'

'Keep up,' Kelly snaps dismissively as Mr and Mrs Bukhari take their arguing, along with Munira, back into their house. 'There are other people in this world apart from you, you know, and some of them know things that you don't.'

She prods at my forehead with her finger.

'Hello? Is anyone in there?'

I bat her hand away.

'And how would you know about jiu-jitsu, anyway?'

'Because Cheryl told me about it.'

That bloody Cheryl Travers.

'And what does she know, apart from how to snog and catalogue-staring?'

Kelly frowns and takes a breath.

'It's catalogue-shopping, you idiot, and she knows all about jiu-jitsu and Andrew Harper – some facts about which you might even find interesting – because his sister told her all about him when they were leafing through a *Freemans*.'

'Well, I was only kidding because I already know about Andrew Harper and his jiu-jitsu,' I gabble, acting all nonchalant and not that interested, 'because I saw him practising it after he moved in.'

'Did you really?' Kelly yawns.

'Yes, I did,' I continue, doing my best to ignore her and to sound cool. 'So tell me what you know, if you know anything at all, which I don't think you do, and I might tell you what I know.'

Kelly narrows her eyes.

'Shan't,' she snaps dismissively, 'as a punishment for your incessant rudeness.'

And with that she skips away up the pavement, humming a Bay City Rollers song which, by the sound of it, could be *Bye, Bye Baby (Baby Goodbye)*.

'I am most certainly not rude,' I say, even though she obviously can't hear me anymore. 'And I do know about Andrew Harper and his jiu-jitsu.'

*

It had all happened the previous Saturday.

'Mind your back there.'

When two removal men were trying to wobble a wardrobe out the back of a Pickfords van that was parked up next door but one.

'Careful and keep it steady.'

Kelly was looking at eyeshadows in Munira's bedroom.

'Bend your knees.'

I was outside, digging holes in the front garden with a teaspoon after getting bored spying on Mrs Douglas.

'Backwards, forwards and now down.'

At which point I climb onto the garden wall to get a better look at the commotion coming from the back of the removals van.

'Up, up and now down, down—'

The removal men stop their shuffling at this point, place the wardrobe they have been struggling with down onto the pavement and one of the removal men smiles down at me.

'It's a lot bigger than it looks, you know. In fact, it's a right real handful.'

He winks at me as the other removal man smirks and lights a cigarette.

I blush but I don't move from the wall.

'You alright there, young fella?'

'Yes, thank you.'

My mouth is suddenly full of spit.

'I'm perfectly fine, thank you.'

Then Andrew Harper appears from the other side of the van, carrying a box with "Books + Cassettes" written on the side.

'Hey,' he says. 'I'm Andrew Harper.'

'Hey,' I say, feeling suddenly very spotty. 'I'm Noah Tribe. Are you moving in?'

Andrew Harper is a bit older than me, has short brown hair, a cleft chin and is wearing a pair of faded Wranglers with a bright red Gola T-shirt.

'Yeah. We've come down here from Salford,' he says, and then he carries his books and cassettes into his (new) house.

'Well then,' the removal man says, still grinning at me, 'I'd better get back to work, I suppose.'

'Yes,' I say, suddenly not interested in him or what he has to say. 'I think you'd better have.'

*

Kelly is only slightly impressed with my little Pickfords story when she returns to the garden from Munira's bedroom.

'He's just a stupid bum face,' she sighs, after I sort of tell her everything that had happened, having first made sure that no one (i.e. Andrew Harper) can hear us as I babble out the slightly amended facts as quickly as I can. 'And he's an idiot.'

Kelly only called Andrew Harper that because of his Manchester accent, though deep down I can tell she fancies him.

'Cheryl says his dad works in accounting,' Kelly continues, climbing up onto the wall next to me, 'and they're getting a Range Rover.'

Munira clomps out of her house, wearing oversized platform shoes, big white sunglasses and swinging a silver handbag in her left hand.

'It's bright blue, Cheryl reckons,' Munira says, taking a pink lipstick from the bag, 'and it's not second-hand either. Where are they now, anyway?'

'They've gone to Sainsbury's,' I say, wriggling about because I have been on the wall for too long and my bum has started going to sleep. 'And what do they want a Range Rover for? They're not farmers.'

Kelly leans forward, nearly slips off the wall and pouts in Munira's direction. 'His dad's very handsome,' she says, obviously meaning every word. 'If you like that sort of thing.'

What sort of thing?

'And I don't know where they're going to park it, either,' Munira says, clomping up and pursing her lips, as Kelly purses hers. 'Because they're not small, are they?'

She starts smearing pink lipstick on my sister.

'Well, they sound a bit weird to me,' I say, as casually as I can.

Then I jump off the wall.

'And anyway, I'm not interested in any of it. Andrew Harper and his stupid dad can have a bloody yellow Allegro, for all I care.'

Kelly frowns.

'Do you have to swear so much?' she asks as I walk away.

But I ignore her and instead go back into the house, where Granddad is sitting at the bottom of the stairs, carving a figurine.

'What do you think?' he asks proudly, holding up the hideous monstrosity for me to see.

'It's lovely,' I lie. 'Is it a bear?'

'No,' he says, a little hurt. 'It's a mouse.'

26

The next day I am drawn to Mum's bedroom window by the tap, tap, tapping of Andrew Harper, once again practising his jiu-jitsu outside.

'One, two, one, two—'

Down on the street below, Andrew is wearing a pair of England shorts with a *Starsky & Hutch* T-shirt and kicking a tree.

'Wow.'

'Do you think she's also watching?'

Behind me, Kelly has managed to sneak into the room without me hearing her creeping about (and not for the first time).

'Well?'

She nods to the wall dividing us from next door.

'Is she, possibly?'

'I dunno.'

'Really? You surprise me, Mr Mastermind.'

Kelly stands on tip-toes to get a better look at the boy outside energetically kicking the tree.

'Cheryl says they snogged when she went round to see his goldfish—'

His goldfish?

'And she said he really likes to stick his tongue in and move it about when he does, apparently.'

Kelly turns and starts to walk away, clearly already bored.

'There was lots of spit and moaning,' she says, closing the door as she leaves the room. 'And his tongue is extremely large and energetic.'

'Is it really?'

I touch the curtain cloth.

'Now that is interesting.'

*

Within an hour I am in the front room with Andrew Harper, having previously made sure that the windows are firmly shut, even though it is still very, very hot outside.

'Do you want some lemonade?'

'No, thanks. I'm alright.'

I had asked Andrew if he'd like to look at my comics after he called up the hallway to see if anyone was in because the front door was wide open. And now here he is, right beside me, and no longer kicking the tree (but still in his England shorts), sitting back to front on one of Granddad's dining chairs and reading a copy of *Shoot* spread out on the table.

'Are you going to stay in Plumstead long?' I ask, trying to sound as bored as possible as I rock my chair next to his.

'Yeah, a couple of years, probably,' Andrew grunts, not taking his eyes off the comic. 'It depends how it goes with Dad's new job.'

'A bit rubbish, though, isn't it?' I say, turning the page of my *Look-in*.

'It's alright,' Andrew says after a while. 'It's better than Salford, anyway.'

Pause.

'What's Salford like?'

Lick of the finger.

'It's alright.'

Turn of the page.

'Though it's a bit boring.'

We continue to rock lazily on our chairs and I do everything I can not to look at his legs, which are tanned and very muscly.

'So, do you like it here instead, then?'

Pause.

'Yeah.'

I'm wearing football shorts as well – old red ones with an equally old white England shirt – and right now my brain is trying to figure out a way to get Andrew to try on my shirt without him getting suspicious so that I can see him wearing the full England kit.

Which will probably be a bit too small for him.

'There's nothing going on round here, though. You have to go into Greenwich if you want to do anything exciting.'

'How far's that, then?'

'About twenty minutes on the bus.'

My eyes are going up and down Andrew's legs and I can feel my face is going red.

'We've sort of got the same England kit on,' I say as casually as possible, though my voice does go up at a bit at the end. 'Funny that, isn't it?'

'Yeah,' Andrew sniggers, 'really funny, mate.'

And then he turns another page of *Shoot*, more interested in a boring interview with Kevin bloody Keegan (who's obviously using the interview to promote Brut 33, because in one of the photos he's even pointing at a bottle of the stuff) than he is in swapping football kit with me.

So I give up on the whole England shirt idea.

'We play this game in here, me and my brother,' I say, the words tumbling from my mouth before I have a chance to sort them out properly. 'It's really mad but good as well.'

I lean back and turn my chair so that it's facing his.

'Oh yeah?' Andrew says, obviously not listening to a word I'm saying before he turns another page of his comic.

'Yeah,' I say.

And the leg of my chair catches one of the legs of his as we continue with our parallel rocking.

'And it's pretty cool.'

Then his eyes leave the comic and we're both looking at each other as we lean over the front of our chairs and we're both shining because of the heat.

'What's that, then?'

'Well, we both get on the same chair…'

'Yeah…'

'And then we push it like this…'

I push my chair forward and our rocking collides.

'OK.'

And for a moment our forearms touch and the hairs on his forearm gently stroke mine.

'Then we keep doing it until the chair falls over and whoever is the one that pushes it over is the winner.'

I'm making it all up as I go along, of course, but he doesn't know that and for a moment he doesn't say anything and suddenly I'm worried about what might happen if he does say something like, "You're making it up, you are," or "Don't talk bollocks," and my brain is rattling off all the things I could say in response, even though they would all probably come out as, "No, I'm not."

But then he just says, 'OK,' climbs off his chair and steps up to mine. 'I'll give that a go, mate.'

I slip back in my chair and look up at his cock (which is outlined in his England shorts and right in front of my face).

I don't say anything.

'OK.'

I want to swallow, but I don't (even I know that would be a bad idea), so instead all I do is stare at his cock and hold the spit in my mouth as Andrew says, 'Shall I get on then?'

And my heart's really going now.

'Cool, mate.'

I lick my lips.

'Go for it.'

And I swallow at last.

'Cheers.'

Then I push myself back, so there's space between me and the back of the chair ('Brilliant'), as Andrew swings one of his legs over and suddenly we're facing each other.

'Ready?'

'Yeah.' He grins and I reach behind him, take hold of his neck with one hand and the back of the chair with the other, and Andrew slips his hands around my waist.

'Go for it, mate.'

So now he's looking right at me and smiling a little bit as well and up close I can see the bum fluff on his cheeks and a chip on one of his front teeth whenever he opens his mouth and his waist is hot and soft under my fingers.

His breath smells of bananas.

'Do you want to start?' Andrew asks.

So I push with my free hand on the back of the chair and we rock forwards.

'Cool,' Andrew says, smiling even more than before, and then he presses himself into me and we roll backwards.

'Ha!'

I push forward again and this time we move in the opposite direction, as Andrew slips against me.

'Ye-ha!'

And then we move back and he rolls down a bit, his cock rubbing against mine and it's harder than it was before.

'This is cool,' Andrew laughs, as the speed of our chair rocking increases. 'It's a really good laugh, mate.'

Then he tightens his grip and pulls me closer and we're both rolling almost frantically against each other and now I'm laughing.

'This is great!' I yell out loud, just because I want to and regardless of who might hear. 'Ride 'em, cowboy!'

And suddenly Andrew's face is really close to mine and his mouth is open.

'This is good...'

And his forehead rubs against mine, as he slides to the left because of all our sweat.

I breathe into his ear. 'Yeah?'

And the chair is rocking backwards and forwards and going faster and faster and our cocks are rubbing up and down and down and up against each other under our shorts.

'Mate...'

Then Andrew opens his mouth and some of his spit falls onto the end of my tongue.

'Yeah?'

I turn my head so my mouth is in front of his.

'Mate...'

'Yeah?'

'What the bloody hell are you doing with my dining chairs?'

I turn my head.

'Oh... shit.'

Granddad is standing in the doorway holding a dead rabbit by the ears.

'Fuck!'

'What did you say, young man?'

Granddad shakes the rabbit in our direction, as me and Andrew topple over, the back legs of the chair make a loud cracking sound, and we both tumble onto the carpet.

'I haven't finished paying for those!'

Spots of blood fly off the rabbit and hit Andrew in the face as he leaps up, darts around Granddad and runs out the door.

'You wait till your mother gets back, Andrew Harper.'

Then Granddad turns and pulls me to my feet.

'And as for you...'

The front door opens and bangs shut as I look out the window, just in time to see Andrew leaping and clearing the front gate and running off down the road.

'You are in big trouble this time.'

But before Granddad can do anything I shake myself free from his grasp, bob beneath the dead rabbit and run out of the room as quickly as I can.

Granddad kneels down and carefully retrieves what is left of the broken chair from the floor.

'Two more months,' he says sadly, picking up pieces of splintered wood from the carpet. 'That was all that was left, just a couple more bloody months.'

In the hallway Kelly is sitting on the stairs, admiring her nail varnish.

'I could hear you two all the way in my bedroom,' she says, before standing up. 'And you were making a right racket.'

'No, we weren't.'

She's lying, I can tell.

'Yes, you were.'

Then she swans off down the hall and opens the front door.

'In fact, I heard each and every disgusting word and gesture,' she says flatly, before going out and slamming the door behind her.

'And would you stop slamming that bloody door!' Granddad shouts from the front room.

But I don't care about the door-slamming, or about what Kelly may or may not have heard, because I'm so excited I can hardly think about anything.

'Sorry!' I shout back (though I don't know why I'm saying that as I didn't slam the front door in the first place), and then I run up the stairs and into my bedroom, where I shove a chest of drawers against the door and throw myself face down, giggling, onto the bed.

'Phew.'

I want to shout, 'Ye-ha!' and I want to laugh as well, but all I do is close my eyes and grip my stomach and whisper, 'Andrew Harper,' over and over and as quickly as I can.

'Andrew Harper! Andrew Harper! Andrew Harper!'

27

And then, after a month of hot sunshine and fly-swotting, it happened.

'Could you come downstairs, please?'

Bad news.

'Oh no.'

Being called downstairs was usually the cue for an announcement of some kind that might lead to suitcases being clicked open and tears on the stairs.

'I'd like to see all three of you in the front room if you don't mind.'

Lying on his bed, Daniel puts down the pen he has been using to colour a whale in his *Big Book of Animals* and stares blankly at me, green felt tip all over his face.

'Can you hear me up there?' Mum shouts up from the bottom of the banister. 'Or am I saying all these things simply and purely for my own benefit?'

Kelly sticks her head around my bedroom door.

'She's put the lights on in the front room and closed the curtains,' she whispers grimly. 'And that can't be good, can it?'

'I wouldn't have thought so,' I say quietly.

Daniel rolls off the bed and pushes past Kelly to get onto the landing.

'Is there anyone else down there?' I ask, pulling Daniel's duvet straight. 'Uncle Brian, perhaps, or Uncle Terry? I heard a car pulling up earlier.'

Kelly comes in and sits on the bed.

'Do you think it's about—'

'No, it can't be,' I say quickly, cutting her off before she can say any more.

And then I feel guilty about being so horrible.

'You smell nice.'

'Thanks,' Kelly says a little sadly. 'It's Chanel No 5, from the big bottle Dad brought back from Berlin.'

'Mum never liked that perfume, did she?'

'I don't think so,' Kelly sighs. 'She said it brought her out in a rash.' She scratches at her chin.

'They were talking with the door closed last night.'

Oh, no.

'Really? What about?'

'Sittingbourne.'

Oh, no, no, no.

'In your own time,' Mum shouts from downstairs, almost as if she has been listening to us the whole time. 'I've got my heated curlers in and have to take them out in a minute so, please, do hurry up!'

Then the door to the front room opens and closes.

'How do you know?' I ask, pressing my hands together. 'Because it can be so easy to get things wrong when the door is closed.'

'I went downstairs and listened.'

I slip off the bed.

'After you, then.'

'You coward,' Kelly says.

*

'I've got some really good news!'

Mum claps her hands together and then touches at the heated Carmens pinned to her scalp.

'Some wonderful and uplifting news.'

The air is sweet with the smell of slowly cooking hair.

'Unique and special, even.'

171

On one side of the dining table Daniel and Kelly stare ahead, becalmed terror on their faces, while on the other Granddad sniffs and slowly turns a page of his *Daily Mail*.

'Remember when we visited your nan last year?' Mum asks, showing us her palms in a display of reluctant excitement. 'And all the fun we had, despite the rain and the sudden arrival of the Sittingbourne fog?'

A vision of incontinent dogs and slippery carpets swims into view.

Kelly shivers.

'Yes,' she says at last.

'Well, your nan has invited us to stay with her again while I do some work at the local garage.'

'The petrol station,' Granddad corrects her without lifting his gaze from the newspaper.

Mum narrows her eyes.

'Yes, the petrol station, if you must.'

'Oh, I do,' Granddad says, standing up and folding the paper under his arm. 'Because I think you will find that is what it is, even if it does sell firewood.'

He moves around the table.

'I'll put the lamb on,' he says, before heading for the door, 'and get some mint from the garden.'

'Will any of those men be there?' Kelly asks, her voice suddenly all hard and tight.

'No, my darling. There's only Derek at the moment and he'll be gone by the time we arrive.'

Mum slowly starts extracting the pins from her curlers.

'As soon as they can find someone to take care of his...'

Polite cough.

'...special needs.'

Dirty Derek, Nan's most loyal and surprisingly mobile lodger (taking into account his use of a wheelchair to get about – though that was before the police got involved because of a scandal at the lido), together with his little, snarling dog that never let you near the

172

television, were the whisky-stinking Dastardly and Muttley of North Kent, that had practically ruined Easter the previous year, after we had descended on Nan's impromptu and with teeth gritted, for an evening of Twister and food poisoning.

'And then it'll just be Afia, Jacinto and the other one...'

'Baako?' Kelly suggests coolly.

'Baako. Yes, that's it.'

'I don't think we should go,' Kelly adds, looking to me for support. 'Because there's just not enough room, is there?'

I dig my nails into the top of the table and stare ahead.

'Oh, nonsense.' Mum chuckles, taking a Carmen from her hair before poking at the curl it has left behind with a spiked comb. 'Now that Derek is leaving there'll be plenty of room, even with the three African children. And besides, you can share with your half-cousin Beverley while the boys have the back bedroom.'

'But Kelly's right,' I say, gulping down air. 'I mean, we can all stay here, can't we, while you work at the petrol station? After all, it's not that far away.'

I look at my sister, a little lost at having over-extended myself like that.

'Is it?'

'An hour and a half, with a change at Gillingham,' Kelly mutters. 'Though the connecting train only has three carriages.'

Mum puts down her comb, picks up a can of Harmony hairspray and begins shaking it across the table at us.

'Now you listen to me...'

She presses hard on the top of the can and douses the air above our heads in thick, heavy lacquer.

'Your grandmother has kindly offered for us to stay with her rent-free – Rent-Free! – and for as long as we like or until we get back on our feet, whichever comes soonest, and that is a very kind and generous thing for her to do.'

'But—'

'No buts, young man, and this is, I might add, the perfect time for you as well, what with your new school in the autumn and taking into account Brian and Barbara's current little difficulties…'

Kelly turns and gives me her best "told you so" eyes.

'I'm not going to a new school—'

'Yes, you are. So you should be both grateful and understanding, instead of being all sulky and resentful.'

Mum returns to the coaxing and the poking of her hair.

'Rent-Free!'

'I thought it was only going to be for a short while?' Kelly asks carefully.

I clutch at a table leg.

'Well, yes, and just until we have saved enough money to get our own place and Brian and Barbara have had a chance to consider what's best for the both of them in the long run.'

'But—'

'But nothing!'

Mum puts down her Harmony and picks up a Rothmans from a box of Duty-Free in the middle of the table.

'Because by then we'll be sorted out, once and for all.'

She lights the cigarette and blows smoke into the lacquer cloud above the table.

'And then our moving days will be over at last.'

I want Kelly to say something, anything, but all she does is bite her lip and look down at the tablecloth.

Mum smiles sweetly at us.

'Now, if you'll excuse me, I have bingo to go to.'

She moves around the table, kisses Daniel on the top of the head, pecks at Kelly and then dabs me on the cheek.

'And it's the Big Jackpot Night tonight, my darlings.'

She suddenly pauses in her pecking and dabbing.

'Are you wearing my No 5, Kelly?'

'Just a little,' Kelly says, a little sadly. 'I quite like it.'

Mum walks towards the open doorway.

'And so you should, it smells good on you.'

She smooths down the front of her sweater.

'Now, I won't be back until much later, so please don't stay up, and don't give your grandfather any trouble in my absence, either.'

We listen in silence as she zips up her jacket in the hallway.

'See you in the morning, my darlings.'

Then the front door opens and shuts with a half-hearted bang.

Kelly turns to me.

'We're really done for this time,' she says.

'No, we're not,' I gabble, finally letting go of the table leg. 'Actually, I think it's going to be alright.'

I don't believe it, of course, but feel like I have to say something.

'Really?'

'Yes.'

But Kelly looks like she is going to cry any minute and I know that if she does I'll start crying as well and then Daniel will start crying and everything will be hopeless. So instead all I do is rub Kelly's arm and try to smile.

'It'll be fine,' I say with as much conviction as I can muster. 'And I'm sure it'll be a lot of fun in the country, what with the animals and everything.'

Kelly's eyes fill with even more shiny tears.

'Wild dogs, horse shit and rapists is what it'll be.'

'Rapists?'

And now I am worried.

'What, in Kent?'

'Everywhere,' Kelly says, her voice hardening. 'Even in the Garden of bloody England.'

Daniel slips off his chair and heads for the door.

'And where do you think you're going?' Kelly asks, wiping quickly at her eyes, but Daniel just stares at her before disappearing into the hall.

'Do you want boiled or mashed?' Granddad shouts up from the kitchen. 'And there's no pudding, just so you know.'

'OK,' I say a little too quietly.

'I don't think he heard you,' Kelly says, getting up slowly from the table.

'I know,' I say, even quieter than before, but by then she has gone as well.

28

The next night we are huddled with Munira in the two-man at the bottom of the garden and plans are afoot.

'Sshh, I hear something.'

Kelly turns off the torch she has been holding under her chin.

'There it is again!'

Outside the tent, a cat sneezes.

'Is that a fox?' Munira asks, sounding genuinely scared.

Daniel grabs my hand with curiously sticky fingers.

'I don't think so,' I say, trying to sound as brave as I can (but holding on to Daniel just in case). 'I don't think you get foxes this close to the road.'

'It could be Dusty from Number 22,' Munira whispers.

'But Dusty's only got three legs,' Kelly whispers, before turning the torch back on, 'and one of those doesn't work properly.'

Then the cat squeals and pads up and down beside the tent in a sort of wonky fashion.

'Crikey!'

'That's Dusty alright, but I think he'll be going soon,' I say, keen to get back to the matter in hand. 'Or at least he's stopped making weird noises.'

Kelly sort of snorts.

'Right then, where were we?'

'Andrew...'

'Oh yes.'

It had been two weeks since Andrew Harper had jumped over the garden gate, followed soon after by his dad knocking on the front door because of what had happened in the front room.

Me and Kelly hid at the end of the landing whilst all the knocking was going on down below.

'This is going to be bad,' Kelly whispers in my ear after the sixth rat-a-tat-tat, 'and very embarrassing – for you, I mean.'

'Do you think so?'

'Sshh. I can't hear anything.'

We press our ears even closer to the banister.

'Alright, alright,' Granddad grunts, making his way up the hall as slowly as he can. 'Can't you see I'm coming?'

'What do you think he's going to say?' I whisper to Kelly as the front door opens. 'Because now I really am worried.'

'He's going to be complaining about you, you dirty bugger,' Kelly snaps, not taking her ear from the banister paintwork. 'Now please do try to be quiet!'

Downstairs Granddad opens the front door, puts his hands on his hips and then grumbles in the doorway.

'Now he's raising his voice,' I say, trying to control myself, 'and I think he's really angry.'

'No, he's not,' Kelly sneers, pushing herself even further into the banister. 'In fact, if you listen properly, you'll hear that he's laughing at something.'

'Really?'

Then Granddad says, 'Goodnight, Bill,' and me and Kelly shoot across the landing and back into our rooms as quickly as we can.

'Holy cow!'

Over breakfast the next morning Granddad announces casually that Andrew will not be coming round again and that he will be staying with his cousin in Devon for the rest of the summer.

'Because it is for the best, all in all.'

There had also been some talk about Army Cadets on the part of his father, though as Kelly is quick to point out, Andrew Harper is, strictly speaking, a little too old for the Army Cadets.

Not that any of that matters, not really, because I just know that I'll never see Andrew Harper again.

'It's all just so unfair.'

'Oh, he'll be back in a few months, I'm sure.' Granddad chuckles, as he over-stirs his tea. 'They can't keep him away from Mineral Street forever, you know. Where the Luftwaffe failed, the chartered accountants of this world are hardly likely to succeed, now are they?'

But I do worry because in the end I didn't even get to say goodbye before Andrew left and now here I am, sitting in a tent at the bottom of the garden, petrified that everyone might think it was because of what we did in the front room (which it was, obviously) and that I was being sent to Nan's as a punishment and that I'd never see Andrew Harper again.

Probably.

'Do you think he'll go to another school?' I ask after Dusty has finally stopped with all his squealing and wonky walking.

'I think, from the way his dad was going on, that they might move to a different part of the country or even to another country altogether,' Kelly says with obvious glee (just in case I haven't quite got the message). 'So, are you happy now, errant chair-breaking boy?'

But I just ignore her.

'Granddad said they couldn't keep him away forever.'

'Well, I think by now that he might have changed his mind, having had an opportunity to re-evaluate all of the relevant facts and opinions in the matter,' Kelly says with a triumphant flourish.

Pause.

'What?'

'Oh, you heard.'

Kelly places the torch back under her chin.

'Right then, shall we continue with the more important issues in hand?'

Outside Dusty rolls about in the grass and starts purring, only this time even closer to the tent than before.

'It's alright,' Kelly whispers as we watch the cat shadow dance on the tent fabric. 'He's just looking for something to eat.'

At which point the flaps of the tent burst open and Granddad pushes his big fat head in.

'So, there you all are!'

Munira, Kelly and Daniel scream and jump back and I have to grab hold of the tent pole to stop it from falling over.

'Granddad!'

Daniel drops the half-melted Mars Bar he has been secretly licking (but then catches it at the last minute in his gooey, chocolaty fingers and pops it back into his mouth).

'And what the bloody hell is going on in here?' Granddad asks, looking suspiciously around the cramped interior of the tent.

'We're playing games, Grandfather,' Kelly says, flashing the torch in his eyes. 'Simple amusements to keep us entertained and from under your feet.'

'What the…'

Granddad flinches and attempts to wave the torchlight away.

'Do you mind?'

Munira smirks but manages to hide her laughter behind her hands.

'Sorry, Grandfather, dear. You were saying?'

'Well, just make sure you roll the groundsheet up properly when you've finished,' Granddad mutters, before slipping back out through the tent flap. 'Otherwise, it'll only get mouldy and damp before the morning.'

And with that, he stomps away through the grass and back to the house.

'As I was saying,' Munira whispers in a highly dramatic fashion for no reason whatsoever (apart from the fact that she is trying to be just like my sister, as usual), 'you can stay with us if you want. Dad'll have the extension finished by the start of the new term and then the three of you can live in there.'

'But she's not going to let us stay with you.'

'And who's "she"?' Kelly asks rattily, turning the torch on me.

'Is she the cat's mother?'

'Don't do that, please, Kelly—'

'You shouldn't speak about Mum like that, it's not her fault.'

She returns the torch to under her chin.

'Parents have to work and if that means going to where the work is, then that is what they have to do and what we all have to do as well – it's the law and social services and the way things are meant to be.'

For a moment no one says anything.

'Oh, I don't know about you lot,' I sigh, wiping the chocolate mess from Daniel's chin with my thumb, 'but I think this move to Nan's is going to happen no matter what we do.'

Then Daniel pushes the remains of the Mars Bar back into his mouth and a thick string of caramel runs all the way from his lips to his fingers.

'We could always run away,' I think and say at the same time, though I'm not sure that is possible once the words have left my mouth. 'Or something like that.'

Kelly frowns.

'And hide in the extension!' Munira adds brightly, though it is obvious from her face that she doesn't know how that could work either.

29

Two days later the air is heavy with the flying ants that have recently caused such a panic amongst the younger, more easily frightened children in the street.

'It's gone all hot again,' I say to Kelly as we kick at the gate in the front garden and stare at the road. 'And I wouldn't be surprised if it keeps getting hotter, either.'

Nobody knew where all the large winged insects were coming from, or where they went to when the wind turned and they suddenly disappeared, but everyone was in agreement that it was a matter of some concern, even though the only inconvenience the ants seemed to cause was when they flew into your hair and couldn't get themselves free again.

'I suppose so,' Kelly replies after a while. 'It might even be the heatwave back again, according to The News.'

'Yeah,' I say, waving vaguely at the ants. 'I suppose it could be.'

'Bloody monsters,' Kelly snaps, trying to bat the ants away. 'I wish they would all just fly away home and never come back.'

'Leave them alone,' I admonish her with as much enthusiasm as I can muster, taking into account the oppressive heat. 'They're only ants.'

Kelly turns and stares at me.

'Ant boy.'

We stop our kicking and lean back against the gate.

'I most certainly am not!'

'Yes, you are. You love ants. In fact, you're practically insectoid.'

'That's not even a word, real or otherwise.'

'Yes, it is. Or at least it should be.'

Asghar and Munira come out of their house.

'Mum said no,' Munira sighs wearily.

And then the four of us stare at the road and the new red Cortina that has recently appeared outside of Number 42.

'Nice car,' Asghar says, trying to wave the ants away.

'1600cc,' I say, taking something of a guess at the Cortina's engine size. 'And it's not that old, either.'

Whatever its age, the Cortina was certainly long and lovely, and we had still not seen who the driver was, despite our close watching since it had arrived a little mysteriously just under a week ago.

'Automatic?'

'Manual, with a lowered suspension.'

And I don't know if that is true either.

'Cool.'

Something rattling and rumbling advances down Griffin Road and I immediately tell from the sound of its overheated engine that it is a van and not a car and that it has nowhere near 1600cc horsepower.

Or 1300cc, come to that.

'Well, here we go,' I say, as Kelly wraps her arms around Munira's shoulders. 'Best to say goodbye now and get it over with.'

At which point a small grey removal van comes juddering around the corner, with Mum in the front seat bouncing Daniel up and down on her lap.

'Oh God,' Kelly moans into Munira's hair.

Through the windscreen Mum waves at us and then lifts Daniel's hand so he can wave at us as well.

'I wouldn't have thought that was too safe,' Munira sort of sobs, all muffled and wet on Kelly's shoulder. 'Or sanitary, come to think of it.'

Kelly hugs Munira even more tightly than before.

'I'm going to miss you,' she hiccups into Munira's hair, moving back to wipe urgent tears from her face. 'You taught me how to cook and get rid of spots and everything.'

Spots?

'And I really do mean that.'

For a second Munira looks like she can't say anything else, probably because of all the high emotion and everything, but then the driver of the van honks his horn and all of a sudden Munira babbles, 'You're the best friend I've ever had,' and then she hugs Kelly all over again.

'Oh, Munira.'

'Oh, Kelly.'

The van kangaroos up to the kerb and then makes this thin whining sound as Daniel licks at the windscreen and Mum says something to the driver that makes him laugh.

'I'm going to miss you so much, Munira.'

Kelly's shoulders start going up and down because of all her girlish sobbing and I suddenly realise how much better girls are at this sort of thing than boys, which makes me a bit jealous, to be honest, because I just know that I could never be like that, even if I wanted to be.

Which I don't.

Obviously.

'So long then,' Asghar says, interrupting my pondering on the differences between the sexes. 'You take care of yourself, mate.'

I hold out my hand.

'And you, mate. All the best.'

'Make sure you come back on your holidays,' Asghar continues, squeezing my hand as tightly as he can. 'We can play football on the Common whenever you want, even if it is raining.'

'Will do,' I say, as the girls finish their crying and Asghar attempts a smile. 'You can count on that.'

And I want to hug him, right now and there in front of everyone, and rest my nose against his neck, but it just doesn't seem the thing to do somehow. So instead, all I do is shrug and punch his arm.

'That's that then,' Munira sobs, wiping at Kelly's face. 'Please make sure you write to me.'

And then her voice goes all hiccupy all over again.

'Oh, God…'

'She will,' I say, taking hold of Kelly's arm and steering her away. 'Don't you worry. Letters by the dozen there'll be and postcards. Just you wait and see.'

'You stupid little wanker,' Kelly hisses, turning to me as Mum gets out of the van.

'You hoo!'

Kelly elbows me in the ribs.

'You haven't heard the last of this, you cruel gay bastard, not by a long chalk.'

Cruel gay bastard?

'Please do come on,' Mum gushes, deploying the over-excited voice she always uses whenever she wants people to do things they don't want to do. 'After all, Sittingbourne is beckoning, along with the next fantastic chapter of our lives. So let's not keep anyone or anything waiting. Now, where is that wonderful grandfather of yours?'

30

After Nan died, never to rise coughing and wheezing from her sickbed ever again, we gathered for her cremation in something of a daze, one squally and chilly Saturday in September.

We didn't talk about what had happened.

Well, not during the actual cremation, anyway.

'It's all just such a shock.'

Instead, what we did was say the things that we knew we were supposed to say and then carried on in our little state of devastation until we were all absolutely sure (without any shadow of a doubt) that the ordeal truly was over and that Nan was indeed dead.

'I can't believe it, to be honest with you.'

This from Simon, muttering to himself the minute we emerge from the taxi at the gates of the Bluebell Hill Crematorium.

'It's just the distressing nature of it all, isn't it?'

Though, to be fair, it had been something of a traumatic week all round, what with the attacks on the Twin Towers and everything.

'It's all just so much to take in,' Simon adds, after taking a deep breath and turning his coat collar up against the wind. 'I mean, I've had to stop watching CNN or listening to Radio 5 Live – though I never really liked that station in the first place.'

At which point I want to say something sensitive, or meaningful, but before I get the chance Rachel takes her brother's hand and leads him towards the gates of the crematorium.

'Oh, you'll be alright,' she reassures Simon kindly, leaving me to pay the taxi driver. 'You just need time for the full reality of it all to sink in, that's all.'

It was the modest, unforced nature of Nan's passing that had caught everyone by surprise more than her actual leaving of us or the lack of any form of conclusive drama once the end did come.

'It's like post-traumatic stress disorder, in its own non-traumatic way, but it'll all become less upsetting to you, eventually,' Rachel continues, as she and Simon reach the entrance to the crematorium building. 'Though don't worry, because it is over, and you can trust me when I say that to you.'

Though you did have to sympathise with Simon, because one minute there Nan was, at the back of everyone's thoughts and fears, pulling strings and scratching memories, and the next the crematorium conveyer belt was being prepared to send her short, narrow coffin trundling its way into the inevitable fires that she had demanded be waiting for her, once, when she made a little (and slightly infamous) speech at Charlotte's wedding, three years previously.

'Can I have everyone's attention please, including the bride and groom, thank you.'

Nobody wanted to remember that particular reception.

Even if they could not forget it.

'I'd like to say a few words about what happens when I'm not around and you all have more important things on your mind than your old nan and her inheritance – if there's any left of it, that is.'

Charlotte's wedding photographs rarely came out of the drawer after that, no matter who asked to see them.

'Because if I'm not burnt I'll be coming back to get the whole bloody lot of you when you're asleep and in your beds,' Nan continued, by now enjoying her cackling performance at the end of the top table, a glass of warm white wine tremblingly held aloft in her bony, blue-veined hand. 'And then you'll all wake up with my fingers at your throats and you can trust me when I say that.'

Nobody dared breathe a word.

Charlotte looked like she was going to cry.

'And I'm not joking either, so you can stop with all your sniggering at the back.'

To us, her relatives and unloved ones, Nan was like Stalin in curlers, though by the end she had become more like Khrushchev in a nightie, tidied away and wound-down as she went Alzheimer's bonkers in an old people's home nobody wanted to visit and which had once been on the cover of *The Kent Messenger*.

TIED TO A COMMODE AND LEFT TO DIE – IS THIS REALLY HOW WE SHOULD TREAT OUR LOVED ONES?

Most of us knew where the old people's home was (Chatham) and yet we all felt the cold lure of busy, busy, busyness whenever the suggestion was made to "go pay your nan a visit".

'Before it's too late, because it will be, eventually,' Mum had threatened me, Kelly and Daniel once, one cold, grey pre-millennial morning, as she struggled to pull on a new jacket that was two sizes too small for her. 'And then what will you do?'

At this point, Daniel looks like he is going to say something, but then he just frowns and stares down at the carpet.

'Perhaps she just wants to be left alone?' Kelly ventures carefully and at last. 'What with all her many precious memories and everything.'

Kelly had been stuck in traffic on the A2 with Dean and the kids for the past three hours because of an overturned lorry near Rainham, so she had every right to be a little tense at the prospect of a visit to her old nan when all she wanted to do was to spend the afternoon with a nice cup of coffee having a gossip.

I decide to do the decent thing and button up my coat.

'Nonsense, my darling,' Mum coos icily, before pulling a scarf around her neck. 'Your grandmother has no reliable memories left anymore; the Alzheimer's has taken care of all of those. Now gather yourselves and put on your gloves for the journey ahead, my sweet darlings.'

'But I—'

'But nothing, my girl.'

*

Five days later, after Nan had failed to make it through a sudden and particularly energetic attack of pneumonia, I got a call just after midnight.

'Wait, wait, wait...'

On the other end of the mobile signal, Kelly is busy chewing on a Nicorette and jabbering the news as I stumble about in the dark.

'Are you sure?'

I'm groping for the light switch at this point so am more than a little confused by the shocking news my sister has blurted out with a certain amount of barely concealed glee.

'But me and Mum saw her only a few days ago.'

'And what was she like then? And answer quickly, please, because my phone needs charging.'

'Pretty crazy,' I say, shuddering at the cold because I left the bedroom window open before going to bed. 'But she looked like she still had a couple more years in her. Or a few months at the very least.'

'Well, it's true. Mum just called and told me.'

For a second I instinctively bristle because Mum had not telephoned me first.

'And has she checked the corpse?'

'You're a vicious gay sod, you are,' Kelly says quickly, barely stifling her laughter. 'Anyway, according to Mum, they're going to cremate her and scatter her ashes over the pet cemetery—'

'Oh, dear God, no—'

'Oh, dear God, yes!'

At which point we both fall into a miserable silence while the full magnitude of the shocking news sinks fully in.

'What's happening with Nan's stuff?' I ask after a while, genuinely interested for some reason.

'Mum says she's going to sort it all out with Beverley and Ron, but I think she's giving everything that can't be sold to the Sue Ryder. Well, it'll be either that or the Oxfam.'

'Really? But I thought Nan hated any kind of charity.'

'Because it was the work of witches, being orchestrated by the devil using his oh-so-cunning means?'

'Exactly.'

'But she's not around now, is she, to give any kind of opinion, sensible or otherwise?'

'I suppose so,' I say, climbing onto a chair and closing the window with something of a bang (which makes me feel guilty because of the neighbours). 'Though you'd have thought they would have respected her wishes at the end.'

'Maybe, even if that does actually mean anything,' Kelly says wearily. 'Anyway, what does any of that matter now because she's finally dead, isn't she?'

Then she disappears as her phone battery finally gives out.

And I am left standing on a chair in my bedroom.

31

'She was calling me Fern Britton at the end.'

We are in the hospital waiting room.

Waiting.

'Fern bloody Britton!'

Mum gives me her best "can you believe it?" eyes, touches at her feather cut and then returns to staring out of the window.

I don't know what to say (or who Fern Britton is), so I keep quiet and try to see past Mum to what she is staring at.

'And that was when I was close enough to her chair for her to see and hear me properly, so it couldn't have been her eyesight.'

Sitting next to us, on a white vinyl sofa that has coffee stains on it, Beverley clutches a giggling Bethany to her chest and joins me in peering past Mum out the window.

'Well, that couldn't have been good,' Beverley says finally, gently bouncing her daughter from side to side. 'Not for you, or her either, I would imagine, Steph.'

Mum turns and leans back against the sofa.

'She said all the newsreaders were ganging up on her and that they were planning her murder.'

Beverley, a smaller, middle-aged and red-haired version of Mum, at this point looks even more confused than she did before.

'They communicated their foul intentions in code, apparently,' Mum continues, lowering her voice for no good reason. 'She wouldn't watch Sky News at the end. She said she found it all just too upsetting.'

Beverley rolls her eyes.

'Oh dear, oh dear.'

And then she pauses and lifts the three-month-old Bethany, whom Nan had so confidently declared Beverley should not give birth to (because of the evil inside her and so forth), and kisses the giggling baby on the cheek.

'Who's gorgeous and special, then?' she asks joyfully. 'Yes, you are, my beautiful baby girl.'

Despite Nan's dire warnings, Beverley had gone through with her pregnancy and, with her husband Ron beside her tightly squeezing her hand, the red-faced baby had eventually popped out with a slither and a start and an umbilical cord wrapped around her neck, her little legs kicking.

'Why Sky News?' Beverley asks after a while, as Bethany yawns and rubs her face against her mother's breast.

'Because they were watching her from the Sky News Centre, or so she said. They'd been looking in on her room ever since Eamonn Holmes started at breakfast. She heard them whispering when they were looking down at their scripts, apparently.'

'Eamonn's no longer on it, though, is he?'

'I've no idea. I listen to *Today*.'

Bethany burps.

'It's a cruel disease, though, isn't it?' I say without thinking, my mind returning to our previous visit to the old people's home and the shrunken old woman in a high chair, her dentures snapping up and down each time she made one of her little pronouncements on Beverley's swollen midsection and the anti-Christ that lay therein.

'It's just a normal baby,' I had shouted, making sure I was close enough to Nan's ear to be heard, even though she ignored me each time I spoke. 'Beverley's had the ultrasound and shown the photos to the vicar, just to be on the safe side, and everything.'

'And what would he know? It's the devil, I'm telling you. You can see its eyes through the wall of the womb.'

Not quite the memory Beverley hoped to hold dear as Bethany

kicked, fidgeted and got evermore ready for her grand entrance; though by that point Beverley was more concerned as to whether the doctors would need to perform a Caesarean and helicopter the baby out (like a gorilla or a whale or one of those animals you see on the Discovery Channel) as the pregnancy had been going on for so long by this point.

'Cruel, but somehow fitting,' Beverley says, at last, standing up with her heavy bundle of joy as Ron comes pounding into the waiting room, a Morrisons bag in his good hand.

'I've had to park in the Disabled,' he says excitedly, as he bounces over to us. 'Though there's no need to worry because we're near the entrance.'

'Oh, Ron,' Beverley sighs gently, shaking her head at the sweating bear of a man standing before her. 'The things you say out loud when we have company.'

And then they kiss and Ron leans forward, gently kisses the baby and Beverley wipes sweat from Ron's forehead with the palm of her hand.

'What have I done now?' Ron asks, though the truth was he had been sweating a lot for months now: a response to the denial of alcohol and, more recently (and God help us), the cigarettes which Beverley was forcing upon him to ensure that he made it through to being the decent father he so clearly wanted to be.

'There you go,' Ron says, plonking the Morrisons bag down onto the sofa. 'That's all her perfume and bibles. The rest of it was all medical and ready for the incinerator, so I didn't think it was worth keeping.'

'What perfume?' I ask, as the contents of the bag clink and settle beside me.

'Those bloody perfume bottles,' Mum sighs as she gets up from the sofa. 'If they weren't in a particular order and facing in a certain direction then the world was coming to an end and we would all end up in Hades dancing on hot coals.'

I shake my head.

'Alzheimer's is a nasty disease.'

'Nasty nothing – that was when I was your age.' Mum chuckles, as Ron and Beverley walk out the room hand in hand.

'Silly bloody woman, God rest her soul.'

*

There were few tears at the cremation and more mourners than I expected, what with the weather and the terrorist attacks and everything.

It was also a relatively sedate affair, though I did notice a certain nervous eyeing of the coffin throughout the service, almost as if everyone wanted to be certain that its lid would not be popping up at the last minute as those long, tattooed fingers came out, searching for some nice, warm flesh to cling on to.

'It's funny, really,' Kelly muses, as we watch the coffin disappear through the purple velvet curtains that hide the living from the incinerator, 'but now I feel almost sorry for her.'

I take a quick look round.

'She might have done a lot worse,' I say casually. 'Nobody could have come. So actually, she couldn't have been that unloved.'

'Or feared,' Kelly mutters grimly. 'Though I don't think there is a man on earth that could have convinced Granddad to come, even if he were able to.'

'Which is hardly surprising, taking everything into account.'

'Possibly,' Kelly sighs. 'Though God knows Mum did have a bloody good go at persuading him.'

By the time the velvet curtains have closed for good and we are all shuffling out to the car park, all of us looking forward to the sandwiches waiting for us back at the pub and the bet-laying as to who might be next, the whole thing had started to feel like something of an anti-climax.

'I'm glad that's over,' Kelly says, as she checks her phone for text messages the minute we get outside. 'I need to get back and pick up Dean and Adam from their judo class in an hour.'

I look across the car park to where Ron and Beverley are bickering and strapping Bethany into the back of their new Zafira.

'I didn't know they were doing judo. Isn't Adam a bit young for that?'

'No, they do special classes for the under-10s and he loves it.'

She snaps her phone shut with a flourish.

'We originally started him on the kung-fu, because of all the happy-slapping, but he didn't get on with all the walking up and down, so then we moved him over to the judo and now he's more than happy with the pyjama-pulling, though Dean's put his back out a couple of times.'

'And are you not planning on joining us later, after all the judo and its associated potential physical injuries?'

Kelly narrows her eyes at me and then sighs and looks back at the crematorium, any potential fight suddenly gone out of her.

'I just want to forget all about it, to be honest,' she says, reaching into her bag for her car keys. 'Or at least not to have to talk about it all night long with the rest of them.'

'I understand,' I say.

Then she turns back, unsmiling, her face pale and drawn.

'And you know why, don't you?'

'Yes,' I say, as she leans forward and kisses me gently on the cheek. 'I think I do.'

32

1976

'It's the smoking that'll do her in,' Granddad whispered to me, as we hide from Mum's little van in the front room. 'It's why she'll go before I do. I knew that the first day we met and I'll be proved right in the end, just you wait and see.'

He wipes away the hot tears running down my face.

'Did she always smoke a lot, Granddad?'

'From morning to night and even between mouthfuls whenever she was eating, though I think she's now down to two packets a day. Mind you, when I first met her she was on three, so it's progress of a sort.'

'Where was that, Granddad?'

'In an air-raid shelter near Bethnal Green.'

'And do you still love her?'

'Until the day I die and then afterwards, no matter what the bloody divorce papers say and regardless of what happened after.'

Nan did, however, marry again some time after leaving Granddad, eventually taking the hand of the saintly Robert Bridge on the same day that Elvis and Priscilla Presley tied their own matrimonial knot in Las Vegas, though Nan would also find herself a widow in the end, which didn't surprise anyone.

'But does she still love you, Granddad?'

'Not for a quick chance or in a moment, I'm afraid.'

The rumour was that Nan had killed off the ever-faithful Robert (who had difficulty walking due to blood clots in his legs) so that she could get the house on Church Lane that he came with.

'It's a gift from the Almighty up in heaven, it truly is.'

Though nobody could prove anything.

'And up in heaven is where Robert is right now, I'm sure of it.'

It was following seven years of an occasionally happy marriage that Robert eventually passed away, at the height of the three-day week, stumbling down the stairs in an accident that was possibly precipitated by his worsening blood clots.

Or so the coroner said.

Though there remained some speculation about that, right up until Nan's eventual and equally sudden demise twenty-eight years later.

'In thanks to Robert, God rest his soul, I will be lighting a candle and saying a prayer of commiseration later this evening, and you can be assured of that fact, my departed wobbly-legged love.'

It was one of Nan's more reliable little speeches, every time she had a large enough audience to hear it and a drink in her hand.

'Due to Robert's generosity of spirit, I now have this roof over my head which, what with the guard dogs and the high garden fence, is practically safe, and I will forever be eternally grateful to Robert for it and especially now that his soul has finally left us.'

The fact that few taxis would venture as far as the house on Church Lane (even with its high fence and guard dogs) didn't bother Nan as, thanks to Robert's fortuitous kindness, she was also bequeathed two very large gardens (one front and one back), a toilet on the ground floor and gas fires in all the main rooms.

Indeed, if you ignored the lorries that trundled past every few hours on their way to the cement works, it was everything Nan could have ever wished for.

'Bless you, sweet Robert, and rest in peace knowing that your walking stick will never be thrown out while I'm still alive, I can assure your benevolent spirit of that very fact, my sweet love.'

Though I couldn't help but notice that said walking stick did end up as part of the back garden runner bean frame, not long after Robert had been buried.

But I didn't say anything about it.

Not even to Kelly.

'So rest at last, my wonderful, departed darling.'

At which point the tears would inevitably fall and the glass would be shaken (usually because it was empty) and sometimes there might even be polite applause from whichever audience was party to Nan's little performance at the time.

'Though he was all fine and dandy until Ted Heath came on the television,' I heard Mum whisper once to Moany Aunt Barbara as we watched the *Eurovision Song Contest* less than a month after the funeral.

On the TV screen, one of the ABBA women was bobbing about, grinning and generally being stupid for the cameras.

'And then the next thing you know, he's on the oxygen with his legs up in traction and she's off down the High Street picking out new curtains.'

'The red ones with the blue border?' Moany Aunt Barbara asks at this point, aghast and bored with the television.

'The very ones – and she didn't get them on HP, either.'

'But then again, Marjorie always was an instinctive homemaker, wasn't she?'

'Not that you'd notice, no.'

Regardless of her homemaking skills, Nan was in her own house at last, which at that point was owned by the Gas Board, where Robert had worked most of his adult life, emptying meters and writing down dubious gas readings along the East Kent coast. As a result, and as his widow, Marjorie could remain as a tenant of the Gas Board until her death or until she chose to leave (which, as everyone accepted, was unlikely to happen any time soon, even if she had somewhere else to go).

Which she didn't.

'She always has the option to move into one of those retirement communities,' Moany Aunt Barbara suggests carefully, as ABBA join hands and bow to the *Eurovision* audience. 'Or she could possibly be sectioned.'

'Oh, I can see that working.' Mum laughs. 'After all, we're not the kind of people that like to go quietly, are we, Barbara? And certainly not when we're being pushed.'

'As I think I've learned over the years, thank you, Stephanie,' Moany Aunt Barbara shoots back, a little affronted at Mum's ridiculing of her querulous suggestion. 'And it has been a lesson hard learned, I can tell you.'

'Very well then. So let's just leave it at that.'

'Yes, indeed. As I think we should.'

Though as it turned out, within five years of Robert Bridge's death, the Gas Board house would be the only building left standing on Church Lane, once the cement works it led to had been scaled down and everyone else had moved away.

All except Nan, that is, who no longer had to work full-time, or to please Robert Bridge, with his blood clots and trembling legs, because by then he was dead and she was doing part-work running up party dresses for Freemans, and everything was just fine and dandy, what with the dogs and her newly adopted African children and the (very, very) high fences that surrounded them all.

'A lot of people may not like it here, but it's perfect for me,' Nan assured anyone who took the time to drop by for tea. 'Apart from when the gypsies go by, of course.'

Or after it snowed, when Nan was cut off from everyone except the rent collector, or when it rained and the house became a sodden haven for stray cats in the middle of a treacherous river of mud, poorly illuminated by occasional street lights, and gossiped about by local schoolchildren.

'This is and will forever be my beautiful and wonderful home, all because of the love of a good husband for his wife.'

*

I just can't stop crying.

'Five minutes, my darlings!' Mum trills from outside, as Kelly begrudgingly stacks suitcases into the back of the van. 'Then we really will need to venture forth and onto the motorway!'

'Now, you be good to your nan,' Granddad says, wetting one corner of a handkerchief and wiping at my cheeks. 'She's not long for this world and deep down – very, very deep down – she remains a good Christian woman with her heart in the right place.'

'Which is where, Granddad?'

'Right next to her purse, which is always stuffed with cash.'

'We really must be leaving. Now, where's Noah?'

'And remember to keep clear of the dogs and especially that nasty little one that sleeps under the coffee table. I had to hit it with a spade once to get it off my leg. It was never the same after that.'

'But I don't want to go.'

'Now, now, you…'

Granddad takes me in his big fat arms and rubs my back.

'It'll be alright,' he says kindly. 'Just remember to take care of yourself and, more importantly, to look after your mother, because you're the man of the family now.'

'Yes, Granddad,' I say, trying not to cry any more. 'I will.'

'And don't worry about all those tales concerning your evil old grandmother, young fella.'

He releases me from his bear hug, licks a fat thumb and rubs my face.

'Because she's not as bad as people make out.'

'Really?'

'No, she's as human as the rest of us. She's just got a few more demons than most people, that's true, but they only come out when she thinks about everyone that's gone and the mistakes she's made.'

Mum appears in the doorway.

'I think we should be going,' she says gently. 'Otherwise, we'll be late for tea.'

'Goodbye, Granddad. I'll write to you the first chance I get.'

'Goodbye, Noah.'

Then he smiles one last time.

'And don't forget to say hello to Marjorie for me.'

*

'Your grandmother was very successful in putting food on the table while your granddad was away working,' Mum announces from the front seat once we reach the motorway and pass the turnoff for Chatham. 'And there were always lamb chops on Tuesdays, even in winter.'

Kelly looks like she is going to be sick.

Daniel snores in her lap.

'And it is a very kind offer on her part to let us stay in her house while I work and save some money for all of us.'

I want to cry all over again.

'Though, just remember, when you go to the shops, never cut through the trees. There was a nasty incident there once with Beverley and a drunken tramp from Sheerness. Your nan didn't press charges, but it was a valuable warning of the potential dangers of unsupervised woodland, nonetheless.'

In the back of the van, with her back pressed against the suitcases to prevent them from toppling over, Kelly looks at me and vigorously shakes her head. 'When was that, Mother?' she asks above the roar of the van's overburdened engine.

'Oh, don't worry, my darling,' Mum shouts back, 'because it was long before they painted the lines on the road and repaired the street lighting.'

She swivels round in her seat and grins at us.

'Exciting, though, isn't it? Like a real journey into the future unknown. Adventures about to begin!'

We hit a pothole and carrier bags filled with leather belts and knickers spill everywhere.

'Yes, Mother,' Kelly and I reply in unison.

'Adventures about to begin.'

33

With our little delivery van rattling and hissing outside after its long journey on the motorway, me, Kelly and Daniel stand and sweat in the doorway of Nan's lounge, watching Beverley having her hair done in the middle of the carpet.

'Hello, Beverley,' Kelly says, wiping at her forehead as casually as she can. 'It's very hot outside.'

'Hello, Kelly,' Beverley says, wet-eyed and wincing as Nan weaves away with a hairbrush above her head.

'Yes, it is, isn't it.'

'She has to have her hair cared for every day. Otherwise, it becomes impossible to brush and then we have no choice but to cut it,' Nan announces in a loud, scratchy voice from where she sits on the edge of the sofa as Beverley twitches nervously between her bony knees.

'And that would be a real tragic waste. Would it not, Beverley?'

Sitting on its hind legs in front of the two of them, Nan's little mongrel dog, Pickle, fixes me with its good eye and starts to growl.

'Yes, Nan, it would be and that is God's truth,' Beverley yelps.

'Because after a good long bath, when an innocent girl's hair is at its moistest and most pliable, is when it is best handled,' Nan continues, a long snake of ash hanging from the cigarette at the corner of her mouth. 'And that is how the magic of the brush is best worked. Do we not understand that fully, Beverley?'

Pickle growls some more and then turns and waddles over to a half-empty bowl of water in the corner of the room.

'That we do, Grandmother.'

'And what is a woman without the beauty of her hair?'

All eyes to the headscarf wound tightly over Nan's scalp.

'So long as it is kept clean and well-cut.'

Cough, splutter, peel of the cigarette from Nan's lips.

'For a woman is, in her essence, a head of beautiful hair.'

Beverley waits patiently and obediently saying nothing more, one careful eye on the dwindling cigarette above her as the brush resumes its back and forth, transforming her long auburn tresses into the indestructible plait that had long ago become her trademark and inescapable curse.

'It's always best to have well-groomed hair,' Nan continues, 'as a sign of appropriate respect for others and as something that can be passed from mother to daughter.'

She taps fresh ash onto the carpet.

'Now hand me the ribbon from the coffee table, Beverley, and stop your crying, there's a good girl.'

'Sorry,' Beverley mutters, quickly wiping her hand across her face. 'I think it must be my hay fever.'

Nan narrows her eyes in our direction.

'And has your mother explained all of the house rules to you?'

Daniel blinks.

'No, Nan,' Kelly babbles.

Nan sighs, inspecting the ribbon as Beverley hands it to her.

'Don't get into strangers' cars, never pet the local strays and remember that there are worse things in life than playing in the road – like sitting in front of the television all day and stuffing your faces till the cows moo home. Is that not correct, Beverley?'

'Yes, Grandmother.'

'And only Beverley may enter any part of the house between the hours of nine and five outside of legitimate school days, as she is a gift and a joy to behold,' Nan continues, affectionately stroking Beverley's shiny plait. 'She alone may also enter and enjoy the comforts of this lounge at whatever time she pleases, for she is so very special indeed.'

I would eventually come to understand just how special Beverley was, even though Kelly would (inevitably) discover that particular secret before anyone else during a partially wet Christmas afternoon after we had all gathered at Uncle Brian's for a running buffet of cold turkey and warm coleslaw.

Come join us
Family all
for Festive Fun
& Joyous Celebration

That was our first proper get-together since Robert had died and Nan was still dressing all in black or, at least, in very dark grey.

'It's for the required prolonged and meaningful mourning or until the year is out, whichever comes first.'

Moany Aunt Barbara, however, wanted us all to enjoy the "Festive Fun & Joyous Celebration" regardless of any unfortunate family tragedy or the rainy weather that set in as we arrived.

'And don't worry, because we won't be staying long,' Mum whispers quickly to me, Kelly and Daniel, before shaking rainwater from her umbrella on Moany Aunt Barbara's doorstep as we shiver and pray for the front door to open. 'It's just to give out the presents and to find out when the house is going on the market.'

She rings the doorbell again, this time more firmly than before.

'So no sulking or I'll make you play in the garden.'

'But it's raining,' Kelly hisses.

'I am fully aware of that fact, thank you.'

At which point the front door opens and Charlotte and Beverley appear with tinsel in their hair.

'Beverley, darling. So you were able to make it after all!'

Dad was not there that year and, despite Mum's heartfelt protestations that he was needed in Northern Ireland, she still spent the rest of the evening the victim of pitying looks over the potato salad and of gin-soaked tears in the conservatory.

'Though that's the life of the Forces wife,' Moany Aunt Barbara consoled her in the middle of a special episode of *Some Mothers Do 'Ave 'Em*. 'It's a hard and lonely existence and it's not going to get any easier, my dear, and certainly not until he's discharged – honourably or otherwise.'

Kelly, Charlotte and Beverley stayed upstairs for most of that night, painting Colour by Numbers on the landing whilst talking in low, even tones that were indecipherable to the rest of us as we ran whooping up and down the stairs.

'We three girls need only the company of our female sex and not the annoyances of you stupid boys, so go away and stop making so much noise.'

Then, when they did eventually re-join us, blank-faced and covered in eyeshadow, the three girls were completely wordless.

'Do you think they've got an ouija board up there?' Cousin Thomas asked his brother in a fearful whisper as the girls descended the stairs one by one. 'Or perhaps a voodoo doll?'

Ignoring her cousin's frightened speculating, Kelly took hold of Beverley's hand at the foot of the stairs, before following Charlotte into the kitchen for a helping of trifle under cling film.

'Come join us,' Charlotte intoned mysteriously, as the girls gathered around the breakfast bar and the kitchen's fluorescent lights blinked into life, 'as we feast at the bowl of cream and sherry-soaked biscuit in jelly in celebration of what we have leant here this very special evening.'

Whatever had been said upstairs that night over the acrylic paint would remain a secret until years later, though if I had looked closely enough that hot summer afternoon in 1976, as Nan brushed the last of the life from Beverley's hair, I would have seen the truth staring me in the face sitting right there on the lounge carpet.

'Boxes to the right of the door, bags to the left,' Mum trills to the van driver as she marches up a garden path towards us. 'And do try not to squash my shoe or hatboxes, as they are very valuable and I do not wish to have to replace them, thank you.'

'Kelly, you come with me,' Beverley says quickly, springing to her feet as Nan drops her dead cigarette into an ashtray. 'You're going to be sharing my room at the front of the house, just like we're sisters!'

She rushes over and gives Kelly a quick hug.

'And you boys are in the back bedroom,' Nan wheezes, wiping cigarette ash off her slacks. 'I've had the mop round and I've even taken the precaution of opening the windows, so you had better be grateful.'

At which point I make the mistake of stepping into the lounge.

'Oh no!'

Beverley quickly yanks Kelly aside, as Pickle scuttles for safety under the coffee table.

'You never ever come into this lounge during the daytime,' Nan snaps, narrowing her eyes and pointing a bony finger in my direction. 'Only Beverley may enter here. Did you not pay attention to the rules as I kindly explained them to you only a few short minutes ago?'

Nobody dares breathe a potentially dangerous word.

'Well?'

Opening the front door, Mum sneezes and mutters, 'Oh dear,' under her breath.

'I did, Nan,' I say quickly, the words sucking the oxygen out of my lungs as they leave my mouth. 'Every word of each rule fully and completely understood. Honest.'

Daniel's left leg starts shaking.

'And I promise on my father's life that I won't make the same mistake again.'

'Well, make sure you don't. Now, go up and sort out your bedrooms and then get outside and enjoy the sunshine,' Nan growls, before taking a seat at her sewing machine. 'Because it is good and healthy for you. They said so on the radio just the other day.'

'Yes, Nan,' I say, taking Daniel's hand and pulling him more fully into the relative safety of the hall. 'And I promise I won't disobey your rules ever again.'

'Good. Now get out, the whole bloody lot of you.'

At which point the sewing machine roars ferociously into life.

'Come with me,' Beverley whispers, leading me, Kelly and Daniel to the foot of the stairs as Mum glides up the hallway.

'That's it, you go get yourselves sorted out,' Mum says merrily as she turns into the lounge, 'while I have a little chat with your grandmother.'

She slams the lounge door shut behind her and then reopens it to let Pickle bounce into the hall.

'This is going to be the best fun ever!' Beverley squeals, running up the stairs as the lounge door slams shut again. 'You can't imagine how boring it's been here with no one nearly my age to speak to. We are going to have such fun,' she continues. 'And just wait until you meet the wonderful African children!'

She shakes her plait from left to right.

'Do you like it?' she asks, taking the plait and caressing it over her shoulder. 'It's never been this long and it smells so very clean and nice.'

'But isn't it…' Kelly asks, searching for the right words and then, not finding them, carrying on regardless, 'painful, always having it brushed like that?'

'After a while, you get used to it,' Beverley says wistfully, careful to keep her voice down. 'Honestly, you can get used to anything if you really have to.'

Kelly's face is Sphinx-like.

'Why's that, then?'

'Just because.' Beverley shrugs, beckoning us up the stairs. 'Otherwise, things just get all tangled up and then everything goes wrong, wrong, wrong.'

Behind the lounge door, Nan laughs a loud, cackling laugh.

'Afia!'

Beverley ushers us urgently up the stairs and onto the landing.

'Quickly,' she hisses, 'and then I'll show you my new colt if you are quiet and good.'

We nip across the landing and into Beverley's bedroom, which smells of leather and saddle soap.

'That sewing machine's a bit noisy, though, isn't it?' Kelly asks as she looks around the room. 'Especially that motor, what with its rrrrrr and ahhhhh all the time.'

Beverley frowns.

'Yes, but I only notice it when *Magpie* is on, otherwise you—'

'Just get used to it,' Kelly drawls, rolling her eyes as theatrically as possible. 'I think I understand.'

'Now, do come on,' Beverley gushes, slapping the sides of her thighs. 'Because if we can get everything unpacked we'll be allowed to take Minstrel for a ride!'

'I'm alright, thank you,' I say, sniffing something not quite right in the air. 'Besides, I don't think we need to worry about unpacking everything because we're only going to be here for a short while. Mum promised.'

Kelly raises her eyebrow again.

'I think,' she says very slowly, 'it might be a good idea to have a ride on that colt of yours, after all, Beverley.'

34

'You should open a window or, at least, use some of the carpet cleaner Afia's got under the sink.'

Kelly presses herself up against the window of my bedroom as a firework explodes in the smoky night sky outside.

BA-BA-BA-BANG!

'I hate fireworks,' she continues, drawing a line in the condensation on the window with her finger.

'And the smell of urine.'

It was because of Jacinto that Kelly was talking like this.

Nan had tried everything to control Jacinto's bed-wetting after he, Afia and their middle sister, Baako, were deposited into her care all the way from Nigeria by their grateful parents, with God's best wishes and a cash payment every four calendar weeks.

But nothing had worked.

'It's like a swimming pool in here that hasn't had its water changed,' Kelly mutters, staring out at the night sky.

Afia said it was because Jacinto was lazy, and Nan said it was because he was mad, but I thought he was just a miserable kid who wets himself when he has nightmares.

Daniel hops into the room and jumps onto my bed.

'God, I hate it here,' Kelly sniffs, before squeezing her nose between finger and thumb. 'Though it's Afia and Baako that I feel sorry for.'

'Really?'

'Yes, really.'

She opens the window and laughter blows in from the recreation ground up the road.

'Me too,' I say, meaning every word, 'though I think it'll probably be alright once the floorboards dry out a bit.'

'You could try putting talcum powder on the carpet and then hoovering it up,' Kelly sighs wearily, staring out the open window.

'It might make something of a difference to the general odour.'

'I could do, but I don't think talcum powder is going to do much,' I say without even bothering to think about the possible benefits of Kelly's slightly novel suggestion. 'If anything at all.'

Daniel rolls over and hides under the duvet.

'Anyway, we're not going to be here for that much longer, are we?' Kelly turns and stares at me.

'How long do you think before we go back?' she asks.

'Not much longer,' I say, unravelling Daniel from the duvet. 'A couple more months, I reckon, and then we'll definitely be going home again.'

'You said that just after when we first got here and you said the same thing about Mineral Street. "We'll be back with Dad before the month is out," you said.'

Which is true. I think.

'No, I didn't.'

'And, "We'll only be here for a short while," you said,' Kelly continues flatly, before drawing another line on the windowpane.

A rocket zips up into the night sky behind her.

ZE-ZE-ZIP!

'You said it would be a couple of weeks at the most and now we're even at new schools.'

Which we were – Sittingbourne Boys Secondary School (for me, obviously) and Sittingbourne Girls Secondary School (for Kelly, which she had hated from the start).

'That bloody, stupid shit hole.'

Meanwhile, Daniel had been set up to attend a "Special School" just outside Rainham, though there was some discussion about whether its minibus could come this far out to pick him up and take him home again.

'I think we might be back at Granddad's by Christmas,' I say, after pondering for a bit, 'and then we'll be going home for sure.'

'Do you think so?'

'Definitely.'

'Good.'

Kelly comes over and sits on the bed.

'Because I want to be back as soon as possible and I don't care what they say at that stupid school about all the messing about.'

'I wouldn't worry about that,' I say, not entirely convincingly.

'After all, those teachers are just idiots.'

We both lie back on the bed and stare at the cracks in the ceiling.

'What do you think Granddad's doing right now?' Kelly asks after a while.

'Getting the dinner on, probably,' I say, suddenly feeling very hungry.

'Chicken?'

I think for a moment.

'No, it'll be lamb with boiled vegetables and roast potatoes, I reckon.'

Kelly swallows.

'Do you think he's missing us?'

'Yes,' I say immediately. 'He's probably missing us a lot.'

Without warning or a creaking of the stairs, Mum sticks her head around the door and wrinkles her nose.

'Only until we can get back onto our feet and I can save a little bit of money, my darlings,' she sing-songs, trying to breathe through her mouth. 'So don't you worry yourselves, because the time will literally fly by!'

'How long exactly?' Kelly asks, sitting up and crossing her legs. 'If you were to make a best estimate?'

'Oh, I'd say no more than a month or two,' Mum replies, her eyes roaming the room. 'Now, if you'll excuse me, I've been invited to some wine tasting at the Sittingbourne Social Club, so please don't wait up for me.'

Then she disappears, la-lahing her way down the stairs.

'You know, it might not be so bad,' Kelly says with no hint of conviction to her voice, before laying back on the bed. 'And at least it's quiet here.'

'I suppose so.'

Daniel picks his nose and fidgets about, too bored to settle, too lazy to get up.

'Will you stay still, please?' Kelly snaps at him. 'I don't want a repeat of last week, thank you very much!'

The previous Tuesday Daniel had been sick on Kelly's dressing gown because he had eaten too much Angel Delight after dinner (though Beverley said that was because it was made with sour milk).

'You're only going to vomit again if you carry on and I'm not doing any mopping up this time.'

Baako, on the other hand, said it was because Daniel had been eating washing powder in the garden.

And I believed her.

'Now stop all your unnecessary fidgeting!'

Daniel blows a loud childish raspberry and then wiggles about even more.

'Mind you, Beverley survived it here, didn't she?'

Downstairs Nan's sewing machine starts to drone almost reassuringly as raindrops smack against the window ledge.

'That's true.'

Another rocket shoots up into the sky.

WH-WH-WHOOSH!

'I'm off now, darlings,' Mum shouts up the stairs, and then before we can answer, the front door opens and shuts.

'What if she doesn't come back?' I ask, as the rain suddenly comes down even heavier than before and I think of Mum getting wet outside.

Daniel looks at me funny.

'Then Dad will have to come and get us,' Kelly says immediately. 'It's the law.'

I turn and stare at her.

'And just where did you get that from?'

Outside a taxi roars away up the road, obviously in the wrong gear for the pace of acceleration the driver is clearly aiming for.

'I looked it up in the library.'

Downstairs Pickle starts whining.

'You couldn't have. You're not even a member.'

'Yes, I am. I joined with Beverley.'

I put my arm around Daniel's shoulder and sit him up so that we are both now staring at our sister.

'I can even show you the library card if you like.'

For some reason I want to kiss Daniel on the top of his head, so that's what I do. But then, before I can kiss him again, he wriggles free and flops back down onto the bed.

'Well, I'm still not convinced,' I say, nudging Daniel with my knee. 'I mean, just look at the African children. And who knows they're even here?'

In the hallway Pickle starts howling.

Kelly puts her finger to her lips.

'Ssshh.'

The rain patters more violently against the open window.

'Bloody rain,' Kelly scolds no one in particular. 'This house is all rainwater and damp if you ask me.'

'Well, it can rain for as long it likes,' I say, thinking and talking at the same time. 'And for as hard as it likes, for all I care.'

'And then we could sail away in the house,' Kelly chips in. 'After we turn the whole thing upside down so that the roof becomes the hull?'

She snuggles herself in between me and Daniel in an attempt to get warm.

'And then we can sail around the world and have adventures?'

'That we can,' I say, putting my arm around Kelly's shoulder. 'And then we'll never have to come back to Nan's or Granddad's, come to that, because we'll finally be free.'

35

Da, da, da, da, da, da
De-ala-lud-da, da, da, da, da
De-ala-lud-de-a-lut-da, do, alooo…

Kelly sits up on the bed, concern written all over her face.

'Oh no.'

I want to get up to close the window, because of the rain, but can't be bothered because I'm so comfortable.

'Isn't she supposed to be at the bonfire party?'

'She got out of it because of period pain.' Kelly yawns. 'Nan put her on aspirin and sent her to bed.'

Period pain?

'Not that she's stayed in it all that much.'

I narrow my eyes and study the thin strip of orange light across the landing running along the bottom of Beverley's bedroom door. On the other side, as I well knew, Beverley would be dancing about in front of a flaming gas fire, very possibly clutching an album sleeve to her chest and imagining she was dancing with Agnetha and Anni-Frid (or possibly with Björn and Benny).

Boomamin, boomamin, boomamin, boomamin
Boomamin, boomamin, boomamin, boomamin…

'Bloody hell,' Kelly snaps. 'She's not even playing all of the songs, just the intros, and I don't know why she likes ABBA so much. They're not even that good.'

Which is certainly true.

Though the truth was that Beverley had long ago become obsessed with ABBA in a way that was a mystery to us all, and particularly to Nan, for whom popular music was considered a dangerous distraction from her sewing and Afia's homework.

'It's the devil's music,' she had warned us sternly after Afia put the Top 20 on in the kitchen that very first evening we arrived. 'You think it's harmless and fun and then, before you know it, you're on heroin and having orgies just like the Rolling Stones.'

Afia put her washing-up brush down momentarily and made the sign of the cross over her chest.

'Now turn it off,' Nan snapped, pointing a bony finger at the radio, 'and concentrate on those bloody dishes.'

Beverley had saved the money she'd made from helping out at the stables and then bought the ABBA album with the helicopter on the cover from the record shop opposite the train station.

'Isn't it great?'

She simply could not wait to show it off to us.

'No, not really.'

Or at least to wave it about in front of our faces.

'And don't you just love the white jumpsuits they're wearing?'

Another waft of the album, obviously not listening.

'Well, they look like decorators to me.'

Which they did, to me.

'Oh, what do you know about pop music, anyway? Because this is the greatest collection of songs I have ever heard.'

It was also the first album that Beverley had owned and, for the next couple of days, after it appeared in a flutter of girlish squealing (on the part of Beverley and, though she would later distance herself from her initial heartfelt hysteria, on the part of Kelly, as well), it was played again and again until we all knew the running order of Side One and Side Two, as well as where the needle jumped during *Tiger* because Pickle had got over-excited and bumped against the record player on the album's first play.

'I want them to play *My Love, My Life* at our funeral,' Beverley sobbed, as Kelly blew the dust off the stylus and Nan threaded a needle. 'Promise me you'll make sure they do that?'

Our funeral?

Perhaps they had become closer than even I had imagined.

'Of course I will,' Kelly reassured her, high emotion throttling her voice. 'And if not that then certainly *Dum Dum Diddle.*'

'Oh, please, girls. It's not even music,' I said, rolling my eyes and heading for the hallway after failing to find the pair of tweezers I was looking for in one of Nan's small vases. 'And frankly, it's nothing compared to *Aladdin Sane* or *Young Americans.*'

'You should be in the bloody garden,' Nan growled half-heartedly as she manoeuvred a frilly collar around the sewing machine. 'In fact, the whole bloody lot of you should be getting some fresh air into your lungs and following my simple and easy-to-follow house rules.'

'That David Bowie, he's just an old poof,' Kelly snorted at this point, before giving two fingers to Nan's back. 'And he's a Nazi. It said so in the papers.'

'Am I just talking to myself?' Nan spluttered in a puff of cigarette smoke. 'Or just to Pickle?'

I rolled my eyes.

'Oh, really? And what would you know about Nazism?'

'Quite a lot. We learnt about it in History.'

'Get out!'

I turned and walked away as slowly as I could.

'You and that David bloody Bowie,' Kelly sneered, following me one sulky step behind out into the hallway. 'Why don't you go and marry him if you think he's that brilliant? Which he's not.'

The door to the lounge slammed shut behind the two of us.

'Is Beverley not coming?' I asked, suddenly aware that we were alone in the hallway.

'No,' Kelly said, unlocking her crossed arms. 'She's promised to polish the horse brass and to mix some feed down at the stables.'

'My arse, she will.'

*

Another firework explodes in the night sky.

BANG!

'Are you going to the bonfire later?'

'I don't think so.'

'They're going to burn a dummy of Jim Callaghan.'

'Who are?'

'Some of the lads from the park.'

I hate those bloody idiots.

Beome, a beome, boom, boom
Beome, beome, boom, boom...

'Oh, bloody hell!'

Kelly climbs off the bed and inches her way out onto the landing and towards Beverley's bedroom.

'And she's got the volume turned up full as well.'

'What are you doing?' I ask, strangely fascinated by Kelly's silky gliding along the wallpaper.

Beside me, Daniel looks equally mesmerised.

'Sshh,' Kelly hisses.

Downstairs Pickle starts howling.

'You'll need to get in there quicker than that,' I say, trying my best to be as encouraging as possible.

'Will I, really?'

'Otherwise, Beverley's going to blow our cover and we'll all have to go out into the garden.'

Kelly narrows her eyes at me from the other side of the landing.

'I am doing the best I can,' she half-whispers, pushing her hair behind her ears. 'And there is a method to my actions, I'll have you know.'

'It's only a matter of time, so please hurry your method along to some kind of conclusion,' I say, really meaning it.

'Do you want to do it?' Kelly snaps, not whispering at all and staring right at me funny. 'Because you can, you know.'

'No, thank you.'

Blink.

Now with more narrowing of the eyes.

'Because your method looks perfectly capable of success from what I can see.'

Eoooooohhh, ohhhhh, oh, ohhhh
Oh, oh, oh, ohhhh, oh, ohhhh...

'Sorry to bite your head off,' Kelly half-whispers once again. 'It must be because of the rain and the very loud ABBA.'

Then she creeps nimbly up the landing.

'And because you clearly seem to believe that you are in some sort of camp James Bond film or something.'

'She means *Live and Let Die*,' I say, pulling Daniel back down onto the bed just as he starts to slip away. 'Or possibly *The Man with the Golden Gun*.'

Ohhhhhhh, ohhhhhhhhh...

'You see, the trouble with ABBA,' I continue, holding tightly on to Daniel as he wiggles on the edge of the bed, 'is that they lack the special qualities that make an artist like David Bowie the star that he so obviously is. Because he is, you know. Everyone says so. He's like all of The Beatles rolled into one single and vaguely bisexual package.'

Daniel tries to get away with renewed vigour, but I hold on to him by the back of his jumper.

'And I don't care what people say because he is not a drug addict or a Nazi.'

Daniel finally escapes and bounces down onto the carpet.

KAPOW!

Burning white drizzle lights up the night sky.

'You bloody philistine!'

Up the landing, for some reason, the ABBA gets even louder as the floorboards creak under Kelly's carefully placed feet.

'In your own time, sis...'

The floorboards stop creaking.

'Oh, fuck off,' Kelly hisses loudly before the floorboards start creaking again. 'You stupid, bloody Nancy boy.'

Downstairs the door to the lounge opens and Pickle finally stops howling.

'Just look at the state of you!' Nan shrieks for some reason before the door closes, then quickly opens again. 'And you can turn that bloody racket down. I can't hear the telly down here what with all that thump, thump, thump!'

The door to the lounge slams shut for the last time as, across the landing, Beverley's music finally dies down.

'Thank God for that,' I say to Daniel, as he hurriedly climbs back onto the bed, before making "Put-Ker-Putt!" noises and shooting at something above our heads (aeroplanes, probably, or possibly vampires).

'Honestly, mate, if I hear *Knowing Me, Knowing You* one more time I really will go Aladdin Sane.'

But Daniel just ignores me and keeps on shooting, narrowing his eyes so he can get the winged ones fully within his sights.

Chung de-chung de de-chung...

I roll my eyes.

'Oh boy.'

Chung, de-chung de-chung
Chung de-chung de de-chung
Chung, de-chung de-chung…

'Still, not long to wait now, matey.'

PUT-KER-PHUTT!

'Just a couple more weeks and then we'll all be back at home in time for Christmas. Just you wait and see.'

BANG-GA-GA-BANG!!

36

'Noah, Noah, come quickly!'

Afia, waving her arms about as quick as rain, leaps from the open front door and springs onto the lawn.

'Duke's wobbling on his legs and making wheezing noises.'

I am high on the swings next to a giggling Baako, blowing white breath into the cold morning air and trying to get as high as I can.

'Noah, please!'

So I'm not that interested.

'Stop your shouting and flapping, why don't you?'

Afia clutches at her head as if to stop it from exploding.

'Forgive us, Baby Jesus, for our sins and mistakes in this world and please do help me get Noah off the swing.'

In the lounge Pickle starts barking and jumping up at the window.

'Aaaaffiiiiaaaa! Come and help me with the washing!'

Without another word Afia rushes back into the house as Kelly emerges, wiping her hands on the front of her jeans and pulling a grinning Jacinto in her wake.

'Why is Afia crying?' Jacinto asks, a fat thread of snotty spit hanging from his chin.

'She's not crying, she's screaming,' Kelly says, pinching at Jacinto's snot thread, before shaking it off as quickly as she can onto the grass. 'Or howling, to be more precise.'

Jacinto sneezes.

'And just why is Afia screaming?' Kelly asks, turning to me and Baako.

I kick my feet into the patch of earth in front of the swing and push its chains out with my hands.

Baako continues swooping up and down beside me.

'I dunno.'

Jacinto drools onto the grass and grins, watching his sister as she giggles into the sky.

'Afia's just being stupid.'

Jacinto was usually grinning, regardless of what was happening in the world around him, because he was a bit mentally handicapped, or "backward" as Nan told us when we were first introduced. 'You have to speak very, very slowly and do drawings if you want him to understand you. It's because of his' – another tap at the wrinkly forehead – 'mental badness.'

'Baako, what's going on?' Kelly asks, as Afia once again races out of the house.

'It's Duke!' Afia sobs, before her sister can answer. 'He's had an ailment.'

Duke, Nan's latest dopey-eyed guard dog, part-Alsatian, part-bloodhound and a gift from the man who delivered the cloth for Nan's part-work ('Free of charge, because there's no garden at the new flat and to help keep you and your good African children safe') had been ill for weeks, wheezing, drooling and farting in front of the television. Beverley was convinced that it was because Afia was feeding her the poison that Jimmy (who lived next door and looked through the windows when we were changing for bed) had given her for the rats that lived at the bottom of the garden.

'But be careful with it, because it's powerful, dangerous stuff.'

Me and Afia killed those rats not long after Bonfire Night when it was raining and cold.

*

'They're not really rats,' Afia assured me, shaking the jar of poison, all ready to do the murderous deed, as we hovered in the mud where the rats' nest was. 'And I don't care what Nana says on the matter because it's just not true.'

'What are they then?' I ask, keen to get on with the job in hand. 'Because they certainly look like rats to me.'

'They're field mice.'

'Field mice? This isn't *Watership Down*, you know.'

I snatch the jar of white powder from Afia's hand and sprinkle the poison onto the mud behind her back before she can stop me.

'There, now at least she can't complain that we haven't done what we were supposed to do.'

'Do you think we should use all of it?' Afia asks, all mysterious and frowning as I stand back to survey my handiwork.

'No. Why?'

I wipe rainwater from my forehead and try to look nonchalant.

'It's just that there might be more of them later on, that's all.'

Afia holds out her hand.

'Here, give me the jar. I'll take care of it.'

'Well, if you're sure. Because it's dangerous stuff, you know.'

I hand her the jar as Afia smiles.

'Good. Now let's get inside. I've got a steak and kidney pudding in the oven.'

Which turned out to be delicious.

We had it with boiled potatoes, cabbage and mushroom gravy, and nobody argued that night.

*

Right now, however, Afia is all arms flapping and running round and round the swings like she is going to take off any minute.

'Afia, please!'

Which she very well might do the rate she is going.

'I am begging you, Baby Jesus,' Afia sobs, frantically crossing and re-crossing her chest, 'please forgive us all and save our dear beloved dog, Duke, from going to meet You up there, in Your sweet heaven—'

'Afia!'

'If that is indeed where you are eventually going, you sweet smelly dog.'

'Afia, please.'

I kick with my legs and the swing goes even higher than before and then it shakes a bit like it is going to topple over in that magical way that makes it so exciting whenever you get near the top.

All I want to do is laugh.

'Poor, smelly dog,' I yell, tipping my head back, suddenly giddy from all the up and the down. 'Because it's not long now before you're going to be completely dead, dead, dead.'

Five minutes later we are gathered in the lounge, just in time to watch Duke's final stumble in front of the television.

'See. I told you he wasn't well,' Afia says, crossing her arms. 'And now how do you feel?'

In the kitchen the washer-dryer starts its spin cycle.

'Shut up, Afia,' I snap, as Duke comes to a sudden stop in the middle of the carpet. 'He's going to be fine. He's just got a little food poisoning, that's all.'

'Oh, really?'

Duke howls, totters and then hits the carpet with a loud thump.

Baako puts her hand to her mouth.

'Oh my sweet Lord Jesus!'

A lamp falls to the floor.

'Afia, are you going to help me with these delicates?' Nan shouts up from the kitchen. 'Or am I doing them all by myself?'

'Be with you in a minute, Nana.'

Baako goes to kneel next to the dead dog, but Afia holds her back.

'Don't, Baako, it could be catching,' she says, as the last of the air wheezes out of Duke's lungs. 'Like myxomatosis, but for dogs.'

'Do you think he's been poisoned?' Kelly asks.

All eyes turn on Jacinto, who has a blue ribbon in his hair and a chocolate bourbon in his mouth.

'Even if unintentionally.'

Afia coughs discretely.

'What?' Jacinto asks, sugary drool falling onto his T-shirt. 'He looked at you before he fell over, Afia.'

We all turn back to the dead dog on the carpet.

'Perhaps it was the shock,' Afia mutters, leaning over the body. 'Seeing the Christmas tree all lit up might have done him in.'

'Oh, this is only going to get worse,' Kelly sighs gravely.

'Where's Mum?' I ask.

'At the Broken Coach & Horses,' Kelly says, poking Duke with the toe of her shoe. 'They're giving out Christmas puddings as prizes at a darts match, apparently.'

'Isn't she a bit above all that?'

'It's only for the fun of it, she says, and, anyway, you know how Mum likes to think ahead.'

Afia straightens the lamp.

'There,' she says cheerily, 'that's all better, now, isn't it?'

'Aaaaffiiiiaaaa!'

'Coming, Nana.'

Afia steps carefully over the dead canine body.

'I'll tell Nan,' she says, as she disappears out the door. 'And I'll do all the comforting that may be required as well.'

Kelly chews thoughtfully on her lower lip.

'Come on,' she says. 'The sooner we get on with this, the better.'

'Afia's acting weird,' I whisper to Kelly as we troop out into the garden to look for the best place to bury the body, just as Nan starts shrieking in the kitchen. 'She keeps singing to herself and smiling and then nodding for no good reason.'

Kelly picks up a broken walking stick and drives it into a flat spot on the lawn. 'I wouldn't worry about that,' she says, patting garden dust from her hands. 'She's just been at Nan's secret gin, that's all.'

'But she's not even old enough to drink!'

'Yes, I know. But it does get so boring in the kitchen, what with all the cooking and washing-up and the drying of the dishes. Now come on, *National Velvet*'s starting on ITV soon and Nan's only going to stay upset about Duke and the washing for so long.'

'Fair enough.'

And we race each other back into the house as quickly as we can.

37

'Oh, this is just too awful for good Christian words.'

In the lounge, Nan prods Duke's body with a slippered foot and wipes warm Daz down the front of her housecoat.

'It's almost as if he waited until I'd finished paying for the carpet, as well.'

'Dead, Nana, no doubt about it,' Afia says, as Nan gingerly bends down and presses her head against Duke's chest. 'Just look at the way his tongue is hanging out.'

'What a shocking way to go. And it's all so very mysterious.'

We all stare down at the body.

'Well, don't just stand there,' Nan snaps. 'Get it bloody well buried so I can put the washing out and start a new part-order.'

Baako appears in the doorway, holding an old potato sack.

'Don't worry. I've wiped it with some disinfectant,' she says before anyone can say anything.

Afia narrows her eyes at her.

'Have you really?'

Baako spreads the sack out next to the body.

'Well, with some Fairy, anyway.'

'Oh, for heaven's sake,' Nan shrieks, shaking her curlers at the two African sisters. 'It's a dead animal – God rest his poor canine soul – not the newborn Baby Jesus. Now, just get on with it!'

'Yes, Nana,' the two girls reply, almost in unison.

And with that, we roll Duke onto the sack and then part-carry and part-drag him out into the hallway, while Nan finally gets to work on her pile of two hundred little girl party dresses.

'And make sure you don't get any hairs on any of my satin, either,' Nan warns, before closing the door to keep the heat in. 'They're a special order for Freemans.'

In the hallway I take hold of the two front corners of the sack, while Afia and Kelly grasp the two back corners and Baako leads us out into the garden, clutching a small posy of flowers picked from the kitchen's window box.

'Make this quick, Baako, please,' Kelly snaps, as we drag Duke's body across the grass. 'My film's starting in a minute.'

'And I've got to get Nan's coloured wash out and the chicken carved,' Afia adds, wiping sweat from her forehead. 'And it's a big bird, I'm telling you. Heavy.'

'Where's Beverley?' I ask, grateful for the short break in the dead dog-carrying.

'Having a bath,' Kelly mutters ruefully. 'Her new Avon order came today.'

For a second we all look up at the bathroom window and listen to Beverley warbling *Dancing Queen* in the bath.

'Well, come on then, Baako, you stupid girl,' Afia snaps as soon as our moment of yearning is over. 'We haven't got all day.'

'OK, Afia. No need to shout,' Baako pouts, taking out a little bible from her pocket as we pick up the body once more and carry it to its designed burial spot.

'Oh dear God…'

'We have to do these things right,' Baako continues, in that even, solemn tone of hers that drove the rest of us mad. 'It's what Mum and Dad would want us to do.'

'Baako!' Afia shouts, waving her arms about for no good effect (though her frustration is justified). 'Please do think of the chicken!'

Inside the house, someone starts banging on a window.

'What's that?' Kelly asks, momentarily startled.

In the lounge, Jacinto's face is pressed up against the glass.

'Just look at him, the jammy bastard,' Kelly complains bitterly. 'And I bet she's turned the fire up full, as well.'

A wrinkly hand reaches around Jacinto's chest and pulls him in and away from the nets.

'Dear Lord above, who knows and sees all and who watches over us no matter what we do, please look down on us today as we come to You as Your faithful and honest servants and children,' Baako intones, trying to follow the tiny holy words on the pages of her bible as they blow about in the wind. 'For we need Your grace and love in this, our hour of sadness and loss—'

'Do please think of the chicken, Baako!'

I try my best to keep Duke's dead fat body from slipping to the ground, though it's hard because of the weight and the greasy sackcloth which keeps sliding through my fingers.

'Baako, faster!' Afia squeals. 'I am begging you, in the name of the roasting poultry!'

'And so,' Baako adds quickly, snapping the bible shut, 'we bury Duke, our much-loved companion from the world of dog, and ask you, Dear Lord, to take care of him as he runs to You, all the way up in heaven.'

'And amen to that,' Kelly murmurs, letting go of her corner of the sack. 'He was hurting my wrist, as well as chipping my nail varnish.'

And then Baako tosses her posy into the grave and we roll Duke into the hole in the ground, where he falls all crooked and bent in one corner.

The muffled whirling of the sewing machine in the lounge comes to an ominous halt.

'Afia! What about that succulent bird?'

Then the sewing machine starts up again.

'You don't mind covering him up, do you?' Afia (sort of) asks, before running back towards the house. 'After all, I did help with the carrying.'

Kelly picks up a spade.

'And I bet she doesn't wash her hands before she bastes that chicken,' she says, shovelling earth into the hole. 'The dirty cow.'

I pick up the other spade and join her in her soil-tossing.

'Amen to that, sister.'

And another animal is put to rest in Nan's pet cemetery.

'Now speed up your shovelling.'

*

Nobody knew how many dogs were buried in the garden, not even Nan, truth be told.

Or cats, come to that.

Beverley's first Alsatian, Manchester, which used to stand about looking straight ahead, went first, buried next to the birdbath, followed by Bonny, who used to be Nan's guard dog, before going a bit blind and nearly being put down.

'She's keeping a sad eye over us even now,' Beverley had sobbed, before checking her watch to make sure she wasn't late for the stables, as Bonny's burial came to an end one grim Saturday in March. 'And she always will be, as long as there is a bump here on the lawn.'

After that, little moulds of earth would spring up every year or so, as more pets went under the roses. Then, after Beverley's one and only rabbit got run over by a milk float, that went under the lawn as well, buried in a shoebox.

Until it was Duke's turn to be laid to rest in the pet cemetery.

'It's only right to bury each and every one properly,' Nan pronounces later after Baako has laid some fresh flowers on top of Duke's grave. 'And it's good for the garden as well, as it makes the soil fertile and rich because of all the bones.'

Behind Nan's back, Afia makes a sort of vomiting face.

'Now, come on, you two,' Nan continues, losing a slipper as she makes her way back towards the house. 'There's fresh ironing to do and I'm not doing it all on my own.'

'Be with you in a minute, Nana,' Afia sing-songs, grabbing my arm to stop me from walking away. 'We just need to pat down the earth first.'

She digs her nails deep into my flesh and puts a finger to her lips.

'Well, pat faster then.'

'I used the rat poison,' Afia says quickly, as soon as Nan has disappeared back into the house, 'to put him out of his misery.'

'What misery?'

'The misery of living with her.'

She nods towards the open front door.

'And now he's free and with Baby Jesus.'

'Oh, dear Lord.'

'Our one and only God—'

'That's canine murder, that is.'

'It's for the best. She used to kick him when he was crying.'

'But still…'

I shake myself free from Afia's painful grasp.

'How much is left?' I ask, rubbing my arm.

'Enough to kill two fully-grown men or three women.'

My mind suddenly goes blank, like it doesn't want to think anymore, in case it comes up with something really bad that it won't be able to put back again once it's out in the open.

'Come on,' I say at last, as Afia starts giggling into the wind.

'You've got socks to pair.'

38

'Just look at the state of this. It's not right.'

Come Saturday morning, Nan is in the kitchen, leaning on the chest freezer and peering at a till receipt as it winds away from her trembling hand down towards the lino.

'You need to get a job, you do,' Nan says, waving the receipt at me over the top of a stack of Safeway carrier bags. 'Even if it's only part-time and not very rewarding – something like delivering papers or cleaning out the horses with Beverley.'

'Get a what?'

'A bloody job,' Nan coughs, phlegm spluttering everywhere. 'You need to start earning because of all your eating.'

She pops a fresh cigarette into her mouth.

'I mean, can't you see the financial evidence right here, in my good Christian hand?'

More waving of the supermarket receipt.

'And look at how long it is – Christmas shopping or not.'

She rolls the cigarette lazily from one side of her mouth to the other.

'And where do you put all the custard creams, that's what I want to know—'

'It's just with my tea. I don't think—'

'Oh, don't you worry,' Nan sighs kindly. 'Because I've seen it all before.'

She searches in the pocket of her housecoat for a lighter that works.

'Michael and Brian were the same when they were your age.'

'Did they have growing pains too?'

'No, they were greedy little pigs,' Nan snaps, retrieving a box of matches tied with a pink ribbon from her pocket. 'Human dustbins, they were, never satisfied with three square meals and a warm cocoa before bedtime.'

Behind her, Afia trudges into the kitchen with the last of the shopping, her ears alert to our conversation.

'And you can keep your mind on your work,' Nan snaps, puffing a quick cloud of smoke in Afia's direction as she passes, 'rather than listening to other people's legitimate discussions.'

Afia starts opening and closing cupboards for no good reason.

'He eats like a pig, Nana, and he needs to pay for his food,' she says, nodding and grinning maliciously at me. 'We just can't keep up with all the consumption.'

Nan narrows her eyes and drills holes into the small of Afia's back, before shuffling herself out of the kitchen. 'Get yourself a job after Christmas is out the way,' she says over her shoulder, the till receipt trailing behind her up the hallway, 'and start paying your way or bloody well get out.'

'She's onto you, man.' Afia giggles, turning to point at me once the coast is clear. 'And now she's got you good and proper – work for Noah, money for Afia.'

I want to argue, or at least to put up some semblance of an argument, but what she is saying is true, as recently all that I could think about was food and no matter how much I ate (or when), nothing seemed to satisfy my constant appetite.

'Where is it?' I ask, stopping Afia's giggling in an instant.

'Where's what?'

'You know what.'

For a moment it looks like Afia is going to put up a fight, but then she frowns, wipes her hands on a tea towel and opens the cupboard under the sink.

'You tell no one, man,' she says, reaching deep into the back of the cupboard. 'It's our secret and not a word, otherwise, Christmas will be ruined good and proper. And New Year along with it.'

She pulls out the familiar jar, filled halfway with sparkling white power.

'Promise?'

She holds out the jar.

'Well, do you?'

I reach for the jar, but at the last minute, Afia snatches it back.

'Promise me, Noah.'

'I promise,' I say, meaning every syllable. 'It will be our special Christmas secret.'

'And not a word, not to anyone.'

'Not a word.'

Afia finally hands over the jar.

'Amen to that, then.'

And the jar of poison is mine.

*

'Have you eaten any of these chips?'

I'm standing with Kelly in the middle of the road after a quick run to the fish and chip shop, but I'm not really here.

'Well, did you?'

Instead, in my mind, it's still yesterday afternoon and I'm hiding a jar of white powder under my bed as Afia keeps a look-out on the stairs.

'Because it looks like you've got more than I have.'

And right now my thoughts are on other, more important, things than Kelly (who is being even more annoying than usual).

'Of course I haven't.'

Which is a lie.

'And anyway, that's just a stupid thing to say. Why would I want your chips when I've got my own?'

I defiantly toss a hot chip into my mouth.

'Where's Mum?'

It looks like it might rain any minute.

'She's not back yet.'

Thunder rumbles lazily in the distance.

'But she's been gone for hours.'

Kelly lifts her bag of chips to her face, briefly closes her eyes and inhales deeply.

'I know that, stupid, but according to the latest intelligence reports I have received she is looking at carpet pattern and curtain combinations on the High Street.'

All of a sudden any thoughts I have about white powder are gone and it's just me and Kelly arguing about chips and interior furnishings in the middle of the road.

A rumble of thunder explodes closer than before.

'You liar. Where is she really?'

And for the first time, I notice that Kelly is wearing a grey vest with Number 18 on the front (even though she isn't eighteen, it's not even slightly warm and the vest is an old one of mine) as well as a new pair of pink flip-flops.

And just where did she get those from?

'Well?'

It finally starts to rain.

'Don't speak to me like that,' Kelly snaps, waving her bag of chips at me. 'It's not nice, you know, and I am not lying.'

She twirls a tightly knotted pigtail in her free hand and then tilts her head as a drop of rain splats on her forehead.

'According to my sources, Mum will also be staying at a friend's house until tomorrow,' Kelly continues, before popping a steaming chip into her mouth. 'However, I have heard no reports as to who that friend is, though I do know it is a He and not a She and that Mum met him while working at the petrol station.'

'That's just another big fat lie, that is.'

A second twirl of the tightly knotted pigtail.

'Do you think so?'

'Yes, I do, actually.'

I suddenly don't want my chips, which are soaked in salty vinegar anyway (though I continue eating them regardless).

'A deceit of mine or hers? Which do you think it is?' Kelly asks, all blank and annoying and clearly under Beverley's evil influence in some way, even though Beverley is not even here.

Something is very wrong.

'Hers, stupid.'

Kelly pokes her hair behind her ears.

'Don't think I don't know what you and Afia have been up to,' she says, calculating and fishing and wilfully ignoring my earlier question. 'What with all your whispering and giggling in the kitchen when you think no one is around.'

I look her straight in the eye and scrunch up my chip paper with the last of my chips still inside.

Which I don't care about.

'You know nothing.'

Kelly narrows her eyes like she is genuinely angry.

'Oh, I know everything, and if Nan finds out, you'll be in big trouble and you can have no doubt on that front.'

'If she finds out what?' I give Kelly one of my hard looks and blow rainwater off the tip of my nose. 'Because now you're just bluffing like the big fat bluffer you are.'

'I most certainly am not!'

'You most certainly ruddy well are.'

Kelly wants to spook me.

I can tell.

Just so that I blurt something out.

But I'm not going to.

'And anyway, you're the one that's a big fat bluffer, not me.'

Which is completely untrue, as I am not even remotely overweight.

'Now you're just trying to turn my words against me, you horrible cow, and that's my T-shirt you're wearing,' I say, sucking in my stomach.

237

Kelly's eyes twitch.

'I know far more than you think I do and I have no need to turn your words against you because you're nothing but a stupid fool and an idiot.'

She puts her free hand on her hip.

'And besides, this is a vest and not a T-shirt, and it looks better on me than it does on you because I've got a better figure than you have.'

She suddenly takes hold of my hand, sniffs it and then leans forward and smells all over my neck and head like she's some great detective or something (though she has been reading a lot of Sherlock Holmes lately, so she could be on to something here).

'Knock it off, why don't you, you bloody cow!'

I try to push her off, but she's got a tight grip and is much stronger than she looks.

'You've had a steak and kidney pie as well as the chips!' Kelly squeals, finally letting go of my arm. 'And just you wait until Nan finds out about that!'

I'm suddenly spooked by her quick (if partial) deduction of what I've been up to at the fish and chip shop, but I think I'm covering it pretty well.

'It was only a pie while I waited for the chips and because they let me have it for half-price because it fell on the floor.'

'Did they really?'

'Yes, they did, and it's not like it's a three-course meal or anything.'

'Oh, Nan's not that naive where food is concerned and she'll be able to tell if you've spoilt your appetite before dinner.'

Which could be a major offence, especially if it happens at the weekend.

'Well, it's a bit of luck dinner's not for another hour then, so that I can run around the garden and work up a proper appetite if I have to.'

Kelly frowns, clearly not believing a word of it.

'I suppose so,' she says flatly, before crushing her chip paper into a greasy ball and crossing her wet arms. 'Though you're going to have to do a lot of running and you're going to get very wet if you do so.'

She turns and walks through the gate into the garden, her flip-flops making sucking noises on the wet concrete as she goes.

'Anyway, you missed all the excitement while you were away doing all your pathetic pie-stuffing.'

I follow her through the gate, letting it swing shut behind me (which we're not allowed to do, even if it is raining).

'Much more exciting, indeed.'

Kelly suddenly turns and blocks my path.

'Dad's coming,' she squeals, her face lighting up. 'And he's on his way already.'

Quick swipe of rainwater from her face.

'And I even know when he's going to be here.'

Then she grins, obviously having looked forward to this moment for a very long time.

'He phoned earlier. I took the call and Nan was watching, trying to listen to what Dad was saying, but she couldn't and I was like, "Yeah," and, "OK," and, "No," and then I handed the phone to Nan and she laughed and said, "That will be lovely," and, "Goodbye," in that stupid pretend voice of hers and told me that Dad was coming round next Saturday for tea.'

She takes a deep breath and grabs hold of my arms.

'And he says he's got news!'

'Does she know what the news is?'

She being Nan, obviously.

'No, I don't think so. He said it to me and not to her.'

Then she looks away, momentarily confused.

'Or at least I think he didn't say anything to her about his news, though he could have, I suppose, after he spoke to me, now I come to think about it—'

'Oh, who cares?'

I take hold of Kelly's waist and she grips my elbows and we bounce up and down, hugging each other in the rain.

In the house Pickle jumps up at the window and gets caught in the net curtains.

'This is it,' I say, as Pickle goes into a frenzy of barking and scratching. 'Because now Dad's finished arguing with Mum and we can all go home.'

I don't know if that is strictly true or where home is anymore, come to that, as we had no home, strictly speaking, and Kelly must have realised that as well, but she doesn't say anything (probably because she wants it to be true just as much as I do). Instead, all she does is keep bouncing up and down with me getting wet in the rain.

'I know, and isn't it lovely?'

And even though Kelly smells of salt and vinegar and damp chip paper I give her a big kiss and we hug and dance and don't care if Nan can or can't see us from the lounge.

39

The last time I saw Dad (before he unexpectedly and drunkenly re-entered our lives on the night of the 2001 General Election, waving a bottle of champagne and pronouncing, 'William Hague will see off that bloody fraud Tony Blair, just you wait and see') was just before New Year's Day 1977.

Dad had a bright yellow Allegro back then.

'Be not afeared of the colour and be assured that it will grow on you as it did on me, eventually.'

Dad truly loved that car.

'And it has outstanding rust protection for such a curiously proportioned vehicle.'

When I was little Dad had a big black Ford Zephyr that smelt of soap and leather and which would slide me and Kelly, giggling and terrified, across its slippy-shiny front seats every time Dad turned the wheel.

'Don't you worry about the smell, you two.'

Quick winding-down of the driver's window.

'It's just a little' – cough – 'water on the' – cough – 'engine, that's all. Nothing to worry about.'

Daniel had not been born then and Mum did everything she could not to get into "The Hearse", as she called the Zephyr, not until after Daniel's birth anyway – a decision that would prove to be more than a little precipitous after "The Hearse" turned over on an ice-covered autobahn just outside Bonn, nearly killing my unborn brother in the process.

I grazed my arm that night and Kelly bruised her forehead.

'But it could have been a lot worse if you think about it.'

Dad, obviously, always the optimist.

'And how, exactly, could it have been "a lot worse"?'

Even if Mum was a little more sceptical.

To this day Kelly has a small scar from that night, just in front of her right ear. Sometimes she tells the story of how she pulled me from the car through the shattered back window then sat with me until a German fire engine arrived, and the firemen cut Mum and Dad free from the slowly burning wreckage in front of us.

'*Es wird alles gut werden.*'

After that Dad was never drunk at the wheel ever again.

Sort of.

'Daniel's was a difficult pregnancy in many ways,' Mum would remark later to Mad Aunt Joan, after pondering the scars left from a myriad of stitches on her left knee, 'and I'm happy to say my last if I'm being completely honest with you.'

Dad had a vasectomy not long after.

'Just to be on the safe side.'

And much to Mum's grim-faced satisfaction.

Before "The Hearse" we had a bright blue Volkswagen 1600, which rattled as if it was going to explode any minute (even when idling) and which was incapable of doing more than a spluttering eighty miles an hour.

That was when we were living in Münster and, though the Volkswagen only lasted one winter, during that time we quickly got used to scooping out rainwater from its footwells every Saturday morning before venturing out on one of our regular expeditions into the West German countryside.

'It's important to make the most of the world around us,' Mum would declare breezily as we sleepily piled out of the house, zipped up and ready for another fresh adventure.

'Even if the particular part of the world happens to be so very Germanic.'

My parents' desire to enjoy my father's various postings in West

Germany was certainly sincere enough, even if their grasp of the actual language and local customs mainly consisted of energetic pointing, the odd faltering waving of a textbook (whenever the pointing became too confusing) and the regular and over-amplified use of the word "*Ja!*" at every opportunity.

Then, one day, the 1600 exploded on a petrol station forecourt in Minden and, two weeks later, "The Hearse" entered our lives.

'On balance and after due consideration,' Dad confided to us years later at Granddad's funeral, 'I would have to say that Zephyr was the best car I have ever owned. When it went to the scrappers it was the end of an era, no matter what your mother says.'

For a second his voice faltered.

'Though, that said, it did cost a fortune,' he continued sadly, as he stared down at his loafers, 'and after the accident it was more or less a total write-off, to be honest.'

'I imagine that must be a very painful recollection,' I said, delicately touching his arm to underline my attempt at empathy. 'And have you given any thought as to what you might replace the Rover with when the time comes?'

'Oh, that's just another sad and upsetting loss,' Dad answered, his voice fading away. 'And I can't imagine it's going to be the last one either, motoring or otherwise.'

*

It started snowing on Saturday, just after lunch.

'Oh my God! Oh my God! Oh my God!'

Me and Kelly are in the kitchen when the first fat flakes blow haphazardly against the window.

'Snow!'

Afia is baking cakes and sniffing chops, while Kelly is helping her by frowning and weighing self-raising flour.

I have my head pressed against the side of the fridge-freezer, listening to its motor.

Mmmmmmmmmm, brrrrr, mmmmmmmm…

It had been threatening to snow on and off for days and now, at long last, here it was.

'This is a good sign,' Afia announces excitedly, taking a break from her baking to lean out of the window and catch some of the white snowflakes on her tongue. 'Because it is a true and honest declaration of God's love and His hopes for all of us during this proper festive season.'

'Well, it's that and the Arctic front moving in from Russia,' Kelly adds, before joining Afia in her snow-tasting. 'Yum, yum.'

Away from the Arctic front (and Moscow's no doubt cunning intervention in the workings of British domestic life), the telephone had been ringing all day with calls from excited relatives confirming they would be coming to Dad's welcome party, motorway closures permitting, of course.

'This is going to be the best family get-together ever!'

The house had been busy all week with the sound of vacuuming and sweeping and of Pickle barking and squeaking every time he got trod on, which he did often.

'Oh, get out the way, you silly dog.'

Even I was doing my bit, mopping the kitchen and taking out the rubbish (though that soon got to be very boring), while Afia and Kelly studied cake recipes and argued about which jelly to use in the trifle.

Mmmmmmmmmm, brrrrr, mmmmmmmm…

'What's that smell?' Kelly asks, closing the window and sniffing the air.

'Disinfectant,' I say, lifting my head from the fridge-freezer. 'Nan's doing the hall carpets. So make sure you've got your slippers on, otherwise you'll only get your socks wet.'

'You're just a total idiot, you are,' Kelly mutters, wiping her hands on a damp tea towel. 'And it's unhygienic to lick white goods, you know.'

'I am not licking. I am listening.'

'To what?'

'To this...'

Kelly presses her head to the other side of the fridge-freezer's cold, enamelled surface.

'I can't hear anything,' she says, straining to hear (anything at all), 'apart from a low and boring sort of hum.'

'I know. It's nice, though, isn't it?'

Outside a van beeps its horn.

'And what the bloody hell is that?' Afia asks with a start.

Kelly peels herself away from the fridge-freezer.

'Because it sounds very mysterious to me.'

'My new material delivery is here,' Nan shouts up the hallway. 'So cut your chattering, go bring it in and watch you don't get any snow on the satin.'

I check my hair in the mirrored glass of the window.

'I'm meeting up with some of the lads from the park later—'

'I thought you hated those idiots?' Kelly asks, narrowing her eyes at me. 'Or have you changed your mind for no good reason whatsoever?'

'I don't hate them at all, and yes, I have,' I say, more to myself than to her, 'because they're funny and know how to have a decent kick-about and sometimes that is all that matters.'

'A kick-about in this weather? Have you lost your stupid boy mind?'

'It's just a bit of snow...'

More urgent beeping on the part of the van.

'Afia!'

'And what makes you think we're even that bothered about your ruddy kick-about?' Kelly asks, before coming behind me to touch up her hair in the glass. 'Because we're not, you know, not even slightly.'

Outside, the driver leans out the van window and then yells as loud as he can, 'Come on, love. The heater's melting our legs off in here!'

'I think they're becoming a mite impatient,' Kelly says, wetting a curl as Afia disappears at speed up the hallway.

'Mite?'

'It means a "little bit".'

'I'm not joking about the melting legs, either,' the van driver continues as Afia races out the front door and slips on the garden path. 'And the heater smells of melted plastic – which is probably poisonous – so hurry up!'

'Afia! What's taking so long, you stupid girl?' Nan shrieks, before collapsing into a fit of nicotine-infused spluttering. 'I mean, can't you hear the agitation in his voice?'

I pull on my new leather jacket (a suspiciously early and expensive Christmas present from Mum) and zip it up all the way.

'I might be out until The News is on,' I say as casually as I can, 'as some of us have some serious goal-scoring to attend to.'

Then I kiss Kelly on the cheek, for some reason.

'Bye.'

Kelly narrows her eyes even more.

'Well, don't start drinking with those louts in between any goal-scoring,' she says coolly as I dart up the hallway. 'After all, you know how sick you get if you even have a taste of alcohol.'

'You're the one that's sick – sick in the head,' I say as cleverly as I can, though not so loud that Nan might hear and then stop me from going out. 'And besides, it's only a kick-about, not some bloody party.'

'Oh, shut up with all your swearing, will you?' Afia snaps, clutching a cellophane ball of blue satin to her chest as we pass on the garden path. 'And don't come back drunk.'

Behind her, the material delivery van speeds away up the road in a cloud of snow and exhaust smoke.

'Just what is it with you girls and your obsessions with alcohol?'

I spin round so that I am running up the slippery white path backwards, no longer caring who can hear me now that I am free.

'Because I will not be coming back even slightly drunk, no matter what does or does not happen, and you are all going to be proved wrong on that front, just you wait and see!'

40

'Wake up, you stinky, smelly bastard.'

I open my eyes and suddenly everything is cold, bright and very, very wrong.

'Hello?'

Beverley and Kelly are standing at the foot of my bed, wearing white jodhpurs, red riding jackets and black riding hats.

'Can you hear me?' Kelly snaps, her face a picture of icy disdain. 'Or am I talking only to myself and Beverley?'

Something strange has happened between scoring a goal at the bottom of the park in a frenzy of snowy arm-waving and whatever is happening right now.

'What's going on?' I ask, my voice coming out all crackly and hoarse.

'Got a bit of a sore head, have we?' Kelly asks, trying not to laugh.

Next to her, Beverley does her best to stifle a smirk.

'A little bit of a migraine, perhaps?'

It is all almost demonic, like something out of a Hammer horror film (if not quite so gory).

'Oh my God.'

All that Beverley and Kelly need is to be holding hands and wearing slightly more creepy outfits (matching pink and blue jumpsuits perhaps or bloodied wedding dresses) and the grisly scene would be complete.

BRIDE OF FRANKENSTEIN GOES RIDING
(WITH HER STUPID FRIEND)

Beverley puts a hand to her mouth.

'You smell terrible,' she says, looking like she is going to be sick any minute. 'And I do believe that you might have had an accident, if you get my drift.'

I peel my head from the pillow.

'I don't feel well.'

Kelly smacks at the duvet with a riding crop she has cunningly hidden behind her back and then taps it in the palm of her hand.

'It's a bit of luck Nan hasn't found you like this or she would have made you come down to the paddock with us as a punishment.'

She whips the bed again, narrowly missing my arm.

'That bloody horse—'

'He is not "that bloody horse",' Beverley snaps, nostrils flaring. 'He is my darling Minstrel and he is beautiful.'

She straightens her riding hat.

'Very beautiful, in fact, and sleek with it.'

I rest my head back on the pillow and close my eyes.

'Oh, dear Lord.'

*

Minstrel had been Beverley's "special present" for her tenth birthday, after she had started her *Famous Five* phase, hanging about the paddocks and hawking sugar cubes in exchange for equine affection. The colt was Beverley's dream come true, almost literally, apart from the work involved in actually keeping the thing, of course.

'Minstrel is quite simply a pony that is my very own,' was how she had put it after being introduced to Minstrel by a slightly nervous Nan, doing her best to avoid piles of horse shit as she tottered about the stables in her slippers. 'And I love him more than Marc Bolan and Donny Osmond put together.'

'We'll have none of that T. Rex talk here, thank you,' Nan snaps, slipping on the stable's cobblestones. 'It turns young girls' thoughts to more... illegitimate... pleasures.'

Since then Minstrel had become a slightly wobbly distraction for whenever The Bay City Rollers were out of the country, or the housework needed doing, and a growing drain on Nan's increasingly stretched finances.

The sewing machine had never been busier.

'It's like being in *Black Beauty*,' Beverley gushed not long afterwards to Kelly (who had never really been the horsy type), as Nan unfolded notes from her special purse with the small padlock. 'When I'm on Minstrel I can almost hear the theme music in my head.'

'But what about the, you know, smell?' Kelly asked, wrinkling her nose. 'Because it is quite disgusting.'

'Oh, I let Tony take care of all the clearing-out and rubbing.'

'That bloody Irish boy and his jailbird father,' Nan coughed, snapping her purse shut. 'They're nothing but trouble, the ruddy pair of them.'

Beverley rolled her eyes and immediately looked around to make sure no one could hear their conversation.

'Oh, Grandmother, really.'

Apart from being "that bloody Irish boy", Tony was sharp-eyed, easy to laughter and proud of his missing front tooth, which he had lost in a brawl outside Woolworths the previous summer.

'From fighting over the Pick 'n' Mix is what I heard,' Nan muttered ruefully, not bothering to lower her voice. 'He's a bad 'un, and his father has littered many children all over the county, so be warned, my girl.'

Tony passed the house each morning on his way to his manure-tossing, an unlit cigarette behind one ear and with a whistling tune on his lips.

'Because it's better to follow a song than the word of the governor.'

And whenever he strolled by, Beverley was usually waiting, either sitting beside the fence or leaning out the kitchen window, ready to smile and catch his eye.

'Good morning, Beverley, my sweet darlin".'

'Good morning, Tony, you cheeky sod.'

From the first time he flashed Beverley his gappy grin, she was smitten and, judging by Kelly's violent blushing whenever Tony's name was mentioned, she wasn't the only one.

*

'It's alright,' Beverley coos lugubriously, as I raise my head once more from the pillow. 'Nan thinks you've got food poisoning.'

She nods in the direction of the open door.

'I told her you had ingested something that didn't quite agree with you.'

'You told her what?'

For the first time, it fully registers in my brain that beneath the duvet I am naked.

'What are you talking about?'

'You don't remember how you got up here, do you, underage booze boy?' Kelly asks, a malicious smile on her lips. 'Or what happened when you got back from the park?'

I can't think straight.

'Oh no...'

I feel like I'm about to be sick.

'Or indeed what occurred at the garden gate.'

I try to swallow, but my mouth is too dry, so instead all I do is pull the duvet even more tightly around my neck and momentarily close my eyes to the horror unfolding around me.

'No,' I mew.

'We carried you up here!' Kelly proclaims triumphantly, startling my eyes open and pointing at Beverley with her riding crop. 'Step by wobbly bloody step.'

I look at Beverley, who is smiling.

'Oh yes,' she says flatly. 'I had hold of your arms.'

'And I had your feet,' Kelly adds with an unnecessary flourish. 'Don't you remember trying to get in through the back window?'

Beverley bites her lip and a vague recollection of Pickle barking as girlish arms pulled me down from the window re-surfaces in my brain. 'I thought it was a dream,' I croak, gripping the duvet even tighter, 'or a very bad and extremely painful hallucination of some kind.'

'No dream, you drunken pig. We saved your life. You could have been concussed, you know, if you had slipped trying to break back into the house, or you could have choked on your own vomit.'

For a second nobody speaks as I try to wrap myself in the duvet which Kelly begins slowly pulling from my body.

'What do you want?'

'An ounce of tobacco, as a present for Tony,' Beverley says carefully, pausing briefly in her duvet-pulling so that the demand, and the potential consequences of it being ignored, can fully sink in. 'And some cigarette papers, if you don't mind.'

'And just where am I supposed to get either tobacco or cigarette papers?'

'From your stupid new park friends, of course.'

A quick yank of the duvet.

'Alright!' I snap, pulling the duvet out of her hand. 'But I want the money upfront.'

'You have a deal!'

Kelly drops a handful of coins onto the bed. 'By the weekend would be nice,' she coos, tracing her riding crop along the duvet towards my head. 'And now, if you would excuse us, we have a rather important appointment with a horse, a saddle and a two-bar fence.'

And with that the two equine conspirators troop triumphantly out the room, leaving me with a headache and what is left of my dignity.

'A bloody deal, indeed.'

41

'Do you want something to eat? A slice of pizza, perhaps, or a cheese roll?'

'No, thank you.'

I am in the lounge on the phone and Afia has her head shoved round the door.

'Are you sure? The rolls are nice and crusty and they've got that just-from-the-bakery smell.'

Nan is snoring under a blanket on the sofa, her false teeth rattling in her open mouth.

'Or I could grill you some bacon.'

Afia drops her voice to a whisper.

'I don't think she' – Nan, obviously – 'even knows it's in the fridge.'

'Afia, please...'

I put my hand over the telephone receiver.

'No bacon for me, thank you. I find bacon sandwiches a bit greasy at the best of times.'

'There's also some fresh fruit. You could have a banana if you want. Bananas are filling and they're good for you. Monkeys like bananas.'

At the other end of the line, and somewhere near a whining horse, Kelly giggles, obviously in no great rush to return to the phone.

'No bananas, thank you. They make me sleepy.'

'Please yourself. They're only going brown anyway.'

I move the telephone receiver to my other ear.

'I could get you an orange if you like. Or a pear—'

'I am actually on the phone here...'

Afia flaps a J-cloth over her shoulder.

'Well, don't be too long, if you don't mind. I need to phone for a taxi to take her' – Nan again – 'to her whist drive once she wakes up.'

'I'm back,' Kelly squeals loudly in my ear. 'And sorry about the delay, but Minstrel needed a very thorough rub-down.'

'Kelly, I'm running out of time...'

I don't mean to sound so demanding, not really, and the second the words leave my mouth I regret not so much the words themselves but rather the snotty tone they are wrapped in.

'Do we know what time?' I ask, as calmly as I can, one careful eye on Nan as she snorts and turns on the sofa. 'Or do we even have an estimate as to what the time it is likely to be?'

And it's not even Kelly that I'm annoyed with.

Which only makes things worse.

'What time, exactly?' Kelly asks sweetly.

And now it's my sister's turn to be snotty.

'Has Mum told you the arrival time?'

Afia rolls her eyes and disappears from the doorway.

'Well, nothing has been confirmed. So I can only go on what I've heard...'

'Of course...'

'And what exactly is that supposed to mean?'

It is always important to remain absolutely calm whenever Kelly gets like this.

'What do you mean?'

'Because either you want to know or you don't.'

'I do, I really and honestly do. So please carry on telling me whatever it is that you are going to tell me. I'm sorry.'

'It's just that all I get is complaints about the so-called gossiping and the trunking and it's just not ruddy fair when all I'm trying to do is help.'

'I said I'm sorry.'

Jacinto walks into the lounge balancing a sausage on a plate and then, seeing Nan on the sofa, turns around and walks straight out again.

'Afia!'

'Alright then…'

Baako shoves her head around the door, pokes her tongue out at Nan and then disappears back into the hallway.

'Mum said something about three o'clock,' Kelly continues, clearly in no mood to be rushed. 'Though I couldn't work out if she meant Dad is coming to the house at three or that we are going to be eating at three because Minstrel was making a noise and Beverley was in a bit of a mood.'

Kelly's voice drops to the level of a whisper.

'Plus, I think she was a little bit distracted by Tony when I was speaking to her—'

'What did you say?' Beverley immediately asks in the background. 'Because I heard that.'

Which doesn't make any sense at all.

'Anyway,' Kelly continues, raising her voice again, 'three o'clock is, I would say, the safest time to have everything set up and ready.'

'Three sounds like a weird time to eat to me.'

'Do you think?'

'That must be the time that Dad gets into the station – if he is coming by train instead of driving – rather than when we're going to be sitting down for the grub.'

'"The grub"?'

I close my eyes and take a very, very deep breath.

'Anyway, I'll speak to Afia and get everything organised and we'll set up the recon for one.'

It is because of Dad that I am talking like this.

'Or possibly for two.'

Kelly, however, could not be less impressed with my assured use of such military terminology and organisational skills if she tried.

'Set up the what for when?'

'The look-out and the walkie-talkies for one or two,' I say quickly, as Afia re-appears, brandishing a very large and extremely brown banana.

'Oh,' Kelly says. 'Understood, I think.'

'Otherwise, we won't be ready for when he does get here. And is there any news on what time Mum is arriving?'

'No. She said she'll be back as soon as she can get away from the petrol station.'

That bloody petrol station.

Afia peels the banana and starts eating it.

'Alright then,' Kelly sing-songs, before continuing as sweetly as she can. 'And did you manage to get the tobacco we ordered?'

*

Two days later I am up a tree on Church Lane with a pair of binoculars around my neck and a walkie-talkie in my hand.

'I've got some bad news,' Kelly squawks on the walkie-talkie.

'You're supposed to say "over",' I say, jamming my thumb on the Talk button. 'Over.'

Kelly's voice comes back even more distorted than before. 'I didn't want to say anything earlier,' she squeals, 'because I knew you'd get upset. Over.'

'I don't get upset at things. Over.'

'Yes, you do. You can get hysterical over anything out of the ordinary. Over.'

'That's just ridiculous, that is. Over.'

Because it is.

'No, it's not. Over.'

'Yes, it is. Over.'

Pause.

'Well, do you want to hear my news or not?'

'OK then. Whatever it is and which is certainly not going to annoy me or make me hysterical. Over.'

'Mum has to stay at a friend's because of a funeral and she won't be coming later on after all.'

For a moment I look at the walkie-talkie, not sure what to say.

'Over.'

The walkie-talkies had been my idea.

Cousin Martin had left them at the house a couple of years ago (possibly because he wasn't a walkie-talkie kind of guy, stamp-collecting being more his kind of thing) and now, thanks to me, they were out of their box and being put to some good use at last.

I press the Talk button.

'A funeral? Really? Over.'

'It was probably the best she could come up with in the time available,' Kelly says quickly, and then the walkie-talkie goes quiet. 'Or something similar. Over'

I put the walkie-talkie down.

'That's the worst excuse I have ever heard in my life,' I shout as loudly as I can. 'And plausible excuses are, I might add, my business.'

Kelly drops from the tree at the far end of the lane in a bundle of blue denim and a knitted purple jumper.

'Right.'

She marches towards me, shouting something over her shoulder and, though I can't quite make out her face, I can tell that she is really, really angry.

'You ruddy bastard!'

I jump down to the ground and hit the Talk button.

'Five minutes, everyone. I just need to clarify a couple of things with Kelly and then we'll all be back on. Please stay up your trees. Repeat, stay up all your trees. Over.'

Kelly's face is a grimace of barely controlled rage as she stomps towards me.

'You drive me mad sometimes, do you know that?'

'Oh, really?'

Behind us, sitting in two of the trees on Church Lane, Beverley and Afia were maintaining their positions on their respective boughs and, if only Kelly would get back up hers, we would have the four-tree formation that I had planned the previous evening and our surveillance operation – which I had named "Big Daddy" for obvious reasons (though I was the only one using the name, I noticed) – would be complete.

'I mean, just what is your problem?' Kelly demands, waving her arms about. 'Is it because you want to be at the head of the welcoming committee or something?'

Bloody girls.

'No.'

Dad is late, that is why Kelly is being so angry.

'Really?'

'Yes.'

After all, we had all been up our trees, waiting and looking out for over an hour now, everyone was tired and Kelly was not cut out for this kind of endurance surveillance, anyway.

'And is it not enough that we are risking breaking our necks and giving up the best part of our day, not to mention the whole of last night, trying to set up these stupid walkie-talkies – which don't even work properly, I might add – when Dad might be coming by taxi? Have you even thought of that possibility, Planning Boy?'

'He would never do that,' I say quickly. 'He's a military man and he would have to march up from the station. It's how they're trained—'

'And you're still going on about it!'

Kelly waves her arms about.

'After all this time—'

'A funeral?' I spit back.

The words are out of my mouth before I can think.

'And what's wrong with that? People die, don't they?'

'A funeral, on a Saturday? On this Saturday?'

'Figure approaching at eleven o'clock,' Beverley squawks over the walkie-talkie. 'Could be male. Over.'

Not taking my eyes from my sister I squeeze the Talk button on my walkie-talkie.

'Acknowledged. Over.'

Kelly places her hands on her hips.

'And who cares? Really and honestly, who bloody well cares? He's coming, we're here and soon everyone else will be here as well. Isn't that enough, even for you?'

'Operation False Dawn,' Beverley cuts in. 'It's just Tony, walking one of the stable dogs. Looks like it could be Boxer. Over.'

Kelly lifts her walkie-talkie.

'Tony? Is he coming this way? Over.'

'No. He's heading for the recreation ground. Over.'

Kelly suddenly looks like the fury has gone out of her.

'I just think it's not that important,' she says carefully. 'Mum doesn't want to see him and, as her children, we have to respect her wishes – it's the law and the way that families are and should always be. So does it matter whether she's making it up or not?'

I suddenly feel really angry and stupid at the same time.

'I hate her for this,' I say at last. 'She's ruined everything.'

'She might still come, later. Before we start the meal.'

I want to sit down and cry, and it is only because I am pressing my teeth together really hard that the tears do not come. I try to breathe and know that I won't be able to speak because if I do my voice will come out all wobbly and embarrassing and it will all be a nightmare.

Kelly put her arms around my shoulders and gives me a hug.

'Come on,' she says.

Her hair smells of Vosene.

'I'm sure he's going to be here a long time,' she whispers, all kind and delicate in my ear, 'and that Mum'll be able to get a lift back before he has to leave, funeral or no funeral.'

The walkie-talkie in her hand suddenly squawks back into life.

'Male figure approaching. Without a dog this time. Over.'

'Besides,' Kelly continues, licking her thumb and wiping at my face, even though I'm not crying or anything, 'he's late as it is. So he's not going to be going anywhere soon, is he?'

'Target sighted,' Beverley shouts, falling from her tree.

Kelly jabs at her walkie-talkie.

'Are you sure?'

'You have to say "over",' I say, grabbing my binoculars.

'Over!'

Kelly turns and runs off down the lane.

'No doubt about it,' Beverley yells back. 'He's got a backpack on and he's heading in your direction. Now it's up to you, Number Two. Over and out!'

I rub my eyes, put the binoculars to my face, turn the focus ring and there, in the middle of the road, is a tall figure getting bigger and bigger and marching right towards us.

And running up to him is Kelly with her arms wide open.

'Dad!'

42

When I reach him, Dad is holding Kelly's hand and kicking up mud as he and Kelly march towards the house.

'Carry your bag for you, mister?' I ask (for some reason), once I breathlessly catch up with the two of them. 'Because it looks very heavy to me.'

Kelly sniggers and covers her mouth with her walkie-talkie.

'Please, let me help you.'

I take a much-needed breath.

'If that's OK with you, of course.'

Dad stops marching and peels off his backpack.

'Here, be my guest, young fella,' he says, handing the backpack over to me. 'Your assistance is very much appreciated.'

'Oh no!'

My knees immediately wobble as I twist and turn, trying to bounce the backpack up onto my shoulders.

'Not too heavy for you, is it, son?' Dad chuckles, grabbing hold of my arm to stop me from falling to the ground. 'Balance your weight there.'

Kelly turns away, her shoulders shaking with barely suppressed laughter.

'No, no,' I bluster, pulling on the straps of the backpack, 'don't you worry. I'll be fine.'

I bend my knees and bounce the backpack further onto my shoulders.

'What have you got in here, anyway? Bricks?'

'No, just a few presents.'

'Presents?'

For some reason, the backpack doesn't seem so heavy.

'For your mother and grandmother.'

And now it is an unbearable burden.

'Oh, right.'

'I promised them some perfume and cigarettes. You know how women are.'

He winks at me and then walks away.

'Honestly?'

'Yes.' He laughs over his shoulder. 'Ravenous beasts they are, son. Though they're also easy to please if you know what you're doing.'

Beverley and Afia catch up with us, take one look at the backpack I am still trying to balance on my shoulders, and then run off after Dad and my sister.

'We saw you from the trees,' Kelly splutters, swinging Dad's arm backwards and forwards. 'We were spying on you and using walkie-talkies to keep in contact.'

She waves her walkie-talkie in the air.

'We had code words sorted out for when we saw you and everything.'

'That was my idea,' I say, trying to catch up. 'I set up the walkie-talkies and then got them working with new batteries because you have to set them up first...'

I want him to be proud of me and to see how I am like him.

'So that way they can tune into each other. Because if they can't they don't work properly—'

Dad suddenly stops walking and we all stumble to a halt in his wake.

'A strategic plan, eh?'

He drops to one knee and holds out his hand to my sister.

'Here, give me that.'

Kelly hands over her walkie-talkie and Dad turns it on, listening carefully as it hisses into life.

'Well, well, well. What do we have here?'

We all lean in closer and strain to hear some meaning in the static.

'What is it, Dad?'

Because one of us has to ask.

Dad narrows his eyes at the walkie-talkie.

'That's very clever,' he says, turning the volume down before standing up again. 'And impressive in its forward-planning way, I would argue.'

He hands the walkie-talkie back to Kelly.

'You could have a career in military intelligence, you know.'

'Could I? Could I really?' Kelly gushes. 'I've just never thought—'

'No, not you. Your brother.'

'Oh.'

Dad takes hold of Kelly's hand and the two of them turn and march off down the road towards the house.

'He's the coolest man in the world,' I say, without thinking, 'and I don't care what Mum says.'

'I'm going to show him Minstrel,' Beverley says, running off after Dad and Kelly.

'The best father in the whole holy universe,' Afia says, sprinting off to re-join the others.

'In the whole solar system,' I say, even though there is no one left to hear me, but I don't care, because it is true. 'Wait for me!'

*

'What do you think they're doing in there?'

It is two hours later and me and Kelly are on the swings in the garden even though it is starting to get really cold, listening to the sound of laughter and Leo Sayer spilling from the house.

'I mean, they can't still be looking at photographs, can they?'

On her swing, Kelly sways lazily from side to side.

'I don't know,' she says coolly, eyeing the house. 'Perhaps they're just very, very drunk.'

Which is certainly an option.

'Or possibly playing cards.'

The front door opens and a distant relative emerges, pointing at the sky.

'I don't think Nan's got a full deck, though, has she?'

Kelly looks momentarily confused.

'No,' she says carefully. 'She can't have because Jacinto has hidden all the aces.'

The pointing relative disappears back inside.

'Oh, dear.'

This had been going on for ages now. A few of the relatives had even come over and asked me and Kelly how we are getting on, pushing pork pies and ham sandwiches in our faces, before returning inside the house for more beer and cigarettes.

'They might have got the Scrabble out, I suppose.'

'Or the Monopoly. In which case we could be here for ages.'

I get off my swing, take hold of the washing line and sway left and then right, even though I have been told by Nan not to something like a thousand times.

'Do you think he's given out some presents?' I ask at last.

He being Dad, of course.

Kelly continues to study the house.

'He's not Father Christmas, you know.'

'I didn't say he was. I was just, you know, asking.'

'I wonder why he's come now,' Kelly asks, more to herself than to me. 'Do you think it has anything to do with Daniel?'

'No, definitely not.'

'Because he's no trouble—'

'That's only because he doesn't say anything.'

'And he's cheap to feed.'

'He's not a cat—'

'Yes, I know that.'

'I'm just saying.'

'Anyway, I don't think it's got anything to do with Daniel.'

Kelly swivels on her swing.

'Beverley says Mum's been spending a lot of time in Elm Grove.'

I roll my eyes.

'Oh, really.'

Beverley was fast becoming Little Miss Super Spy and, what with that and the way she had recently taken to trotting around Sittingbourne on Minstrel (even though she knew she shouldn't, because of the danger to cars and the horse shit and everything), she was fast becoming very, very annoying indeed.

'So what?'

I swing again to the left on the washing line and then back to the right.

'Anyway, all Beverley goes on about these days is Elm Grove. Elm Grove this, Elm Grove that – it's just a road, you know.'

'A grove...'

'A grove then, whatever that is.'

'It's like a cul-de-sac,' Kelly says authoritatively, 'but with more trees.'

'Really? How intriguing.'

Afia sticks her head out the front door.

'You know you're not supposed to do that,' she says, all loud and over the top and nodding in my direction. 'Because of the danger to yourself and the risk of the washing line snapping.'

'Oh, piss off, Afia,' I say, and immediately my face goes red because of the swearing.

Afia disappears back into the house pretty sharpish.

'That was a bit rude,' Kelly says.

Inside the house, the sound of laughter grows louder.

I swivel around and cross my legs.

'Besides, the bigger question is not why she is spending all of her time in Elm Grove – which doesn't mean anything one way or another now that Dad is here – but why is she not spending any of her free time with us?'

'It's because of her work,' Kelly says automatically, clearly not believing a word of it. 'She has to put in... the hours.'

'But she works at a petrol station, not down a coal mine.'

I swivel the other way round.

'I know,' Kelly snaps, looking down at the ground. 'Beverley says it's because of Mark, her new friend that works on the pumps.'

I lean more heavily on the clothesline and push my stomach out as far as I can.

'Really?'

'Yes.'

'Interesting.'

'If you say so.'

'And when did Beverley tell you that?'

This could be bad news, come to think of it.

'Last night, after she put the bedroom light out.'

Behind me, there is some kind of commotion inside the house as someone starts banging at an upstairs window, but I pay no attention.

What we are talking about is, after all, far more important.

'And what else did she say?'

The banging inside the house gets even louder.

'Just that she went round his flat and that then they went to see someone in Elm Grove.'

'Oh… bollocks.'

I suddenly don't know what has made me more angry: Mum, for the irritating Mark connection, or Kelly, for not telling me about all this earlier. In the quick silence that follows I realise that it is my sister who is more in the wrong because she has known about these things all along and not said anything about them to me until now.

'Oh, that doesn't mean anything,' I say, really believing what I'm saying, despite everything. 'And besides, Mark's probably just a good and decent friend. So who cares about him and what they get up to together?'

Deep breath.

'And even if they are doing stuff, which I'm sure they're not, it's probably got nothing to do with us anyway.'

The front door opens and Nan totters onto the step, her hands pressed against the base of her back.

'Noah,' she squawks, shaking cigarette ash onto the doormat, 'could you come on inside, please?'

43

Afterwards, everything was different.

'What happened?'

Kelly, being nosy as always: all eyes and ears, her brain going ten a minute like a counting machine.

'Nothing, really. She just wanted me to say hello to someone.'

She being Nan, obviously.

I thought very carefully before I said that because I wanted the lie to be good enough to put Kelly off (though achieving that was hard enough at the best of times).

'To whom, exactly?'

'To Deaf Aunt Annie.'

'Deaf Aunt Annie?'

'She's one of the Welsh relatives from Mountain Ash.'

Kelly clearly does not believe me when I say this.

'Is she really?'

'Yes. The Welsh relatives came down on the National Express.'

'Bet that took a while.'

'Yes, but it's cheaper than the train and there are fewer stops.'

'Was anyone sick?'

'I don't know—'

'Because I would be. Due to all the bridges along the way.'

I shake my head to get rid of Kelly's words that are buzzing about in my ears like flies.

'Maybe they were. I don't remember whether they said so or not.'

Though the truth was I could remember everything: from releasing the clothesline and it pinging back above my head; to walking into the house and the laughter from the lounge getting louder and louder; all those relatives, most of whom I had never met, and Dad, sitting in the middle of the room, like a long-lost king returning to his people.

'There was a lot going on. Too much to take in, really.'

'Though you'd remember if they said they were sick or not – especially if it happened on a hot coach. I mean, you'd remember that, wouldn't you?'

I remember thinking that it was odd that, as I went into the hall, Nan was not there waiting for me because, after all, she had been the one that had asked me to come in, in the first place.

'Dad was surrounded. They just couldn't leave him alone.'

'And what about Nan?'

'She was sitting at her sewing machine.'

'Even with all the guests being there?'

'Even with all the guests being there.'

'Well, that's not very sociable.'

'No, not really.'

What happened between reaching the front step and my eventual leaving of the house was not exactly a secret, though I thought the little Mountain Ash story I had made up for Kelly (something effective enough to distract from Afia's later no doubt extremely detailed gossiping but which was also evasive enough to put Kelly off the scent so she would not be that interested once Afia started her babbling) was clever and effective.

For the first minute or two, anyway.

'And it certainly wasn't very polite of her.'

When it did happen, the important thing, I immediately realised, was to prevent it from turning into another one of those incidents that we'd all have to carry around forever and which we'd never be able to escape, no matter how hard we tried.

'Not polite at all, in fact.'

So it was best to just pretend that absolutely nothing of any importance had taken place and, if you do pretend like that hard enough, people are willing to believe anything, whether it is true or not.

'To ignore your own guests, it's just not the done thing. And especially not at Christmas.'

'It's not Christmas yet.'

'It very nearly is. It's yuletide and peace to all men. They've even got crackers in Woolworths.'

Because what I wanted most of all was for everything to go back to how it was before and, if that was not possible, then for us all to move on to whatever was coming next, because it didn't matter, not really, and certainly not after what happened did happen.

It was nothing; it was just more trouble.

And stupidness.

'What did Dad say, while all this was going on and you were saying your special "hello" to Deaf Aunt Annie, who was not sick in any way coming down on the coach from Mountain Ash?'

'Nothing.'

Actually true.

'He said nothing.'

Inside the lounge, everyone was on chairs collected from around the house. Some were perched on the arms of the sofa or the dog-hair itchy armchairs. A few of the lucky ones were jammed into the sofa itself (tipped slightly forward due to the collective weight of all those fortunate perchers and because the sofa springs had given out years ago), though for everyone else the choice was between mismatched chairs from the back of the house or stools that had been brought down from the attic and which smelt of paraffin.

'They all said I had grown a lot since they had seen me last.'

Another lie.

Obviously getting good at this.

'But a lot of them have never seen you before. Well, not outside of photos, anyway.'

Though perhaps not that good.

'That's right. Sorry.'

The chairs were arranged around the walls of the lounge in a courtly semi-circle as Pickle scurried up and down in front of the coffee table, weighed down as it was with plates of half-eaten sandwiches and bowls of crisps.

He wanted the food.

He could smell it.

'That bloody dog. And I bet he licked the plates.'

Dad sat grinning to the left of the sewing machine, a can of beer in his hand.

'Was he drunk?'

'I don't think so. He looked like he was just merry. After all, he was only on Carlsberg.'

Everything in the room was for Dad and, to a lesser extent, for Nan. The chairs all radiated out from them and those that were doing the appreciative perching were their courtiers.

'You wanted to see me?' I asked as I walked into the room.

The hum of conversation fell away.

'Is there something you want, Nan?'

My father looked up and smiled gently but said nothing.

'Because I can come back later if you're busy.'

On the other side of the room, hunched over a crumpled copy of *The Daily Mirror* spread out on her sewing machine, Nan didn't seem to hear me at first. Then she said without turning round, 'Come closer, please, Noah.'

Pickle started to growl.

'My, hasn't he grown?'

Nan was going to give me something or my father was going to give me something, I could just tell, and for some reason, I thought it would be a key or an envelope with a key in it or perhaps a card with the address of our new house on it and Elm Grove would just go away because it was not needed anymore.

'Stand before me, please.'

And then I did what Nan asked because I just knew that what was

271

going to happen was going to be good and I was smiling to myself, but also for my father because I wanted him to see that I understood and that I was grateful, that I was in on their little conspiracy.

'Closer, Noah.'

We were both on the same side, my smile said to my father.

This was our little secret.

'Yes, Nan?' I asked expectantly.

I had almost forgotten about her. She had become secondary to what was going on, unspoken between me and Dad.

It was like she wasn't even there.

'Closer.'

And though I could not see everyone, I could feel each pair of eyes on me. Because everything was just so perfect, like one of those games that adults play at Christmas (or on your birthday) when they deceive you and make you think something bad or boring is going to happen and then they tell you the truth and give you a present and suddenly it is the best thing in the world.

'Noah?'

Because then you don't have to pretend to be glad or to be happy because you just are. Adults are like that; sometimes they lie to you, but it is always for your own good and, just as long that you accept that fact and play along, things always turn out right in the end.

I turned from my father and faced my grandmother.

'Yes, Nan?'

Dad said nothing.

He just looked at me and then I realised it had been Nan that had called me in, so obviously she was the one who was going to give me my present. And as my eyes moved from my father to meet hers she pulled back her hand and slapped me across the face.

'You little bastard.'

Suddenly I'm facing the closed door I had walked through only a few seconds before, and it is the sound of the palm on my cheek now ricocheting around the room and the sudden overwhelming urge to cry that is more shocking than the pain of the slap itself.

Everyone is staring.

Dad is watching.

He still doesn't say anything and I daren't look at him.

I don't want to look at him. Instead, all I do is turn back and concentrate on one thing.

Do not cry; whatever you do, do not cry.

'What have I told you about pulling on that washing line?' Nan demands, narrowing her eyes at me. 'You know it can't hold your bloody weight.'

I can't speak because I know that if I try to my voice will come out all wrong and then I'll start crying straightaway.

'I'm sorry...'

Then I have to stop.

I'm finding it difficult to breathe and my chest is rising and falling in hiccupping gasps, so all I can do is look down, careful that the motion of my breathing does not shake any tears out and onto the carpet.

'Now, get back out there and do as you're told.'

'Yes, Nan,' I say, my voice as unsteady as a whisper. 'I will.'

'You bloody well better.'

I turn and walk back towards the door, not taking my eyes from it for a second, and open and close it behind me as quickly as possible, just in time for the music to start up all over again.

From a Jack to a King
From loneliness to a wedding ring...

Then the tears come, out in the hallway. But, since I still have to face Kelly, I quickly wipe my cheeks and walk back into the garden, which is cold and bright.

I played an Ace and I won a Queen...

In the lounge, Pickle starts barking and yelping.

And walked away with your heart...

'He's not come for anything,' I tell Kelly when we are back together on the swings. 'He just wants to see her. Probably to drop something off or to give her some money.'

I stare at the road beyond the confines of the garden and Kelly takes my hand, her swing bumping lazily against mine.

'Oh, OK.'

Kelly doesn't say anything after that, not for a long time anyway, and she stops asking about what happened in the lounge (though the truth is, she would have heard everything – it was pretty loud – everyone would have heard it). Instead, all she does is look back towards the house as organ music begins to wobble through the air.

'Is that real?' she asks after a while. 'Or a record?'

Nan had a Bontempi with a tablecloth on it in the corner of the lounge, next to the telly. She complained it used too much electricity, which was why she rarely plugged it in.

'I think it's one of her albums,' I say without thinking.

Nan's slurred singing joins the now off-key organ music.

Give me joy in my heart, keep me praising
Give me joy in my heart, I pray
Give me joy in my heart, keep me praising
Keep me praising till the break of day.

'Though I could be wrong.'

We rock to and fro on the swings, listening to the racket coming from the house, as the light begins to fade and the relatives we don't know start to leave, accompanied by stuttering car engines and jokes about drunk driving.

'If we don't see you again, make sure you have a lovely Christmas.'

Until we finally go back inside and eat cold, curly sandwiches in the kitchen as Afia makes a cup of tea and gently sings to herself over the washing-up.

Sing hosanna, sing hosanna
Sing hosanna to the King of kings
Sing hosanna, sing hosanna
Sing hosanna to the King.

We didn't get to say goodbye to Dad and he didn't tell us he was leaving. Instead, Afia crept back into the kitchen, once the last of the beer cans and wine bottles had been put in the bin, and told us as carefully as she could that a taxi had taken Dad away because he was too tired to walk back to the station.

'And you have to be careful at this time of night due to the ice on the roads where the street lights don't work properly.'

Afia suddenly takes a quick breath, her face a mask of concentration as she works out what to say next.

'Ice on the road. Right…' Kelly says, helping her out as we listen to the gentle hum of the fridge-freezer and Pickle barking at the closed front-room door because he wants to be let into the hall.

'And that can be very dangerous for a man who has drunk as much as your father has,' Afia continues with renewed vigour. 'Which was a lot, I can tell you. I had to stop counting the empty cans in the end because there were just so many of them.'

Me and Kelly stare at each other as the barking goes on in the lounge and Afia hovers nervously in the kitchen doorway.

'Well, I'm going to bed,' Kelly says, at last, getting up and dusting breadcrumbs from her jeans. 'I've got to get up early in the morning, to help Beverley with the mucking-out.'

Then just before she leaves, she comes over and kisses me on the top of the head – which is strange because she has never done that before – and rubs me in the middle of the back.

'Goodnight,' she says tenderly, before leaving me and Afia alone.

'Wait,' I almost whisper to Afia as she turns to follow my sister out of the room. 'Not yet.'

Afia narrows her eyes and crosses her arms.

'What do you want?' she asks, suspiciously sniffing the air for potential trouble. 'I've got sleep to attend to as well, you know.'

'How much of it do I use?'

My voice is like someone else's and all hard and metallic and not me at all.

'How much of what?'

More narrowing of the eyes, before Afia quickly looks up the hallway at the closed front-room door.

'You know what.'

Because she does. I can tell.

'Noah, don't, please. Rat poison is only for rats—'

'And sometimes for dogs...'

Afia puts two fingers to her lips, then carefully shuts the kitchen door. 'Only to end misery and pain and not for any other good Christian purpose.'

'If you say so...'

She jabs a finger in my direction. 'And what do you want to use it for, anyway?'

'For her.'

Her being Nan, obviously.

Afia presses her lips so tightly together that her cheeks bulge.

'Don't do it, Noah,' she says at last, before taking a deep breath. 'Not even she is worth a crime against our good Lord Jesus Christ and His hope for love amongst us, even with all the sinning.'

Quick nod of the head towards the closed door.

Just in case I don't get the message.

'Because evil only creates more evil and violence more pain.'

Then she presses her palms together and squeezes them hard like she is praying with all of her might.

'And how would you give it to her?' she suddenly asks, releasing her praying hands with a flourish. 'She's not an idiot, you know, and

277

has a taste for anything that's not right. She always knows when the milk is about to turn, even before it goes sour and becomes cottage cheese in a teacup.'

Up the hall, a still-trapped Pickle starts whining.

'So rat poison is not going to get anywhere near her lips, I'm telling you. Not even if you dilute it a lot or bake it in a cake.'

'I'm going to put it in her drink when she has her coffee and rum.'

It's like I've thought it all through already and I've been looking through books from the library (even though I'm not even a member), but the truth is the thoughts and the words are coming together in the kitchen between me and Afia and they are only starting to make sense when they are all out in the open.

'She won't taste anything then. Well, not after the third mouthful, anyway.'

Though that is probably true. After the second glass of rum Nan usually starts mumbling and falling asleep and not bothering if we turn over the TV.

'Oh, she's not going to be fooled by warm rum.'

Afia presses her hands on either side of her head and then quickly shakes any potential murderous plans out of it.

'No, Noah, no. It is a crime and a sin against God and will put us both in prison and on the front page of the *News of the World*.'

'A crime against God?'

Afia steps forward and wraps her long, bony arms around my shoulders. 'Against everything.'

'But I hate her so much…'

I want to cry again.

There is a part of me that wants to but I can't.

'I hate her and I hate him and I hate everyone…'

Afia pulls me into her blouse, which is soft and warm.

'God's grace will take care of her,' she whispers in my ear, before slowly stroking my hair. 'One way or another, the evil witch will be beaten by our beautiful God and He, not the poison of the rats, will get her and then we'll all be free at last.'

'Do you think so?'

The fight has gone out of me now, I can feel it.

'Honestly?'

And all that is left are words and questions and waking up tomorrow.

'Of course. God always wins in the end. Even if it takes Him years, He always gets His justice.'

'Justice?'

'For all and everything. Now, where's the poison?'

'Under my bed, behind the suitcase.'

Afia squeezes my shoulder. 'I'll take it out in the morning and flush it down the drain.' Then she releases her fingers from my hair, straightens her back and smiles at me. 'Now you get to bed before the evil witch comes out.'

Which could happen. After all, Pickle would have to be let out sooner or later.

'And trust in God, because He will get her. You'll see.'

And then she leans forward and kisses me in the middle of the forehead with her soft, warm lips.

'Goodnight, Noah. Sleep tight.'

45

Before you get to Sittingbourne's All Saint's Church, just along from the Co-op supermarket and the new houses with their own driveways on Tonge Road, you come to The Broken Coach & Horses public house.

COACH PARTIES WELCOME

There also used to be a Sittingbourne Social Club next door: a grim whitewashed bungalow popular with couples marrying on a budget, but that was boarded up years ago following a food-poisoning scandal that made two columns on page six of *The Kent and Sussex Courier*:

PUB TOAD IN THE HOLE GAVE ME THE TROTS

The Broken Coach & Horses stands at the top of Church Road and across from the Sittingbourne Recreation Ground (actually an expanse of poorly maintained grass and broken benches on which me and Kelly would sometimes sit, watching five-a-side football when there was nothing good on the telly, or if Nan had forced us out of the house to play).

Which was often.

'Well, this is bloody boring,' Kelly sighs, staring straight ahead. 'And it's bloody cold.'

Just as she has today.

'We could always go back and watch *Doctor Who* if you want,' Kelly continues, clearly trying to be nice and kind (if only to get in from the cold). 'And I'm sure Nan won't mind too much, especially if she's been drinking.'

Which I am not particularly interested in doing (even if Nan would let us) as I have far more important things on my mind right now than Cybermen and Daleks.

'Oh, that's just totally rubbish,' I snort, secretly not believing what I am saying. 'And it's for little kids, really.'

'Do you think they need a new Doctor?' Kelly asks as pitch-side fighting breaks out in front of the fire-damaged bench we are sitting on. 'Because Tom Baker is just too eccentric, if you ask me.'

'I think so. And some new monsters because the current ones are simply too unbelievable.'

'Especially those stupid Sea Devils, with their silly rubber masks and ridiculous eyes.'

Then Kelly falls silent as a woman drags a brawling footballer off the pitch by his ear.

Presumably his wife.

'I liked Jon Pertwee,' I add after a while, as what's left of the football fighting dissolves into a melee of finger-pointing and half-hearted shouting. 'He was funny and wise.'

It starts to rain with a stop and a start.

'I don't think I have ever seen a game here that has not ended in some kind of a fight,' Kelly sighs, ignoring the rain pattering around us, as the footballers' finger-pointing continues. 'Or at least in a heated and unnecessary argument involving fists.'

'Come on,' I say, jumping off the bench. 'We need to be back by four. Afia's making shepherd's pie.'

'She's a good cook,' Kelly says, reluctantly joining me down on the damp grass. 'Especially when she makes pies. Is she planning on making another pie before Christmas? A steak and kidney pie, perhaps, or a chicken and mushroom?'

'I think she is – beef and onion, probably.'

'I can't wait for her New Year dinner,' Kelly says, suddenly animated by all the talk of pies. 'Christmas is just going to be the usual if you ask me. But Mum says New Year is going to have a special Italian theme.'

I hate it when Kelly does this.

'And when did you speak to Mum?'

'Last night, on the phone, when you and Afia were giggling in the kitchen.'

Afia had put Pickle on the table and lifted his front legs so that it looked like he was dancing to *Save Your Kisses for Me*, which was playing on the radio.

Until Pickle nipped her on the wrist.

'We were not giggling. We were doing the drying-up.'

Which is a lie, obviously.

It suddenly stops raining and then starts again almost straightaway.

'Bloody Britain,' Kelly mutters, as we leave the recreation ground and pass The Broken Coach & Horses. 'It can't even get the weather right.'

'That's true. It's just a bloody stupid country.'

'Mum also said that we might all go for a nice drink at some point,' Kelly continues, nodding towards the pub. 'To celebrate the season and to discuss something that might or might not be important.'

'And why did she say that?' I ask, immediately bristling with jealousy because Mum and Kelly have clearly been discussing things behind my back again.

'Because she likes Christmas and has something she wants to talk to us about, I suppose.'

Which is a blatant lie.

'Well, she must be joking about the nice drink,' I snigger, 'because Christmas or no Christmas it's the drinking hole of the damned in there. And everyone knows it.'

'Who's everyone?'

'Just everyone.'

Kelly frowns and makes a sort of "mmmmmmm" sound, though what I'm saying is true because The Broken Coach & Horses never seemed to have any customers in it, regardless of what day it was.

'And is that a genuine and provable fact?'

According to Afia, it was because of the state of the toilets.

'With any evidence at all behind it?'

We both stop and peer at the pub which, as usual, appears to be empty.

'I would say so.'

In fact, beyond its empty car park and litter-filled water trough, The Broken Coach & Horses was notorious in Sittingbourne for being little more than a maze of tatty public rooms and dark dusty bars divided strictly along lines of membership and tradition.

'And if Mum thinks going in there at Christmas is a good idea she needs to get her head examined.'

After all, not even Nan liked going to The Broken Coach & Horses and she was one of its private members.

'It's fifty pounds a year to gain access to the private bar and you also get free membership of the darts team, if you want it, though of course not that many do,' was how the pub landlord put it to her, after Nan took us to The Broken Coach & Horses at the end of our first week in Sittingbourne "as a welcome to the area".

'Because it is a very interesting town and the locals can be very accommodating.'

Cough and a splutter.

'When they need to be.'

I never really understood the divide between the public and private where pubs are concerned, apart from the fact that at The Broken Coach & Horses there was a door between the two domains through which you could not pass without the full and proper membership having been being paid in full.

'Stop right there.'

Because if you did, then you risked potentially stern words on the part of The Broken Coach & Horses barmen (or women) who were always on the look-out for potential rebels, whether they had full pockets or not.

'I can see you, you know.'

Yank of a pump handle.

'Even if I am filling a glass.'

And then there was The Broken Coach & Horses Family Room, right next to the toilets, which was a haven for fold-away chairs and broken toys donated by the local Oxfam.

'You will find two boxes of childish amusements at the back of the room and which are always full to the very brim with fun and various games.'

The Family Room had its own jukebox (that never worked), little round red vinyl-topped tables and a tiled floor that was always slippery with discarded crisps and slowly drying Coca-Cola, no matter how many times it was mopped.

'About twice a week with Dettol, when the cleaners are in.'

Nan would occasionally take us to The Broken Coach & Horses after we had been suitably welcomed to the area, "to at least get you all out of the bloody house".

When we went, none of us ventured into the Family Room, because nobody ever did and especially not families with actual children.

'After all, it's just not fun, is it?' a mother had complained, famously, one Saturday lunchtime after taking a quick, disgusted look around the Family Room's cold, miserable interior. 'And especially when you could be outside, sitting under a parasol in the warm sunshine enjoying the weather.'

And with that, she picked up (actually picked up!) her small son, turned round and carried him out of the pub.

'Snotty cow,' one of the barmen muttered as she left. 'And all because we didn't have any smoky bacon crisps, as well.'

Though to be fair, the disappointed sun-seeker was from one of the new houses on Tonge Road and they enjoyed their own form of fraternisation, usually involving a drive up the motorway to Chatham or Maidstone or the occasional indulgence at the local Harvester (fifteen minutes along the A2).

*

'Have you been to a Harvester before?'

The Monday after Granddad's funeral we decamped to the very same Harvester during an ill-judged and poorly planned family get-together, even though we knew that the food was only partly cooked on the premises once it was ordered from the menu.

'It's prepared elsewhere and then brought on lorries and heated up when you ask for it,' Kelly explained grimly as she fiddled with an unopened packet of Silk Cut. 'Which is why the service is so fast, I would imagine.'

None of us complained.

'Well, it's best not to make a fuss,' Dad said rather confusingly as we pondered Kelly's words and stared at each other, waiting for a waitress to arrive at our table. 'After all, they're only doing their job and it is a Bank Holiday.'

Kelly slowly peeled the cellophane from her Silk Cut.

'Nobody's making a fuss, Dad—'

'I was simply pointing out—'

'We could always—' Mum ventured after a moment.

'I wouldn't,' Dad added quickly, squeezing her arm. 'That probably wouldn't be a very good idea.'

'Right you are,' Mum squealed, jumping a little at Dad's touch. 'I won't do that, then.'

At which point we all returned to staring at each other in becalmed and hungry silence.

*

Two days after the punch-up on the recreation ground I received a letter from Dad suggesting we go to The Broken Coach & Horses for a drink the first Sunday after Boxing Day.

I couldn't understand why because there was no reason, not really. So when the letter arrived, at first, I ignored it, because then it would have to go away and I wouldn't have to write back and say, "Sorry, but I just don't have the time to meet you".

Or something like that.

Kelly, however, has other ideas the minute she finds out about the letter and its mysterious contents.

'See what he wants,' she says quickly, while still reading the letter (which I had hidden inside a copy of *Look-in* until Afia flicked through it when she was nosing about in my room pretending to do some cleaning). 'After all, he must have something important to say otherwise why bother writing in the first place?'

'Oh, I don't know,' I say, a little confused by Kelly's sudden attack of reasonableness. 'It could be some kind of trap.'

'Some kind of trap?'

Cue much furrowing on the part of Kelly's eyebrows.

'You've been watching too many episodes of *Doctor Who*, you have, regardless of who is or isn't playing the Doctor at any particular point in time.'

Pause.

'What?'

'Never you mind. Anyway, I wouldn't worry about it,' Kelly continues, carefully folding the letter and wiggling it back into its envelope. 'I mean, meeting for a simple drink can't be too bad, can it? Though it is a mystery why he's writing now after all that has happened.'

We both look at the envelope and ponder the mystery of the invitation.

'Do you think he's got cancer?' Kelly asks suddenly.

'Or perhaps he might even have met someone.'

Kelly knits her brow even more tightly than before and then chews thoughtfully on her lower lip.

'Though I thought he already had, actually.'

'Do you think so?'

I mean, I had thought about such a possibility over the preceding months, but Kelly and I had never actually speculated openly on the subject.

Until now, that is.

'Beverley was saying just the other day that he might want to, while he's still got it in him.'

'While he's still got what in him?'

Kelly looks away and swallows awkwardly.

'Life,' she says, at last, her voice trailing off.

'Or something similar to it.'

46

Of course, despite my outward appearance of cool nonchalance my brain was still going ten a minute, working on "what if?" scenarios. I never learned, not really. That was always my problem, and the questions were still being asked later that night, inside my head and against my will as I read and re-read Dad's letter with a torch under the duvet.

I will only be back in Sittingbourne for a short time. Then I have to leave on tactical and military business, so it would be useful to see you again and to properly talk this time.

Military business?
Tactical?
The presents Dad had brought with him that fateful day earlier in the month were collected under the Christmas tree (white, plastic and brand-new from Woolworths), though they were mainly, we noticed, for Daniel and Beverley, apart from a big bottle of whisky for Nan, which she said couldn't wait for Christmas Day to open.

And how is your mother?

When you next speak to her could you please remind her that she still needs to send the post office savings book back to me?

That big, oversized whisky bottle would soon sit at the end of Nan's sewing machine, its contents gradually going down bit by bit as the days went by and as Christmas drew inexorably nearer.

'Because I told you I couldn't wait for Christmas, didn't I?'

When she drank the whisky Nan sang songs to herself that nobody remembered, slept in for a bit longer than usual and, on those very special days, Beverley even got to leave the house without having her hair plaited.

'But don't say anything. If she does wake up, tell her I'm in a deep, peaceful sleep and cannot be awoken, not even for a raging house fire.'

A raging house fire?

'Because she will understand, believe me.'

Until, finally, on Christmas morning (and with a certain amount of expectation), we, at last, get to see the presents that Dad had left all those weeks before.

*

'I'm going to change my hair-do to a Farrah Fawcett,' Beverley announces with a festive flourish (and for no good reason) as she and Kelly wipe the special Yuletide cutlery in the kitchen. 'First chance I get, and I'm going blonde as well.'

'Once you start bleaching it you'll never be able to stop,' Kelly cautions her, carefully rubbing the dessert spoons before putting them away. 'It's a long, expensive road from that point on.'

'Yes, but that's just the high price you pay for beauty.'

'Well, I suppose so,' Kelly sighs, apparently defeated by Beverley's inescapable logic on the matter. 'Though I still don't think it's fair on your follicles.'

'Presents after dinner, my Christmas darlings,' Mum trills with misplaced urgency from the landing, before descending the stairs in a new jumpsuit and a cloud of Charlie. 'Once a few seasonal visits have taken place.'

She tra-la-la-las her way into the lounge, where Nan is tutting over the television.

'I think I prefer it like that,' Beverley says, not sounding like she believes what she's saying. 'I mean, it's something to look forward to then, isn't it?'

Kelly shakes a Christmas cracker next to her ear as two minicabs pull up outside.

'They're here!' Beverley gushes, tossing the last of the cutlery onto the table before dashing up the hall. 'Coats on, everybody.'

'Well, those taxis must have cost a fortune,' Kelly says, marching up to the front door and crossing her arms in a gesture of disapproval at the commotion building around us. 'At least twenty pounds, I reckon.'

Which seems a lot to me.

Outside, the minicabs come to a steaming halt at the gate.

'We're just going to pop round to say hello to your grandmother's friend, Abigail Stevens,' Mum announces, ushering Daniel up the hall, before kissing me and Kelly on the cheeks as quickly as she can. 'She's not going to be around much longer – Abigail Stevens that is, not your grandmother – so we said we'd drop by for a mince pie and a cup of tea. We won't be long, though, don't you worry, because we will open all the presents just as soon as we get back and I promise you on that seasonal fact, my sweet Christmas darlings.'

'What's the matter with this mysterious Abigail Stevens?' Kelly asks, trying to hide her excitement at the sudden burst of festive freedom about to envelop us. 'Is she dying or close to it?'

'No, love. She's emigrating to Australia.'

Beverley darts past, zipping up a new and very pink blouson jacket.

'And try not to eat all the Quality Street,' Nan screeches, as she pulls on her posh mackintosh. 'Because I know how many are in the tin and I'll be counting them on my return, you can mark my words on that front.'

She bats Afia around the head as she appears in the hallway together with Baako and Jacinto, all three of them pulling on matching green parkas.

'Stupid bloody girl.'

Then they all tumble out the front door and into the garden.

'Merry Christmas, my darlings,' Mum shouts to those of us left behind, before skipping gaily up the path. 'And I mean that from the very bottom of my heart.'

'I thought it would snow again by Christmas morning,' Kelly sighs, as we watch them fuss about, trying to cram themselves into the minicabs. 'But the weather just doesn't seem to have the right idea.'

The doors to the minicabs slam shut one by one.

'They warned it might rain on the radio,' I say, as the first of the cars pull away. 'Though not until later in the evening.'

*

Two hours later, me and Kelly are laid out at either end of the sofa, watching TV with Nan's tin of Quality Street propped up on a cushion between us.

Two piles of multi-coloured foil are growing on the carpet and Pickle has been banished to the garden.

'Exactly when is ABBA going to be on?' Kelly asks through a mouthful of toffee.

Top of the Pops is on the television.

'Later on, I reckon, after Cliff Richard.'

Noel Edmonds, who is pretending to be at a Christmas dinner in the *Top of the Pops* studio, starts cracking jokes with Dave Lee Travis, who looks a bit confused.

'What do you think the last song will be?'

'*Never* bloody *Forever*, it'll have to be,' I say without thinking.

'I suppose so, though he's a bit rubbish, isn't he, Demis Roussos?'

'He's super rubbish and very, very fat.'

We continue our chewing as Legs & Co. start bobbing about on the screen.

'God, this is boring,' Kelly sighs, before getting up. 'Shall we have a drink?'

'I'm not sure.'

'I know where the vodka is hidden.'

'Oh, OK then.'

I look at the clock and feel sick because of the Quality Street.

'Where are they?' I ask, beginning to worry about when Mum might be coming back and when we will be eating. 'Because it has been ages.'

'She's still with the so-called Abigail Stevens, I suppose,' Kelly says, suddenly sounding very sad. 'And getting drunk in the bargain, I would imagine.'

'But at least they won't be eating because they've left us to cook the Christmas dinner, so they're not being totally selfish, are they?'

Kelly blinks and swallows.

'I'll get that vodka,' she says grimly.

I don't want to drink the vodka, though, not really, and I don't think Kelly does either. She is just being clever and stupid because it is Christmas and we are on our own.

'Don't worry,' I say, trying to sound like I am perking up for no real reason. 'Because I'm sure everyone will be back soon.'

Though all I want to do is to eat the turkey, which is slowly cooking in the kitchen oven and filling the house with its sweet meat smells.

'No, they won't. In fact, they won't be back for ages yet,' Kelly sighs, almost as if she has just remembered what I have just said. 'So do you want a cheese sandwich instead of that vodka to keep you going, Hopeful Christmas Boy?'

'Yes, please,' I say, popping a chocolate Brazil into my mouth, as Noel Edmonds wraps tinsel around his neck and makes a face like he is being strangled. 'And some Twiglets too, if you don't mind, as I think we may well be waiting to eat that turkey for some time to come.'

*

When the minicabs pull up again, two hours and forty-five minutes later ('And that'll be another twenty quid'), both Mum and Nan are very drunk and extremely happy.

'Did you see the place settings, Stephanie? Now, that's what I call class. And it's good to see a hostess trolley that's used for its intended purpose and not just to keep the tea towels in.'

'Oh, you are so right, Mother, and what a lovely centrepiece.'

Then, later on, we (finally) get to eat the turkey that has been roasting all afternoon, together with hard, hurt-your-teeth roast potatoes and soft, squirty Brussels sprouts, before donning brightly coloured paper hats and playing Mouse Trap.

Until Mum and Nan fall asleep, that is, and the rest of us can escape to the kitchen to poke with our fingers at the warm, gooey Christmas pudding that nobody wanted to eat as dessert.

'This is almost very lovely,' Kelly slurs (she has drunk some white wine with her dinner), before scooping a big dollop of Christmas pudding and cream into her mouth. 'It is indeed perfectly fat and sweet.'

'It's from Marks,' Afia says with a certain relish, before dropping another spoonful of cream onto the pudding from a great height. 'She pretended she made it herself, but I saw the boxes hidden in the bin.'

She being Nan, obviously.

We don't care, though, and, if anything, the Marks & Spencer connection makes the pudding taste even better.

'It's just delicious,' I say, licking cream from the back of my hand. 'And it's even better than ice cream, in my opinion.'

Which it is, sort of, though I do like ice cream more, as a rule.

'Do you hear that?' Kelly asks, suddenly grabbing Afia's sleeve.

We stop our licking to listen to Mum and Nan as they snore in between the laughter on the telly.

'This is the best Christmas ever,' I say, the words sing-songing in my mouth before demanding to be set free. 'And I'm not just saying that because of all this pudding.'

Because it is true.

Kelly stares languidly at me across the table.

'I think,' she slurs very slowly, 'you might well be right in saying that, Christmas Pudding Boy.'

And then we return to our sugary feasting until Nan and Mum eventually wake up with a confused start ('What's happening, Stephanie? I can't feel my toes!') and we all rush into the lounge to open our presents, which are quite good.

'Merry Christmas, everyone!'

I get a denim jacket and an ABBA annual (which I give to Beverley, who I think should have had it in the first place), while Kelly gets a round suitcase that has a doll's head and make-up inside and Daniel gets an Action Man.

'Wow!'

I want the Action Man but don't say anything because, strictly speaking, it is for kids. 'Even with gripping hands it lacks the sophistication required by someone of my age,' I say, eyeing the box keenly, despite myself.

Kelly snorts beside the fairy lights.

'You're fooling no one,' she says, as Beverley sniggers behind the back of her hand.

Dad, we discover, bought us jigsaws.

'Jigsaws?'

And when we have finally stripped the Christmas paper fully from the long, narrow boxes stacked on top of each other under the Christmas tree it is a genuine disappointment that I think even shocks Mum.

'Such a considered... purchase... and so very like your father.'

My jigsaw is of a castle (1,000 pieces), while Kelly's is a white kitten (500 pieces) and Daniel's is a creepy clown (150 pieces).

'Baako, clear the table of the wrapping paper,' Nan snaps, as we all stare in silent shock at the jigsaw boxes. 'And make us all a nice cup of tea with your sister, so that we can all enjoy some After Eight mints.'

Later on, we try to put the jigsaws together before we go to bed, at least to show willing, but don't get to finish them before *The Morecambe & Wise Show* starts on the television.

Thankfully.

'I don't think he thought very hard about our presents,' Kelly whispers, stuffing a handful of peanuts into her mouth after we get a chance to stop pretending to put the jigsaws together. 'But at least he made an effort, no matter how small that effort was.'

'Do you think so?'

'Well, possibly. Though the effort had to have been very, very small in the first place, if it truly existed at all, that is.'

'So small as to be barely measurable?'

'Not even with a microscope.'

Kelly thinks for a minute, rolls peanuts around in her mouth and then swallows.

'Agreed,' she says finally. 'And unfortunately.'

47

By Sunday all the jigsaws have disappeared.

'I think Nan must have given them away,' Kelly sighs, as we search under the beds and then in the bin, which is overflowing with Christmas paper and crumpled crackers beside the front gate. 'Either that or Jacinto's buried them in the garden for the pets to play with.'

I am holding a broken Buckaroo! in my hand.

'But why would he even want to do that when the pets are all dead in the first place?'

'Because that's what he does. He buried my netball and Daniel's yo-yo and we only found them again because Pickle dug them up by mistake.'

'I'd better get the spade then,' I say, and we troop back into the garden just as a yellow Allegro pulls up to the gate.

'Hello, son,' Dad says, getting out of the Allegro. 'And hello to you too, Kelly.'

'Hello, Dad.'

Dad leans purposely on the Allegro's roof and then grins at us over the top of the fence.

'I thought you'd come by taxi,' Kelly says, wiping her hands on the back of her jeans. 'Or that you'd walk up like you did last time.'

'I don't much like taxis, as a rule,' Dad says, patting the roof of the Allegro. 'Very expensive, I tend to find.'

He leans through the open driver's window and honks the horn for no good reason.

'What a sound!'

I stare at the car in a state of shock and confusion.

'And what do you think of this little beauty?'

Dad walks round to the front of the car and pats energetically on its bonnet.

'She was a genuine steal.'

'Was "she"?' Kelly asks, biting hard on barely suppressed laughter. 'I mean, really, was "she"?'

'Oh, yes. And these things never rust,' Dad continues, carefully adjusting a wing mirror. 'You can complain about a lot of things where BL is concerned, but its rustproofing is incredible – and it's guaranteed, as well.'

'But it's—'

'The cheapest second-hand car I have ever purchased. Can you believe it?'

He steps forward and the three of us awkwardly shake hands over the fence.

'Yes, I can,' Kelly mutters, before turning and trotting away back to the house. 'Without any doubt or second-guessing whatsoever and thank you very much for asking.'

After which it's just me with Dad and a fence between us.

'Right then.'

And the truth is, I want to hug him despite what has happened, though he would have to do something for that to happen, and since he doesn't, no hugging takes place.

'So here we are again.'

Instead, all we do is stare at each other, then at the Allegro, then at each other again, until Dad opens the driver's door and ushers me through the garden gate to admire the Allegro's brown interior.

'Are you ready for a proper adventure, son?'

He turns the ignition as soon as I climb into the car.

'I suppose so.'

'Because that is exactly what you are about to get.'

And we slowly crawl away from the kerb.

'Just you and me and this little beauty.'

I pull at the seatbelt, which seems to be jammed.

'You know, I think this is the best motor vehicle that I have ever had the pleasure of driving.'

'Where are we going?' I ask, as I finally pull the seatbelt over my shoulder and lock it into place. 'Because I haven't got my jacket or told Mum what we are doing.'

My head suddenly fills with visions of restaurants and the kind of country pubs that advertise in the middle of *The Kent Courier*.

'Well, I thought we could drop in at The Broken Coach & Horses,' Dad says, fighting with the gear stick. 'It's where I used to take your mother when we came to visit your nan and there was nothing on the telly. Did you know that?'

'No, I didn't.'

I stare through the windscreen, daring each passing lorry to swerve and force us off the road and into the kerb.

'Well, it's true. The Broken Coach & Horses was actually where I proposed to your mother, though that seems a lifetime ago now, in calendar terms, anyway.'

We bounce over a pothole.

'I went down on one knee in the beer garden and even got a round of applause from the other drinkers.'

I spontaneously grip at the glovebox as Dad finally finds the gear he has been looking for.

'Did you really?'

'Oh, yes. Though I did have a twitch in my back for a couple of days afterwards because of the way your mother was leaning on me before I had a chance to stand up properly.'

COACH PARTIES WELCOME

'And here we are!'

With no further warning, Dad turns the steering wheel and we career into The Broken Coach & Horses car park without indicating.

'Though of course, your mother was very touched by all the clapping going on around us, despite the pain in my back. She even got a little bit unnecessary because of all the high emotion in the air and everything.'

Dad slams on the brakes and I bolt forward, the seatbelt the only thing preventing me from crashing through the windscreen.

'There you go,' Dad announces, proudly grinning at me. 'Now, where's the best place to park, do you think?'

I peer through the windscreen at the car park, deserted except for a brown Reliant Robin propped up on bricks in a far corner.

'I think over there,' Dad says, not waiting for me to answer, and we putter into a diagonal space next to the bins.

'Did you see that?'

'See what?'

'How nippy it is? Have you ever seen such a precise three-point turn?'

'Is that what it was?'

'Yes.'

'It's just that I thought—'

'No, no. It was a three-pointer, and I should know, having driven so many tanks for a living.'

'Tanks. Right.'

'Now, let's get inside and you can tell me all about yourself.'

He reaches over and rustles my hair.

'Because we never got to have a little talk last time, did we?'

'No, Dad, we didn't.'

'So, let's get to the bar then.'

*

Once inside the pub we don't talk about anything much.

Instead, all we do is watch the only other customers play a game of darts as Dad tells me about his latest posting in West Germany, and I listen to what he says whilst clutching a glass of warm lemonade without ice.

'So it's back to the Rhine for me in a couple of months but with more lads to take care of this time and some brand-new amphibians to play with.'

Dad grins at me across the little table we are sitting at.

'Because amphibians are a lot of fun and they require a hell of a lot of manoeuvring.'

'My new school's going well,' I blurt out.

Then I stop talking, not knowing what to say next.

'Well, I'm very proud of you, son,' Dad says kindly, once it is obvious that I am not going to say any more on the subject.

'Really?'

'Yes.'

'Though it is a lot harder than I thought it would be.'

Dad smirks, for some reason.

'Because it is. Or it was, at first, I mean.'

At which point Dad looks almost painfully confused and we both lapse into uneven silence.

'Would you like to hear some music, Dad?'

'Yes, that would be nice. But nothing too glam rock, if you don't mind. I'm not a fan of Gary Glitter and never have been.'

'OK, then.'

I get up and walk over to the jukebox, push some coins in and select *You're So Vain*, *Space Oddity* and *Virginia Plain*.

Dun-a-lun-a-lun-dun-dun-a-lun-a-lun...

But, unfortunately, *You're So Vain* is scratched and has to be cancelled by the barmaid before the start of the first verse.

'That's a terrible shame,' Dad says, as a grim silence descends once again on our table. 'And you didn't even get your full musical money's worth, either.'

The silence then gets even heavier as a dart hits the pub dartboard with a loud *thwack!*

'Well, I'd better get you back as you'll only have things to do, I would imagine,' Dad announces suddenly, as another dart hits the board, this time with a sulky thud. 'After all, it is getting late—'

'Is it?'

'And I have things to do before I need to depart Sittingbourne.'

'Yes, I suppose so.'

'Plus, I don't want to get into any trouble, not with your mother. I had enough of that when we were together.'

'Fair enough.'

Almost relieved at the chance to escape, we get up and leave our little table, march out of the pub, climb into Dad's strange yellow car, and then drive back to Nan's house as fast as the Allegro's wheezing engine can take us.

'You look after yourself,' Dad says, pulling up the handbrake after reversing up to Nan's front gate. 'And good luck with all your new schoolwork.'

I unclick my seatbelt as he holds out his hand.

'You too,' I say, shaking the hand as quickly as I can. 'And enjoy driving all those amphibians.'

I climb out of the car and slam the passenger door shut.

'Oh, and thanks for the jigsaws.'

'Did you manage to finish yours?' Dad asks, frantically winding down the driver's window.

'No, I think there was a piece missing.'

'But it was nice, though, the photograph. That's Leeds Castle on the box, that is.'

'Yes, I know...'

Then, before I can slap the roof, Dad gives a quick wave of his hand and the Allegro jerks away from the gate and shoots off up the road, honking its parpy horn as it goes.

'You bastard,' I mutter under my breath, as the little yellow car disappears finally from view. 'You ruddy, rotten bastard.'

*

'What was he like?'

I am in the bathroom brushing my teeth as Kelly creeps in behind me, careful not to creak the floorboards.

'Hello. I didn't know you were still awake.'

Dad is long gone and all I want to do is go to bed.

'Sorry. I thought you had finished,' Kelly says nervously.

I put down the toothbrush and spit gooey white and blue toothpaste into the sink.

'He was OK.'

Which is a lie, obviously.

I quickly wipe my mouth with Daniel's *Thunderbirds* towel, which smells suspiciously of chocolate.

'Did he seem tired?'

'Yes,' I say instantly.

For a second neither of us says anything.

'Oh, OK.'

I can't look at her, even though she is staring right at me, and my sudden attack of cowardice makes me feel small and very ashamed.

'Well, maybe just a bit. But that could have been to do with all the driving he must have had to do because it is a long way to drive.'

I fold up the towel and place it back on the rack next to Afia's, which is scrunched up and damp.

'I suppose that must have been the reason,' Kelly says after a while. 'After all, he's surely very busy, what with the tanks and the obstacle courses he has to deal with and everything.'

I try to think of something to say but can't, so I just look down at the sink.

'I wonder if he'll come again?' Kelly asks eventually, her voice rising with the false optimism she is always able to deploy when she needs to. 'To see Daniel, perhaps?'

'Of course he will,' I say, rubbing her right shoulder and looking at her properly for the first time. 'Otherwise coming out of the blue like that would just be cruel and unusual, wouldn't it?'

'Yes, I think it would be.'

Kelly's eyes are wide and wet with tears, but the rest of her face is a mask of defiance.

'Anyway, I'm sure he just needs to sort a few things out first.'

'Of course he does, and then, after he's done that, he'll be back, won't he?' Kelly says, her tone starting to brighten a bit.

'I have no doubt about it and I'm sure he'll be all done in a couple of months.'

Kelly wipes at the corners of her eyes and reaches for the towel rack.

'And then he'll ask to see me as well, don't you think?'

Her hand settles on Afia's towel.

'Not that one,' I say, offering her Daniel's towel instead. 'Yes, of course he will, you'll see.'

And then Kelly hugs me and smells of the Avon talcum power that Beverley got from Mum for Christmas. Beverley loved that talcum powder the minute she unwrapped it (probably because it came with a matching soap and flannel).

'Thanks,' Kelly says.

'No problem. Now, you get to bed before Nan comes upstairs or Afia grasses us up.'

Which was always a danger. I could already hear Pickle scratching at the door to the lounge.

'And then I'll tell you everything Dad had to say in the morning.'

Which would also give me enough time to work out what he could have said, if he had been bothered.

'Goodnight then,' Kelly says, as downstairs the door to the lounge creaks opens and Pickle scurries into the hall.

'Goodnight, Kelly. Sleep well.'

48

The following Monday, after the adults' New Year hangovers have passed and the last of the Christmas rubbish has been taken away by the bin men, Mum comes in from work bearing gifts.

Never a good sign.

'Downstairs, everyone, please,' she shouts up the stairs the minute she is in the hallway. 'I have something special and pleasing for you all.'

I am actually with Kelly on the carpet in the lounge, watching John Craven's *Newsround*.

'Who's she bloody well shouting at now?' Nan asks, as she hunches, struggling with a jammed needle, over her sewing machine.

'Can you hear me up there?'

'Silly bloody cow,' Nan hisses under her breath. 'Voice like a foghorn even on a clear day.'

The door to the lounge flies open and we all pretend to be surprised.

'Mother!'

'Not so little ones!' Mum squeals, waving two Allders carrier bags at us. 'Gifts galore will shortly be forthcoming.'

Nan grunts out a puff of cigarette smoke, presses on the sewing machine pedal and drops ash onto the carpet.

'And I've got something extra special for you, beyond the pleasing sophistication of what is in these bags,' Mum continues above the renewed rattle of the sewing machine. 'And do you mind?' she snaps, eyeing Nan's back peevishly. 'As I'm being positively kind and giving here.'

A quick cloud of cigarette smoke appears above Nan's head as the sewing machine comes to a controlled stop.

'Thank you.'

And then, before any of us can say anything (or indeed ask what she is going on about), Mum steps aside, revealing an unsmiling overweight man in thick square glasses and an ill-fitting grey suit, hovering in the doorway.

'This,' Mum burbles, 'is Mark and he is very excited about meeting you all today. Aren't you, Mark?'

Mark says nothing.

'I said, "Aren't you, Mark?"'

Mum elbows the less than effusive Mark quickly and sharply in the ribs.

'Mark, please!'

One of the Allders bags rattles.

'Well?'

Mark looks a little startled.

'Yes,' he says at last, slowly and evenly.

'And, what are you?'

Nan peers over her shoulder at the commotion in the doorway.

'I am very excited about meeting you all today, thank you.'

And then Mark's eyes descend on Kelly and he smiles, slowly and surely, like a snake eyeing a distracted mouse.

'I have been looking forward to this moment for a very long time indeed.'

Kelly gets up from the carpet, steps forward and holds out a hand.

'Hello,' she says, her voice all cold and hollow. 'I'm Kelly.'

Mark looks her up and down and then holds out a big pink paw.

'Hello,' he says, his voice suddenly a lot brighter. 'I am Mark Preston.'

'Pleased to meet you, Mark Preston,' Kelly says, shaking the paw.
'Likewise.'

Mum claps her hands together.

'That's the way to do it.'

She grins at me and then nods at Nan, who bites hard on her cigarette.

'Now, let's all get to know each other, shall we?'

Afia appears frowning in the doorway.

'Tea and coffee, please, Afia, my darling,' Mum trills without even looking at her. 'And don't forget my sweetener, dear.'

Afia disappears back into the hallway.

'She's on a diet,' Kelly says, still holding Mark's hand. 'To both control the weight and ward off the risk of potential diabetes.'

'I know,' Mark says wearily, releasing my sister from his grip. 'She has told me all about it many times and in great detail.'

I stand up, shake pins and needles from my leg, and take hold of Mark's free hand. 'Nice to meet you. I'm Noah.'

'I know who you are,' Mark grunts, not that interested in what I'm saying.

'Well, isn't this civilised?' Mum gushes.

She steps forward and puts her Allders bags down on the coffee table.

'Now, shall we have a look at what Mark has very kindly bought for you both?'

'Yes, please,' Kelly says, with not a trace of excitement in her voice.

'And let's all sit down while we do it,' Mum clucks. 'Because no doubt we've got lots and lots to talk about. So why don't we get to know each other properly and in a more civilised fashion?'

She plonks herself onto the sofa and pats her knees, for some reason.

'Who would like to go first?'

'Shall we wait for the tea and coffee?' Kelly asks. 'Before we get so especially cosy.'

Mum narrows her eyes.

'No, because proceeding without refreshments is the appropriate method with which to continue in this instance, I would say.'

She silkily strokes at the cushion next to her.

'Kelly, you can sit between me and Mark, my darling.'

Kelly turns, sits down on the sofa in one quick movement and then stares straight ahead.

'Now let us begin to get to know each other.'

Though the truth was we already knew all about Mark Preston.

'Where shall I sit?' I ask.

'You can stay where you are,' Mum snaps.

Because he had stayed over at the house a fortnight ago, after his work's Christmas party, when he was giggling and drunk and losing a shoe on the stairs (before running off for work the next morning so as to be out of the way before anyone else was up).

Or so he (probably) thought.

'You've got to admire his vim,' Kelly whispered, as we watched him huffing and puffing his way up the lane from our perch at Beverley's window. 'Though he's going to be in trouble at the mill if he doesn't get a move on.'

At which point she smirks and lets go of the curtain.

'The fat bloody idiot.'

*

'He's a very pleasant man,' Nan croaked with a certain amount of enthusiasm later the same morning, as Beverley had the last of the resistance brushed from her hair. 'He's doing nicely at the paper mill, has an extremely good pension and his last wife was very responsible indeed.'

Her brushing comes to a sudden halt at this point as she comes over momentarily confused, before correcting herself. 'Because she's not dead yet – not yet by a long chalk.'

She takes hold of Beverley's hair and starts plaiting in double-quick time.

'I met her at bingo once, and very quiet and refined she was, even if she did have a strange taste in finger jewellery.'

She pauses briefly in her plaiting, peels the stump of a dead cigarette from her mouth and drops it into an overflowing ashtray on the carpet next to her right slipper.

'Bloody good manners, though.'

Cough.

'And she's raised those two girls of hers the right and proper way. Very well spoken, they are. Never a hint of a backchat from any of them.'

The hairbrush jabs in the direction of Kelly and me as we shiver in front of the fire.

'And it wouldn't hurt you two to learn some proper manners either. The rudeness I get from you two in this good Christian home.'

One last yank of Beverley's hair.

'Fucking awful, the language in this house.'

The hairbrush comes banging down on the coffee table.

'Now, get off to the stables to play with the horses otherwise you're going to be late for the baling and God knows what trouble you'll be getting yourselves into without the distractions of good Christian work to keep you busy. So get a bloody move on!'

'It was something to do with another woman,' Beverley opines coolly, twenty minutes later, as we slouch our way to stables – Kelly and Beverley in front, me behind. 'Everyone knows about it, though no one talks about what happened.'

I swing my duffle bag high in the air (which is heavy with a big bottle of Coca-Cola that Afia had packed for us while Nan was doing the hair-plaiting) and catch Kelly in the middle of her back.

'Fuck off, will you?' Kelly snaps, shoving me away.

'Well, don't get too close then,' I answer back, rubbing at where her hand has made contact with my shoulder. 'And don't swear so much. It's not ladylike.'

I swing the bag again but make sure not to hit her with it this time.

'He was having an affair with a next-door neighbour but one. Apparently, his wife only found out about it because she came home early after getting bored halfway through watching *Murder on the Orient Express*. They were at it on all fours in the middle of the hearth rug when she walked in and that's the truth.'

'You mean they didn't even make it into bed before going at it?' Kelly asks, clearly incredulous.

'Not even into the bedroom,' Beverley replies coolly.

'Well, I never, the dirty sod.'

'Like dogs, they were, and making horrible noises when they were doing it, or so I heard.'

*

So it wasn't that we didn't like Mark Preston per se.

It wasn't even that we didn't know everything we needed to know about him (apart from Beverley, of course, who could well have done because she knew everything about everyone). It was just that we didn't want him in our lives. He was an intruder and, because of that, he had to be repelled.

'He's been controversially married before, as you well know.'

This being Beverley's latest salvo, whispered later that night, as the three of us hide under the eiderdown in her bedroom.

'That first wife now lives on the other side of Faversham,' Beverley continues conspiratorially. 'And he has indeed got the two children that Nan was going on about, that I can confirm, and both are girls. He sees the first wife on a regular basis and sometimes they even go to Margate together, despite the repercussions from the divorce.'

She lowers her voice even further.

'He's very generous on such family outings, according to my sources, though she only gets the most basic of maintenance payments.'

'And how do you know all this?' I ask, growing weary with Beverley's very breathless tale. 'After all, that's a lot of valuable private information you seem to have there.'

Beverley was becoming more expert at finding things out than she ever had been before. She said she wanted to go into the police and you could see why.

'Noah, please...'

She holds up a hand.

'I can't reveal everything that I have learnt to you tonight, I'm afraid.'

Then she shakes her head.

'In fact, all I can say on the matter is that the Guides have their ways where such information-sharing is concerned.'

'What does he do at the mill?' Kelly asks calmly, chewing thoughtfully on her lower lip. 'With regard to his work, or otherwise.'

'It's something to do with the mulching. But whatever it is, it certainly involves a lot of overtime as he's very regularly in The Broken Coach & Horses and is always quick at getting a round in – which is often, according to my more alcoholic sources.'

We all fall silent, digesting this latest titbit and in particular the latter details, which could be important.

'OK,' Kelly says finally. 'I think I understand.'

Which is a curious thing to say because I certainly don't.

'One last question, though – why are they always in Elm Grove?'

'Well,' Beverley continues, quickly sitting upright and pulling the eiderdown from our heads (which I am glad about to be honest because it's getting too warm under there and I am starting to worry that we might suffocate), 'according to Jane Lenders, they've been looking at number 31 in the Grove with someone from the council.'

Jane Lenders, Beverley's new-found riding partner from Tonge Road always seemed to be hanging about outside the Co-op and had her fingers in many of Sittingbourne pies.

'I don't believe it,' Kelly says at last.

'Jane Lenders is always right,' I gush, despite myself. 'She knew Paul Douglas had run away even before the police had caught up with him.'

'They were there only last Thursday,' Beverley says, eyeing out my sister. 'And if you don't believe me, you can ask Jane Lenders yourself. She'll be outside the Co-op tomorrow morning before we do the clearing-out at the stables.'

Kelly climbs off the bed and strides towards the door.

'I think I will,' she says calmly, before taking a decisive hold of the doorknob, 'and I'll do it on my way to school if you don't mind.'

I turn back to Beverley as Kelly clomps her way out of the room and across the landing.

'It's a difficult time for her,' Beverley says casually, reaching for a *Jackie* from a pile of comics on the floor. 'So don't worry about her doubts on this particular subject.'

'It is true, though, isn't it?' I ask, gulping down my fears.

'Oh yes,' Beverley says, turning straightaway to the Agony Aunt page. 'Number 31, Elm Grove. You'll see.'

49

We very rarely ate together at Nan's.

It was one of the unwritten rules, partly because Nan liked to eat at her sewing machine, just as she liked to sleep on the sofa, and partly because Mum was seldom around. So any meal that involved Afia extending the big dining table in the through room which led to the kitchen (really a storeroom that smelled of paraffin) and getting the best cutlery out always signified some kind of special occasion, no matter how dreadful it might turn out to be.

'What are you doing?'

As I ask, Afia is squeezing a thick line of Fairy over the top of the dining table in a big slow green circle. 'I've got no time for you today,' she squeals, waving her arms about in case I don't quite get the message that high drama is clearly in the air. 'There's too much to do and not enough time to do it in – and that's just the way it always is for me.'

More waving of the arms.

'I don't know why I carry on sometimes, but it's got to be done, it really has. So all I can do is suffer.'

She starts smearing the Fairy around the tabletop with a pink bath sponge.

'I'm a slave to this house – it should be illegal.'

I felt sorry for Afia (most of the time), I really did.

As the eldest of Nan's three foster children, she was responsible for everything that Nan could not (or could not be bothered to) do.

And although, strictly speaking, it should have been Beverley doing all the running-about, together with the shopping and the cooking as well as the inevitable washing-up around which the house seemingly revolved, because Beverley was Nan's Little Princess all the real housework usually fell to Afia.

Slightly predictably.

'Sometimes it's all I can do not to dial 999, it really is.'

Though, as Nan was always quick to point out if challenged on Beverley's regal laziness, Beverley did have Minstrel to take care of, even if all that involved (as far as I could tell) was well-timed plait-twirling on Beverley's part as she got the beguiled, sexually frustrated stable hands to do her mucking-out for her, while they did their best to hide their aching erections.

'No one's died, have they?'

For a moment my mind goes through all the names of the relatives I could just about remember.

'No.' Afia giggles. 'No recent deaths in the family, fool.'

More smearing of the detergent goo on the table.

'After all, if someone had died I'd have my black dress on, wouldn't I?'

Bubbling Fairy drips onto the carpet.

'Oh my God, we haven't got Important Company, have we?'

Afia giggles again and for the first time, my eyes focus on the swollen Safeway bags sitting on top of the draining board.

'Oh, yes.' Afia chuckles, picking up a tea towel. 'A very special visitor will be joining us this evening so everyone can have a very important conversation over dinner and not complain about my cooking for once.'

She begins scooping Fairy bubbles into the tea towel.

'Are you sure?'

Important company or special conversations were always a problem.

'Oh, yes.'

Usually, they involved uncles, aunts and cousins coming down to sniff the furniture and endure the tea, though a visit from another wing of the family was usually preceded with troubling and unsettling news – tears over tightly folded letters, telephone conversations that just get louder and louder, that sort of thing.

'Because Mum hasn't said anything to me or Kelly.'

This time, however, there had been no such early warnings and only Mark (bloody) Preston to worry about, though no other dramas to get the tears flowing.

'It's not some cousins marrying each other or someone having an operation around the heart, is it?'

I'm getting a little desperate now.

Afia stands back and reviews her soapy handiwork.

'None that I am aware of, though your cousin Peter does have the shingles.'

The air sparkles with chemical cleanliness.

'And no one's been sent to prison that we are unaware of, have they?'

'No. Now get out of my way as I've got cooking and table-arranging to do.'

She points at the door.

'So move! Before I tell Nan you're causing me trouble.'

I am not causing trouble, obviously.

Though of course the threat of causing trouble and the punishment that the accusation of causing trouble could bring was Afia's standard way of getting what she wanted. So although I'm not worried or concerned in any way whatsoever because of my undoubted innocence in the matter, I leave the room as quickly as I can.

'If anyone needs me, I'll be out the back,' I say as nonchalantly as I can, before running up the hall as quickly as possible. 'And I won't be coming back in for some time yet!'

Afia continues her wiping of the table and rolls her eyes.

'Oh, who cares,' she sighs wearily before drying her hands on the front of her jeans. 'Because I most certainly don't.'

50

When I get outside I find Kelly and Beverley in the back garden watching Tony flex his teenage biceps on the other side of the fence.

'Oh, Tony, you're so funny!'

I roll my eyes.

Now, this really could be trouble and, by the sound of Beverley's over-eager giggling as she pushes her (non-existent) breasts at him, Tony can only be fully aware of the danger so obviously staring him in the face.

'You're so clever. You just make me laugh out loud sometimes, you really do.'

Tony smirks and then, when he sees me, quickly stands back from the fence.

'So, I'll see you tomorrow then,' he says, suddenly all businesslike and over-amplified. 'For the morning exercises?'

'Oh yes, we'll be there, nice and early.' Beverley giggles, elbowing Kelly out the way so she can get even closer to the fence.

'Because breakfast can wait, don't you worry.'

The fence begins to slowly tip over into the path.

'Now, don't you be late this time.' Tony chuckles before walking off, whistling over his shoulder.

'Oh, we won't.'

Kelly joins Beverley in her giggling, even though Tony now has his back fully to the pair of them.

'And don't you worry about us,' Kelly squeals. 'Because we'll be right on time, I promise!'

The fence looks like it is going to fall over any minute.

'You two are so pathetic,' I say, shaking my head. 'And his dad's a jailbird, probably, which only makes it worse.'

Which is sort of true, because Tony's dad had done time (according to Afia) and even if he was sexy (though I had long ago vowed never to share that opinion with anyone and, least of all, not with Beverley or my sister, who seemed to have madness in their blood whenever Tony's name was mentioned), he was also best kept at arm's length due to the rampant criminal tendencies evident in his family line.

'Oh yeah?'

Kelly and Beverley both stand back and the fence quickly rights itself without the burden of their heaving bodies to weigh it down.

'His father is not a jailbird,' Kelly pronounces authoritatively. 'And anyway, you don't even know what a jailbird is.'

Her eyes narrow and meet Beverley's.

'Besides, we were just talking about the work at the stables.'

'My arse you were.'

Beverley suddenly starts grinning.

'I don't care,' she gushes, her voice going all girlish and sing-song. 'Because I think he's dreamy.'

She takes hold of Kelly's elbows.

'And his dad's got his own flat, just off the High Street, which is why Tony can walk home from the stables whenever he wants.'

'How many bedrooms?' Kelly asks, suddenly all excited. 'And how many of them are doubles?'

I sigh as loudly as I can (though I am also interested to hear where this is going).

'Only two, but his dad's has a king-size bed and a fitted wardrobe,' Beverley squeals, 'and they decorated the flat themselves – in terracotta, with a beige dado.'

Now that the conversation has turned to home furnishing I quickly lose interest.

'Listen, do you know what this special dinner's about?'

Kelly looks at me, blank-faced.

'Special dinner?'

Beverley narrows her eyes even more.

'Apparently, your mum's going to be making a little announcement,' she says casually.

'Really?'

Now it's Kelly's turn to look startled.

'What kind of announcement?'

'And is it a good announcement or a bad announcement?' I ask, advancing on Beverley before she can answer.

'That's for you to decide,' Beverley purrs, slowly crossing her arms. 'As I am sure you will be able to do, as you are so obviously aware of the formalities of diplomatic relations and such and such.'

'What?'

Kelly steps back so that she is standing right next to me.

'Spill the beans,' she says, a hint of menace to her voice.

Beverley steps even further back from the fence.

'Let's just say that all of my observations – which, I should point out, you were very quick to spurn not so long ago – are about to be proved correct. Not that I hold it against you, because I don't, though it would be appreciated by myself if you could at least acknowledge that my predictions are moving towards realistic fruition.'

Kelly suddenly moves forward and grabs Beverley by the arm.

'Kelly, you're hurting me,' Beverley complains, trying to shake her off (though that's impossible once Kelly gets a fight in her).

'Please, you've got the skin.'

Kelly digs her nails even deeper into Beverley's quickly reddening flesh.

'Alright!'

Kelly lets go of Beverley's arm, who immediately starts rubbing at the welts left behind.

'They were talking about it on the phone this afternoon.'

Before Kelly can even open her mouth Beverley holds up a hand.

'And I only got half of it because your mum was at the garage and then her money ran out, so all I can do is tell you what I know and no more.'

For a moment Kelly doesn't say a word (probably because she is flummoxed by Beverley's sudden usurping of her established role as the Queen of Trunking – because that is an official title, and I should know because I was the one who made it up).

'Alright then.'

Beverley pulls her plait over her shoulder and starts stroking it, like a Bond villain stroking a cat.

'Mark Preston's coming over with a bottle of red wine so that he and your mum can tell you something.'

'Tell us what?' I snap, suddenly frustrated by all the plait-stroking and the way Beverley is deploying each word for maximum effect instead of just getting on with it. 'This really is becoming intolerable and annoying, you know.'

'They're taking the house in Elm Grove and they've already signed the tenancy agreement,' Beverley says quickly with a grin. 'And they've got a moving-in date worked out as well.'

I can feel my mouth dropping open.

'Isn't that good news?'

Beverley bounces on the spot.

'For you, I mean, not for me.'

She suddenly stops bouncing and looks at Kelly.

'Oh, no.'

Then her face screws up and she starts to go red.

'Because now I'm not going to have anyone to ride Minstrel with and everything.'

Kelly starts to cry.

Oh, dear.

'I am so happy,' Kelly sobs, opening her arms and wrapping them around Beverley. 'Thank you so much for all your trunking.'

And then they weep into each other's hair, leaving me with no one to hug or to cry with, even though I don't want to cry. I'm just happy.

So instead I open my arms and give the both of them a big hug, until Beverley shoves me off because I am squeezing one of her (non-existent) breasts by mistake.

*

That night, for the first time in ages, Nan lets us put the hot water on so that we can all have a bath instead of a shower.

She also lets us play music out on the landing.

'But only this one time, mind, because this house is not a dancehall or a discotheque – whatever that actually is.'

On hearing the news, Beverley pulls the speakers of her record player out onto the landing (as far as she can without the leads coming out the back) and plays *Arrival* all the way through (even though we had all got bored with it a long time ago), and we all sing along to *Dancing Queen* and *When I Kissed the Teacher* while we wait for Kelly to finish in the bathroom.

'I only need a couple more minutes, that's all,' Kelly shouts over the top of the music, not sounding particularly bothered about who has to go in after her. 'And then I'll be well and truly done.'

I bang on the bathroom door the first chance I get.

'But you've been in there for nearly an hour. I don't need that amount of time.'

'Well, you don't have to moisturise, do you?' Kelly shouts back through the door. 'Or do your eyebrows.'

'What does that mean?'

'It means pain and dedication for the purpose of beauty, and that's all you need to know.'

'Well, dedicate a bit faster, please, because I need to have a bath.'

Beverley nips across the landing, clutching a wet towel and wearing a new blue polka dot dress that Nan bought for her in the market. 'Don't tell anyone,' she whispers, as she flicks the towel across the banister. 'Just in case it makes the wallpaper smell a bit damp.'

'OK,' I say, and bang on the bathroom door again.

'Kelly, please!'

Holding a Wombles towel in his lap, Daniel watches us blank-faced from the top of the stairs.

'Kelly!'

'Oh, piss off, will you.'

I give up on the door banging and instead pick Daniel up by the arms and swing him around, just as Beverley re-appears on the landing singing *SOS* like one of the ABBA women.

'You're not going to be sick, are you?' Beverley asks as Daniel swoops through the air before landing back down on the carpet.

Daniel shakes his head.

'Good boy.'

She smiles and kisses him on the cheek.

'Because if you were I'd have to clean it up and I've just done my nails.'

Then she pats him on the top of the head and wafts away back up the landing.

'Kelly, hurry up! There's definitely a queue forming out here,' Beverley says loudly, winking at me and then returning to her bedroom to spray Panache about.

'I'm coming, I really am!'

Then, like a miracle, the bathroom door opens and Kelly emerges, Queen of Sheba-like, a yellow towel wrapped tightly under her armpits. 'Fuck off!' she mouths in my direction, before dashing, giggling, for the safety of Beverley's bedroom.

'Come on,' I say, picking Daniel up again. 'The bathroom is ours and now it is man territory.'

*

An hour later, after we have put on our best clothes and Kelly has (finally) finished doing her make-up (or rather Beverley has finished putting the make-up on her), we come down the stairs as a bright and bath-fresh foursome.

'Don't you look smart,' Afia sighs approvingly, as Mum comes up the hall in her best dress, 'though that Mark Preston has been held up, so you'd better sit down and don't make a mess, please.'

Beverley sighs, rolls her eyes and then follows Afia into the kitchen.

'Darlings!' Mum gushes, opening her arms to wrap me, Kelly and Daniel tightly to his chest. 'A truly wonderful evening awaits us all, because not only is Mark Preston going to make a very special announcement, but we have also been offered a truly lovely council house in Elm Grove – in Elm Grove, my darlings! – and isn't that just the most exciting news for all of us!'

For a moment no one says anything, as my eyes meet Kelly's across the top of Mum's heaving breasts.

'New adventures about to begin!' Mum continues, underlining her words as firmly as possible. 'Do you not agree, my darling?'

Then she releases us from her loving grasp, and me and Kelly look at Daniel, and then the three of us look back at Mum.

'Yes, Mother,' me and Kelly say in grim unison.

'New adventures about to begin.'

Noah's Cultural Appendix

99 ice cream. A description for an ice-cream cone with a chocolate Flake (specially produced for this purpose) shoved into it.

A to Z. A range of British street atlases dating back to the 1930s. Before the internet, most cars in the UK had at least one well-thumbed and dog-eared *A to Z* in it for people to bicker over.

ABBA. A Swedish pop group, formed in Stockholm in 1972 by Agnetha Fältskog, Björn Ulvaeus, Benny Andersson and Anni-Frid Lyngstad, and one of the most commercially successful acts in the history of popular music.

Action Man. An action figure launched in the United Kingdom in 1966 by Palitoy as a licensed copy of Hasbro's American "movable fighting man", G.I. Joe.

Adolf Hitler. If you need to learn about who Adolf Hitler was you're reading the wrong book.

Al-Qaeda. A militant Sunni Islamist terrorist organisation.

Aladdin Sane. The sixth studio album by David Bowie, released in 1973.

Allders. An independent department store operating in the United Kingdom, until it went into administration in 2005.

Ambre Solaire. Suntan lotion with a vaguely lustrous and continental character.

Angel Delight. A powdered dessert product produced in the United Kingdom, designed to be mixed and whisked with milk to create a mousse-like sweet dessert.

Arctic Roll. A frozen dessert comprising a vanilla ice-cream roll covered in jam and surrounded by sponge cake. Actually tastier than it sounds.

Argos. A British catalogue and outlet retailer. Gives a taste of what it must have been like to shop in the Soviet Union.

Army Cadets. The Army Cadet Force (ACF) is a national youth organisation sponsored by the British Ministry of Defence and the British Army.

Arrival. The critically-acclaimed and commercially successful album released by ABBA in 1976.

Austin Allegro. A small family car manufactured by the Austin-Morris division of British Leyland between 1973 and 1982.

Austin Maxi. A medium-sized five-door hatchback car produced by Austin and British Leyland between 1969 and 1981.

Avon. A direct-selling company specialising in beauty, household and other personal care items, mainly targeted at women. "Ding dong, Avon calling", etc.

Baner Cymru. The flag of Wales, which consists of a red dragon passant on a green and white field.

Basil Brush. The fictional anthropomorphic fox from *The Basil Brush Show* and a mischievous character and raconteur, particularly popular with children. Best known for his catchphrases "Ha Ha Ha!" and "Boom! Boom!".

The Basil Brush Show. A British children's television sitcom series starring Basil Brush.

Battle of Britain. A German Second World War military campaign, during which the Royal Air Force defended the United Kingdom against large-scale attack by the Luftwaffe.

Bay City Rollers. A Scottish pop band whose popularity was highest in the mid-1970s.

The Beatles. A British rock band. Rather famous.

Benson & Hedges. A British brand of cigarettes.

Bette Davis. An iconic film, television and theatrical actress, regarded as one of the great American performers (though she was actually English/American).

The Bill. The soapy ITV police drama that ran from 1984 until 2010 and which usually featured stern-faced actors, either running up and down alleyways or discussing their marriages over cups of instant coffee in the station canteen.

Black Beauty. An 1877 novel by English author Anna Sewell. With fifty million copies sold, *Black Beauty* is one of the best-selling books of all time.

The Blitz. The German bombing offensive against the United Kingdom that principally took place between 1940 and 1941.

BMW 3 Series. A luxury car manufactured by BMW since 1975. Slightly dull but very, very desirable.

Bontempi. An Italian musical instrument manufacturer, best known for making low-priced, plastic-cased chord organs in which the sound is produced by air being forced over reeds by an electric fan. Not at all annoying to listen to.

Boots No7. Launched in 1935, Boots No7 is a brand of skincare and anti-wrinkle creams popular with all kinds of women (as well as men).

British Airways. Once "The world's favourite airline", though not so much since the dawn of the Millennium.

(British) Empire. Comprised of the dominions, colonies, protectorates, mandates and other territories ruled or administered by the United Kingdom, this was the largest empire in history and, for over a century, the world's foremost global power.

Brut 33. The brand name Brut was used for a line of men's grooming and fragrance products first launched in 1964 by Fabergé. In 1968 a budget range was marketed as Brut 33 because it contained thirty-three per cent of the fragrance of the original product.

Buckaroo! A game of physical skill, intended for players aged four and above, and made by Milton Bradley, a division of the toy company Hasbro.

BUPA. A private healthcare not-for-profit company originating in the United Kingdom. Not particularly liked by the Liberal Left.

Butlin's. A chain of holiday camps in the United Kingdom, founded by Billy Butlin to provide affordable holidays for British families.

Bye, Bye Baby (Baby Goodbye). A hit single by the Bay City Rollers.

Carlsberg. A 5% pilsner beer created by Carl Jacobsen, son of Carlsberg's founder, JC Jacobsen.

Carmen. Heated hair curlers.

Casualty. A BBC1 medical drama and the longest-running emergency medical drama television series in the world. Not exhausted by its long run in any way.

CB radio. A system of short-distance radio communications, typically on a selection of forty channels within the 27 MHz (11m) band. Keep on truckin', etc.

Chanel No. 5. The first perfume launched by French couturier Gabrielle "Coco" Chanel. Iconic.

Cider with Rosie. A 1959 book by Laurie Lee that sold over six million copies worldwide. Charming or slightly stifling (depending on your point of view).

Cluedo. A murder mystery board game featuring characters with silly names.

CNN. An American cable and satellite television news channel, founded in 1980 by American media proprietor Ted Turner.

The Co-op. Used in brand form by co-operative societies in the United Kingdom which operate as retail outlets.

Coke. Cultural shorthand for Coca-Cola, a carbonated soft drink produced by The Coca-Cola Company. Sweet and sassy (not unlike the author of this book).

Colour by Numbers. Painting to a pre-set design. Messy.

Commander Koenig. A fictional character from the television series *Space: 1999*, played with great seriousness by Martin Landau.

Community Support Officers. Non-warranted, civilian police support staff that arrived in 2002, thanks to New Labour.

Cornish ice cream. A form of ice cream, first made in Cornwall with clotted cream. Delicious.

Coronation Street. A stalwart of the ITV evening schedule, *Coronation Street* appeared in black and white on British television in 1960 and shows no sign of going away. More dramatic in its current format than previously and on television much more often today than it used to be.

Countdown. A British game show involving word and number puzzles, broadcast on Channel 4. Also, the first programme to be aired on the channel when it launched in 1982. Reassuringly dull and predictable.

Cybermen. A fictional race of cyborgs who are among the most persistent enemies of the Doctor in the British science-fiction television programme *Doctor Who*.

Dad's Army. The hugely popular BBC television sitcom about the British Home Guard during the Second World War, broadcast between 1968 and 1977. Movie versions have proved to be less successful.

The Daily Express. A British daily national (very) middle-market tabloid newspaper.

Daily Mail. A British daily middle-market tabloid newspaper and the United Kingdom's second-biggest-selling daily newspaper after *The Sun*.

The Daily Mirror. A British national daily tabloid newspaper founded in 1903.

Dancing Queen. A Europop song by ABBA and the lead single from its *Arrival* album that starts with something of a hysterical piano rush (*Eoooooohhh, ohhhhh, oh, ohhhh, Oh, oh, oh, ohhhh, oh, ohhhh…*).

Dandelion & Burdock. Consumed since the Middle Ages and originally a light mead fermented from dandelion and burdock, over the years Dandelion & Burdock has evolved into a sweet carbonated soft drink.

Daleks. Similar to Cybermen but rather more ridiculous.

Dastardly & Muttley. The villains (one of which is a dog) from the cartoon series *Wacky Races*.

Dave Lee Travis. Radio 1 DJ and *Top of the Pops* presenter, otherwise known as "The Hairy Cornflake" from his time on the Radio 1 Breakfast Show.

David Bowie. The Thin White Duke.

David Cassidy. An American actor, singer and songwriter, well known for his performance in *The Partridge Family*, which then led to him becoming a teen idol and a pop singer in the 1970s.

Daz. A laundry detergent first introduced in 1953. Powerful and bright and certainly not posh.

Demis Roussos. A Greek singer, songwriter and musician whose hit song *Forever and Ever* stayed at the top of the UK Singles Chart in 1976 as part of *The Roussos Phenomenon* EP.

Dettol. An antiseptic disinfectant used for skin disinfection, cleaning surgical instruments and wiping around the home (usually in the kitchen and bathroom).

Discovery Channel. An American cable and satellite television channel famous for its nature and geography documentary series. Expect to see lots of sharks.

Doctor Who. The British science-fiction television programme, produced by the BBC since 1963.

Donny Osmond. An American singer, actor, radio personality and former teen idol. In the mid-1960s he and four of his elder brothers found fame as The Osmonds pop group. Cue lots and lots and lots of female screaming.

Dum Dum Diddle. A song by ABBA, recorded for the *Arrival* album.

Duty-Free. A catch-all term for items free from the payment of certain local or national taxes and duties.

Eamonn Holmes. A journalist and broadcaster from Northern Ireland, best known for presenting *Sky News Sunrise* and *This Morning* before moving onto GB News.

EastEnders. Grim-faced and slightly nonsensical BBC soap opera that landed in 1985 on BBC1 with a flurry, a death and lots of cockney bickering.

Elvis and Priscilla Presley. The former King of Rock and Roll (and his wife).

Encyclopaedia Britannica. A general knowledge English-language encyclopaedia. Sort of like Wikipedia before the internet arrived.

Esso. The trading name for ExxonMobil and its related companies which once had a tiger as an advertising motif.

Eurovision Song Contest. The longest-running annual international television song competition, held primarily among the member countries of the European Broadcasting Union (EBU) since 1956.

Fairy. An iconic brand of washing-up liquid produced by Procter & Gamble in England and launched in 1950. Fairy Liquid has traditionally been green, prompting the well-known advertising jingle "Now hands that do dishes can feel as soft as your face with mild green Fairy Liquid".

Famous Five. Shorthand for a series of children's adventure novels written by the British author Enid Blyton. The novels feature the adventures of a group of young children (Julian, Dick, Anne and George), as well as George's dog, Timmy.

Farrah Fawcett. A popular American actress and model who rose to international fame when she posed in an iconic red swimsuit for a poster (which then became the best-selling pin-up poster in history) and who also starred as private investigator Jill Munroe in the television series *Charlie's Angels*.

Fern Britton. An English television presenter, best known for her television work with ITV and the BBC.

The Forces. Shorthand for the (British) armed forces.

Ford Anglia. A popular, frog-faced, family small car, last produced (in one form or another) in 1967. Cute.

Ford Cortina. A car built by Ford in the United Kingdom in various guises from 1962 to 1982 and the country's best-selling car of the 1970s. Boxy and rather wonderful.

Ford Focus. A compact car manufactured by the Ford Motor Company since 1998 and which became more boring with each incarnation.

Ford Granada. A large executive car manufactured by Ford from 1972 until 1994.

Ford Mondeo. A family car first manufactured by Ford in 1992.

Ford Zephyr. A car manufactured by Ford in the UK from 1950 to 1972. A little tank-like and rather butchy.

Freemans. A British catalogue clothing retailer and its printed catalogue.

Fresca. A somewhat frothy soft drink advertised on television by a sunglasses-wearing bear.

From a Jack to a King. A country music crossover hit for Ned Miller, *From a Jack to a King* has been covered extensively by various artists since its original release in 1957.

The Gas Board. Collective term for the regional operators of the domestic gas market in the United Kingdom up until the privatisation of the sector.

George (W) Bush. An American politician who served as the forty-third President of the United States from 2001 to 2009 and who was in office when the 9/11 terrorist attacks happened.

Give Me Joy In My Heart. A traditional Christian hymn based on *The Parable of the Ten Virgins*.

GMTV. The ITV breakfast show broadcast from 1993 to 2010 and which was essentially the same as *Good Morning Britain* (which it replaced), though not at all like the second *Good Morning Britain* (which came after *GMTV* had finished broadcasting).

Gobstoppers. A type of hard confectionery, usually round and normally between 1 and 3cm across.

Gola. A sporting goods manufacturer based in England.

Golf GTI. The GTI version of the commercially successful (which is putting it mildly) small family car produced by Volkswagen.

Grundig. A German manufacturer of consumer electronics, domestic appliances and personal care products.

The Guardian. A left(ish) British newspaper, available Monday to Saturday and internationally via its news website.

Guinness. This Irish stout always seemed to be a favourite of older members of the family, until it became somewhat fashionable and then suddenly everyone was (apparently) drinking it.

Hammer Horror. A series of British Gothic movies made from the mid-1950s until the 1970s.

Happy-slapping. A fad originating in the United Kingdom around 2005, in which one or more people attack a victim for the purpose of recording the assault (commonly with a camera phone or a smartphone).

Harmony hairspray. Sticky and smelly.

Harold Shipman. A notorious serial killer and GP, convicted in 2000 of the murder of fifteen people.

Harvester. A family farmhouse-style restaurant chain in the United Kingdom.

Health and Safety. A multidisciplinary field concerned with the health, safety and welfare of people at work. Became something of a cultural-political obsession in the UK in the early noughties.

Henry Kissinger. An American diplomat who was the United States Secretary of State and National Security Advisor under Richard Nixon and Gerald Ford. Famous for his shuttle diplomacy.

Homer Simpson. A fictional character and the main protagonist of the American animated sitcom *The Simpsons*.

Hostess trolley. A trolley used to convey food around (mainly) middle-class homes. Somewhat popular in the 1970s.

Hoover. An American vacuum cleaner company whose Hoover brand name became synonymous with vacuum cleaners and vacuuming in the United Kingdom.

HP. A hire purchase (HP) is an arrangement whereby a customer agrees to a contract to acquire an asset by paying an initial instalment (e.g. forty per cent of the total) and then repays the balance of the price of the asset plus interest over time.

Hubba-bubba. A brand of bubble gum that took its name from the phrase "Hubba Hubba" as used by military personnel in the Second World War to express approval.

I Will Always Love You. A song originally written and recorded in 1973 by Dolly Parton. Whitney Houston recorded a version of the same song for *The Bodyguard* movie which, as a single, remained at Number One in the UK Singles Chart for fourteen weeks in 1992 (though it felt much longer at the time).

IRA. The Irish Republican Army (IRA) was one of several paramilitary movements in Ireland dedicated to Irish republicanism (the belief that all of Ireland should be an independent republic). It was also characterised by the credo that political violence was necessary to achieve this goal.

ITV. The British commercial television network, launched in 1955 to provide competition to the BBC, and which, before the arrival of Channel 4, was only the third television channel in the UK.

Jackie. A weekly magazine for girls published from 1964 until 1993. Particularly popular in the 1970s.

Jackie Collins. An English novelist and younger sister of Dame Joan Collins (forever known humorously and affectionately as "the lucky bitches" thanks to French and Saunders).

Jaime Sommers. A fictional character from the science-fiction action series *The Bionic Woman* (1976 to 1978), portrayed by the American actress Lindsay Wagner.

Jamaican Rum. A dark rum that works well in cocktails and with drunks.

James Bond. 007. Ta da da da, da da da, daar, da, da, da, da, etc.

James (Jim) Callaghan. The British Prime Minister from 1976 to 1979 and Leader of the Labour Party from 1976 until 1980.

Jiu-jitsu. A Japanese martial art and a method of close combat for defeating an armed and armoured opponent in which one uses no weapon or only a short weapon.

John Craven's Newsround. A children's news programme launched in 1972 and fronted by John Craven until his departure in 1989. Worthy and slightly patronising.

John Major. Prime Minister of the United Kingdom and Leader of the Conservative Party from 1990 to 1997.

Jon Pertwee. An English actor, entertainer and cabaret performer who starred as the third incarnation of the Doctor in *Doctor Who* between 1970 and 1974.

Kenny. An English pop and glam rock band that released several hit singles in the UK in the mid-1970s including *The Bump* and *Fancy Pants*.

Kent and Sussex Courier. An English regional newspaper, published in Royal Tunbridge Wells.

The Kent Messenger. A British weekly newspaper serving the mid-Kent area.

Kevin Keegan. An English former football player and manager.

Khrushchev. Nikita Khrushchev was a statesman who led the Soviet Union during part of the Cold War, as the First Secretary of the Communist Party of the Soviet Union from 1953 to 1964, and then as Chairman of the Council of Ministers, or Premier, from 1958 to 1964.

Knowing Me, Knowing You. A hit single recorded by ABBA.

L'Oreal. A French cosmetics manufacturer and the world's largest cosmetics company with something of a posh image.

Legs & Co. A *Top of the Pops* all-female dance troupe that appeared on the show between 1976 and 1981. Particularly popular with dads.

Live and Let Die. The eighth spy movie in the James Bond series and the first to star Roger Moore as the fictional MI6 agent.

Look-in. A children's magazine which ran from 1971 to 1994 centred on ITV's television programmes in the United Kingdom.

Look and Learn. A British weekly educational magazine for children published between 1962 and 1982.

Luftwaffe. The German aerial warfare arm of the Wehrmacht military during the Second World War. Famously (and humiliatingly) failed to defeat the Royal Air Force in the Battle of Britain.

McDonald's. The international fast-food retailer and a symbol of modern American capitalism.

Magpie. Sort of like ITV's answer to the BBC's *Blue Peter* but without the latter's serious and slightly middle-class character.

The Man with the Golden Gun. The ninth spy movie in the James Bond series and the second to star Roger Moore as the fictional MI6 agent James Bond.

Marc Bolan. An English singer-songwriter, musician, guitarist and poet. He was best known as the dreamy lead singer of the glam rock band T. Rex.

Margaret Thatcher. British Prime Minister from 1979 to 1990 and Leader of the Conservative Party from 1975 to 1990. The longest-serving British prime minister of the twentieth century and the first woman to have been so appointed, Thatcher was also dubbed "The Iron Lady of the West" by part of the Soviet press.

Marks & Spencer. A major British multinational retailer that sells clothing, home and luxury food products.

Marlene Dietrich. An iconic German actress and singer who achieved international cinematic fame that stretched well into the 1980s. A camp icon (with bells on).

Mars Bar. A British chocolate bar, first manufactured in 1932.

Mastermind. A code-breaking game for two players and also a general knowledge BBC television programme.

Medical Centre. Where Moonbase Alpha's Helena Russell hangs out, in *Space: 1999.*

Miss World. The oldest-running and somewhat controversial international beauty pageant, created in 1951 in the United Kingdom by Eric Morley.

Money, Money, Money. An iconic song from ABBA's *Arrival* album that has a very precise introduction (*Da, da, da, da, da, da, De-ala-lud-da, da, da, da, da, De-ala-lud-de-a-lut-da, do, alooo, Boomamin, boomamin, boomamin, boomamin, Boomamin, boomamin, boomamin, boomamin…*).

Monopoly. A board game where players roll two six-sided dice to move around the game board buying and trading properties.

Moonbase Alpha. The fictional moonbase and main setting in *Space: 1999*.

The Morecambe & Wise Christmas Special. The Morecambe & Wise Christmas shows were hugely popular on BBC1 when broadcast in the 1970s. They were also very, very funny.

The Morecambe & Wise Show. A comedy sketch show originally broadcast by BBC television and the third television series by Morecambe & Wise that began airing in 1968 on BBC2.

Morris Marina. An automobile manufactured by the Austin-Morris division of British Leyland from 1971 until 1980. According to certain sources the Marina ranks amongst the worst cars ever built, even if it did sell very well when it was originally available in the United Kingdom.

Morrisons. A large chain of supermarkets in the United Kingdom.

Mouse Trap. A board game first manufactured by Ideal in 1963 for two to four players.

Mr Mainwaring. The pompous, if essentially brave and patriotic local bank manager who appointed himself as leader of his town's contingent of Local Defence Volunteers in *Dad's Army*.

Murder on the Orient Express. A stiff-backed 1974 British mystery movie directed by Sidney Lumet based on the 1934 novel of the same name by Agatha Christie.

My Love, My Life. A song recorded by ABBA for the *Arrival* album.

National Express. A British multinational public transport company, famous in the UK for its iconic coach services.

National Velvet. A 1944 American hit movie, based on the novel of the same name by Enid Bagnold.

Nazis. Shorthand for a form of fascism that incorporates scientific racism and antisemitism as developed and influenced by German nationalism, the Völkisch movement and the anti-Communist Freikorps paramilitary groups that emerged during the Weimar Republic.

Nellie the Elephant. A children's song from 1956 about a fictional and intelligent elephant that left the travelling circus with a trumpety-trump, trump.

Nescafé. A brand of coffee made by Nestlé and first introduced in Switzerland in 1938.

News at Ten. The flagship ITV evening news programme, launched in 1967.

NHS. The British National Health Service (NHS) began providing its comprehensive health services, free at the point of use and paid for from general taxation, in 1948, and has trundled on ever since.

Nicorette. The brand name for nicotine replacement therapy products that contain nicotine.

Nivea Creme. A popular moisturiser produced since 1911 and famous for its blue and white packaging.

Noel Edmonds. An English television presenter and former Radio 1 DJ that presented *Multi-Coloured Swap Shop*, *Top of the Pops*, *The Late, Late Breakfast Show*, *Telly Addicts* and *Deal or No Deal*.

The number 122 bus. A bus route that runs from Plumstead Station to Crystal Palace.

Oxfam. An international confederation of charitable organisations focused on the alleviation of global poverty.

Penthouse. A men's magazine that combines lifestyle articles and softcore pornographic pictorials. "Classy".

Pick 'n' Mix. A method of commercially dispensing multiple small units of confectionery either in manufactured bags with a fixed number of units per container or by the amount of mass placed in a bag. Popular at the cinema.

Pickfords. A British moving company.

The Pools. A pool-based betting game (actually The Football Pools in the United Kingdom) which invites players to predict the outcome of top-flight football matches in the week ahead. Cheap to enter and offering potentially large winnings, the Pools were once the epitome of working-class escape and wish fulfilment.

Pret a Manger. A British sandwich chain that was, between 2001 and 2008, thirty-three per cent owned by McDonald's somewhat ironically.

Princess Diana. A member of the British royal family who died in 1997 and who was the first wife of King Charles III.

Quality Street. A selection of individual tinned or boxed toffees, chocolates and sweets produced by Nestlé.

Radio 4. The flagship BBC radio station that broadcasts a range of spoken-word programmes including news, drama, comedy, science and history. Popular with the British middle class(es).

Radio 5 Live. The BBC's national radio service specialising in live news, phone-ins, interviews and sports commentaries aimed at the British working class(es).

Radio Times. A British weekly television and radio programme listings magazine once published by the BBC. The Christmas edition was, for a very long time, extremely popular in the run-up to Christmas. Marker pens at the ready.

RAF. The Royal Air Force (RAF) is the United Kingdom's aerial warfare force.

Raleigh Chopper. A children's bicycle, manufactured and marketed in the 1970s by the Raleigh Bicycle Company of Nottingham. Its unique design became a cultural icon and it is fondly remembered by many who grew up during that period (apart from those that went over its handlebars).

Range Rover. A luxury sport utility vehicle from Land Rover, launched in 1970 by British Leyland.

Razzle. Similar to *Penthouse* but not quite so classy. Famous for its Reader's Wives feature.

Reliant Robin. A small, slightly ridiculous three-wheeled car produced by the Reliant Motor Company in England.

Reginald Bosanquet. Much-loved British journalist and broadcaster who was an anchor of *News at Ten* for ITN from 1967 to 1979.

The Rolling Stones. An English rock band formed in 1962.

Rothmans. Cultural shorthand for a cigarette brand with a "sophisticated" image (possibly because of its motorsports sponsorship in the 1980s and 1990s).

Rover 800. A large executive car manufactured by Austin Rover Group (which was originally part of British Leyland) and then by the Rover Group from 1986 to 1999. It was a close relative of the Honda Legend and successor to the Rover SD1.

Safeway. A chain of supermarkets and convenience stores in the United Kingdom that was purchased by Morrisons in 2004.

Sainsbury's. Famous for a long time for being the second-largest chain of supermarkets in the United Kingdom.

Sandals. Shorthand for Sandals resorts and holidays. Imagine a Caribbean island for only the very well-heeled or for those who believe they are.

Save Your Kisses for Me. The winning song of the 1976 *Eurovision Song Contest*, as performed in The Hague, Netherlands, for the United Kingdom by Brotherhood of Man.

Scalextric. A toy that combines a racing track, cars and electricity.

Scrabble. A word game in which two to four players score points by placing tiles bearing a single letter onto a board divided into a 15×15 grid of squares.

Sea Devils. Amphibious cousins of the Silurians in *Doctor Who.* Quite frightening (for younger viewers, obviously).

Second World War. Is there anyone who does not know what this historical event was?

Sherlock Holmes. A fictional private detective created by British author Sir Arthur Conan Doyle.

Shoot. A football magazine published in the UK since 1969.

Silk Cut. A British brand of cigarettes, whose packaging is characterised by a distinctive white packet with the brand name in a purple, blue, red, silver, white or green square.

Sky Digital. Launched in 1998, Sky Digital cemented its place as a relatively expensive provider of pay television with its move from analogue to digital broadcasting.

Sky News. A twenty-four-hour international multimedia news organisation based in the United Kingdom.

Sky News Centre. The beating heart of Sky News, where all the desk action takes place.

Some Mothers Do 'Ave 'Em. A British sitcom starring Michael Crawford and Michele Dotrice, first broadcast in 1973. The series follows the accident-prone Frank Spencer and his tolerant wife, Betty, through Frank's various attempts to hold down a job, which frequently end in disaster.

SOS. The third single from ABBA's self-titled 1975 album. *SOS* was also ABBA's first worldwide hit after *Waterloo.*

The Soviet Union. A socialist state in Eurasia that existed from 1922 to 1991.

Space: 1999. The British science-fiction television programme that ran for two series and originally aired between 1975 and 1977 with huge sets, fantastic models and lots of Proper Acting. Expensive, sonorous and the epitome of cult viewing.

Starsky & Hutch. An American action television series.

Sue Ryder. Shorthand for the network of Sue Ryder charity shops which take their name and establishment from Margaret Susan Cheshire, Baroness Ryder of Warsaw and Cheshire, a British volunteer with the Special Operations Executive in the Second World War, who afterwards led many charitable organisations (and most notably the charity named in her honour).

Sugar Puffs. A British honey-flavoured breakfast cereal made from sugar-coated wheat.

Suzi Quatro. An American rock singer-songwriter, multi-instrumentalist and actress who became a radio presenter.

T. Rex. The English rock band, formed in 1967 by singer-songwriter and guitarist Marc Bolan.

Ted Heath. A British politician who served as Prime Minister of the United Kingdom from 1970 to 1974 and as Leader of the Conservative Party from 1965 to 1975.

Telephone Directory. A listing of telephone subscribers in any geographical area.

That's Me. A jolly song with a cascading introduction from ABBA's *Arrival* album (*Chung, de-chung de-chung, Chung de-chung de de-chung, Chung, de-chung de-chung…*).

Thunderbirds. A charming British science-fiction television series created by Gerry and Sylvia Anderson and produced between 1964 and 1966 using a form of electronic marionette puppetry ("Supermarionation") which combined scale models with special effects to thrilling televisual effect.

Tiger. A banging ABBA song from the group's *Arrival* album.

Titanic. The big, blousy blockbuster movie about the British passenger liner that sank in the North Atlantic in the early hours of 15 April 1912, after the ship collided with an iceberg during its maiden voyage.

The movie is very, very, very, very, very, very, very, very, very, very, very long.

Tom Baker. An English actor, best known for his portrayal of the fourth incarnation of the Doctor in *Doctor Who* from 1974 to 1981 and his narration of the comedy series *Little Britain*.

Tony Blair. A British politician who served as Prime Minister of the United Kingdom from 1997 to 2007 and as Leader of the Labour Party from 1994 to 2007. Controversial.

Top of the Pops. A British chart music television programme, made by the BBC and originally broadcast between 1964 and 2006.

Trotsky. A Marxist revolutionary, theorist and Soviet politician.

Twiglets. A wheat-based snack with a knobbly shape similar to that of a small twig. The taste of Twiglets comes from the yeast extract used in its coating and has been compared to that of Marmite.

UK 2001 General Election. Under the leadership of Tony Blair, the governing Labour Party was re-elected to serve a second term with another landslide during this general election.

Vauxhall Zafira. A multi-purpose vehicle produced in the UK since the late 1990s.

Vicks. Shorthand for Vicks VapoRub. A mentholated ointment for cough suppression due to the effects of the common cold, for muscle and joint aches and pains or (slightly surprisingly) for the treatment of mosquito bites.

Virginia Plain. A poptastic song by English rock band Roxy Music, released as their debut single in 1972.

Volkswagen 1600. A compact family car manufactured and marketed by Volkswagen from 1961 to 1973.

Volkswagen Beetle. A two-door, rear-engine economy car manufactured by Volkswagen between 1938 and 2003. Noisy, cultish and not particularly fantastically equipped.

Volvo. A once slightly staid Swedish motor manufacturer, renowned for its high safety standards and owned, since 2010, by the Geely Holding Group, a Chinese multinational automotive manufacturing company.

Vosene. A brand of medicated shampoo, intended to provide relief from dandruff.

Walkie-talkie. A hand-held, portable, two-way radio transceiver.

The war in Afghanistan. Possibly looked good on paper.

Watership Down. A fantasy adventure novel by British author Richard Adams. Set in southern England, the book features a small group of anthropomorphised rabbits.

West Berlin. A political enclave that comprised the western part of Berlin during the years of the Cold War.

William Hague. A British Conservative politician that represented Richmond, Yorkshire, as a Member of Parliament from 1989 to 2015 and the Leader of the Opposition from 1997 to 2001.

West Germany. The common English name for the Federal Republic of Germany in the period between its creation in 1949 and German reunification in 1990.

When I Kissed the Teacher. A bright and bouncy song from ABBA's *Arrival* album that starts with a carefully strummed guitar (*Beome, a beome, boom, boom, Beome, beome, boom, boom...*).

Woman's Weekly. A women's magazine, launched in 1911.

The World at One. BBC Radio 4's long-running lunchtime news and current affairs programme. Similar to *The World Tonight* and usually an indication, for a certain kind of listener, that it is (probably) time for lunch.

The World Tonight. The BBC Radio 4 current affairs evening radio programme that features news, analysis and comment on domestic and world issues. Usually an indication for a particular kind of listener that it is (thankfully) time for bed.

Wranglers. An American manufacturer of jeans and other clothing items with something of a cowboy vibe.

Wombles. Fictional pointy-nosed, furry creatures created by Elisabeth Beresford and which originally appeared in a series of children's novels published from 1968 onwards.

Yo-yo. A toy consisting of an axle connected to two disks with a string looped around the axle to bounce it on.

Young Americans. The ninth studio album by David Bowie, released in 1975. Plastic Soul sounds just like this.

You're So Vain. A clever, funny and bitchy pop song recorded by Carly Simon. Features Mick Jagger on backing vocals.

Zoom ice lolly. Three different flavours on an ice lolly stick.

Zumba. An exercise fitness programme created by Colombian dancer and cyclist/choreographer Alberto Perez during the 1990s. Somewhat jolly and energetic.